BookMarks

The Shops on Wolf Creek Square

Gini Athey

Editing: Brittiany Koren
Cover art design/Layout: Ed Vincent/ENC Graphic Services
Front cover illustrations
bookcase: © Natalia Mikhailichenko/Shutterstock.com;
storefronts: © LanaN/Shutterstock.com;
book: © Liashko/ Shutterstock.com.;
books: © Gigavector/Shutterstock.com
Map illustration by Logan Stefonek/Stefonek Illustration & Design..

Category: Women's Fiction/Romance
First Edition November, 2016.

Wolf Creek Square Series

Book 1 – Quilts Galore

Book 2 – Country Law

Book 3 – Rainbow Gardens

Book 4 – Square Spirits

Dedication

To Barb R. The words don't say enough, but thank you for your years of encouragement.

And to Peggy O. One of my favorite stores in Green Bay, the books you carried brought me much enjoyment. I wish you many hours of reading in retirement.

Note to Readers

Welcome to Wolf Creek!

In *BookMarks*, Book Five in my Wolf Creek Square series, three members of a family become the new residents in the ever growing community. Millie Ferguson agrees to come to Wolf Creek as a favor for an old friend, Richard Connor, who sees his daughter-in-law, Lily, struggling to run Pages and Toys despite her high-risk pregnancy. A former bookstore owner, Millie agrees to run the bookstore until Lily can return.

During a break from job hunting, Millie's granddaughter, Skylar, visits Millie and is surprised by how much she's attracted to the Square and immediately sees the possibility of a future in this special community. Millie and Skylar are still adjusting to big personal losses in their lives and maybe Wolf Creek Square is the place they can finally put the past behind them.

Millie's sister, Claire, a free spirit who never stays in one place for long, comes to see Millie after years of being apart. Soon, she sees something in Wolf Creek Square that shifts her assumptions about the idea of home.

When Lily is put on bed rest, everything starts to shift and old relationships change as new ones are formed. As opportunities appear, Millie, Skylar, and Claire will have decisions to make.

Nestled in rich farm land, Wolf Creek is a small fictional town west of Green Bay, Wisconsin. Wolf Creek Square is a pedestrian-only area where historical buildings surround a courtyard. Concerts and festivals are held in the Square, encouraging shoppers and visitors to linger and enjoy the atmosphere. Becoming a four season destination, the Square is busy most of the year.

Many of the residents from the previous books (Book 1 – *Quilts Galore*, Book 2 – *Country Law*, Book 3 – *Rainbow Gardens*, and Book 4 – *Square Spirits*) welcome the newcomers to the town.

So sit back and enjoy the bustle of activity on the Square, then visit my website, www.giniathey.com and sign up for my newsletter. You never know what gossip you might find in the newsletter.

Gini Athey
2016

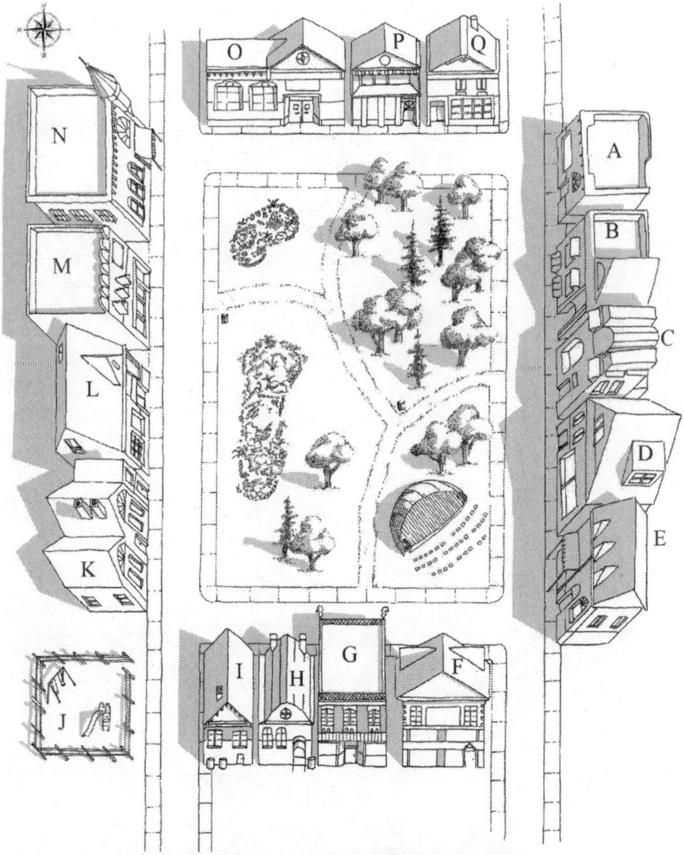

WOLF CREEK SQUARE

A-Farmer Foods
B-The Fiber Barn
C-Rainbow Gardens
D-Clayton's
E-Country Law
F-Art&Son Jewelry
G-Quilts Galore
H-The Toy Box
I-BookMarks
J-Fenced Playground
K-Styles by Knight and Day
L-Vacant
M-Biscuits and Brew
N-Inn on the Square
O-Museum
P-Mayor's Office
Q-Square Spirits

"Books make us laugh,
They make us cry,
They twist our hearts
Before we die."
—Unknown

"Small or large
Picture or word
Pages bound
Silent, but heard."
—Unknown

"When books become friends
The world is at your table."
—Unknown

July

1

Two weeks ago, an old friend called and asked for my help. By the end of our five-minute conversation I'd said yes. Taking a leap of faith, I agreed to tie up some loose ends at home, pack my bag, and make the trip from Minneapolis to Wolf Creek, Wisconsin. Ready or not, agreeing to do a favor for Richard Connor meant my life was about to change—temporarily, anyway. So far, it was looking like a fairly good change of scene. And I'd get to see Richard again.

So, here I stood in a circle of sunlight at the front door of Pages and Toys bookstore looking at the Square in front of me. Fingering the ring of keys to the store was my way of trying to calm the jitters that had started last evening. The keys were old and whatever shine they once had was long gone. The previous owner had run the bookstore for many years, first with her husband and then by herself. In recent years, Lily, a young woman just starting her professional life, had opened a toy shop within the bookstore. A clever idea, but also a smart one, at least from what I saw of the sales figures.

My musing about the shop stopped when Lily Connor herself waved as she came up the steps. I opened the door and was surprised by the intense heat that came inside with her. It was too early in the day to be so hot.

Lily dropped her tote bag on the floor next to the door and took a deep breath. The young woman I'd met in April was about halfway through her pregnancy, and she had a young son at home to tend to as well. No wonder she'd needed some help.

"I've been looking around," I said. "It's quite a store." I gestured at the bookshelves, not quite fully stocked, but still attractive. The children's section, with its wooden toys and puzzles, reflected Lily's expertise. "Overall, it's a smaller space than my shop in Minneapolis was, but it's arranged pretty well."

"Thanks, Millie. You know, I've been trying to keep up with it since Doris had to leave, but it's not easy." She grinned. "But you've waited long enough for a trip to Biscuits and Brew—or B and B as most of us call it. If you're going to be here through the summer and beyond, you need to stay in touch with people on the Square and begin to feel at home here."

Lily had called last evening and insisted on taking me to morning coffee at the café, Biscuits and Brew. I didn't argue. It was time to venture out.

I locked the door behind us and Lily led the way, not that she needed to. Last spring I'd been on the Square during a visit with my granddaughter, Skylar. We came to visit Richard and see the small town shopping destination he'd enthusiastically described. It was easy to understand why Richard, who knew I'd sold my own bookstore, took a chance and called me to help out in this mini-crisis on the Square. Doris Parker, the previous owner was in a care center in another state, leaving Lily to run everything. Judging from how slowly Lily walked in the heat of the early morning, putting all that responsibility on her shoulders was not a good idea.

Although she had a typical pregnancy glow, her face also showed signs of the stress and fatigue she was dealing with, not the least because morning sickness had lingered. But there was more to it than met the eye. This wasn't simply a case of a difficult early pregnancy. Richard had confided that Lily had donated a kidney to Toby, her young son. So, although still in her twenties, she was assigned the ominous label, *high risk*. No wonder her family was concerned.

When we passed Styles, a women's clothing store that

had impressed me on my first trip, Lily stopped to point at the colorful summer dresses in the window. "Next year," she said, with a laugh. "I'll be back into regular clothes then. And as soon the baby is born, Styles will be one of my first stops."

"I carried a full shopping bag out of this store when I visited," I said. "I'll have another look inside soon, especially if it stays this hot. Besides, sometimes new clothes are just what we women need to brighten our day."

"Right you are," Lily said, grinning, "and you can make it part of your new life here on the Square."

I resisted the words "new life," although I didn't say as much to Lily. There wasn't anything in my old life that a change of location would alter, anyway. I had only agreed to come to Wolf Creek to help run the bookstore on a temporary basis. Maybe take the burden off Lily as she gradually cut back her hours and then stay on until she was ready to return, at which point more permanent arrangements would need to be made for the bookstore. Although no one cared to talk about it yet, if Lily didn't choose to buy the store, it might have to close.

A variety of greetings filled the air when we entered B and B. I had to pick up on the lingo of the Square and all the shorthand that peppered the conversation. A low whistle from Nathan, Richard's son and Lily's husband, made me laugh, and his antics brought extra color to Lily's cheeks.

"Oh, hush," she said, casting a pointed look his way. "You'd think we were kids."

I smiled to myself. Oh, to be so young.

Behind the counter, owner, Stephanie—Steph—Baker, took our order. Apple juice with ice for Lily and iced tea for me. I reached into my pocket to pay when Steph reminded me she'd already started an open account for me. I'd learned she did that for all the shopkeepers and employees on the Square. "Oops. I forgot. That account has sure made it convenient to pick up my morning tea and lunch-on-the-fly these last couple of days."

"That's the point." Steph grinned and turned her attention to the couple next in line.

I joined Lily at a table where a couple of other women were already seated. The women's table, I'd learned. At a nearby table, a few men were drinking coffee, but Richard wasn't among them. That didn't surprise me, because I didn't know much about Richard's routine, or if he even had one. It wasn't clear to me, either, how much time he spent in Wolf Creek versus his home in Green Bay. Sometimes, I had the feeling he was gradually shifting his focus more to Wolf Creek and less on his original home and practice in Green Bay.

"Hello, I'm Millie Ferguson," I said to the group of women at the table. I'd met them before, albeit briefly since a couple of them had stopped at the bookstore to welcome me to the Square. But I didn't expect them to remember my name, although they were a friendly bunch. I didn't think any of them would take offense if I couldn't match all the new faces with the correct names.

The activities for the upcoming Fourth of July weekend were the focus of the conversation around the table. Megan Reynolds described past experiences of shoppers standing shoulder to shoulder in her flower shop, Rainbow Gardens. Marianna Spencer was kind enough to remind me that she owned Quilts Galore. She then introduced me to her oldest friend, Liz Pearson, whose husband was one of the lawyers at Country Law. It took only a couple of minutes to understand that Liz was a presence in her own right. In addition to being a lively, colorful person, she'd begun doing graphic design for the various shops and joint ventures on the Square.

Lily had given me her take on the three-day holiday celebration coming the day after next. All well and good, but that didn't stop my case of nerves. It was too late to get new book stock, so we'd have to make do with what was there, even if the shop looked sparse. I tried to relax and enjoy my tea, knowing I couldn't control the traffic on the Square or the books for sale. Fortunately, I had a few ideas of how we could move some old stock to make way for the new when the holiday weekend was behind me.

Midway through Megan's second story, Sarah Hutchinson, the town and Square's mayor, checked her watch. Then it beeped.

As a group, the women at the table stood, as did the men, and like wind-up dolls we all gathered cups and plates and took them to the waiting bins. Within seconds, chairs borrowed from surrounding tables were returned to their rightful places, and we all filed out the door.

More nervous doubts surfaced as Lily left my side to exchange words with Nathan. That left me alone to think about my first day working in a bookstore I neither owned nor had a hand in creating. Yet, I assumed the bookstore would be for sale, probably fairly soon. Richard had intimated that I'd be welcome to put in a bid for it if I wanted to. He had doubts that Lily would want to go all in on the shop once she had a new baby to enjoy and tend to. I waved Richard off. Even if I decided to go back into the book business, why would I consider moving to Wolf Creek to do it?

I was only in Wisconsin and on the Square because years before my husband, Bruce, and Richard had been on opposite sides of a case that pitted Minnesota and Wisconsin against each other over a land use issue. The art of compromise had figured in settling that case, and the amicable conclusion led to a friendship between Richard and Bruce. The two later teamed up on the same side of a few class action cases. Even after Bruce died, Richard and I had kept up a friendship.

When Lily and I arrived back at the store, I gave myself a few minutes to look at the displays in the bookstore windows. Lily hadn't changed them since before Doris left. And they looked it. The springtime decorations were sun-bleached and dusty. If I was going to be associated with this shop, pride alone was driving me to clear that space and do something to highlight the holiday.

I got busy putting all the display books on a cart I'd discovered in the basement and had managed to drag upstairs. The sale cart for the weekend could sit just inside the door and a big sign would make it clear we were practically giving away those older books with their faded covers.

I'd also seen a box in the backroom labeled July 4th, so whatever was in that box was what I had to work with.

Lily was busy choosing games and toys to display on a sale table, so I carried the box to the front, determined to get the window decorations out of the way quickly.

My focus was interrupted when Marianna came in. I recalled that she lived above her shop with her daughter and grandson, Thomas. We were neighbors in our living space, because I'd moved upstairs into Doris' apartment. Doris' sister had arranged for the apartment to be cleaned from top to bottom and, lucky for me, her sister decided to leave the apartment fully furnished.

"I'm trying to get ready for the weekend," I said. "You and Megan had many tales to tell this morning and I might as well make an attempt to be ready." To get a layer of dust off my hands, I rubbed them on the towel I'd used to wipe down the display area I'd just dismantled. "You look ready, though, in your patriotic apron."

Marianna grinned and ran her hand over the red, white, and blue patchwork apron. Then she opened her tote bag and withdrew a piece of fabric that was printed to look like bookshelves filled with books. She shook out the fold and held it up.

"Interesting fabric." I reached out to touch the piece. "I was amazed by the variety of fabrics in your shop. I stopped in when I was on the Square back in April."

"It just came in this week. I ordered an assortment of novelty prints and this was among them. I don't want to overstep here, but maybe you'd like to have a vest or apron made out of it. You know, so shoppers can see you're connected with the shop. Or, maybe, use it in a display."

I stared at the fabric and tried to picture wearing a vest. "I've noticed your aprons, and Megan and Nora's smocks at Rainbow Gardens. I also noticed that Zoe over at Square Spirits has a good size broach that designates her shop. The thing is, I don't know how long I'll be here."

Marianna's forehead wrinkled, as if confused. "Oh, I thought you were staying until after Lily has the baby and maybe a little beyond."

"Oh, I am. I'll be here through the holidays." I chuckled. "Come to think of it, it's only July. I guess a vest might be just the thing."

"I'm sure Beverly and Virgie could make one for you," Marianna said.

"Hmm…I don't believe I've met them. Their names sound familiar, though."

"Virgie works at Country Law." She turned and pointed to the Country Law office on the Square.

I knew Richard had begun working part-time for his son and stayed above the office when he was in town. As Richard explained it, he wasn't yet a true regular on the Square. Like mine, his life was in flux.

"And Beverly is Lily's mother. She and Georgia, the paralegal at Country Law, are sisters."

"I hope I can keep that straight," I said with a laugh. "Given time, I'm sure I'll make all of these connections."

With a toy in each hand, Lily came to the front of the store. "Sounds like you're going through the family tree," she said, grinning at Marianna and pointing to the fabric swatch with the wooden truck in her hand. "Wow. Bookstore fabric. Clever."

I nodded. "Marianna suggested I have a vest made to connect me to the shop."

"I want one, too." Lily tilted her head in thought, a gesture I'd seen her do when she considered a decision relating to the shop. "Do you have any with toys on it?"

"Not in this shipment, but I could call the company and special order a bolt if they have one."

"That would be terrific." Lily turned in my direction. "You with books and me with toys. We'd stand out, which was something Doris never wanted. We didn't even wear nametags. She said the toys and books were the focus of the store."

"I'm sure she was right back when she and her husband opened years ago," Marianna said kindly, "but the Square attracts so many more visitors now. The stores can become crowded these days, especially on busy holiday weekends. Customers like to quickly recognize a person who can help them."

"That's us," I said to Lily, pointing first to her and then

to myself.

I asked Marianna if she would hold the fabric for a day or two, and she agreed.

"I can try to reach Virgie later today," I said.

"I'll put it under the cutting table, so it's there when you need it." Marianna turned when the door opened and the bell jingled.

Customers? So early? Well, why not? This was a store, after all.

Marianna left and Lily headed back to the toys as I stepped forward to welcome the two women customers and offer my help.

"We're not after anything special today," one of the women said. "But we'll be coming back over the weekend. I try never to miss the events on the Square."

I stepped back and considered what the customer said just minutes after Marianna had brought the fabric to show me. She assumed I'd want to be part of the Square and make my presence known. I had to be sure I wasn't leaving the wrong impression. I hadn't given any thought to permanently leaving behind my home, not to mention a lifetime of friends. And what about my granddaughter? Skylar was in the process of planning a future based in Minnesota, which had been her home all her life.

Skylar's young life had been interrupted by the same tragedy that had affected me. Her father had been my only son, Mark, and Skylar had lost him and her mother, Carolyn, when the plane they were on slid off the runway and burst into flames, killing all the passengers.

With Bruce gone, too, Skylar and I were alone and she'd come to stay with me during her college breaks. Both of us had been living in the darkness of grief for years. But Richard's call had changed my life, at least in the short-term, and in unexpected ways. I had assumed I would eventually find the wherewithal to create a new life for myself, but I hadn't imagined leaving Minnesota to do it.

When Richard himself had said, "This will be a new beginning for you," I hadn't immediately contradicted him because I thought of this stint in Wolf Creek as a detour, a delay, perhaps. It certainly wasn't a step on a path with a defined destination.

I was deep in thought, with my two customers wandering down the long aisle of fiction titles, when I heard the bell and again saw Marianna come in.

"I forgot all about this when I saw you earlier. Rachel, my daughter, who is actually my stepdaughter, but I think of as my daughter now, is turning twenty-one next week and I'm having a small party for her." She handed me two envelopes, one for me and one for Lily. "Hope you'll come. It will mean a lot to Rachel."

Lily quickly came to my side and took the invitation. "Can Toby come?"

"Of course. We couldn't have the party without both Thomas and Toby." Marianna winked at me and turned toward the door.

The bell jingled again when she left. That bell. At first I wasn't sure I liked hearing that jingling every time the door opened and closed, but since all the stores had them, I decided I had little choice but to get used to it. It wasn't long before the happy sound grew on me and I wondered why I'd ever thought about taking it down—not that I'd have dared. Certain things seemed to be traditions on the Square, and the bell on the door was one of them.

I turned my attention back to the box of decorations, but the store began to fill with shoppers. And it soon became obvious that Lily and I needed a way to identify ourselves with the shop. Customers obviously searching for help sent loud messages. "I'd like to checkout," or "Can someone help me?"

After the morning rush and a hurried lunch, Lily left for home to rest for a couple of hours. That looked to become a part of our routine I needed to adjust to. I was confident that I could manage the rest of the day alone, so I suggested she not come back for the rest of the day. "Won't you need all your energy for the weekend?" I asked.

Lily didn't argue, but waved goodbye and, tote in hand, left quickly.

A few minutes before closing I finally reached Virgie

Saunders at Country Law. She was busy, but not too busy to say yes. She could get a vest made for me and I didn't have to beg. She was used to rush orders and we arranged to meet.

I was prepared to close and figure out dinner, but Richard saved me from that bother when he called.

"I'm here to rescue you after your first day," he said, "and take you to Crossroads for dinner—if you're free."

Was I free? I'll say I was. I was only too happy to accept a dinner invitation from him. I'd never been much of a cook, so having Crossroads, Biscuits and Brew, and the deli at Farmer Foods were three major bonuses of life on the Square.

"Give me a few minutes, though," I said, wanting to change into a crisp, white shirt to go with my beige summer-weight slacks. I dressed up the tailored shirt with a thin, gold chain necklace under the pointed collar.

When I came back down, Richard was already sitting on the front steps of the store. It hadn't cooled off that much, but he looked none the worse when I went outside and locked the door behind me. After we started toward Crossroads, Richard offered me his arm and in spite of the heat, I took it. I laughed to myself. I was just fine with Richard's old-fashioned manners and the feel of his strong arm under my hand.

The restaurant was already filled up by the time we arrived, but Richard had thought ahead and made a reservation. We sat down, and before picking up the menu Richard glanced around the room. A pleasant shiver went through me when his eyes met mine. I didn't connect my reaction to anything more than relaxing after the last two weeks of constant doing, doing, and more doing in order to make the move to the Square. I had successfully navigated a full day as a retailer again and was ending my day with a dinner with an old friend. No wonder I felt good.

Not knowing the restaurant as well as Richard, I told him I trusted him to order a good white wine to go with the evening specials, a Cajun grilled salmon salad.

"Melanie, the manager here at Crossroads, features Zoe's

family's DmZ wines," Richard said, after giving our order to the waiter.

"Keeping it in the family," I said, "the Square's family, I mean." Zoe and her shop, Square Spirits, had stood out to me.

"I'm a bit of a late-comer here," Richard said, grinning. "I'm still trying to keep all the relationships straight. But I'm glad I'm here as much as I am. I might be able to help out somehow, maybe even offer some emotional support. Nathan is very concerned about Lily."

That remark gave me pause. How concerned were the Connors? I didn't like not knowing the full story and hoped I'd learn it soon. I was quite sure the concerns involved Lily's health, and that could influence events at the bookstore.

The food arrived quickly and I dug into my salad and the crusty bread. "Wow, this is delicious. I could eat here every day." I put my fork down and sat back to take a rest between bites. "Maybe I will. Nothing is stopping me."

He smiled. "I wondered why you went so quiet on me. Now I get it. You were hungry. Maybe it's all that hard work you're doing."

I laughed. "I haven't felt this good in a long time. See what your one phone call started?"

"In all seriousness, I had to do something. I was watching Lily trying to do everything and wearing out in the process. She couldn't keep going at that pace all summer. I'm glad I knew an experienced person to call."

He reached across the table to take my hand, but I saw it coming and reached for my wine glass. I wasn't avoiding his touch. Not exactly. I'd been grateful that we had stayed in contact after Bruce's death. His attentiveness and simply knowing he'd lost his wife and understood my grief had deepened our friendship. We had the occasional dinner when he came to Minnesota on business. Then, Richard had come to my side again when Mark died, once again understanding the pain of losing a child, since he'd endured the loss of a son, Chad, and Chad's wife, Linda. The situation was further complicated, because Chad had named Nathan guardian of Toby, a baby Chad and Linda had adopted as an infant. At first that had been part of the rift between Richard and Nathan. Fortunately, that had been resolved.

Wanting to avoid talk of the past, I said, "I guess I'm going to see just how busy the Square will be this weekend."

"Well, we have three new shops," Richard said, raising three fingers, "so that brings more shoppers. The Fiber Barn and the art gallery, Clayton's, opened last summer, and Zoe opened Square Spirits last November. They've brought a lot of new foot traffic to the Square."

I sighed, a wave of fatigue washing over me. "It makes me a little tired to think of the next days—if we're lucky and the crowds are good."

"Then it's time for us to go." Richard signaled the waiter. Within minutes, we'd made our way through full tables and were back on the Square.

The air hung heavy that night and some of the shopkeepers coming and going from Farmer Foods and Crossroads offered listless waves. Richard seemed nervous, not his normal confident self.

"What's on your mind, Richard? You look troubled."

"It's Lily...again. I can't get my mind off of her. You know she donated a kidney to Toby. She's his biological mother, and it was nothing short of miraculous that Nathan ended up here around the time Lily moved back and discovered Toby is her son."

Richard's eyes misted over when he talked about Nathan and Lily falling in love and the fear they might lose Toby when he needed the transplant surgery. They got through that, thanks to Lily. "Now I can't help but worry about her. No one asked for my opinion, but I think she needs to be home resting."

"I suspect Lily is making more adjustments than you realize," I said. "She's tired and the typical morning queasiness has lasted longer than usual. From what I can tell, she'll voluntarily give up some hours at the shop. She went home early today. She knows why you called me, and fortunately, I have energy to spare."

Richard laughed. "Maybe so, but we don't want you burning out, either."

"Don't worry. I'm having fun so far." I pointed to my front window as we approached. "I'll get to that front window first thing in the morning. I'd enlist Skylar's help, but she's camping with friends for the holiday."

"I'm glad to hear she's getting out with people her own age." He grinned. "Speaking of getting out and all that, would you like to go to the fireworks display on Saturday? Folks from the Square usually bring a picnic supper and then stay for the big light show."

Richard seldom mentioned going to something as ordinary as a small-town picnic. He was a man who usually kept to himself. "Have you gone before?"

"Admit it, you're surprised I asked you to an event like a town picnic," he said with a soft snicker. "But…I'll have you know I've transformed. Toby had a hand in that. I've gone out to the lake for the July 4th celebration the last couple of years. As a matter of fact, the boys, Toby and his little pal Thomas, are counting on me to help them make a track in the sand for their trucks." He flashed a wry grin. "Can you picture that? Time to drag out my jeans for the occasion. No suits allowed for the July 4th picnic."

He wore his happiness on his amused face.

"Life sure is different for you here, isn't it?" I asked.

Richard lowered his voice when he answered. "After losing Chad, I needed to change and reconnect with Nathan and Toby. I have Georgia to thank for that. But that's a story for another day." He lightly touched my arm. "You sleep well, Millie. Another big day tomorrow."

I thanked him for dinner and let myself in my front door. After I locked it, he waved and walked away.

Looking into the shop I let out another sigh. I faced another big day. The window display and reordering of pretty much everything for the shop would eat up any available time I had before opening. Sadly, the shop was lacking in what could be considered patriotic books and toys—adult or children's jigsaw puzzles showing the White House or the Capitol Dome or even a map of the 50 states or a garden of flags. There was a stack of children's coloring books, but I made a mental note to order some of the popular coloring books for adults.

As I walked through the shop to the stairs, I lightly touched the books on the shelves with my fingertips simply for the pleasure of touching books. The glow of the antique lamp posts in the Square gave the shop a comfortable feel. *Like home.*

That thought surprised me.

Doris' furniture had surprised me, too, but the more I lived with it, the more I liked it. Once upstairs, I flopped down on the comfortable couch, a little worn and not a modern style, but it allowed a view out of the low front windows. I could relax and still see the activity across the Square. One end must have been Doris' favorite because the cushion dipped in the center. Two soft chairs were set off to the side and separated by a small table and a reading lamp.

The kitchen was the one room that had been recently updated, with a small dishwasher hidden behind a cupboard door. Even more surprising were the stackable washer and dryer installed inside the linen closet of the remodeled bathroom. Bruce would have looked around the apartment and called it functional.

My mind jumped back to my home in Minneapolis, a condo bought only a month before Bruce died. Then months later, deep in fresh grief, I'd completely redecorated the place, choosing the latest trendy styles to fill the space. Mostly for show than comfort.

And wasn't that a strange way to mark time? Before and after the death of a spouse. Psychologists probably had some name for it. After the second major loss, the death of my son, I went to counseling, some of which consisted of joint sessions with Skylar. I'd learned many esoteric terms, but the bottom line was simple: only time would ease the pain of my double loss.

Skylar decided she needed to sell the house she'd lived in all her life in order to move on. I'd seen us both retreating within ourselves, and she even considered withdrawing from college. Convinced that would be a bad decision I agreed she could move in with me. I debated long and hard with myself, but finally said yes. I really *wanted* her close. Selfish me.

I continued sitting in the corner of the couch and let tears pool in my eyes as I remembered those days. Finally, I shook my head to stop the flow of memories. Skylar had since earned her degree, and I was in Wolf Creek, enjoying an unexpected interlude in a new place. If I wanted to move and make an offer for Pages and Toys, no one would stop me, and I was sure I could strike a deal with Doris' sister. I didn't think Lily would actually want the burden of ownership, so the question that remained was: What did *I* want?

2

The next morning, with a large mug of strong English Breakfast Tea in hand, I went downstairs to begin another day. I knew I'd be starting the day by myself, because Lily had left a message while I was at Crossroads that she'd come in after lunch. I didn't mind being alone in the shop and ease into the day. One more day to go before the holiday weekend started. It was best for Lily to rest. She was only a phone call away if I had questions or traffic was heavier than expected.

Sipping my tea, I let my thoughts travel back to my days in the bookstore in Minneapolis. Along with my friend and business partner, Betsy Morgan, we'd scoured the area until we found a small suite in a strip mall. We put our heads together and managed to shuffle around enough shelves to get the maximum use of the floor space. We were always feeling a bit cramped in the narrow shop, but to outsiders—customers—we looked well-stocked. As Betsy put it, the store itself spoke of abundance.

Just before the holiday rush started, Betsy and I would sort the inventory and pull out worn or damaged books, or those that hadn't sold on our sale tables. We'd box them up and call for a pickup from a couple of shelters in town. If we couldn't sell them, someone else could read them for free. Since some of the Pages and Toys stock was looking a little shabby, I could first see what we could sell at marked down prices over the holiday weekend. I'd noted Wolf Creek had a shelter and Green Bay had a few charity resale shops that would probably like the stock I couldn't move.

Whoa. I had to keep putting on the brakes. This wasn't *my* store. Neither was it Lily's, but in Doris' absence, Lily was in charge. Still, I had a feeling she'd be relieved if I took the initiative and plowed ahead to do what was needed to revitalize the shop. I grabbed a pad and made a note of a couple of questions for her about thinning existing stock and ordering new inventory.

After so much reminiscing about the store I'd once owned, I had the urge to call Betsy and have one of our conversations about the novels we were reading, just finished, or hoped to start. I'd come to Wolf Creek on fairly short notice and hadn't tied up all my loose ends. The minute I picked up the phone, my fingers remembered Betsy's number.

"The Book Shelf."

Her clipped voice made me laugh. "Hi, Betsy. It's me, Millie."

"No. Can't be. My friend Millie disappeared! Must be an imposter."

"Oh, come on, it hasn't been that long."

"Oh, yes, it has," Betsy insisted. "So update me quickly, my friend. I'm expecting a school bus load of small kids. Going to be chaos here in about five minutes."

"Always some drama going on," I said with a laugh. It was as if I'd seen Betsy only last week. "If it wasn't the little kids, it would be getting the tea ready for a reading. You were always sure we'd run out of room."

"And we almost did. More than once."

"Yet you always managed to get me laughing." And so often I'd needed a good laugh, but that was in another era. In a series of short phrases I quickly condensed the last three years of my life. "And that's the short version of how I ended up as a temporary bookstore owner."

"Give me your phone number. I have an idea you might like, but a yellow bus just arrived. I'll call you back."

I gave her the number and then the line went silent. But Betsy left me intrigued. That fueled me to get to work on the window display with new enthusiasm. My old bookstore hadn't offered window space, so having a substantial area to arrange in an appealing way was a new challenge.

I draped a flag I found in the box over a small red-painted chair from the children's corner of the shop. Then I added a few toys and a copy of the biographies of founders of the country, including a new book about Martha Washington. I added another book, *A Year of Celebrations*, opened to pages describing the Fourth of July.

I called the window done, but I stepped outside to check on my hasty handiwork. Maybe it was mostly luck, but the window looked good, if I did say so myself. I was about to step back inside when I heard Virgie call my name as she approached. I waited for her to cross the Square, happy to see her and eager to talk about the vest.

Virgie looked pleased when she said, "Beverly and I can make your vest tonight, but I need some measurements. And we need you to choose a style, either fitted or loose."

"You'd give up an evening to sew?" I asked.

Virgie laughed. "We spend many evenings sewing. We do a rush order when we need to, but even though I'm getting your information, we're selling it to you as a special order through Styles. We work with them exclusively on orders placed in Wolf Creek."

"No problem. Come on in. I don't want you taking measurements right here in the middle of the Square," I teased. I laughed to myself at the cartoon picture that would make. Sixty years old and being measured like a model.

Efficient was the word that came to mind as Virgie measured from one direction and then another, once I decided that a fitted vest suited me best. On the small side anyway, and a fan of tailored clothes, I'd have been swallowed up in a loose vest.

Virgie finished recording the numbers in her small notebook. "I'll bring it by in the morning to see if you like it."

"Your reputation precedes you, so I'm sure I'll be very happy."

She was about to open the door when she turned back. "Are you planning to have a book club here? A couple of us asked Doris about starting one, but she was never interested. Probably because she was wearing out, to tell you the truth.

And it would have been one more thing for her to keep track of."

"I'll have to give it some thought. I'm still getting my feet wet." It occurred to me that Virgie, and maybe a few others on the Square weren't aware that I was only temporary help for Lily.

Virgie nodded and then turned to leave. "I have to run. We've got clients coming in early today."

To the jingle of the bell, I thanked Virgie for making time for me. The bell didn't sound again as the door closed because a man came in just as Virgie left.

"Is there something I can help you with?" I was glad to see a customer to start the day.

He approached the counter. "I hope you can. Over a month ago I ordered three books on woodworking, but nobody's called to let me know if they'd come in."

His tone was polite, but not exactly friendly. I held up my finger to indicate I needed a minute to gather my thoughts. "I've just started here, and I was told about a box of special orders Doris had been handling. As you may know, Doris is no longer here."

I looked under the counter, where I spotted a box filled with books. I needed to address the contents of that box. No time like the present. If this man's books were stashed there and he hadn't been called, other customers were probably waiting, too.

I explained a little more about the situation I'd jumped into as I sorted through the books, finally coming across a book on woodworking. I held it up and the man nodded. I found the other two near the bottom of the box. By the time he left carrying a shopping bag, I sensed all the mishandling was forgiven and he'd be back. I left the box of books on the counter, determined to track down the people who were waiting for their special orders.

I was certain that at one time Pages and Toys worked within a system Doris and her husband had established. They'd undoubtedly had a routine to open the shop each day. Now it was up to me to make sure simple, easily forgotten details didn't threaten to ruin the whole day. I flipped the sign to Open and turned the spotlights on in the window and over the shelving. I checked the register for cash and declared myself ready.

I started the open hours by pulling out a few books from the box of special orders, but that's as far as I got. Shoppers, real shoppers, not browsers, soon filled the shop. As soon as one group left, another filed in. By the time Lily came in through the back door, I was thrilled to see her. I needed food to reenergize me.

As soon as she got to the counter, I raced upstairs and took big bites of half a turkey sandwich I'd bought at Farmer Foods. I washed it down with a glass of water. I would have preferred a tall glass of iced tea, but the pitcher was empty.

Later, between customers, I had a minute to ask Lily about the special orders. She shook her head and sadly told me about Doris either duplicating orders or not ordering the books at all.

"I delivered some books to Zoe that Doris had ordered," Lily said. "She added them to her stock at Square Spirits. Then I added the duplicate books to the shelves. I think what's left in the carton are the special orders, but Doris' records are skimpy."

"Do you know some of the people who ordered frequently? We could call and ask if they've been waiting for books."

Lily agreed to go through the boxes, the computer, and the handwritten notebooks Doris had used to help her keep track of things. I had to accept that we wouldn't be able to solve all the problems in one day.

The afternoon slowed enough so that by closing time, Lily and I had straightened up the shop. The next morning, it would be easy to open up for holiday business. I ended my day with a cool soak in the tub and a hodgepodge of leftovers from both Farmer Foods and Biscuits and Brew. I sat at the window and enjoyed the rich chocolate chips in my last B and B cookie while I watched a Boy Scout troop practice raising and lowering the flag, presumably for Saturday's holiday commemoration.

I was happy to hear Richard's voice when he called. "I have it on good authority that the bookstore was busy today," he said. "Lily stopped in on her way home and told me all about it."

"Well, we had only a few issues to sort out amidst wall to wall customers. It was a great day."

"So, Millie, quick change of subject here," Richard said. "What about the fireworks on Saturday. You never responded to my invitation one way or the other."

Ouch. I hope I hadn't hurt his feelings. Of course, I wanted to go. But Richard had a way of making anything we did together sound like a date, and that made me uneasy. "Oversight on my part," I said in a light tone. "I must have been tired. Yes, I'd like to go and see everyone from the Square. Lily mentioned it a couple of times today. She said Toby couldn't wait."

"Good. I don't want to be the only senior citizen in our group."

"Hmm…are you calling me old?" I was teasing. At only sixty, I didn't think of myself as a senior citizen. Or Richard, either, for that matter.

"Old? You're not old, Millie. You're seasoned, with lots of wisdom."

"Seasoned? Sounds like I'm a roast?" I giggled, and it felt wonderful.

Well, why not? It had been a long time coming.

"Millie, you must be really tired or maybe you're just in a great mood, but in any case, I'll say good-night so you can rest up for tomorrow—and the weekend."

"Both, Richard. I'm tired *and* in a happy state. And that's just fine."

When we ended our call, I sat looking out the window awhile longer, but knew that with three days of intense work and a party in the middle of it, I needed to get to bed. I turned off the light and when I found my comfortable position in bed, I sighed. A happy sigh.

* * *

Two days of intense heat brought record numbers of people to the Square. Many were looking for indoor entertainment in the form of books or games. They all hoped for a break in the temperature so they could enjoy hanging out at the lake. As it was, the heat shortened any trip outdoors, even to the waterfront. Almost all the shoppers browsed the sale cart and table, and usually bought one or two seriously low-priced books from the stock I was trying to move. No one seemed to mind that some of the book jackets were faded or even a little ragged. Likewise, Lily cleared out some of her old inventory to make room for new products and a fresh look.

This kind of sale was good for holiday weekend shopping, but the more we added to the sale table, the more depleted the store looked. It was past time to place orders—and institute a new system to keep track of inventory. Writing sales slips by hand, even with abbreviations, was too time consuming. I later found I couldn't remember what items I'd written on the slips.

The question kept returning to who would make the decisions about changes. Would Lily take over, or was I gradually moving closer to taking charge, even if only for these next months? I wanted to defer to Lily, simply because she'd worked with Doris, but currently, members of Doris' family, who were the most silent of silent partners, legally oversaw the bookstore and the building for Doris.

Whatever the situation, the middle of a holiday weekend was not the time to make big decisions. Or was it? Maybe it was the perfect time to implement whatever worked for the weeks and months ahead. I knew the uncertainty weighed heavily on Lily, although she never mentioned it. Nor did she seem eager to discuss what would become of the toy portion of the store once her baby arrived.

I had no sooner unlocked the door Friday morning when a couple entered with three young children. Oh, boy.

"Welcome," I said. "Glad you stopped in. Can I help you find something in particular?"

The man spoke first. "Last year my son bought an action figure—Jesse James. He's part of the Wild West series."

I could only nod as I had no idea where this conversation was going.

"A young woman told us that Wyatt Earp was going to be for sale this year." He laughed. "My son remembered that and has pestered us all year about coming back to get one."

I watched the youngster shift from one foot to the other in anticipation. I didn't know how I was going to tell them I'd only been in town for a short time and didn't know which toys we carried. But if I was going to help Lily, then didn't I need to know the toy inventory as well as the books?

Fortunately, I was saved from fumbling around to make an excuse while I searched, because Lily arrived and greeted the man by name, Andrew. She nodded to the rest of his family. She gave me a broad smile and waved the little boy back to the toy corner.

"I've been saving Wyatt for you."

When the mom and the three kids followed Lily, Andrew headed for the sale table, clearly hunting for a bargain. With no one else in the store, I stood behind the family as Lily explained all the features of the action figure to the young boy. Then she handed him the flyer that showed next year's offering. She had a way with kids, no question about that. No wonder she'd been good at courting repeat customers. I only hoped she would be here when the boy returned next year.

I also watched the way Lily focused on helping the other kids choose a toy to their liking. Each child was an individual. As a previous bookshop owner, I knew how personal book selection was for both kids and adults. I'd watched booklovers read back cover blurbs for hours before finally settling on their choice. It was the same with children and their toys.

I ventured to ask the mother of the family if she was interested in finding a book for herself.

She shook her head, leaning in to confide, "I'm spending my fun money at The Fiber Barn. One of my friends told me all about their fabulous yarn."

"Well, thank you for coming to our shop and bringing your kids."

I stepped back to the front of the store when I heard the bell jingle and for the next several hours I never left the register, except to head to the back room to hunt for more bags with the Pages and Toys logo printed on the front. Luckily, I didn't have to bother Lily to help.

At the end of the day, Lily and I leaned against the counter, relieved that we'd managed to get through the afternoon. But I couldn't let Lily go home without asking her about ordering new inventory.

"Frankly, Millie, I'm going to let you handle that," she said, "and you don't have to ask for my approval. There aren't enough hours in the day for me to do one more thing. Ever since Doris left, it's been difficult to keep up with everything, especially the inventory." She grabbed a cold bottle of water from the small refrigerator under the counter and perched on the stool by the register.

Her shoulders slumped and she consciously lifted them, a move I viewed as her way of fighting off a wave of fatigue. "I can't sit too long or I'll crash. I've got to put more toys out for tomorrow."

"Let me help," I said. "That way, I'll learn the toy end of the shop and you won't feel so pressured to be here."

"Great idea." Lily shook her head with a note of sadness. "Unfortunately, Doris insisted she was too old to learn about them."

Since I hadn't known Doris, I kept quiet. It was certainly possible that Doris was aware of her limitations and no longer able to adjust and take in new information. Lily chose not to elaborate.

Feeling thirsty myself, I grabbed a bottle of water and saw we had only two bottles left. I wrote a note on a slip of paper and put it in the pocket of my new vest. Virgie had delivered it that morning, but as much as I liked how the vest looked on me, I was disappointed that no one, not even Lily, had commented on my wearing it. Maybe Lily had been too busy to notice, but admittedly, I was always a bit of a clothes maven, and the sleek tailored fit was flattering. But even more, I was a colorful walking advertisement for an equally colorful shop.

I put my feelings aside when, water bottles in hand, Lily and I wandered to the toy corner. Once again, I saw the evidence of organized displays and cleverly chosen inventory. The toys in storage in the back room were efficiently shelved in the same order as they were displayed in the shop.

Finally, I asked the hard question that had been on my mind since my arrival. "Will you have time to keep your space here and sell toys after the baby comes?"

When her eyes glistened I knew I'd hit a nerve and probably hadn't been the first to have asked. "Nathan and I are thinking I need to at least consider being a stay-at-home mom for a while." She shrugged. "As you've no doubt heard, I missed Toby being a baby and Nathan doesn't want me to have to choose between the baby and the shop. But on the other hand, I do love selling toys. Right now, though, I'm too tired to think clearly about it."

"Tired today or every day?"

"All the time," she admitted, turning away to finish filling the open places on the shelves. Then she began stuffing the packing material into the large empty box.

"Leave that. I'll take care of it when I put mine in the recycle bin."

"Thanks." She looked at her watch. "It's time to pick up Toby at Sally's Daycare. Then we have to think about dinner, but that's not really a problem. Nathan and I usually end up throwing together a meal from Farmer Foods. But overall, we have little time for ourselves."

I threw up my hands in a helpless gesture. "Hey, I'm only one person and I treat myself to take-out almost every day. It's been a busy day on the Square, and from what people tell me, we'll be as busy tomorrow. I'm just grateful there *is* a Farmer Foods and a B and B, not to mention Crossroads."

She cast a knowing smile my way. "I like the way you think. And you're right. We're *always* busy in July."

Smile or not, Lily's voice was flat, not the strong or upbeat tone that would carry her through a summer season of shoppers and visitors. She grabbed her purse and tote, and gave me a quick wave when she pulled the door closed. I'm sure she didn't hear the little bell jingle.

I watched Lily, with her head down, on the diagonal

walkway across the Square, the quickest route to Sally's. I considered what I could do to ease some of the pressure on Lily, but at the same time, I wondered if it had been her idea to bring in someone to help over the next months. Had she told others in her family how tired she was every day? Richard came to mind. He was the one who'd called me, but I still didn't know if Lily approved, or if her father-in-law had stepped in and taken over. He'd explained Lily's reality of living with one kidney. Were it not for Richard, I'd still be in the dark about that. It was no wonder Nathan was bringing up the idea of Lily staying home with the new baby.

As I mulled over Lily's situation, I walked up and down the aisles of books, noting large empty areas. Not the right image for a successful business, and now that Lily had given me the freedom to order books, I wouldn't delay. That alone gave me a lift—a small taste of the freedom and the creativity afforded owners of retail stores.

I slept fitfully that night, almost as if afraid of what the weekend might bring, but excited as well about having a hand in sprucing up Pages and Toys. Sure enough, as Lily predicted, Saturday was a repeat of Friday. By afternoon I'd answered many questions about the toys as well as the books. Two more customers had books in the special order box, and I came up with a short explanation of the reason they'd accumulated in the box. I didn't want to go into any more detail than necessary to explain the reason Doris left.

Early in my marriage to Bruce, he'd explained the basics of what privacy meant in his life as an attorney, and throughout our marriage I understood that he knew things about people in town I wasn't privy to. The habit of privacy carried over, and I'd learned the lessons well. That's why, regardless of the kindness of the questions customers asked about Doris, I said as little as possible. If they wanted more information to satisfy their curiosity, they had plenty of people on the Square to ask. I'd kept the policy in place when it came to Lily as well.

To thank those who had been caught up in our special order mishap, I gave each customer a 10% on-the-spot discount and a gift certificate for a future purchase. I mentioned it to Lily when she came in and she was totally agreeable.

Meanwhile, I found myself getting back into the groove of working hard and enjoying every minute. I looked forward to going to the lake with Richard and spending time with people from the Square I hadn't gotten to know.

***

Richard buzzed the back door and led me to his car. We soon became one of many cars on the road to the lake. As we drove along, I recalled the picnics of my childhood. My mother had fried chicken and made potato salad and fruit sticks on Saturday in preparation for a Sunday afternoon in the nearby park or at the public beach. I could still recall the memory of my dad laughing and playing with my sister and me. He worked hard to provide for us, yet we never felt he resented the responsibility.

"We should have gone with Nathan," Richard grumbled when a small car beat him to a front row parking spot.

I just laughed, thinking of us crammed in with Lily and Toby and all the food and blankets. "Nathan and Lily have their hands full with Toby. We can manage ourselves and stay out of the way."

By the number of cars in the lot and on the road, my idea of a small town fireworks display needed rethinking. Fortunately, Richard was quick to locate another parking spot and flashed a big smile when he pulled the key out of the ignition. "Let's go. The boys are waiting for me."

"Go ahead, then. I'll find my way there," I said as I climbed out of the car.

"No, no. I didn't mean that," he said, grabbing a tote from the backseat. "You have no idea what it means to me that Toby asks me to play with him. And with Thomas, Marianna's grandson." He finished his thought as he led the way down the path toward the lakefront. "I made so many mistakes with Chad and Nathan, and then again when I started out with Toby. I was making the same bad choices all over again. Nathan was smart, though. He moved Toby away from Green Bay—and from me."

Years ago, Richard and I had talked a little about some of our mishaps and losses, and I was painfully aware of his many regrets. But as it turned out, Richard had been given a second chance to be with Nathan and Toby. "Like you and I have said before, all that's water under the bridge. You've been given a second chance to embrace the future, and that includes Nathan and Lily and their wonderful, little guy."

"And the future is now," Richard said with a laugh.

We'd come to a fork in the path and I saw the lake visible through the woods to our right. "Look at that crowd. Seems like everyone from the Square is here."

Richard staked out a spot next to Sarah and Sadie. He shook out the blanket and spread it on the ground. I was glad both women were happy to see us, but almost immediately Sarah stood up and left. Richard wandered off, too.

"So glad you joined us," Sadie said. "I came last year and had a ball. With more of us on the Square, the group just gets bigger and bigger." Sadie's multiple bracelets danced in the sunlight when she shooed a fly away. I'd seen those bracelets on other occasions. Come to think of it, I'd not ever seen her without them.

"Richard said the picnic would be fun," I said. "He wouldn't take no for an answer. Now I'm glad I'm here."

Sadie grinned. "Sometimes we need others to nudge us forward."

Suddenly, Toby ran past Sadie and me and headed toward Lily and Nathan, who were talking with Zoe and Elliot. Or was it Eli? I needed to find a way to tell those twins apart. Especially, because one brother was Georgia's guy and the other was Zoe's. I saw them both at their store, Farmer Foods, almost every day.

Not far from that group, Megan waved a red-checkered plate in the air to get everyone's attention. "Hot dogs and burgers are ready. Grab a plate everyone." She stood next to a table laden with bowls of salads, bags of chips and pans of treats. More food than our group could possibly eat, but since I hadn't asked Richard what he planned to bring or offered to pick up something myself, we'd come without anything to share. Mildly annoyed with Richard, I knew I wouldn't show up to another potluck empty-handed, whether I came alone or with someone. That "rule" had been imprinted on my conscience from my childhood days. Not that I noticed anyone keeping score over who brought what.

When Sarah rejoined Sadie and me, I followed the two women around the table and took a small spoonful from each dish so I could try everything. Sadie had begun filling in the painful details of how she ended up in Wolf Creek, starting with her husband's conviction for financial fraud. Lowering her voice, she admitted that she and her son Clayton had been reduced to using phony names in order to at least try to maintain anonymity. No luck there. Their cover had been exposed when they'd run into Art Carlson, the jewelry artist on the Square and an old friend from the New York art world.

"Turns out the world really *is* that small," Sadie said with a laugh.

"It seems that every person I've met, even the young people, have a personal story of loss and survival," I said. I refrained from saying that I'd traveled that road, but hadn't decided that Wolf Creek was my endpoint, even though the Square appeared to be filled with happy, energetic, and enterprising men and women living full lives—or that was my impression. Whatever tragedy had hit and changed their lives, they hadn't been permanently damaged or crippled by it. Could I say that about myself? I didn't want to ponder the answer too long.

When we got to the end of the line, Reed Crawford offered us a choice, lemonade or iced tea. "Want me to carry this for you?"

I spoke before Sadie had a chance. "Oh, you, young whippersnapper. We're not helpless yet."

Reed grinned. "Sorry, Millie, I didn't mean it that way. But if you do need help, I'm in the building right next door."

"Thank you, Reed. I'll remember that."

Ignoring my remark, Reed carried our cups of iced tea and handed them to us after we settled back down on the blankets. Then he was gone, probably off to help someone else. Richard joined us a few minutes later, his face red from exertion and a smile that went from ear to ear.

I couldn't resist teasing him. "Looks like it takes a lot of energy to be a granddad." On a daily basis, Richard's life seemed filled with one serious issue after another. Seeing him laugh warmed my heart.

He had filled his plate to the edge causing a few chips to fall onto the blanket when he sat down. He picked one up and popped it into his mouth, then winked at me.

"I'll never tell," I said.

"Me, either," Sadie said, laughing.

We concentrated on our food and, in my case, anyway, did some serious people-watching.

As dusk approached, Steph made her way through the group with her box of star-shaped cookies, frosted in white with red and blue sparkles.

"Take all you want," she said.

"I can't resist them," Sadie said. "But they're almost too cute to eat. Almost." She took a bite out of one of the three she took. Richard grabbed a handful, too, but I managed to keep it to two.

Before the fireworks, Megan and Rachel packed up the food and filled the coolers nearby, while Reed and Nolan Crawford carried bags for us to dump our used plates and napkins.

Somehow, sitting in the company of these people, who had been nothing but friendly, made Minnesota seem far away. More to the point, home seemed far away, as if it belonged to the past. This group of people inspired me. It was going to be such fun to be among them for the summer and share in their festivals.

Everything around me seemed vibrant, especially the sight of Richard keeping Toby out Lily and Nathan's way so they could help serve food.

I turned to Sadie, who had been in Wolf Creek over a year. "What made you stay in Wolf Creek?" I asked. "It's obviously such a small place compared to New York. I feel that way coming from Minneapolis. Yet I find myself with a degree of contentment as I think about the months ahead."

"It's an easy answer for me," Sadie said with a quick shrug. "Clayton found Megan here and I was tired of running. By the time Clayton asked Megan to marry him, I'd made friends with most everyone on the Square. Don't get me wrong. I loved New York, but because of my husband, my life there was gone. I'd been run out the city. So, it seemed safe here."

Richard had returned with Toby, who plunked down on the edge of the blanket and ran his truck back and forth across the sand, oblivious to all of us, including Richard.

"Sadie just told me she's only been in town for a little more than a year, but she's happy here," I said to Richard. "Like you."

"Grandpa moved here to be with me." Toby looked up, and then slid over so his shoulder touched Richard's arm.

Oops. Little ears were always alert. I needed to remember that when I talked to Lily in the shop and Toby was there. There might be some things in our conversations, especially about the new baby, I wouldn't want Toby to repeat.

Toby stayed with us for the fireworks and a hush fell over the crowd of people who had gathered. The quiet lasted until the fireworks started and then we all exclaimed at once over the designs of the bursting lights over the lake—from streaking comets to budding flowers. The show lasted close to half an hour, but once it was over the picnickers began to pack up and make their way back to the parking lot. We hung back and waited for the crowd to thin. Nathan and Lily wandered over to collect Toby, and then waited with us, while Sadie took off with Clayton and Megan.

Richard's was among the last dozen cars to turn onto the road back to the Square. On the way home, Richard entertained me with stories of Toby and Thomas' antics. "They're very entertaining," he said, adding that he needed some new toys for his apartment. "Toby has outgrown the classic wooden trains and the puzzles are way too easy. He's not challenged anymore."

"I'm not surprised," I said. "Kids outgrow toys the way they outgrow books."

"I'm learning that. I worked out a deal, though. If I get

some new things—racing cars and action figures are the new interest—then we'll go through the old bunch and pass them on to Thomas." Richard grinned. "He was okay with that."

"You should hear yourself," I said. "You're talking about trucks and cars and action figures like they're a new corporate case you've taken on."

"Oh, these toys are way more important," he said with a laugh.

I added a few details Lily had told me about the latest action figures. Richard looked at me like I'd revealed hidden knowledge.

He parked the car behind Country Law and we walked into the Square and stood in front of Pages and Toys. A soft breeze rippled the leaves, moving the hot air around.

"One more day and I'll have finished my first holiday weekend on the Square."

Richard frowned. "Did I make a mistake calling you, Millie?"

"Why would you think that?" I was surprised by the question.

He tilted his head from side to side as he considered his words. "Well, I see how tired Lily is every day. Running a shop isn't easy. I've wondered if you've decided you don't want to work that hard anymore."

"Look, I've lost five years of my life to grief, and like you, I welcome a change like this, even if it's only temporary."

"Oh, Millie. I…"

I put my fingers over his lips. "Shhh. Let me finish." But he scrambled my thoughts when he kissed my fingers. I pulled my hand back, surprised at his forwardness. "I only want you to be honest with me about Lily's situation. Is she going to be able to work all summer? She's tired a lot. I don't know if I should count on her half days or closer to fulltime."

Without warning, Richard sighed in relief. "Whew…and here I thought you were going to tell me you'd decided to pack and go home."

"No, no, I'd never leave Lily in a lurch like that, not to

mention Doris' family." I paused. "Besides, I like it here. I enjoyed helping customers today and being around the books."

Richard stared into the Square, his forehead wrinkled in thought. "The truth is, I don't know how to answer your question about Lily. It's as if Nathan doesn't know what Lily wants right now, either. And Lily doesn't know how she's going to feel physically. As you can imagine, Toby is a handful."

He turned back and looked straight into my eyes. "I can promise you this, Millie, I'll remind Nathan and Lily that they have to keep you in the loop. After all, if Lily can't carry her weight, you'll need to budget for part-time help in the shop. You can't do everything any more than Lily can."

If I hadn't moved quickly to unlock the door I was sure Richard would have kissed me. Kind of presumptuous of him. We'd always been strictly platonic friends. Oh, I found him plenty attractive, but I hadn't given serious thought to inviting another man into my life again. Was I ready for that?

Well, why not?

A thousand reasons why not flooded in.

"Thanks, Richard," I said, half inside and half outside my door. "It was great to go to the lake with you."

"It was nothing, Millie, nothing."

His parting grin and wave were good-natured. Maybe he realized he'd better not move too quickly.

I waited until Richard moved away from the door before going to the stairs. Tomorrow would be a pivotal day in my life. First order of business was carving time to put in a major book order, and second in line was perhaps trying to get a better handle on Lily's situation. No matter what she decided, I'd cope. I sat at the desk in the back room downstairs letting the new ideas for books and arrangements and special sales wash over me. Managing a bookstore once again. What a life!

3

The next morning Richard called early. "How about meeting me at B and B for coffee…oops, tea in your case?"

"Okay—I'll see you there in forty-five minutes." He didn't need to know I was still in bed, nor did he need to know that I'd sat downstairs working and planning until well after midnight.

"Better hurry. You're a working woman now and about to start another fabulous day on the Square." He had a laugh in his voice as he spoke. "I don't go over to B and B that often, but I do know a lot of bonding goes on. That's part of the charm of the Square."

I laughed. "You don't need to oversell the place. I've already said yes."

Another laugh.

I hurried to dress and join the group at B and B, hoping Richard would keep his distance. I didn't need rumors about us starting to buzz through this little Square, especially since I didn't know what level of friendship I wanted with him. I certainly didn't need someone escorting me everywhere. Forgoing my morning toast, I decided to get a muffin with my tea.

I needn't have worried about Richard clinging. He was already at the men's table and simply waved when he saw me, but that same pleasant shiver traveled through me.

With a sense of relief, I slid onto an empty chair next to Marianna at the women's table. The women were deep in conversation about weekend sales. Everyone agreed the shops as a group had broken another record for foot traffic—and for shoppers willing to spend money on the high-quality items the Square had become known for. No wonder they were so upbeat.

One thread led to another, and soon the talk turned to Rachel's birthday party. The women batted around gift ideas that ranged from goofy fun items to new clothes from Styles. As I sat there in the middle of the discussion about a young woman I barely knew, I decided it was best to simply give her a gift certificate for Pages and Toys. It was a puzzling scene though, because the women talked about the gifts even as Rachel moved around the tables serving muffins and breakfast platters to other patrons.

Marianna touched my arm lightly. "They're only teasing her," she explained. "She loves to get gifts of any kind, and all these women know that. She would be happy with nothing more than a new pair of jeans."

"I think she and my granddaughter would enjoy each other," I mused. "They're about the same age. Skylar is twenty-two."

"Bring her to the party if she's in town. There aren't many people that young on the Square."

Sarah's watch beeped and like a unit responding as one, everyone stood and filed out. Sarah's watch was like the bell at the beginning of the school day or the old style factory whistle that signaled the start of a shift. The Square was ready to welcome another day of shoppers and visitors.

I didn't wait for Richard, but hurried to unlock my door, don my vest, and turn on the lights. After being with the others at B and B, it was easy to pretend I was already the proprietor of the bookstore on the Square. Within minutes, I was absorbed with the reality of a steady stream of shoppers that lasted until late afternoon. Lily had been equally busy in the toy corner and we both periodically replenished the shelves as we had done the day before.

Lily reviewed her list for reordering. "I can't believe how fast toys are selling this summer. This hot weather sure is driving sales."

"The books are moving, too, and we need more bags."

I had an opening and I took it. "Since we're talking about orders and what we need here, how are you feeling after putting in such a full day?"

"Tired." She grinned. "That's my answer every day. But the nurse tells me it's normal for the first trimester. My morning sickness is lasting longer than usual and that's sapping my energy. That, and the heat. I hope I spring back soon."

"Yes," I said, "but I need a favor from you. A commitment, really."

Lily frowned. "Really? That sounds serious."

I laughed. "Not really. I don't want to probe every day how you feel. It's like meddling in your business, and as a rule I don't do that with anyone. But if you find you need to cut back, I may need to bring in some help."

Lily tapped her knuckles on the side of her head. "Of course. I should have been thinking of that." Her shoulders slumped. "Sor…ry."

Her feigned hangdog look brought on another laugh. "I only mentioned it because I made a commitment to Doris' family—and to your father-in-law—that I'd run this place as if it were my own. I don't want to let understaffing cost us sales."

"So," Lily said slyly, a smile tugging at the corner of her mouth, "you like us? And Richard speaks *highly* of you."

My face warmed. "Lily, please. I've known Richard for years. We're *friends*."

"Okay," Lily said, closing her laptop. "If you say so." She checked her watch and put her computer in her bag. "And you have my word. You're entitled to know where things stand with me."

Flashing her signature bright smile, Lily quickly headed out the front door.

Wow. Was she smiling about her life? Happy to be picking up her little boy? Or was she looking so happy because of Richard's actions and what she hoped for his life?

Either way, it didn't matter to me. For the first time in five years, I was looking forward to weeks and months of full, productive days.

***

I decided to call Skylar after coming back from an impromptu dinner at Crossroads, initiated by Marianna and Art. Clayton and Megan were there, and Sadie had called to ask me to join them. But, as much fun as I had chatting with new friends and hearing about their families, I missed my granddaughter. When Skylar had been away at school the house seemed empty, but when she came home on her breaks, the rooms were filled with her young energy. Simply by being herself, Skylar had a way of lifting my spirits. We had shared tragedy and loss, shed tears together, but we slowly worked our way through crushing grief, in part, at least because we clung to each other.

I hurried upstairs and fixed a glass of iced cranberry juice and sparkling water, which made it a festive drink—at least to me. Then I walked to the window overlooking the Square and toasted myself and my contentment in Wolf Creek. I guess having made so many connections in town and having budding friendships added to the sense that I'd made not only the right decision to say yes to Richard's request, but it was a personally rewarding one, too. Having enjoyed my moment of private celebration, I called Skylar.

"Hi, Gram," she said, answering on the third ring. "A little late for you to be calling, huh?"

I laughed. "What? It's not even 9:00 yet."

"Just teasing, Gram," she said, "but it's good to hear your voice."

"I'm checking in to see how you are, but I'm also feeling so good this evening that I couldn't resist calling."

"What's the reason for such a good mood?" she asked.

"I have that feeling when we know something is just right. Like the feeling you had when you chose your major. Or, when you decided to sell your house. It wasn't a one hundred percent happy choice, but it was the right one. Coming to Wolf Creek and taking a chance on this temporary position is turning out well." I paused to take a breath. "And, I've just come back from dinner with new friends, and I was out at a Fourth of July fireworks celebration the other day, and business is booming here in Wolf Creek. The shops—and their owners—are so interesting."

"Wow, Gram. You do sound happy," Skylar said, her voice overflowing with what sounded suspiciously like forced enthusiasm. "I'm happy for you."

"I hear a 'but' somewhere in your tone," I probed. "This is about moving forward, Skylar. That's why I'm feeling good."

"Oh, I *am* glad for you. You seemed happy there last April when we visited." She paused. "It was like you belonged there."

"That's how I feel this very minute, honey, like I'm where I belong, at least for now. Who knows how I'll feel when it comes time to pack up and go home?" I felt a pinch in my stomach. It was too early to talk about packing up. I walked away from the window and sat in one of the chairs. "That's enough about me. Tell me about the camping trip?"

"Uh, well, I didn't go."

Silence. I waited for her to explain.

"Everyone had a partner but me, so I played sick and stayed home. I didn't want to go camping with a bunch of couples."

I sensed it took effort for her to sound neutral, which prompted me to refrain from sounding overly sympathetic. The last thing she needed was her grandmother's pity over a missed camping trip. "Well, if you feel like that again, come to Wolf Creek for a break. It's not such a long drive. To tell you the truth, we were so busy I could have used your help." That was no exaggeration.

Skylar sighed. "I wish I'd thought of that. It would have been fun. And a change for me."

I heard the longing in her voice. She couldn't hide it. I hadn't heard that tone in quite a long time, not since she was struggling to choose her major and commit to a career.

"How about this? Why don't you come for a visit *now*? You're done with school and you haven't found a job yet," I argued. "And I'm meeting people here— In fact, I've been invited to a birthday party next week for a young woman only a year younger than you." Before she found a reason to say no, I added, "I'd love to see you."

"Well, I'll give it serious thought, Gram," she said with a laugh in her voice. "And I'll call back tomorrow. I want to hear much more about all that's going on where you are. You do sound…well, happy is a good word."

Happy? My heart beat faster. Skylar and I hadn't used that word to describe our lives in years. For all that time, being *okay* had been good enough.

"Well, why not?" I said.

Skylar laughed. I knew she was amused that I used my old standby expression.

I laughed, too, because just hearing the sound of her laughing lifted my spirits.

"So, let's leave it that you'll call me and let me know about a visit." I paused. "I think you'll like it here. And besides, it's a visit, not a major life decision."

"Will do," she said, ending the call.

I stood and went to the window again, my favorite spot in the apartment. The Square still had walkers and a few Crossroads diners and hotel guests coming in and out. I was sure I was right about Skylar enjoying a visit here. If she came soon, she could go to Rachel's party with me. I wondered if she'd react to a change of scene the same way I had.

Turning twenty-one had been a milestone for Skylar, and a dizzying one for me. She was a legal adult, and oh, boy, had she used that privilege—and in the most grown up of ways. After selling the home she'd been raised in, she consulted a financial advisor for guidance with the proceeds of the sale, along with the financial settlement she'd received after the death of her parents. With that money no longer held in trust, she seemed to have a good sense about preserving it and using it well. She could have bought herself a new home, but by moving in with me, we had mutual support as we worked through our devastating losses, but also figured out the best way to rebuild our lives. I'd been an observer, watching from the sidelines as Skylar made one decision after the other. Coming to Wolf Creek to manage the bookstore was the first major decision I'd made without involving her.

I slept fitfully, probably because I'd begun to count on a visit from Skylar. I had to check my own feelings and try to stay detached. I wanted to see her myself, of course, but I couldn't shake the feeling—call it intuition—that the visit would be good for her. I kept up the patter of self-talk about Skylar being free to do as she pleased. Finally, when the sky brightened and dawn approached, I got out of bed and began fixing my morning tea. My major task of the day was to focus on taking charge of the bookstore for as long as I had the responsibility for it. In some ways, I had to start treating it as if it were my own.

Once downstairs, I started with the biggest immediate issue, that of getting enough books in the store to be considered close to being well-stocked over the summer. I also had to think about holiday orders and making sure every nook and cranny of the shop offered something to buyers. As a mental side note, if Skylar came for a visit, I'd have her pack up some of my winter clothes and stash them in her car.

I smiled to myself thinking about how much I enjoyed a challenge, and that meant getting deeper into the business itself. It didn't take an entrepreneurial genius to understand that behind the scenes, the shop had areas that had fallen into disarray. *Shambles* was the starker word that came to mind. The question remained about how much I should do. But no matter who took over the bookstore, increasing inventory and having a solid inventory control program was needed. I might as well make my own life easier for the next six months and have a system in place for the new owners down the road. Since Square Spirits was the newest shop on the Square, I figured Zoe probably had the latest in efficient retail software. I'd pay her a visit.

As I wrote item after item on my list, I was taken back to the days when Betsy and I pooled our resources and opened our bookstore. We were engaged and excited. Funny, that's how I felt about the job of streamlining Pages and Toys and producing good sales numbers for the summer and holidays. I guess it came down to the adage: Once a saleswoman, always a saleswoman.

I looked up to see shoppers on the Square and hurried to unlock the front door. The minute I flipped my sign to Open, shoppers appeared and my lists disappeared under the counter. I was occupied with the steady stream of people that continued all day. My first break happened when Lily arrived for the afternoon. I called B and B for a to-go salad and ate it upstairs while Lily took over.

Lily was worrisome, though. Some of her natural brightness had diminished over the previous few days. Or, more accurately, it came and went. She was no longer the reliable, energetic woman she'd been when she felt well and strong.

Lily left about an hour before closing, and with only a trickle of browsers left on the hot afternoon I closed a few minutes early to walk to Square Spirits at the other end of the Square.

I could see that Zoe was winding down for the day, but in her gauzy tunic and dark slim-legged pants, she still looked peaceful. Most of all, she appeared happy.

"You're right at home here on the Square, aren't you?" I asked when I'd finished my questions about her software.

Zoe glanced around at the bowls of stones and racks of cards and journals. The wine shelves were full, and a large amethyst piece sat prominently on a shelf that drew attention to the array of gemstones she had for sale. "I've never been more content. I'd gone through a difficult time in my life, and when I decided to come here and open my shop, I finally found home."

"That's a familiar story on the Square, isn't it?" It was an observation more than a question. Richard crossed my mind, which led me to ask about Eli. "And am I right in saying you met a special man here—Eli, is it?"

"I sure did," Zoe said with a laugh. "I sure did. Eli owns Farmer Foods with his twin brother, Elliot, but he's also growing grapes on the family farm and my brother is helping him learn about making wine."

Some of her long, dark hair had fallen forward across her shoulder and she self-consciously smoothed it back. "We're living in the apartment Eli renovated above Farmer Foods. I'm using my place upstairs for private readings, an extra office, and storage space. The kitchen is handy for making quick meals when I'm working. It's a guest apartment on occasion as well."

I considered how lovely she looked in the flowing tunic in a light lilac shade. She matched her shop. "Sounds like things fell into place. Your work and your personal life."

Zoe nodded. "I can't say it often enough. I'm happier than I've ever been."

I couldn't help but study Zoe's mature, serious expression, even in happiness. There was nothing giddy or flighty about her. That didn't surprise me, though, because even after meeting her the first time, she struck me as a person of depth.

I picked out a bottle of wine and a chunk of green calcite for myself, and a round piece of polished rose quartz I had a hunch Skylar would be drawn to. I commented that Skylar had found her shop fascinating last April. "Skylar spent quite a bit of time in here during our visit. She brought scarves and journals and stones to her friends back home. So, while I'm here, I believe I'll pick up a gift certificate for her."

When Zoe pulled one out from under her counter, I noticed her distinctive logo on the form and asked who designed them.

"Liz Pearson. She's married to Jack, one of the Country Law attorneys. She created them for me and reconfigured the banner for my website. She's one of the people involved with the one-stop wedding business that Megan started last year."

"Lily has told me a little about that business. Mostly about the attention it's brought to other shops on the Square," I said. "I'll need to get up to speed on that—and a million other things. Lily and I have tended to talk in quick conversations of about five minutes each, but I'm trying to get an in-depth sense of what's going on."

I held up the certificate when Zoe handed it to me. "I

need to contact Liz. She can help me get a supply of gift certificates." I could see selling a lot of them. "They're a favorite holiday gift item for all retail shops."

With that, I paid for the items as I admired the small crystal Zoe had put in a small organza bag. "What a nice welcome," I said, turning to leave.

"I hope you'll be as happy here as I am," Zoe said.

I nodded to thank her, then went on to my next stop, Farmer Foods. I was almost at the front door when my cellphone rang.

"Hi, Gram," Skylar said, her voice chipper. "I'm accepting your invitation. I'll be there tomorrow. Is that okay?"

My energy soared. "That's wonderful. I'm so happy. But, leave a little room in your car for a box or two of things I need here. I'll have to call you when I'm back in the apartment. I'm at the grocery store now."

"Buy a lot of food—and plenty of treats," she said with a laugh. "I plan to stay for a few days."

"Music to my ears."

Half an hour later, I left the store with two full bags. Despite their weight, I walked with a lighter step than I had when I'd started across the Square. Between Zoe's positive attitude and Skylar's call, my day became extra special. I hadn't realized how much I missed my granddaughter.

I put the food away and readied the spare room. Meanwhile, I entertained myself by adding more items to my growing lists. Long ago, I'd faced facts. I would always be an incorrigible list maker.

4

The next afternoon, Skylar sent a text to tell me she was on her way. She still hadn't arrived when the sky darkened and a thunderstorm made for an exciting few minutes on the Square. It passed quickly, but left the ground wet and the trees dripping. At least the rain had cooled the air for a few minutes before the sun came out again.

Near closing time, I heard the buzzer at the back door. I assumed it was Skylar, but when I opened the door a delivery man said, "Three boxes for Toys."

"Bring them in. I'll sign for them. Lily isn't here at the moment."

"Doris used to sign for her, too. You new here?"

"I am, and I'll have boxes for the bookstore coming soon. By the way, I'm Millie Ferguson." I extended my hand.

"Good to know," he said as he shook my hand. He didn't linger and was soon on his way.

As the truck disappeared down the alleyway, I spotted Sklyar getting out of her car. I ran to her and enveloped her in a tight hug. "Come in, come in. Let me help you take in your luggage."

She lifted two large suitcases out of the backseat. "We can get the other stuff later," she said. "I've got another one completely filled with your things, and a couple of cartons of odds and ends for you in the trunk."

We rolled the luggage into the shop. "No unpacking yet, Gram. Right now I want to have a look at the shop you're tending."

Like so many young women were doing, Skylar had

left her shoulder-length hair loose. The sun brought out the highlights in her light brown hair, and the color on her cheeks gave her a radiant glow. Just looking at her sent a ripple of happiness through me. With her bright smile and hazel eyes sparkling, she reminded me so much of her father. Even as a young boy, Mark had always had the look of a kid who knew how to have fun.

I locked up and turned off the shop lights so we could go upstairs and start our evening with a glass of DmZ white wine. "Bought right here on the Square," I pointed out, lifting my glass for a toast. We clinked our glasses and took a sip.

Skylar and I each claimed an end of the couch and pulled our legs underneath so we could see each other as we talked.

"To Gram," Skylar said, holding her glass out again, "for jumping into a big project—another one."

"And to you, for deciding to take a break from your job hunting and enjoy a visit."

I met her glass halfway. Another clink, another sip.

"So, how is it going here?" Skylar asked.

"Very well. The days are full and time races along." I filled in details about the work of putting the shop in order and getting things operating smoothly again, including the unorganized special orders. "In some cases, Doris ordered the requested book twice. That confirmed Lily's early suspicions that Doris was spiraling down. Lily ended up taking some extra stock down to Zoe to see if she could sell it. Meanwhile, I keep the sales tables filled with damaged books and those with faded covers."

"Sounds like a huge job. I can't wait to help."

"And I need it." I explained the uncertainty about Lily and how long she'd be able to work. "She's already down to afternoons. I can see she doesn't feel very well. Richard is concerned about her."

"Speaking of Richard, how is he doing?"

Skylar had a special interest in Richard because he'd represented her after her parents had been killed. He'd been both skillful and sensitive when he'd negotiated the settlement. She had nothing but good to say about him.

"He's busy going back and forth between Green Bay and the Country Law office, and he's involved with his grandson, Toby. He's had considerable fences to mend on a personal level, but like you said, he's a terrific lawyer."

"I think he's a good man," Skylar said with a shrug. "Whatever is in his past, I'm glad to hear he's trying to fix it."

Deciding we were becoming far too serious, I got up and assembled dinner from the food I'd picked up. After dinner, Skylar finished unloading the car and we shuffled things around to make room for the new clothes. We said our goodnights and went off to our separate rooms. It was so nice to have her here.

***

Unlike me, Skylar liked her coffee in the morning—the richer and creamier, the better. I could see she'd be one of Steph's biggest latte customers.

After we ate, Skylar got to work getting a layer of dust off some of the shelves. She was especially interested in the toy corner and the toys arranged on shelves with their companion books. When Lily came in, she and Skylar soon had their heads together comparing notes about recent studies that observed kids and toys, and the ways children actually used their toys. The conversation was a testament to how much Skylar had learned on the way to her degree in child psychology.

As it turned out, Lily had stocked some of the latest toys that encouraged imaginary play. Leaving the two of them chatting, I finished cleaning up, using my own imagination to rethink the arrangements for the books.

That evening, Richard showed up at the front door around closing time and insisted on taking Skylar and me to Crossroads for dinner. His pleasure at seeing Skylar touched me. Having suffered losses himself, he was particularly sensitive to what Skylar had gone through.

We had plenty to talk about over dinner, especially because Richard kept us laughing with his stories about

Toby. Taking Skylar's expertise seriously, he asked her opinion about the rapid way the young boy was outgrowing the simpler toys, always reaching for something that stretched his imagination.

Skylar didn't hesitate to pass on what she'd learned about typical eight-year-olds and their ability to create their own worlds. According to Skylar, not everything was about video games and the latest electronic device.

"Lily said the same thing," Richard said. "She's so happy to see kids in the toy corner of the shop discovering things they can't find on TV or a computer screen."

Undeniably, I took pride in the dedication with which Skylar had immersed herself in her field. "Skylar and Lily have already taught me a lot," I said to Richard. "I can see a lot more goes into the way Lily chooses her toy stock than I'd known."

That night, Skylar and I stayed up until almost midnight talking about the changes I could make immediately. "The summer business is going to transition right to the busy holiday season and I want to be ready," I told her.

"The summer, the holidays, it all sounds so exciting, Gram. I wish I could be here with you."

"Really?"

"For now, anyway, at least until I find something back home. Budget cuts have pretty much eliminated a possibility for me to find a job in the schools."

Home. The place she called home seemed distant to me now.

***

The next morning, shortly after I unlocked the door, the little bell announced Rachel's arrival. Her shift at Biscuits and Brew had just ended and she wanted to remind me of her birthday party. "It's going to be simple, but fun. I hope you can come."

I called out to Skylar, who was straightening the shelves of kids' books. She joined us at the counter.

"I want you to meet Rachel Spencer, the birthday girl," I

said to Skylar, doing a quick introduction.

"*Skylar*…interesting name," Rachel said. "Nice to meet you. You should come to my party with your grandma. Everyone is welcome, and besides, there aren't very many young people on the Square." Glancing around, she added, "Such a great store. I buy all my little boy's toys and books here."

"I'm glad to hear that," I said. "Some new children's books and toys came in just yesterday. Lily put most of them on display already."

"Come on back and have a look," Skylar said.

The two went off together, but when customers started coming in, Rachel was quick to leave. I had a feeling that Rachel had come in more to meet another young person than to shop.

Sarah stopped in around lunchtime. She looked around and smiled before flashing a quick thumbs up sign, no doubt a response to the number of shoppers milling around. It had been clear from the beginning that the quality of the shop, even the look of it on the Square was a concern for Sarah. Part of my job was to reverse that trend.

Sarah left when a customer approached and asked about guidebooks for sailing the Great Lakes and fortunately, we had a collection in stock to show her. But once again, I made a mental note to check for new titles about boating and boatbuilding.

When Lily arrived in the afternoon, she was immediately absorbed into the shoulder to shoulder shoppers. At one point, she mentioned that our sales tables were empty again. I'd anticipated that the reduced-priced books would sell, but they were going at a faster rate than expected. So was Lily's older stock of toys.

With Skylar's help, Lily came up with a one-table arrangement that was fuller and more appealing. By the end of the day, I was stunned that only three books and one toy remained.

"This is a good problem to have," I remarked.

"Wow, Gram," Skylar said, "have you ever seen crowds like this?"

Lily perched on the stool behind the counter. "It'll be like this, or close to it, 'til the end of the year. Only weather keeps them away."

"That's exciting. It's great to see the kids showing so much interest in wooden toys and puzzles," Skylar said. "Seems like kids take a longer time deciding on the toy they want than adults take when they're picking out books."

Skylar leaned on the counter and pointed for Lily to hand her a bottle of water from the fridge. "One for Gram, too. We don't want her to get dehydrated," she teased.

"The doctors want me to drink a lot because of the baby," Lily said, "and I only have one kidney, so I have to be extra careful."

Apparently unaware of the seriousness of having one kidney, Skylar said, "Bummer. Then you probably have to pee all the time."

Lily grinned, not taking offense at all, while Skylar opened one bottle and was ready to give it to me. I shook my head.

The door had opened and a customer came in. She was looking for a last minute birthday gift for a young girl. I put my hand out to stop Lily from getting off her perch on the stool to help her. Instead, Skylar guided the woman back to the toys. I smiled to myself over the easy familiarity she had with the customer.

I waited until Skylar's voice faded in the back before I asked, "You all right, Lily?" A rhetorical question, because it was obvious Lily was about done in.

"Just tired. I didn't sit behind the counter much today. I'm glad Skylar was here to help. She sure knows her toys."

"Her education was focused on child psychology, and she was always fascinated by the inventive way kids use toys. I'm sure she enjoys helping customers. She can take over restocking the shelves after we close. Skylar won't mind helping out."

"You're right. And I need to get home. I don't have the energy to even take care of customers right now." Lily grabbed her purse and tote, and left with a wave and the jingling bell.

I couldn't help but be concerned about her, but I also had to ask what would happen to the toy business as her pregnancy continued. While Skylar helped the customer, I grabbed more of our shopping bags from the back room.

What a mess it was! I had a big job ahead of me. Each box had to be gone through, and given Doris' condition before she left, I couldn't predict what I'd find. I hadn't mentioned it to anyone, but books were turning up in odd places, as were outdated calendars and greeting cards. I found a few hardback books tucked into the cartons of shopping bags, and a stray coffee mug in a box at the back of the storage area.

As I stacked the fresh supply of bags under the counter I realized I needed to ask Lily if she'd ordered more. We hadn't worked out the finer points of running the shop. Had ordering supplies been solely Doris' job? Hoping I could catch her before she got involved with Toby or fixing supper, I called her on her cell and learned she'd put ordering more shopping bags on her to-do list, but the day had been so busy it never got done. I also heard the exhaustion in her voice.

"Why don't I take care of that from now on? Especially because you need to cut back your hours a little. I can place an order tonight and you don't have to think about it again."

"I'm sorry, Millie. Doris took care of things like that, and then I started trying to pick up the slack. I admit I'd only begun to understand how many supposedly little tasks she'd taken care of when she was well."

"No problem. Remember, I owned a bookstore once, so the only thing that's surprised me so far is the number of shoppers on the Square every day," I said with a laugh. "Now that's the kind of surprise I can handle. You try to get some rest."

Several customers came and went, and Skylar and the shopper were still in the back in the toy corner. Finally, they moved to the front of the shop, still chatting about the Laura Ingalls Wilder doll and book she'd chosen.

"You might warn the mom that once kids read the first book in the series they're usually hooked," I said. "We carry most of the titles, and so do many libraries."

After she left, Skylar and I spontaneously did a high five and I locked the door.

"Time for a big cappuccino, Gram. I know—tea for you. My first day and what fun it's been."

"You go upstairs. Put the meatloaf in the oven. I'll be up as soon as I place an order for bags."

"Don't forget gift cards and tissue paper, too, as long as you're doing an order. That lady has to make another stop because we didn't have them."

"Right you are," I said with a sigh.

Skylar headed upstairs while I took care of those final items for the day, grateful for my granddaughter's fresh eyes to help me look at the shop. Tired but happy, I'd begun to be bolder in the shop, making more decisions and using my own creative skills to make it feel alive and thriving.

Well, why not? For six months it was basically mine.

It didn't take long to eat dinner and put the kitchen in order. *Thank you, Doris, for adding the dishwasher.* While Skylar was in Wolf Creek I wanted to take advantage of her time with me, especially since I didn't know when she wanted to go back to Minneapolis. But that was a topic for another day. We finished our evening sitting on the couch, sipping wine, and watching the night descend on the Square.

Just before I went off to bed and left her to stream a movie on her laptop, I asked her if she'd make a note of everything she'd change downstairs. "I want to know what you think the shop needs to give the bookstore a boost of energy—and a modern look, even though it carries traditional toys. I want it to be the best bookstore in the area."

Skylar slyly raised her glass in a mock toast. "As athletes say, 'Go big or go home.'"

I laughed. "Exactly. So fill this notebook with anything that comes to mind. Right now Doris' family just wants it to keep going, and they don't care how I do it. With business so good, I think I can invest in some new promotions."

I crawled into bed content, but even better, I felt alive and brimming with ideas. Funny how my life seemed like an endless road stretched out ahead of me. I knew better, of course. I'd learned, as had Skylar, that life isn't endless. Sometimes it ended in an abrupt, shocking way. But whatever was ahead for me, I intended to give it everything I had.

5

The smell of Skylar's fresh brewed coffee greeted me when my alarm buzzed. I went out to the kitchen to welcome another day and found Skylar at the table, a steaming cup already in hand. She was dressed in a peasant skirt and loose blouse.

"I'm heading downstairs early, Gram," Skylar said. "I know Lily needed to leave at closing time yesterday, but the shelves need restocking and there are plenty of toys in the backroom. I want to get started on that before we open."

"Sounds good," I said, amused by her eagerness to jump in with both feet. I had to bite my tongue so I wouldn't remind her to eat breakfast. Old habits were hard to break, and I had to remember to treat my adult granddaughter as a woman capable of knowing when she was hungry. Besides, I had my hands full making sure I ate a hearty breakfast before plunging into my day.

I took my time and watched some morning news with my tea and toast, waiting until shortly before opening time to join Skylar. She was busy taking an inventory of the toys in the backroom and commented about what was needed. "I wonder if Lily knows we've sold almost all of the puzzles that just arrived. What should I say so she doesn't feel like I went behind her back?"

"Best to just tell her the truth and offer your help. I don't think Lily will be offended." At least I hoped she wasn't. I didn't really know much about her or if the pregnancy had affected her disposition. I wasn't exactly sure if she'd question Skylar's judgment, either, but it was a chance worth taking, especially because Skylar apparently wanted to stay busy.

When the bell jingled, Lily came in with Toby leading the way. Usually outgoing, Toby held back when he saw Skylar, a new person to him.

Lily grinned at her little boy. "Toby, this is Skylar. I told you about her. She's the lady that's helping me with the toys."

Still a little shy, Toby smiled and then looked my way.

"Hi, Toby," I said, "good to see you today. I'm glad you get to meet Skylar. She's my granddaughter."

His grin broadened.

"Go on, Toby. You can get a puzzle or a toy," Lily said. "Last night Toby helped me pick out toys for my next order, so I told him he could choose one because he worked so hard."

Lily turned to Skylar and patted her tote as if it contained gold. "Order info," she said with a grin. "I'd like to run a few things by you."

I slipped away and left Lily and Skylar to handle their work, and Toby wandered back to the toys. I had enough to do, starting with the steps to open the shop for the day. There was a sequence of switches that turned on regular lights and spotlights, but we needed more spotlights. If the shop were mine, I'd add track lighting, but short of that, I could strategically switch bulbs to brighten the dark corners. It didn't make sense to save a few cents on the electric bill, but end up with a shop that had shadowed areas.

With Skylar and Lily occupied, Toby ran to the front of the shop to show me the latest action figure his mother had talked about. Full of his stories and his shyness gone, I noticed what a little charmer he could be.

A few minutes later, toy in hand, he left with Lily to go to Sally's, where he'd be for the day while Lily worked.

Within minutes of opening, a family came in and two solo shoppers needed some help. We were so busy it was late afternoon before I had an opportunity to talk to Skylar about her earlier conversation with Lily.

"You were right about her being open to my help," Skylar

said. "Lily gave me her list and the password to her account. I have her permission to order extra inventory and pick out items I think will sell. I told her that I was happy to help you keep things going—at least as long as I'm visiting."

"That's a good way to put it," I responded. "She rents the space, but she also helps with the whole shop, too. Doris took care of her customers when she wasn't here."

"Lily knows a lot," Skylar said, nodding. "She also mentioned a Sidewalk Sales Day in August and wants lots of toys for it. And she said you'll need more books for that event. Stock turns over quickly—her words."

I laughed. "I'm taking her advice to heart, but tomorrow is another day. Tonight, we need dinner. Let's go raid the deli at Farmer Foods. We can go to Crossroads tomorrow. How about that?"

"I want a fat turkey sandwich and more of those fresh strawberries you had. We need a boatload of food. Good thing you have me to help carry it all. We should stock up and fill your cabinets while I'm here."

"I suppose, but I think I'll be mostly buying what those cooks at Farmer Foods fix."

Skylar grinned. She knew me well. I never pretended to love cooking.

After I locked the door and we made our way across the Square to Farmer Foods, Skylar talked about needing a birthday gift for Rachel. "What are you giving her?"

"Does that mean you'll stay long enough to go to her party?"

"Sure. She invited me." Skylar had a sly smile on her face. "And we need to even out the numbers around here, you know, young versus old." Then she snickered.

Her teasing and listening to her react to her own joke filled me with pleasure. We'd had too many years when we'd shed more tears and shared our sorrow; far more than we'd bantered back and forth and laughed over little things.

Our shopping took over an hour, not only because we filled a cart, but because so many people stopped to welcome us to the Square. By the time we got home, we hurried to eat our turkey sandwiches, made to order at the deli. The glass of wine and a chocolate cookie made us feel like we'd eaten at Crossroads.

We both went downstairs and worked in the shop before heading to bed. Even Skylar looked bushed, in a good way, by the time we went up to our rooms.

***

The next morning Skylar worked on Lily's accounts and the restocking while I kept busy rearranging displays. Lily came in just in time to work the afternoon rush. We took separate breaks for lunch, but I used the time to plan a major order that I hoped would move us through the summer months. Even a few days ago I'd have been reluctant to commit so much money, but it wasn't realistic to play small. The Square itself was the result of shop owners playing big.

Around closing, Richard came in and said, "Supper's on me—for the three of you." He pointed to Lily, Skylar, and me.

Lily shook her head. "I have to take a rain check, Dad. I'm really tired."

Richard frowned. I could see his concern.

"I agree," I said quickly, not really up for sharing Skylar again. I also bristled at his last minute declaration, more than a real invitation. Had he simply assumed we didn't have plans of our own? "I have tons of work, and Skylar and I planned to go over some orders tonight."

That wasn't exactly true, since I'd suggested to Skylar that we go to dinner at Crossroads that evening. But we could change our plans easily enough. Besides, we did have work to do. And plenty of food on hand.

Richard stood there looking a little forlorn. Apparently, he'd been ready to enjoy the evening and the three of us bowed out, leaving us with an uncomfortable silence.

Lily grabbed her tote. "I'll see how I feel in the morning, but I'll be in by noon at the latest. I might actually get here by opening time." Lily laughed, as if she'd made a joke.

No one laughed along with her.

It was an awkward moment, but it ended quickly when

the four of us scattered. Lily took off for Sally's, and as I locked the door I saw Richard walk toward Country Law. I felt a little sorry for him. If Skylar hadn't been visiting, I'd have accepted the dinner invitation and enjoyed his company.

After Richard and Lily left and Skylar went upstairs, I had one more item I wanted to get done. I called Reed Crawford. He answered after a couple of rings, but I couldn't hear much beyond, "Hi, Millie."

"Reed, I can hardly hear you. Your construction noise is muffling your voice. I want to talk to you about installing a sound system. Why don't I walk over?"

I heard him say something about something he'd installed, and I told him I'd be right over.

After locking up the shop, I went next door. Reed had left the door open so I stepped inside. The scent of fresh paint along with banks of bright lights recessed into the ceiling created the image of ready and new—ready for a new owner to occupy.

Reed approached me with a small remote control in his hand. "Listen."

Instrumental music surrounded me, first soft, then louder as he increased the volume. Then he changed the disc, and bluegrass fiddling filled the shop. "It's perfect for music you download and store, of course, but it's also designed to work with a multi-disc player located in the back storage room." He pointed to a closed door at the end of the open space. "The speakers are hidden in the ceiling, the way new buildings are equipped." He smiled. "Clever, huh?"

I considered what he'd displayed, but said, "It's more than I want or need. I could tuck speakers on top of the book shelves for now. But give me an estimate." I could change my mind. I could see from the small collection of CDs Doris had for sale that she didn't sell many. Something else that was yesterday's news, but I had some of my own music to use as background in the shop.

"Got it." Reed made some notes in a little book he held. "I'll price it out and get back to you. Meanwhile, I can install a few small speakers for you—no construction mess and it can be done all at once."

"Perfect," I said. "You can install them anytime, except tomorrow night. I'm going to Rachel's party." I edged toward the front door, eager to wrap up my day.

"That's fine. I'll be at the party myself. I'll come by Sunday morning, if that works for you."

"I'll plan on it. Thanks so much." I smiled to myself as I left, thinking about what a good impression Reed left. I was also pleased to do something to improve the quality of my days in the shop, and music would certainly do that.

After a quick dinner with Skylar, I spent a couple of hours placing book orders from two different distributors. It took that long to reestablish an account that had been listed as closed. Another small mess to clean up. Apparently, Doris had paid old invoices and confused them with the newer orders. Once again, it appeared her deterioration had been swift and dramatic.

As I passed the door to her room, I heard Skylar on the phone. I considered knocking long enough to say goodnight, but I decided to leave her alone to have her conversation. I was ready to give into sleep. Still, I was curious who she was talking to.

***

"Gram, Gram? You getting up today?"

Huh? Where was I? My intense dream had me back in the bookstore in Minneapolis trying to unpack box after box of books. I stacked them in high piles when there was no other place to put them, all the while surrounded by a dozen customers talking at the same time.

"What time is it?" I asked, sitting up and rubbing my eyes.

"Your alarm went off fifteen minutes ago."

I threw off the light blanket and got to my feet. Skylar handed me a cup of tea, piping hot with lemon. "I'll be ready in a minute," I said, sheepishly.

"I'll make you some toast and eggs, and there's orange juice left," Skylar said, turning to leave my room. "Oh, Lily sent a text. She'll be in later, if at all. Not feeling good this morning, but hopes to make the party."

Skylar's go-to breakfast would make a nutritionist very happy. She'd covered three of the daily requirements with eggs, toast, and fruit. Not so for me. I didn't find eggs in the morning appealing, but I had to admit food was about energy now, more than what I liked or disliked. And I needed a lot of energy for these long days.

Skylar finished eating before me and was already dressed for the day in the shop. After clearing away the dishes, she left with a giant mug of coffee. I wasn't in any particular hurry, so I sat with a second cup of tea and eased into the day.

I didn't see much of Skylar that day, but I heard her laughter above the other voices now and then along with bursts from children and adults. The energy in the shop was fun and exciting.

When Skylar rushed to the counter to get a bottle of water mid-afternoon, she smiled and said, "We need more toys."

I shrugged. With a long line at the register, it was obvious I couldn't help her restock.

Busy as we were, we still had an event to look forward to.

6

Richard was only too happy to go to the party with Skylar and me. The three of us made the short walk to Crossroads and once inside, we followed a row of balloons that led us to the private dining room.

Wow. This community knew how to enjoy itself. First the Fourth of July picnic and now a birthday party. I wondered what I'd see when the fall holidays arrived. They worked hard, but made time for fun. They'd made it easy to feel like one of them, even if only for a short time. I was so content my smile hurt my cheeks.

Rachel herself stood by the door to greet us, with Thomas standing next to her. "Thanks so much for coming. Isn't this something?"

Marianna stood nearby, camera in hand, recording the event by taking one shot after another as new people arrived. Alan Carlson soon stepped into our group and introduced himself. When Thomas held his arms up, Alan hoisted him onto his shoulders to give the little boy a panoramic view of the room.

Skylar surprised me by pulling a small, stuffed puppy from her purse and handing it to Thomas. He was surprised—and cheerful. Based on the boy's happy grin, Skylar had made a friend for life.

Alan stuck out his lower lip in a mock pout and leaned forward to look into Skylar's bag. "Nothing for me?"

"Sorry, only for those 12 and younger," she quipped.

We were being moved deeper into the room by the groups of people coming in behind us. I recognized some of the faces when I glanced back. Richard leaned forward over my shoulder and quietly said, "Let's find seats."

I pointed at Sadie sitting at a mostly unoccupied table. "I see Sadie with empty chairs over there."

"Lead on."

I turned to include Skylar, but Alan was introducing her to Reed and another man of similar age, probably Nolan. I'd learned the two men worked for their cousin, Charlie Crawford, but sometimes ventured out themselves. Usually they lived in the places they renovated, although I hadn't seen Nolan when I talked with Reed about the sound system.

Skylar certainly didn't need to keep track of me at the party, any more than I needed to keep an eye on her. She was showing signs of her growing independence. That made me both happy and sad. Living together we'd become close, maybe too close for comfort for someone so young and just starting her adult life. But, because of what we'd gone through together, we'd depended on each other instead of reaching out to the world.

Sadie, glad to have us join her, soon started talking museum business with Richard, giving me a chance to scan the room. Most of the residents of the Square had divided themselves into clusters based on their ages. When I saw Skylar sitting between Lily and Alan, who had Thomas on his lap, I immediately saw how animated she was, intensely involved in the conversation. Nathan tended to Toby, and Reed and Nolan rounded out the group. Sarah traveled between the tables, eventually taking the empty chair next to me.

From the front of the room, Clayton Sommers blew a sharp whistle to get our attention. It worked and all eyes glanced his way.

Rachel stepped up next to him. "I want to thank all of you for coming tonight. Marianna says this is a milestone in my life and I will always remember it. If it hadn't been for her patience and understanding, I don't know how I would have made it through the last three years." She stopped when her voice cracked. She waved her hands in front of her face as if willing away the gathering tears. "Anyway, cake and ice cream coming right up."

Clayton grabbed her arm. "Not so fast, young lady." In his rich baritone voice, he began singing the birthday song. We joined in, then ended it with a hearty applause.

"Thank you, thank you." Rachel made a few simple bows. "Now, cake." She quickly left the front of the room and began cutting the cake on a nearby table, with Nolan adding a scoop of ice cream to each plate. Reed and Alan stood nearby. Seems those two, and others, were always around helping, and tonight they were in charge of delivering the cake plates to the guests.

A server from Crossroads came by offering coffee, tea, and sparkling water for the adults and juice for the kids. Immediately, the noise in the room returned to its previous level. The community had gotten together for a celebration for one of its own and that was special in itself.

"I can't imagine being twenty-one again," Sadie remarked before spooning a bite of cake into her mouth.

"I'm fine with where I am," I said. And I realized I was. Anyway, weren't people always saying that sixty was the new forty? But with a whole lot more wisdom? I hoped so.

I looked to Richard for a comment, but either he chose not to be part of our conversation, or he hadn't given it much thought. I didn't want to get into a philosophical discussion so I didn't press him for an answer.

Sadie continued on about the new exhibits at the museum. "I hope some of the people from the bus tour stop in. You have to come and see the new areas within the museum we opened last month. We've started with the founding of Wolf Creek."

"I assume you have museum brochures," I said, "so if you want to bring some over, I'll add a display of Wisconsin history books and a reminder sign in the window that you're open."

"Oh, that would be terrific. I'll bring some over tomorrow."

Had I offered too quickly? Would I have time to assemble another display?

Well, why not? All it amounted to was taking a few

books out of the window and putting new ones in. The rest of the display would continue the theme of the making of a country.

I was ready to leave about the time Rachel came to the table for one last thank you. I saw others in the room making their way out, so I stood to send a message to Richard that it was time to go. He stood, too, apparently understanding my desire to head home. Rather than coming with us, Sadie said she'd wait for Sarah.

Skylar was still across the room with Reed and Nolan and one of the women from The Fiber Barn. I couldn't remember which one though. I waved, but she was deep in conversation and didn't see me. Oh, well. She knew the way home. Besides, she'd probably have a two-man escort.

Richard said little as we walked the length of the Square. I hadn't been around him enough to see his high and low moods, but I imagined he was like all the rest of us, with good days and bad.

"Penny for your thoughts," I said.

"Nothing, really. My life is changing quickly and it seems I don't have much control over it anymore." His frown indicated confusion about his situation.

"Control? Who really has much control?" My voice was louder than I intended. "Maybe over little things. I have control over what I eat and the clothes I buy, but we don't have much to say about the big picture. We've both learned that lesson the hard way." I'd conveyed a more cynical attitude than I usually associated with myself, but there it was. I couldn't take it back. And wasn't inclined to, anyway.

We'd come to my corner shop. "I'm kind of nervous about Saturday," I said. "It'll be my first bus tour and, from the buzz I hear, mostly from Lily, they are a one-of-a-kind experience."

Richard grinned and waved dismissively. "You'll be fine. Most of the time, there'll be the three of you in the store."

I didn't have the heart to remind him that on the Square, the businesses were called shops *not* stores. Well, maybe Farmer Foods was a store, and I always referred to the shop as the bookstore. So which was it? I didn't answer the question, because I couldn't see that it mattered. Maybe that was a gift being a little older had given me. The ability to decide what mattered and what didn't—at least some of the time. I'd spent too many years fretting over inconsequential things.

"Good night, Richard." I gave him what I thought would be a quick hug, but he hung on longer than I expected, so I moved away. "I'll let you know how the tour goes on Saturday. Busy weekend. Reed is installing a sound system in the shop on Sunday morning."

"Does he know how to do that?" Richard-the-lawyer had returned.

"Oh, I'm sure he does. He just put in a more elaborate one in that building." I nodded to the building next door.

"Could be a waste of money if you need to have it replaced later on."

I waved him off. "Whoever takes over the store can worry about upgrades." Richard was just being Richard.

***

After a really fast supper the next day, Skylar and I went downstairs to finish preparing for the bus tour. She put out every toy she could squeeze onto the shelves and I carried empty box after box to the recycle bin after unloading and shelving the new books that had arrived earlier in the day.

Skylar thought to add water bottles and sandwiches to the small fridge by the register. It felt like we were preparing for a major disaster. Maybe we were.

How the fates love to laugh. Well, laugh they did.

Skylar, Lily, and I could only laugh with them, or we'd have cried. At the last minute "bus" had become "buses" when two tour companies overlapped their dates. That amounted to twice as many shoppers. Oh, my. Sarah stopped in, but seeing us too busy to say hello she went on her way, pleased, I'm sure, by the successful day.

Thankfully, Lily felt well enough to stay most of the day. She sat in the chair in the toy corner or leaned against the shelves whenever she could, but she was never happier than when helping a crowd of kids. Lily had a following, too, and recognized a few shoppers from previous visits, which added to the atmosphere. I noticed she had a way of making each customer feel special.

Two shoppers asked about Doris. When I explained she wasn't able to manage the shop any longer they both commented they were glad the bookstore hadn't closed.

At closing, the three of us let out a long sigh of relief. When we ran a sales report on the register, Skylar and I were stunned by the numbers. Lily just grinned and said, "We have many days on the Square like this one."

As I thought about the shop, maybe I *could* take it over if I chose to. The crowds along with the sales volume we did that day made the idea seem viable—even attractive. My other bookstore had done well, very well, but all-day rushes like the one we'd had weren't typical.

"Hard to beat an adrenalin rush like this, isn't it?" Lily sat on the stool and tapped the counter with her fingers.

Skylar sat on the floor. "No wonder you wanted to partner with Doris and sell toys. You saw the potential and jumped on it."

Lily beamed at the compliment. "If I wasn't pregnant, I'd build the toys into its own business." She sighed. "But right now, I need to get home. Nathan just texted that he and Toby are on the way back with takeout barbecue. I finally feel like I can eat a real dinner."

Lily quickly added a few items to Skylar's list for reorders and took off. I went off to check the empty spaces on the book shelves and do my own reordering. But while I walked up one aisle and down the next, a terrible thought occurred to me.

How would I manage when Lily no longer came to the shop and Skylar was back in Minneapolis?

The reality was I couldn't.

Then worry took over. It stayed with me all evening and into the night.

***

The next morning Reed buzzed the back door and with Nolan following, he brought three boxes into the shop. I'd had Skylar bring my speakers and CD system from home, and Reed went to look at it in the storeroom where we'd left it.

"Thought you were interested in a wireless system, Millie," Reed said frowning. "I'd have to use wires to connect the main box to those speakers. I can return the one I bought if you want to use yours."

"Wires would look tacky." Skylar, who had joined us, made her opinion clear. "I thought you wanted to upgrade, Gram."

Well, nothing like being blunt, Skylar.

"You're right," I said. "We sure don't need the shop looking like a dorm room with an amateur rigged sound system."

"Okay, then," Reed said, "I get it. What I got for you will be perfect—and won't take us long."

"You need my help?" I asked.

Reed gave me a pointed look that silently asked, *Are you kidding?*

I laughed and waved off my offer. "Have at it."

The two men worked, but the whole project probably took a lot longer than needed. Keeping up a running conversation with Skylar took up lots of time, after all. Good thing they weren't working by the hour. Still, they finished up around noon, and all afternoon my shoppers were able to enjoy upbeat Beatles songs with a little country-western thrown in. It was that kind of day.

***

As the days passed, one flowed into the next, and Skylar never mentioned plans to leave. I would let her decision ride for a while and enjoy the rhythm we formed living and working with each other. I talked to Richard now and again. He'd tell me about his day, but would only briefly listen when I started to tell him about an unusual customer or the huge sale I'd made to a family of five before he would interrupt. Hmm…that wasn't the kind of conversationalist I was used to. I couldn't help feeling slighted.

That wasn't the kind of friendship I'd been used to with him, either. He sometimes said I was too busy, using a tone that sounded like a complaint. Too busy for what? I wondered what he meant. I was really far too busy to take any time trying to get him to understand that I loved being busy—even over-busy—every day. I'd have assumed he'd understand my excitement about doing so well in the shop. After all, it was his idea that brought me to the Square in the first place.

By the end of July, I knew for certain Pages and Toys was not a one person shop. I needed help and I needed it before Lily and Skylar left me alone. After dinner one night, Skylar and I relaxed by the window overlooking the Square.

"Honey," I said, "I know you've enjoyed being here and helping Lily and me, but the reality is that I'm going to need help very soon. You'll be going back to Minneapolis…"

She held her hands up to stop me. "Gram, I wish I could stay *here*." She looked away. "But I know we have a home that I should go back to."

"Wait, wait. Are you telling me you'd stay if you could?"

She lifted her hands in the air. "*Yes*."

August
7

I turned the calendar the next morning, admiring the photo of the sparkling clear lake with the snow-capped mountains reflected on the surface. Still reveling in Skylar's answer, I'd have admired just about any landscape I saw that morning. The note about the association meeting that evening put an even bigger smile on my face. Doris had been a member, and as an acting owner I was a member of that group now.

Leaving Skylar to her coffee, I headed off to B and B. All my nervousness about going inside the coffee shop was gone on the morning breeze. I joined the usual group of women and felt like I belonged. My visitor status had changed to voting member.

The topic-of-the-day traveled between light talk about the idea of having dinner or a drink after that evening's meeting and the upcoming Sidewalk Sales Day. Having sold off the old and damaged books, I had nothing to put out for sale but a few slow-moving titles along with a selection of my standard fare. I could fill the sidewalk sale bin with books that included a local connection or atmosphere. I decided to put out a free box filled with older holiday decorations. Skylar might like the job of sorting through the many cartons and choosing what we could get rid of.

I hurried back after Sarah's watch beeped and found Richard sitting on the front steps. A big smile greeted me and he stood when I got closer.

"Good to see you, Richard. What brings you by?"

"A dinner invitation. Let's stay and have dinner at Crossroads after the meeting."

Well, why not?

"I'd like that," I said, surprising myself.

He nodded his approval. "I'll make a reservation."

"Later." I waved and walked through the open door.

My day started with customers who said they'd browse for a while. That gave me time to begin dismantling the front window display. Had a month passed so quickly? As well as I thought my patriotic July 4th theme had worked, that holiday was over and I had to find something new to put in the window.

I went to the back room to find Doris' beat up box labeled "August." I laughed when I opened the box and found a piece of fabric printed with faded beach umbrellas.

But it sparked an idea to depict a water front vacation with lots of "beach read" novels. Previously, the bookstore had stocked the latest bestselling novels only in hard cover, but given that Lily gave me carte blanche to order, I wanted to add a variety of the most popular fiction in paperback. Quite a few shoppers had already asked why we had so few soft cover editions of the newer bestsellers. Good question, and it was time to correct the situation.

When one of the women stood in the doorway and said she wanted to pay and be on her way, I grabbed the box and followed her to the register. I had been away from the front of the store for only a few minutes and was surprised to see the number of customers in the shop. I'd left the front door open to enjoy the cooler weather and entice the visitors to enter, but on the other hand, that eliminated the jingling bell to alert me that someone was coming inside.

I didn't get back to the window project until well after lunch. I knew I wanted sand, maybe a few toys from Lily's inventory, and an assortment of books. Years ago, I'd seen a department store in Minneapolis use sawdust for sand in their summer window displays. That certainly would be easier to handle than bags of sand—and I knew just who to call.

"Sawdust?" Reed laughed. "I live in the stuff. How much

do you want?"

"Enough for a window display."

"I'll be there in an hour with a pail full."

I quickly ordered quite a few paperback copies of newer beach-reads and had them shipped overnight. Using short breaks between customers, Skylar and I managed to spread the supply of sawdust Reed brought by. At the end of the day, he grinned in approval of my beach idea and agreed that real sand would be much harder to clean up.

"It gets everywhere," he said, laughing. "You don't want customers brushing away sand on the pages of books!"

"You're right," I said. "I hope the sawdust stays put. I'm counting on your shop-vac to clean it up."

In his usual good-humored way, Reed waved and left. But I'd noticed him looking around the store. I almost asked him if he wanted something else, but he took off. Then it dawned on me that maybe he'd been looking for Skylar. Well, well. A new development.

And none of my business.

I got to work assembling the display, leaving room for new beach-read books between the toys Skylar and Lily chose and the paper plate settings I'd used from my kitchen, along with a picnic basket and my small cooler. There, job done.

The second window had been more of a puzzle, but one of the first of that day's customers had asked for a book on canning fruits and vegetables. And the display almost made itself. I grabbed assorted books on canning, freezing, and drying foods, along with summer cookbooks and one that focused only on picnics. Talk about specialized. I spread out titles and propped a few against a canning pot I'd noticed in passing on a shelf in the basement. Hmm…maybe Doris had done some canning. The shelves looked as if they'd been specially installed to handle pint or quart size jars. The window was still sparse, but not empty. It needed accessory pieces and I'd seen a few gadgets at Farmer Foods that would fill in nicely.

After only two months I better understood Megan's and Marianna's conversations of the amount of time it took for their windows to be timely and attractive. Betsy and I had split the work and we'd had a couple of part-timers who added their ideas and labor. Now that I was aware of what it took to create displays for two windows more or less on my own, I'd be better prepared for the coming months when the Square would be filled with holiday shoppers. Warmth spread through me just thinking about having Skylar around to help. I wouldn't have to do it all alone, and the shop was doing so well that I could easily justify her salary.

When I climbed the stairs to end the day, I realized with a start how completely content I was. What a revelation! I laughed out loud.

***

The next morning when I unlocked the door I spotted Sarah sitting on one of the benches across the walkway from the shop. I waved, but she was on the phone and didn't see me.

I'd quickly learned that Sarah was the hub of the events and activities that made Wolf Creek Square a shopping and tourist destination. Once a small rural town, it had gradually faded into a near state of decay. *Not on Sarah's watch.*

Like a CEO, she'd checked in a few times to see if I needed help, but I was happy to tell her that with Skylar and Lily at my side, the shop and I were doing fine. I wasn't surprised when a few minutes later the bell jingled and she stepped inside.

"What brings you by so early?" I asked.

"I didn't see you at coffee this morning. Hope we haven't scared you off with it being so busy." Sarah looked around the shop. "Looks nice, Millie. I know you had a big job getting things back on track."

"I had some paperwork this morning, so I couldn't get over to B and B. I sure enjoy the morning group, though," I said to reassure her, although I wasn't being completely truthful. I glanced around. "This is such a good space for a bookstore. Would be a shame if it had to close. Some of the customers have told me that shopping here is one of the reasons they keep renting cottages on the lake year after year. They mean the whole Square, of course, but many specifically mention this shop."

"That's one of the reasons I'm glad you'll be at the association meeting tonight. We like to check in and compare notes about how the season is going."

"Well, I do hope no one minds. I'm only temporary help around here, not an owner."

"For the next few months that means nothing." She waved her hand dismissively. "You'll never know how relieved I was when Richard suggested talking to you. We had a problem and a solution showed up. I wish every problem could be solved that easily."

When the bell jingled and customers came in, Sarah slipped out.

For the next few hours I couldn't keep a lid on my joy at being with customers and simply being around the books. I buzzed around the shop suggesting titles when people needed direction and then waited for them at the register to complete the sale. When half a dozen cartons of new books arrived, I clapped my hands, bringing on a case of the giggles from Skylar.

Lily came in after lunch carrying an armload of catalogs.

I quickly grabbed them when she tried to close the door with both hands full. "What in the world are you doing carrying all of this?"

"I'm not helpless, Millie. Just pregnant, like lots of other women in the world."

Her grit and stubbornness were showing, but I didn't comment.

"Is Skylar here?"

I pointed behind me. "She's been helping a little girl for a while now."

"Girls have a harder time making a decision about toys—and books—than boys do."

"Really? Why is that?" I asked.

Lily sighed. "Girls are more afraid of making a mistake."

Was she talking about the little girl or maybe making an observation about herself?

"As long as Skylar is ordering the toys now, she'll need

these." Lily straightened the pile into a perfect stack. "Toby was a little disappointed that he wouldn't be helping me pick out the toys anymore, but it can't be helped. It's all I can do to come in and do the work when I'm here. The paperwork overwhelms me these days, maybe because I gradually had to take over much of that job when Doris couldn't handle it."

Skylar stepped up to join us when the little girl went down one of the book aisles to find her parents. She carried her toy as if it was gold. I'm sure to her it was. "Why don't you bring him by some afternoon and he can help me put an order together. I'd love to see what he chooses."

Lily grinned. "Oh, he would be so excited to do that."

"Besides, it's still your business," Skylar said. "I'm just helping out for now."

"You're doing more than that. You're giving me peace of mind." Lily laughed. "And, boy, do I need that right now."

The baby must have moved because Lily pushed at her side. "The baby's active today. Moving a lot."

"That's good to hear," I added as I walked away to tend to the large number of shoppers who had filled the shop.

Where did all these people come from? Singles, couples, families. I wanted to greet them all and find a book for each of them to take home.

And I did.

Skylar and I locked the door for the day, and spontaneously slapped our palms in a high five. So many people, so many sales.

"Sure hope that large book order arrives tomorrow," I said. "I already sold two of the books out of the window display."

Skylar turned away, but I heard her say, "I took a toy out of the window, too." She turned back to see my reaction.

Neither of us could stop the laughter.

I was about to turn off the lights when someone made a few quick raps on the door. I retraced my steps to the front of the shop and found a young man waiting for me. I turned the bolt and opened the door.

"I'm sorry to bother you just as you're closing. I've been

invited to a friend's house for dinner and want to bring him a gift. Would you be kind enough to help me find a book for him? He loves biographies."

Me turn down a sale? Not on your life. "I think we can find something he'll like."

He stepped inside and we went down the second aisle to the shelf of books about famous, and not so famous, people. He immediately chose one about Al Capone because of the fugitive's connection to Wisconsin and his friend's interest in history.

He asked if I could gift wrap it for him. I was happy to say yes. Thank you, Skylar, for suggesting we stock paper and cards.

By the time the young man left I had only a few minutes before meeting Richard at Crossroads for the meeting. I used the time to retouch my make-up and run a brush through my hair. On my way out, Skylar stuck her head out of her room and told me to have a good time.

Like Rachel's birthday party, the Wolf Creek Square Business Association meeting was held in the private dining room at Crossroads. Sarah was at the door greeting all of us and handing out the agenda for the meeting.

"We have a few minutes yet before the meeting starts." Sarah waved us to the tables along the back wall filled with assorted snacks and beverages. She turned to greet the next group entering the room.

"Come on this way, Millie," Richard said. "I see Nathan. And Jack and Liz are with him. Have you met Liz?"

"Briefly. At morning coffee." I remembered Zoe saying Liz designed her gift certificates. Maybe I'd have a minute to talk with her about doing one for the bookstore. That stopped me. If the store closed at the end of the year, why would the bookstore need anything new, other than restocking the books? Somehow that seemed sad. I wanted the shop to be a gem of a place as long as it existed. And I'd be there through the holidays, so a sophisticated, well-done certificate would show the shop in a good light, no matter who ended up buying it.

Richard got a glass of white wine for each of us. I took

a sip and found it dry, even with a hint of fruit. Nice. We mingled with the crowd waiting for others to arrive.

At the top of the hour we got to our seats and Sarah started the meeting by talking about the fairly long agenda. She stopped to take a deep breath. "This weekend, we have the Sidewalk Sale Days," she said, "and with all the new shops on the Square since we've had this event, I believe we'll see lots of traffic."

I had a lot to take in, including information about an ice cream social going on with the sidewalk sale. It would be hosted by a veteran's group that helped out at Elliot and Georgia's wedding reception. I recalled hearing something about that, mainly because they'd come to the Square the first time to help the women move into The Fiber Barn.

"And to keep it simple, the vets aren't selling the ice cream, just asking for donations. They'll have a refrigerated truck and vending booth on the corner between Country Law and Art&Son and for the afternoon and evening."

"Hope they have lots of chocolate."

Something about Elliot's dry tone brought a round of laughter. Zoe just rolled her eyes, but even Richard laughed at the remark.

Wow, what a weekend. Even the high school band was playing during the afternoon and into the evening.

"Next item," Sarah said. "Tom Harris is bringing one of his large bus tours on the following weekend. He's promoting it as the Last Bash of Summer bus trip. He called me the other day to confirm the trip and let me know his riders requested Wolf Creek as the destination. I think we should all take pride in that."

Sarah finished up quickly with an overview of the coming holiday season.

I found I wanted time to slow down. When the holidays were over I'd be heading back to Minneapolis. Sitting there with others on the Square, I wasn't sure how I felt about that. My condo in a co-op seemed far away, disconnected from me.

I followed Richard into the main dining room at the close of the meeting. He had called for a reservation, but when Art and Marianna suggested we join them, I was happy to accept and Richard seemed fine with it. Then Clayton, Megan, and Sadie asked for a table to be added, so our group expanded. Finally, the one vacant seat was filled when Sarah joined us. But then Jack asked Melanie, the manager, if we could add one more table so he and Liz could join us. Nathan begged off, needing to get home. Worry lines around his eyes spoke of concern.

It was a fun group, full of easy, teasing banter and reciprocal interest in each other's businesses. Betsy and I had found the same kind of community in the area where our shop had been located. The atmosphere at dinner was really just a more boisterous version of mornings at B and B—minus the separate tables for men and women. I listened more than talked, picking up as much as I could about my neighbors and the pleasure they found in living on the Square.

I was caught off guard when the lights dimmed to signal closing time. The hours had passed so quickly with my dinner companions. We were all more relaxed with the workday behind us, unlike the focus of morning coffee.

Right then, in Crossroads, I began to sense a yearning deep inside of me. For a few minutes, I wanted to slip into the group and become a part of it—for real.

When Richard and I walked to the bookstore we didn't say goodnight right away. Instead, he led me to the bench across the walkway from the shop where we sat and unwound from the dinner.

"We didn't get much time to talk by ourselves this evening."

I detected a note of disappointment in Richard's words. "Was there something you wanted to say?" I asked.

"Toby's other grandparents, Linda's parents, called about Toby's yearly visit." Richard worked his throat to keep the emotions at bay. "That was one of the provisions in the guardianship agreement Chad had prepared. Linda's parents can visit Toby and he can go to see them every summer."

That sounded reasonable enough, but I knew there was more to this story. I was learning it slowly, a detail here and an anecdote there. I decided to be patient and wait for Richard to finish.

"The summer is passing quickly. Given Lily's situation, Nathan doesn't want to leave her now for the trip to Ohio. Since Toby is still too young to travel alone, I'm taking him. I'll be gone for a week."

"Wonderful. What better person for him to travel with than his granddad? You'll have a great time."

"I haven't seen them for years, not since Chad and Linda's funeral."

There was more than sadness in Richard's frown. It gave away apprehension, as if he wasn't used to letting his insecurities surface. So, he wasn't only the hardcore lawyer, he was the caring father, now grandfather.

"It's good for all of you to be together again. Especially for Toby," I said, thinking of my son's wife, Carolyn, who grew up in foster homes. Skylar and I had no one to connect with after her death. I envied Richard this opportunity to expand the number of people who loved Toby.

Richard bit his lower lip. "But Millie, the thing is, I don't want to leave you here alone."

Where had that come from? "What? I'm *not* alone. Why would you think that way? Skylar is here. I'm making new friends and working seven days a week!"

Oops. My tone was sharp. Maybe because his statement implied he had to keep track of me. Talk about alarming. On the other hand, maybe I'd misread his meaning. I realized he was opening up about his feelings for me and I wanted to close that door quickly. We hadn't spoken about the future, and I didn't want to. Not yet. Maybe Richard would become more than a friend one day. But at the moment, I had no interest in being part of a couple.

Switching topics I said, "Speaking of Skylar, I can't even describe how happy I am that she's staying. She and Lily get along well, and now the pressure is off Lily. If she needs a day off, or has to leave early, we'll be covered."

Richard beamed over that news. "It's great they get along. But, between you and me, I've been wondering how long Lily can continue to work. She's still not feeling well."

"I know," I said with a nod. "I see it, and so does Skylar."

Concerns over Lily darkened Richard's mood, but only for a minute. He quickly perked up.

Richard suddenly nudged my shoulder. "What was that you were saying about Skylar?" He nodded toward the end of the Square where Skylar and Reed were walking across the Square with Rachel and Alan.

I grinned. "I guess Skylar had an evening out, too."

I stood to thank Richard and head in. "I'm glad you told me about your trip."

"I'll call you when I get there," he said, giving me a quick hug.

Seeing Richard up close made me see more sides of him. I knew for sure he had the demeanor of a man used to getting his own way, but I had no inclination to cater to that particular trait. Besides, I had way too much on my plate to concern myself with what was on his.

8

The next day Megan pulled me aside as we were leaving B and B after morning coffee. “I’m working with an engaged couple today and I’d like to bring them by to show them your wedding planning books. They need something to ease their wedding worries.” She flashed a bright smile. “I’m supposed to handle their worries, but some are nervous anyway.”

“Sure, anytime,” I said. “I’ll pick out a few samples and have them at the register.”

She turned to Zoe and I heard her mention that she’d bring the couple to visit Square Spirits after the bookstore.

Megan had mentioned her wedding planning business that involved every business on Wolf Creek Square which made it a one-stop shopping destination for couples. I needed to learn more about her concept so there would be a selection of books available. We had only a few good wedding books left on the shelves. Once I was back in the shop, I jotted a note to order more titles and put it in the pocket of my vest.

The couple Megan brought in were young professionals who were going to rely on Megan to coordinate their entire day, in addition to a pre-wedding shower and the gift opening party the day after the wedding. Whew!

They found two books, *Your Complete Wedding* and *On Your Special Day*, to take with them. Megan suggested a guest registry and a photo album, but the couple wasn’t ready to make that decision yet. I got Megan’s hint for me to have a selection of them available too, although she hadn’t said it in words.

By the time our conversation had moved onto the couple describing their honeymoon, three groups of shoppers had come in, the bell jingling with each group. Megan moved the couple toward the door with a combination of kindness and professionalism, reminding them about their next stop, Square Spirits.

I viewed this opportunity of being part of the Square's wedding venture as another facet of the bookstore's image. Doris had been only marginally involved with Megan's business, but I wanted the store to have a good image.

There it was again, my concern for the shop. I couldn't hide it from myself any longer. The Square and this shop were creeping further and further into my heart. At the moment, it was hard to remember that I'd agreed to be here only until the end of the year.

That thought sent another one through my strange brain pathways and led me to make a mental note to call Betsy in the morning. She'd never called back after her visit from the school children. Maybe they kidnapped her and left her on the bus. Oh, boy, I was way overtired. That night, the softness of my bed made sleep come easy.

***

The next morning I lazed around the apartment waiting for Skylar to join me for breakfast. Skylar was one of those women who was instantly awake and on the move the minute they woke up. I preferred to start my day with a cup of hot tea—even in the middle of summer—and use that time to sit at the table and plan my day.

And that was the irony of us living together.

From my point of view, Skylar needed to slow down and relax until the shop opened at 10:00 and I needed to step up and do those pesky tasks that took only a few minutes to get done, but were always on the list. But, in the past we'd been able to find a routine that worked for us, and I was sure we'd be able to find one that matched new demands.

While Skylar made scrambled eggs and toast, I grabbed two cartons of yogurt from the refrigerator and told her about the previous evening's association meeting and dinner.

I noted she was a little less forthcoming about her evening, and I left it alone. Maybe she and Reed and Rachel and Alan had walked off the Square for pizza, but she didn't offer information and I didn't probe. Almost casually, she mentioned that Reed had asked her to hang out on the Square with him on Saturday night after the shops closed. A well-known local bluegrass trio would be playing and the local veterans group would be serving ice cream. They could pick up dinner at a couple of places off the Square after work.

That sounded like great fun to me, but she shrugged and mumbled something about maybe being too tired after working the sale all day.

What nonsense. People her age could work all day and have fun late into the night. I know I had lived that way through my twenties. I tried to keep my thoughts to myself.

But I failed.

"I think it's great you're going out." Chuckling, I added, "And with a man."

Her features formed the perfect skeptical scowl. "What if something happens?"

"As in you might actually like him?"

Skylar snapped the towel at me, but she laughed.

***

That week, the days blended one into the next, but I wasn't drawn to B and B for morning coffee every day. It was pleasant enough, and it was mostly idle talk, most of which was almost too much on the light side for me. I preferred to spend a little time getting laundry done and keeping the place livable. My serious workday started when I unlocked the door at 10:00. Then I kept a steady pace, ending with restocking the shelves and occasionally chatting with Richard on the phone.

One evening, Skylar and I were downstairs when I heard her moaning and talking to herself from the toy area. I went to see what she was fussing about.

"Gram, just look at this?"

Packing boxes surrounded her—full boxes.

"There's no room on the shelves for these." She held up a pixie doll with her own matching luggage, sitting open and overflowing with trendy clothes.

I nodded. "I have the same problem with the books. Too many for the space." I arched my arm toward the shelves that were now filled to capacity, so different from the day I'd arrived. I had extra copies of at least half of the titles in boxes downstairs. Unfortunately, there simply wasn't enough space for all the stock Lily and Skylar had ordered. Miss Pixie Traveler doll had nowhere to land.

The next afternoon when Skylar and I showed Lily the sales totals for July she clapped her hands. "I knew it. I just knew that the shop could do even better if we upped the inventory."

Skylar spoke in a whispered tone, "It's like a small gold mine."

Lily laughed. "It could grow into a big gold mine if we had more space." She patted her stomach. "Right now I think the baby is thinking the same thing."

The Square itself definitely needed more space on Saturday when wave after wave of visitors arrived early for the best deals. Many stayed into the afternoon for ice cream and music. Liz had brought flyers offering specials at B and B and Crossroads, and a portion of the money for these meals would be given to the veteran's group. It would also keep the shoppers on the Square for the day.

In the afternoon, I left the door open so I could hear the music from the local high school band. Unfortunately, I had to keep a close watch on the door to bar people holding cones and cups of ice cream from stepping inside. Food and sticky fingers didn't mix well with books and toys. One woman actually complained when I asked her family to finish eating their ice cream outside before coming in.

"You should have a sign saying 'No food allowed.'"

A sarcastic retort was on the tip of my tongue, something pointing to simple common sense courtesy, but I swallowed back my words.

After the shop closed for the day, Richard stopped by

with two bowls of ice cream. So, we sat on the steps to enjoy the music and the people milling about. He stood when Skylar came out to say hello.

"Whew! What a day. I'm planning on eating dessert first," she said, her body bouncing with eagerness. "Can't wait to get a double scoop."

"Oh, Skylar, I'm sorry," Richard said. "I should have brought you some."

By now she was in front of the shop, just as Reed stepped out of the building next door. Perfect timing. I nudged Richard's arm with my elbow and pointed my chin toward Skylar and Reed, who were heading toward the ice cream stand.

"What do you make of that?" he asked.

"Well, it tells me she can see to getting her own ice cream," I joked. "But, like I told her, it's about time."

Later, we walked toward the band-shell, but I was ready to leave before the Bluegrass band started to play. With Skylar out on a date, I sure didn't want to be Gram hanging around. Besides, I was bushed. When I crawled into bed awhile later, the fiddlers were still going strong, but they didn't keep me up.

The next morning I left Skylar sleepily making herself coffee and took off to B and B. One of Tom Harris' bus tours was the next big event on the Square, so I heard quite a few legendary stories about his tours. Apparently, Tom had spent a couple of days in Rainbow Gardens deciding if he wanted to fulfill a life-long dream of owning a greenhouse or stay with the family business of running a charter bus company. Although he stuck with the tour business, his time on the Square had made him a big fan, and his growing number of tours provided a huge boost in sales.

When I got back to the shop, I once again added a few more books to the window displays and checked the supply of sale bags. I wasn't fond of the bags, perhaps because I wasn't fond of the shop's name. Pages and Toys. So ho hum. Never a good response. But if the shop was mine, what name would I give it?

So deep was I in thought, I startled when Skylar slipped in next to me.

"So, Gram, do you think we could shift the books a little to open up more shelving space for the toys?"

"You figure out where you want the space, and I'll help you move the books—I'll figure out which titles we can thin out." I had four boxes of books in the backroom that needed to be added to the inventory system and shelved. I didn't tell her that, but I felt a little guilty knowing that the sales for the toys almost matched those for the books using much less space. I sighed to myself. Clearly a long range plan would include separate shops, one for the books and one for the toys.

I'd done it again. These businesses were not mine. They were Lily's and Doris'. I was temporary help. Besides, Skylar would soon return to Minneapolis and get back to the business of job hunting. Wasting one minute thinking of the changes I'd make if the bookstore was mine was pointless.

On Saturday morning, just after morning coffee, I saw Sarah hurrying down the walkway toward Pages and Toys. She detoured into Styles and a few minutes later the bell on the front door jingled.

"Millie? Are you here?" Sarah called out.

"Coming." I hurried to the front of the shop with an armload of sales bags. I carried my vest over my arm.

Sarah was tapping her fingers on the counter when I arrived. "Just received a call from Tom Harris. There was a mix up with his assistant, or somebody, and two buses are coming. Is Skylar here to help you?"

"She'll be down in a minute. We'll be fine."

"And Lily?" There was a note of concern in her voice.

"I don't know when she'll be in," I said.

Sarah looked away, into the Square as if she was debating to say more. "If you need something, call me. I'll be around all day."

"Thanks for the support."

She checked her watch and with a wave, left.

Skylar came down minutes before it was time to unlock the door and was typically nonplussed when I told her about the two buses. "I'm glad I had a good breakfast. I doubt we'll get a break today."

"I'm going to put some yogurt in the fridge with a few more bottles of water. Help yourself when you want it."

By the time I went upstairs for the yogurt and came back into the shop the first group of shoppers were checking the sales table. They each wore a "Tom Harris Last Bash" name tag, and that meant the buses had arrived.

Was I ready? You bet.

As busy and crowded as the shop became, I still had fun talking to the women and couples. Even the customers laughed about the prediction that electronic books would make shops like Pages and Toys obsolete.

"That won't happen on my watch," one woman said. "I'm here to buy books for everyone in my family. I like e-books as much as the next person, but for gifts, give me a print book anytime." She grabbed one of the shopping baskets and went on her way to the shelves.

Another customer declined a sales bag for the one book she bought. "Bags are expensive and I'll just throw it away." She opened her large purse and nestled it into one corner. "I'll be back to do some Christmas shopping now that I know you've expanded your inventory of books and toys."

The stream of tour people seemed continuous for several hours. Many arrived carrying bags from other shops on the Square. We were all having a good day.

Around 3:00 a man came in alone, and I grinned when I saw his nametag. Tom Harris.

"Just stopped in to introduce myself," he said. "Megan told me about Doris' departure and suggested I meet the new people working here."

"It is nice to meet the guy responsible for bringing all these shoppers." I was multitasking while I talked to him, completing sales and encouraging shoppers to add their names to the newsletter list. I had one for the shop and Marianna talked often about the kinds of tidbits she included in hers, pointing out that bus tours were a perfect group to encourage to sign up. Tom didn't linger when he saw the line at the register. I managed to say a quick thank you when he left.

By the end of the day my feet hurt, I was hungry and thirsty—and happy with all the empty spaces on the shelves. No wonder I couldn't stop smiling.

I walked to the back of the store where Skylar was still helping a customer. I stood for a minute to revel in watching my granddaughter in action. Such a sales natural. Was it possible she'd found a new direction for her life?

I heard the bell jingle and was surprised to see Reed approaching the counter.

"Hi, Millie. Would you have a book on whittling?"

"Hmm. I don't think so. But let's look at the hobby books." I led him to the back row of shelves where I'd put the craft and special interest books when I'd rearranged the stock. I ran my hand across the books scanning each one. "Sorry, there's nothing here, but I can order one for you."

"Something basic—you know, a beginner's book." He turned when he heard Skylar's voice coming from the counter by the register.

Was he really here to order a book, or had he come to see Skylar? It was obvious to me where his thoughts had gone. Whittling flew out the window. I wondered if he knew how transparent he was.

Still, he recovered nicely. "I saw a TV special a while ago about this man who's been whittling his whole life and makes the most amazing things. I work with wood all the time, but I've never whittled."

The bell above the door jingled and I heard Skylar turn the lock. "Gram?"

"I'm back here with a customer."

"Oops, I locked the door."

"That's okay. Come on back."

Skylar flushed when she saw Reed. "Hi, neighbor. Buying a book?" She flashed a brilliant smile.

"Yes. No. I mean, I want to get a book to learn how to whittle."

"You already make wonderful toys," Skylar said, "which reminds me of something. Has Lily called you to order more?"

Reed frowned and shook his head. "Um, no. I haven't heard from her lately."

"After this whirlwind day, there's only one truck and one train left."

"I have more stored away," Reed said with a grin.

I was not part of this conversation, but being stuck between them and the wall didn't give me an easy escape route. And I wanted to sit down. "You two figure it out. I'll pick out a book, Reed. I'll let you know when it arrives." I scooted between them and headed upstairs. I doubted they noticed I left.

I started water for tea and sat on the couch while it heated. There were a few people on the Square, the last of the shoppers for the day. A family with three small children left B and B. I watched as the kids ran into the Square and around the gardens. How wonderful for parents to know that the children could run free in the Square. No motorized vehicles of any kind were allowed on the Square when the shops were open—and the bicyclers had to leave their bikes in a rack down at the edge of the park.

The kettle was about to boil when Skylar arrived. "Stay where you are. I'll make a cup for you."

"Thanks, honey."

She came to the couch with my tea in one hand and a bottle of water for herself. She walked to the window and looked out. "Reed's asked me out for dinner tonight. I told him I'd call him back."

"Is there a reason you didn't say yes?"

Skylar had talked very little about her Saturday night with Reed, but I hadn't wanted to press her. I sensed she was at another crossroads in her life. She needed to decide what was best for her.

"I'm beginning to like this little town," Skylar said, running her hand down her cheek and chin. "It's so much more than a bunch of businesses. Know what I mean?"

"I think so," I answered, not wanting to speculate aloud, "but I'm curious about what *you* mean."

"It's a *community*, Gram, a thriving, exciting community."

I laughed. "Funny you should say that. I'm feeling the

same way. I've already made friends here that will be hard to leave."

"Would one of those friends be Richard?"

I answered with a quick shrug. I'd known him before arriving on the Square. It wasn't at all like Skylar meeting Reed. But maybe there was more with Richard than I was ready to acknowledge.

Skylar abruptly walked into the kitchen and called Reed. A few minutes later, dressed in a pair of slim-legged jeans and an embroidered peasant blouse and wedged sandals she waved goodnight. As for me, I ate a thick ham sandwich from Farmer Foods and sat on my couch thinking about Richard.

He interrupted my reflections when he called from Green Bay. He'd been busy at the office preparing to be away the next week on his trip with Toby. I told him about the bus tour and meeting Tom Harris. "According to Sarah, that man has brought a lot of business to the Square."

"True enough," Richard said. "Now tell me what you'll be doing while I'm gone?"

"The same thing I'd be doing if you were here. Staying busy, I can say for sure. I'm ordering inventory and assessing demand for the national bestsellers right now. I feel like I have an important mission not to fail Lily or Doris."

"You're doing great, Millie. At least the shop didn't have to close. Not yet."

What? "Are you trying to tell me something?"

"Not my place, but Nathan said Lily was way too worn out to be in the shop today. I was thinking Toby and I shouldn't leave right now, but Nathan doesn't agree. He thinks that with Toby gone Lily will get more rest."

"I think Nathan is right. Skylar and I did fine today. At times, we were too busy to think about being tired. Anyway, Skylar's young and she worked all day and is out for dinner with Reed tonight."

"Again?"

"Ha! Did you hear yourself? You sound like a dad who isn't too sure he likes this development." I didn't hesitate to let my amusement show.

"Oops. Guess I'm still learning I'm not in control of everybody."

And why would you want to be?

"Most especially Skylar and Reed," I teased. "But tell me again, when do you leave for Ohio?"

"Tomorrow morning. I'll stop by before we leave."

"No need," I said, suppressing my irritation. "I'll be completely absorbed restocking shelves and filling the empty spots."

Silence. Finally, Richard said, "Well, then, goodnight, Millie."

Sleep came easy that night, but I stirred when I heard Skylar come in. Mostly, I wanted to hear all about her evening. I'm glad I stopped myself in time, because I heard the low buzz of two voices. I smiled and rolled over, leaving well enough alone.

9

I hadn't given it much thought before, but the next morning I was glad the shops opened at noon on Sundays. After the hectic bus tour Saturday, I needed the extra hours to relax and then restock.

Despite what I'd said on the phone the night before, Richard knocked on the front door around 9:00. I was already downstairs to let him in, but he didn't stay for more than a few minutes. I sensed he was concerned about the long drive and had been clear about wanting to arrive before dark. He also didn't know what kind of traveler Toby would be or how often they'd need to stop.

"I wouldn't worry. Kids usually fall asleep during long drives," I said, hoping to reassure him.

He gave me a hug and, without warning, a soft kiss. Then the bell jingled when he left. He was persistent, I'd say that for him. I wondered if I'd inadvertently encouraged him to act in such a possessive way. And presumptuous. He'd showed up at my door when I specifically told him I'd be busy. On the other hand, I touched my lips and smiled. That warm energy filled my body again. Oh, brother.

We had good, steady traffic all afternoon, although not the record numbers we'd had the day before. I found myself restocking the shelves periodically. A good sign.

Georgia, Lily's aunt, and Beverly, her mother, hosted a small shower for her that evening. Skylar and I had been invited and we joined Marianna and Rachel for the short walk to Beverly's house.

With women only, the teasing and laughter made me feel

close to the women from the Square, regardless of age. Lily asked Skylar to help with the gift opening while Rachel served snacks and dessert. I hadn't seen many of the new style baby clothes and safe toys, so when the gifts were passed around I wanted to learn all about them.

Sitting next to me, I overheard Nora Alexander's low voice saying, "I want a baby, too."

I'd heard about the Alexander Foundation renovating the museum on the Square, but had seen Nora only a few times at B and B. Already a pretty woman, her bright smile and generous attitude transformed her into quite the beauty. She made me want to know her better.

Skylar and Rachel chatted all the way home about the toys and cute clothes Lily had received. Boy or girl? Who knew? Lily and Nathan had kept that secret as tight as evidence in a court case. Never had I heard Lily slip even once when customers came right out and asked. But maybe they'd decided not to find out and let it be a surprise for themselves as well.

"You're quiet tonight, Marianna," I said.

"Ah, you noticed," she said, smiling sadly. "I can't help but worry about Lily and the baby. Staying healthy is critical for her right now, for both of them, really."

"Lily can get some rest now while Richard is away with Toby at his grandparents. They left today," I pointed out. "Maybe that will help."

"They better take advantage of it. They won't rest much after the baby is born," Marianna laughed. "My only experience is with Thomas, and I know it took both Rachel and me to keep him fed, dry, clean, and warm."

By then we'd entered the Square and headed for our shops and homes. I noticed lights on in the apartment Reed and Nolan lived in, the building between Quilts Galore and Pages and Toys. I glanced at Skylar and saw her staring at the lights. A smile tugged at the corners of her mouth.

Maybe love *was* in the air. This Square seemed to have that kind of magical powers—or so I'd been told.

***

Sales fell off the following week. On a couple of afternoons, the Square seemed almost empty. When it became the topic of the day at morning coffee, Marianna and Zoe said they worried about these lulls in traffic when they were new on the Square.

"Families are beginning to head home to get ready for school starting. And it's hot," Marianna said, "but we'll see an upswing of visitors for the Labor Day weekend. Then the fall tours begin." She laughed. "I use these dips to get ready for the holidays. I try to plan ahead, because it gets really busy around here come Halloween."

"I opened in November and I've never had a break." Zoe's bright eyes flashed. "I work with Megan in the Square's wedding business and with Square Spirits to run, there aren't enough hours to do everything."

"You left out Eli." Jessica, from Styles, was quick to point out.

A soft glow covered Zoe's face and neck. From what I'd seen, Zoe and Eli had a natural, easy connection. It reminded me of the way Bruce and I had been together. Even thinking about those times caused something to stir within me.

That evening, Richard called to tell me they'd arrived without any difficulties. He tried to sing a song Toby had taught him, but he couldn't remember all the words. He was happy to hear about the baby shower and how happy Lily looked.

"I miss you, Millie," he blurted.

"Time for me to get some sleep," I said, quickly saying goodnight. He'd done it again. He wanted a response, but truthfully, I hadn't had a minute to miss him. Still, his words sent pleasant shivers on a trip through my body.

***

Lily surprised Skylar and me when she called and said she wanted to see us after the shop closed on Monday. We hadn't seen her since the baby shower.

All day I wondered what she'd say. During lulls between shoppers Skylar speculated, fearing Lily would close the toy business, then swinging to the opposite end of the spectrum and hoping Lily would expand the toy inventory even more. In reality, there wasn't any room to expand the toys without taking space from the books. Whenever those thoughts cluttered up my train of thought, I added worries about the future of the bookstore.

Rather than being relaxed with fewer shoppers and getting caught up on paperwork, the day dragged for both of us.

Lily arrived as I was shutting off the spotlights. When she turned the lock on the door behind her, it was clear she didn't want any interruptions.

"Can we go upstairs?" she asked. "This could take a few minutes."

"Absolutely. Would you like a glass of water or juice?"

"Water's fine." She dipped her head to keep from looking at me.

Skylar bounded up the stairs. Lily followed at a much slower pace and I went up the steps last.

When Skylar offered the soft chairs, Lily suggested the chairs around the table. "If I sit in a soft chair, I'll have trouble getting out of it. Not a pretty picture." She was able to laugh at the image she described.

Skylar fixed glasses of ice water for the three of us and we settled at the table with Lily between us. She took a gulp of water and then pulled a rumpled piece of paper from her purse and smoothed it out with her hand.

"My doctor had a lot to say today." She stopped to take a breath and blew it out. "Starting as soon as I get home from here, I'm confined to bed rest until the baby is born." She put her hand in her lap, like she was connecting with the baby.

The gesture also pulled her away from Skylar and me.

"Tell us more," Skylar said. "Are you in danger? Is the baby okay?"

Lily shook her head. "The baby is fine, and I'm okay, but I have to be extra careful. They don't want the baby born too early. That's what's behind the doctor's concern."

"What happens when the baby is born, Lily?" I asked.

"Well, the doctor can't precisely predict how quickly I'll

get my strength back. I want to nurse the baby, but well… we'll see." She took another sip of water.

We waited. This was Lily's meeting.

"I don't want to, but given everything, it looks like I have to sell my toy inventory and end my arrangement to lease the space. I still think it's a great idea, but I can no longer do it."

"What does Doris' family say?" I asked, curious.

"That's the other thing," Lily said. "They don't want to be long-distance owners anymore. They want to sell the bookstore and the building."

"Do you want to buy it?" I knew the answer, could even see the longing in her face as I asked.

Lily sighed. "Yes, I sure do, but we already own the Country Law building, and Nathan and I are both too busy to worry about dealing with renters for this one. So even if we bought this building, that would mean Nathan would have to figure out what to do about the store. I'll be too busy taking care of the baby and Toby."

Lily passed a sheet of paper covered with figures to me. I could see this was an offer to sell the toy inventory to me. I could sell what was there and order more if I liked, and then I'd own whatever was left when it came time for me to leave. I fingered the paper with the offer, and then slid it across the table to Skylar. She gave no response to the figures Lily had written. Inside, I was proud of the business woman my granddaughter had become.

"This is a big surprise, Lily. How soon do you need an answer?" My mind began to think logically. I needed serious answers. Why not just sell the existing inventory down, I wondered? There was no guarantee that the next owner would want to sell toys.

"By the end of the month. Then I'll sell the toys in bulk, maybe have an online sale. I'll have to end the lease that Doris' trust now holds." Tears started to gather in Lily's eyes.

This had been a difficult decision for her. Her tears told that story. She knuckled them away and grabbed a tissue from her purse. "Nathan keeps reminding me that I can start a new business when the kids are older."

I didn't know what to say about her future and didn't want to dish out platitudes about everything being okay. I didn't know that, but I also had experience with situations that didn't work out. My heart was beating fast and my mind was approaching overload. I needed to talk to Skylar, to hear her thoughts.

Lily reluctantly stood up. She touched the paper on the table. "Nathan and I think this is a fair offer, especially since you've seen the potential of the business."

I stood and Skylar followed my lead. I stepped up to Lily and gave her a hug. "I know this is hard for you. Sometimes, we have to make difficult decisions in life. It looks like you're facing one now."

Lily nodded and straightened her back. Skylar stepped forward and gave her a hug. "I'll walk down with you."

I heard a faint bell jingle and then heavy footsteps as Skylar ran up the steps. "Gram, can you believe our good fortune?"

I went to the front window and watched Lily head toward Country Law. Her shoulders slumped forward, her steps short and slow. She appeared defeated. Sadly, I turned back to Skylar. "It's so sad to see her forced to give in…or maybe give up is a better way to put it."

Skylar approached me and said, "Sorry, Gram. I didn't look at it from her side. I just saw a possibility for my own future—and yours."

At first, I wasn't sure what she meant, but then it dawned on me that Skylar might want to continue the toys as her end of the business. That would mean she'd stay on even after I left. "You need to think hard about this, Skylar. You have a home, friends, a whole life in Minneapolis."

Skylar tilted her head from one side to another, as if considering her words. "The truth is, Gram, you have more ties there than I do. It's not that big a decision for me to leave and start something new."

The way she said the words "something new" told me she was filled with excitement and anticipation over the prospect of a change. "Tell me, then, what's your plan?"

She shrugged. "Uh, well, I don't exactly have one formed. But, Gram, listen to me. When I went out with Reed the other evening, all he talked about was the renovations he and Nolan had finished next door. He wanted to show me, so we stopped there on the way home. Gram, *I saw myself living there*."

She stood at the window next to me staring out, a faint smile adding to her glow. "Every time I think of the cramped space the toys have downstairs, I want to have a whole store filled to the brim with toys. Like Lily's vision." She turned away. "I don't mean to be insensitive about Lily's situation, Gram. I really don't. But it seems like I've been offered an opportunity that I'd be foolish to ignore."

It was beginning to become clearer what she meant. "It's a big decision to make." My wistful tone puzzled me in a way. It was as if Bruce was standing next to me, cautious, but not telling me to be a naysayer. Besides, hadn't I been having similar thoughts?

Telling me she'd be right back, Skylar went to her room. When she returned, she said, "Gram, I have enough money to buy the building next door. I could certainly buy the toy inventory at Lily's price. That's the least of the cost." She paused. "But I think I should slow down and talk to Richard first."

"I planned to call him, anyway. I'll see what he has to say about the offer, but don't be surprised if he tells you he has a conflict of interest. After all…" I shrugged. "We probably shouldn't get ahead of ourselves."

Had I said *we*? I didn't want to wait until the next day, so I called Richard right away. He didn't pick up so I left a voice mail.

For the next couple of hours, Skylar and I killed some time eating dinner and chatting while Skylar kept her eye on a baseball game on TV. When Richard called, I asked him for client-lawyer confidentiality. He became very quiet.

"What happened, Millie?"

"Lily offered to sell the toy inventory to me tonight. As you either know or will soon learn, she's been put on bed rest until the baby is born." I went on to describe the offer she'd presented. "The thing is, though, Skylar wants to buy the building next door to open a full-service toy store. She has the money to make that happen. She hasn't spent a dime of the settlement or from the house sale. All of it is producing income."

"I see. With elaborate financing not an issue, I can see why things are moving quickly. I can't say I'm surprised about Lily's situation." A second or two passed. "To tell you the truth, I'm relieved."

"Lily gave me until the end of the month to decide," I said. "That's a condition of the proposal."

"As Skylar's attorney, and yours, I don't want either of you to talk about this to anyone until I get back on Sunday. Especially because it not only involves the inventory, but also a new plan Skylar wants to put in place. Not that I'm negative about it. She's probably on to something and would be welcomed to the Square. But I do want to talk to Skylar. This is a major move. Ask her to call me tomorrow, mid-morning is best."

Since there was nothing more to say, I asked how the visit was going.

"Surprisingly well," Richard said, his voice reflecting a light mood. "They're great people and good with Toby. They had a terrible loss and sometimes I forget that, especially now that Nathan has his family. But the trip was exciting for Toby and he's having a lot of fun. I think they'll be coming to Wolf Creek for Christmas."

"That's wonderful to hear. For all of you." Our called ended with a quiet goodnight.

Skylar went on to bed. I tried to sleep but couldn't. I ended up on the couch with pen and pencil writing down my thoughts about the Square and the bookstore. What would I need to put a plan in motion? What was involved in making a move? Would Doris' family want to sell the shop to me?

At some point in the night, I'd dozed off on the couch. When I opened my eyes I heard Skylar making coffee before dawn. "Put the kettle on for tea, please," I called.

"Didn't you go to bed?" she asked.

"Too much to think about."

"Did you talk to Richard?"

"I did, and he wants you to call him today," I answered. "He said the middle of the morning would be best for him."

"Was he surprised?"

"About Lily or the offer?"

"I guess about both."

I left the couch and wandered into the kitchen to fix my tea. Skylar had already started to make French toast for our breakfast. A telltale sign. She always wanted French toast when she was stressed and had a lot on her mind.

We ate and dressed quickly without further conversation. I kept quiet about my speculation about the bookshop. Around opening time, Skylar disappeared into the back room to make her call. She came back smiling a few minutes later, but we had customers milling around. When we had a lull, she whispered, "Richard says it's all feasible. It's really up to me to decide what I want."

While waiting for Richard to come back, the two of us managed the shop that week as if nothing had changed—or was about to. The hot, humid weather had returned, which was the main topic at morning coffee at B and B, along with the Labor Day weekend looming ahead. Some were engaged in the typical moaning and groaning about the end of the summer. I didn't know if they wanted summer to continue, or if they were groaning in anticipation of the busy, upcoming holiday months.

Richard and I had a couple of quick conversations, but he was careful not to discuss the personal side of Lily's situation. I wondered if he would have preferred not to represent Skylar—and me—but I was apprehensive about asking him.

Richard's absence gave me time to think about the possibility that I could stay, too. I confided to Skylar that there was really nothing stopping me from making a move as well. At his suggestion when he returned, we met upstairs in my apartment rather than at Country Law. He mentioned too many ears and left it at that.

Our meeting wasn't short. Richard asked Skylar probing questions and made notes about her answers. He was the professional she needed, but also the friend that would look out for her. He assured me that if I decided to join in this complex series of transactions, he could represent the two of us, even with Nathan representing Lily and Doris.

We were about to end the meeting when Richard asked if it would be okay if he called Sarah to see if she was free to join us. That took me back, but when I understood what was behind his intention to get Sarah's approval, I wanted to hear what she'd say.

Within minutes, we heard her knock on the front door and Skylar ran downstairs to let her in.

Sarah was thrilled at the idea. An hour later, it was settled. Skylar accepted Lily's terms, and would make an offer on the building next door—and move into it. That was a clean deal, without complications. Meanwhile, I was almost 100 percent certain I'd make an offer to Doris' family for the store and the building. Wow.

With Sarah present, I asked about changing the name of the shop. If the store was going to be mine I wanted my own mark on it. I hadn't yet let myself think about a new name for the shop, but I was eager now to set my mind free.

After Richard and Sarah left, Skylar and I poured ourselves a glass of wine and sat on the couch. *Stunned*. That word fit. Skylar in particular had acted quickly, while I hesitated to go all in. I needed to think about what it would mean a little while longer. I put a lid on expressing continuing doubts I couldn't quite shake off.

Skylar showed her excitement in every animated gesture and rise in her voice. At one point, she settled down and quieted herself. Then she said, "What do you think Mom and Dad would think about my decision?"

"I think they'd be delighted to see you moving forward with a new life." I snickered. "I also think Mark would have laughed to see me right on the edge of going back into the book business."

Then it happened. Out of nowhere came the name: Bookmark. It was like a flash of perfection. I could honor my son—and Skylar's dad—by naming the store *BookMark*. But every time I said it to myself and then out loud, I'd add an “s,” so, BookMarks it became.

“BookMarks, honey. Wow, I just came up with the new name for the bookstore I haven’t decided to buy yet.”

“Right,” Skylar said dryly. Then she reached across the couch and gave me a hug as we burst out laughing.

“Okay, BookMarks on Wolf Creek Square. I’m 99 percent there. But what about you and your toy store? Any ideas?”

She grinned slyly. “You bet I do. I’ve already made that decision. The shop will be The Toy Box. And my logo is going to be a Jack-in-the-Box.”

“Wow. Give the lady a blue ribbon. So, you’ve already done a lot of thinking about this haven’t you?”

Skylar snickered again and leaned toward me. “I haven’t slept for *days*.”

Maybe so, but she didn’t look it. Skylar’s body vibrated with energy.

I couldn’t capture the yawn that escaped. “Maybe tonight we’ll both get a good night’s sleep.”

“There’ll be lots of excitement once the news gets out. I can’t wait to tell Reed.” Her face lit up even mentioning his name.

I imagined her texting him later, or maybe calling him. It was obvious there was more than casual friendship between them. I couldn’t define what was happening, and had chosen not to ask.

I went off to bed already knowing where my heart was leading—I felt the yearning in the warmth in my body—not so different from what I felt when Richard was around.

***

The rest of August went by in a whirlwind, and then suddenly, thanks to Richard and Nathan, Skylar and I each owned a business and a building next door to each other. Documents were signed, the toys were gone from BookMarks, boxes of deliveries came through both our doors, and one day, Skylar moved into a now empty apartment. Reed and Nolan had moved into their new building on the Square, where they’d once again do the work to renovate it.

As a special thank you for all his help, I took Richard to dinner at the Castle in Green Bay. It was quiet, elegant, and private. Exactly what we needed to get away from the frenzy of the sale and Skylar's move, not to mention the piles of paperwork. But, as we gathered our things to leave, Richard said, "I can't tell you, Millie, how excited I am to have you nearby now. We can see each other every day."

Inside, I groaned. He'd caught me off guard, without time or preparation to explain how excited I was to have this opportunity, this challenge ahead of me. If he expected to be in touch every day, let alone see each other, Richard was bound to be disappointed. But at that moment, I couldn't let his idle remark distract me or even annoy me. I had way too much to do.

September
10

If I'd learned anything it was that big news traveled fast on Wolf Creek Square. By the time Sarah made the two announcements at the monthly business association meeting, she was delivering old news. On the other hand, the camaraderie of the town was apparent in the warm welcome Skylar and I received. In fact, the business meeting turned into a mini-celebration.

With the three-day holiday weekend approaching, Skylar and I wanted to move the toys before the weekend, but there wasn't time to have shelves made and the inventory displayed. Skylar had asked Reed and Nolan to build a shelf for a train to run around the shop. It would be a few feet from the ceiling and above the door so it could be on a continuous track. She'd laughed as she'd tried to describe the tunnels and the way station Reed and Nolan wanted, but the train would be so high no one would see the embellishments.

Things had moved quickly, so fast we didn't have time to have new signs installed before the busy weekend. Disappointing, but what could we expect? Everything had happened in a flash of time.

Marianna reminded me a couple of times that September and early October generally gave shopkeepers a chance to breathe before Halloween kicked off the holiday season that would keep us busy to the end of the year. In spite of all that was ahead to take care of, I couldn't wait for the busy holidays. From what I could see in Skylar's excited expressions and high energy, she felt the same way.

Liz had created a flyer that announced the new name of the bookstore and the opening of the separate toy shop. I could slip that into every sales bag and I put them in the community promotion racks at the museum and B and B. All in all, I was like Skylar's train moving down the track picking up speed.

The box of Labor Day decorations I found in the backroom fueled my disappointment over the delay in getting my new sign. The old raggedy box held a small gold star and an old fragile and faded poster of the World War II icon, Rosie the Riveter.

Leaving Skylar to mind the shop, I ran to Quilts Galore to see what patriotic fabrics Marianna had in stock. But then I saw a bolt of cotton fabric with various tools printed on it. My idea for Labor Day changed immediately.

I called Reed and left a message asking if he would loan me some extra tools he wouldn't need in the coming weeks. With the sawdust already in the window, it would be easy to arrange tape measures, hammers, nails, screws, and anything else I came across that fit a construction theme. And rather than being a chore to put the window together, I found it exhilarating.

Saturday arrived with the sun bright in the clear blue sky, and my labor-themed display was ready. It was almost embarrassing how I admired my own handy-work. The array of tools sent exactly the message that matched the occasion. Besides, I had a pretty fair selection of how-to and home-repair books.

Both in the store and in private, Skylar and I celebrated this new phase of our lives, and we weren't shy about spreading the news about our two ventures. Naturally, Sarah and other owners were only too happy that yet another new store was opening, and an existing one was getting a whole new look. But as often happens with change, not all customers reacted so well.

One shopper remarked that she was sorry to hear that the toys were splitting off, because she'd always bought the toy-book combinations Lily offered.

Skylar, who was completing a sale at the register and

overheard the woman's comment, quickly spoke up. "I can still offer that. And maybe Gram would like a toy or two scattered about her shelves, too." She raised an eyebrow to send a silent question.

"I'm sure we'll try new ways to offer combinations." I hadn't said yes or no to the idea, but I wouldn't reject any strategy that would result in more sales of both books and toys.

I completed the next sale and noted that the supply of bags was low. Again. For two months I'd brought bags out of the backroom almost every day. Seemed like a waste of time and I wanted the new BookMarks to run smoothly and efficiently. With Lily gone and Skylar soon moving next door, BookMarks would be a one-woman show—oops, shop.

Fear loomed. I hadn't given much thought to the mechanics of running the shop alone—I'd been too busy with the fun stuff, which for me, involved coming up with ways to give the shop a new image. A makeover from top to bottom. Rather than letting fear paralyze me, I vowed to take each day and each customer one at a time. Playing upbeat jazz in the shop would help keep me focused and fuel my energy.

Addressing the constant need to resupply the sales bags, I ended up pulling out everything under the counter and cleaned what looked like years of dust out of the corners. I lugged the entire box of bags from the backroom and unloaded it onto the shelf. I estimated the supply would last until my new bags arrived.

I looked at all the miscellaneous papers, trinkets, and odd pens and pencils I'd found in my cleaning spree and had the gumption to throw it all away. A five-year-old retail store furnishings catalog was useless, anyway. It ended up being one of dozens of old catalogs I stuffed into the recycle bin.

I still needed to store the special order books in another box that had seen better days. But a new heavy weight wooden box was on the way. I'd seen one online and ordered it for both its attractive design and its practicality. Job done.

That evening Skylar went off with Reed for a barbecue

at his cousin Charlie's house. Richard mentioned going to Nathan and Lily's to grill hot dogs and hamburgers, but I didn't want to impose on a family already too busy, so I declined Richard's invitation. Besides, I needed a break from people. I considered a soak in the tub, a glass of wine, and maybe the movie I'd heard Skylar talk about at breakfast. What more could a girl want?

As much as I wanted to make all the changes in the shop on my long list, the reality was that it would probably take most of the month or more, to fully make the shop mine. I needed to erase Doris' fingerprints on the shop, but I also knew she and her husband had grown deep roots on the Square. I noticed the museum and the mayor's office included photos of many shops on the Square that had come and gone over a century or more. Pages, later Pages and Toys, were featured with photos in that "hall of fame." For me, it was as if the historical record spoke for itself and I was free to make the kind of changes needed to create BookMarks into a modern shop.

The holiday weekend went by in a flash, mostly because of the large number of visitors, more than expected, according to Sarah. When I'd arrived, I'd been more than happy to clear out the tattered and faded books. Now only a handful were left. The inventory on the shelves was current and varied, just the way I planned it. But that wasn't so alluring to bargain hunters. I pulled out a handful of bestsellers, and like the chain-stores, I offered a small discount, but enough to provide incentive to buy the books. All in all, I did okay.

Late Monday afternoon, when the Square began to empty, Skylar started packing up the toys on display. Somehow, she'd wrangled Reed to construct temporary shelving over the weekend, and he'd enlisted Nolan's help. By the time they were done, some rustic yet serviceable shelves were available, and Skylar could open.

Skylar was as excited to open her shop as I was to take over mine. Two generations apart, we still managed to keep up a steady flow of ideas. Anyone listening could have mistaken us for two sisters getting ready for prom night.

Since I knew I'd never have convinced her to take it slow

or to wait for all the shop remodeling, I stood back and got out of the way as she jumped in with both feet.

I pitched in to help her pack and carry boxes next door, where I began unloading when she went back for another load. It wasn't long before Reed and Nolan stepped up to help, which made the move go much faster. The two guys kept up a constant commentary about the toys and neither was shy about reminding Skylar about the lack of construction toys. Nolan suggested featuring some pink hammers and work benches to appeal to little girls.

I went home as soon as the stock was moved, but Skylar and her friends stayed to arrange things and order pizza. I was drifting off to sleep around midnight when she tiptoed into my bedroom and kissed my forehead. "Thank you, Gram."

I pulled the light blanket up around my chin and slept soundly the rest of the night.

The next morning, Skylar was up early and busy giving me a rundown of her priority list, with furniture being high on the list, like number one.

"Before you buy anything for your apartment, remember that I'm selling the condo. You can have whatever furniture you want shipped here. I'm going to ask Betsy to oversee the moving company's packers, with Ethel's help."

"Ethel?" Skylar was trying her best to understand who I was talking about.

"You know, the woman who manages the co-op."

"Right." Skylar nodded, as if she remembered. Mostly, though she was lost in her own list.

"I'll probably need to go to Minneapolis myself," I said, "depending on how quickly the co-op gets an offer."

"You can't leave now," Skylar said. "Who'd run the bookstore?"

I shrugged. I had no answer.

***

At last, our signs arrived, ready to be installed. Given the choice, I wanted our signs hung on the same day, but they had to be installed early in the morning before the shops opened. I arranged to have Skylar's done first, especially because the sign itself was my gift to her. If it took too much time, then I'd wait for mine.

I'd told a few white lies to Skylar about why my new sign wasn't done more quickly. I made up a story about needing more time to decide the colors and lettering. It was actually Skylar's sign that would take more time to install. It wasn't a simple matter of swapping out one for another, as it was with mine. Her installation would require attaching brackets the building didn't have.

Since it was a gift and I wanted it to be a surprise, I didn't tell her it was arriving the next morning. Fortunately, she'd had Liz do some mockups and had left the drawing she chose sitting on the kitchen table. That meant I'd known what to order for her, right down to the smallest details.

Since it was unusual to have trucks inside the pedestrian-only Square, when a truck rumbled past our building, Skylar went to the window to have a look. When she saw it was a truck from a sign company she let out a happy scream and ran downstairs. I watched her jump up and down around the truck. Then I looked into the Square and saw some other shopkeepers navigating their way toward our corner of the Square. I shook my head. It seemed some of the owners didn't want to miss a thing. I put on my shoes and hurried downstairs.

Sarah waved. I'd notified her that the signs were coming, and she probably texted her list of owners and employees to let them know the truck arrived.

"When, Gram?" Skylar bounced at my side. "How did you…? When…? You're the best." Her words tumbled out. The men finished the brackets on the building and we all held our breath as they uncrated the sign.

The din of low "Ohs" and "Ahs" came from the crowd, followed by rousing applause. Reed picked Skylar up and twirled her around.

I laughed at the sight. *Well, why not?*

The sign was constructed exactly as the drawing showed. A white background with different color letters, but not arranged in a straight line. A colorful Jack-in-the-Box sat in the left corner. They'd followed the scanned drawing I'd sent to the letter.

Sarah stepped forward and talked with the leader of the crew. He gave her a mock salute and then had the truck back up and stop in front of the bookstore.

Now it was my time to be nervous, but when a strong hand took my elbow I relaxed. Richard had arrived. Skylar soon came to my other side.

When the covering on the sign was removed, tears welled in my eyes. The colors I'd chosen reminded me of Mark. Years ago, he'd said he didn't like the bother of trying to match various colored shirts and suits with the perfect ties and socks. Instead, all his suits were either black or gray, so I chose gray for the background. The lettering was black with each letter highlighted with an echo strip of white, for his shirts and burgundy, for his ties.

"It looks like Dad," Skylar said softly.

I slipped my hand into hers. "He's not gone, Skylar. He's here on the Square with us and in our hearts."

The sign installed, the second round of applause from the assembled group brought me out of the past. I stepped over to the installer when he approached with an invoice for me to sign.

"Thank Sarah for letting us stay past opening," he said. "Not having to come back saved us a lot of time."

"I will," I said. "Both signs are exactly what we wanted. Thanks for doing such a great job."

The owners drifted back to their shops to begin their day. With Richard looking on, Skylar and I stood a while longer looking at the signs that marked the true launch of our new businesses.

A man approached the bookstore, but seeing it dark, he turned back to us. "Is the shop open?"

"You bet it is." I turned to Skylar. "See you later." I headed inside, and Richard followed.

As it turned out, the young man was on the Square to pick up a book he'd ordered. "I'm glad the shop didn't shut down after Doris left. It would be another fifteen to twenty miles for me to get to another bookstore."

That pleased me, but I couldn't resist adding, "You do have ordering online as an option."

He grinned. "I know, and I do that sometimes. I like to browse, and talk to the person selling the books."

"That's what we like to hear," I said with a grin. "Thanks, and do come again."

The bell made its happy sound when he left.

"Aren't you busy today?" I asked Richard. He was leaning on the end of the counter while I'd completed the transaction with the young man. It was odd to see him just hanging around the shop.

"Not really. I'm waiting for Georgia to do a search for a land case Nathan gave me."

"Well, then, I have a job for you. I'm selling the condo. I don't need to wait for a buyer because we turn that part over to the co-op when we sell. It's part of the deal. But I need you to handle the 'paperwork'." I made those ridiculous quote marks with my fingers.

"Selling so soon?"

"Why wait? I'm sure there is a waiting list for a condo in that complex, and I'm here now. Lock, stock and barrel."

"Yes, you are and I can see you every day that I'm in town."

I flinched at his words. "Look, I'm going to be extremely busy over the next weeks, Richard, first getting ready for the holiday season and then handling what I hope is an abundance of customers. All bookstores, independents and chain stores, do their best business from Thanksgiving to Christmas. I have to be ready."

Apparently ignoring the point I was making, he asked, "What about your furniture? And your personal stuff? Are you moving it all?"

It seemed I was doing exactly that. "I don't have time to make decisions about what to keep, sell, or give away. I'll have everything shipped here, and then Skylar can take what she wants to set up her place."

"Are you giving everything to her? You know she has enough money to buy her own household things."

"That's not the point. Why buy what we already have?" I'd managed to move past him into the back corner where the toys had been. "I'll want a few soft chairs back here, where I'll hold the book club meetings."

"Book club?" Richard laughed at my announcement.

What was so funny? "Yes, a book club. I've already had inquiries."

He shook his head. Indignant over his tone, I ignored him while I straightened the front racks of books by local authors. When more customers arrived, Richard pretended to be looking for a book, then left. As busy as I was, I got over my irritation with him, and I barely noticed he was gone.

Later that day, Megan stopped by. Gasping for breath, she carried a bouquet of fresh flowers. "I ran across the Square, but I guess I'm more out of shape than I thought. Anyway, this is your official welcome to Wolf Creek Square."

I took the bouquet from her outstretched hands. "These are beautiful. Thank you so much."

"I gave Skylar hers this morning, but then we got busy." She grabbed the door and gave it a quick shake to make the bell jingle extra long. She laughed, and her bright spirit remained long after she'd left.

Every time I looked at the flowers I smiled. I was home.

11

It had to happen sooner or later, and early the following week Wisconsin was targeted for some bad weather. Cold and warm fronts were colliding, and when the resulting storms arrived, shoppers stayed away. I wasn't used to being alone in the shop for such long periods. It was a two-sided coin. The weather gave me time for reorganization and putting in books orders, but daily sales suffered. Busy days had left me no time to breath, let alone study both print and online catalogs and talk to distributors about new titles with strong reviews I could feature on my shelves.

The rainy weather lasted only a few hours, and when the line of storms passed to the east they left behind overflowing flower gardens on the Square and walkways that had become rivers. I had lived in the Midwest a long time, so I knew we'd have weeks in every season that were dominated by bad weather. As long as the electricity wasn't interrupted, I'd do fine.

I was conscious of missing Skylar, even with her living next door. She could have stayed in her room in my apartment, of course, but her joy over her decision had made her want to stay in her own place. As far as she was concerned, making do with an inflatable bed and picnic supplies posed no particular challenge. Our furniture would be arriving soon and having a place to call her own was irresistible. The day she picked up her coffeemaker was the day she set up her home. What more did she need? Her kitchen table was a board across two sawhorses, compliments of what Reed and Nolan left behind.

As the last of the thunderstorms lingered and intensified, Sarah texted each business to let them know the direct path went right through Wolf Creek Square. Damaging high winds and hail were possible. It didn't happen often, but Sarah declared the Square closed to visitors, which gave the shops time to get ready.

The sudden news of an afternoon with a closed shop made me realize that I was wearier than I'd known. I locked the door and went upstairs to fix some tea and wait out the storm with the TV on so I could get weather updates. Live radar out of Green Bay was tracking the storm and encouraged everyone in its path to prepare for electrical outages. I immediately filled the bathtub and every kettle in the kitchen with water.

When the sky darkened, I sat by the window and waited. Richard called to make sure I was inside and okay. He was in Green Bay and planning to stay there until the middle of next week. Just as well. He hadn't yet understood that I wasn't used to having someone around a lot. Even Skylar had been busy with her own life when we lived together.

Richard meant well. I knew that, which is why I dreaded having to set ground rules for our relationship now that I lived in Wolf Creek. That meant figuring out what I wanted. Hmm… I wasn't ready to think that out. Instead, I pushed my tendency for self-questioning aside and watched the storm approach.

Arriving at precisely 4:08, it was exactly as predicted. The wind howled between the buildings making an eerie combination of high pitched sounds over a low bass roar. Wave after wave of torrential rain pelted the window and streamed down the glass. I watched from my place on the couch, nearly hypnotized by the sights and sounds of it.

Suddenly a limb broke from the tree across the walkway and the sound of shattering glass startled me off the couch.

I hurried down the stairs. Sure enough, the window had blown out. Shattered. Gone!

I grabbed armloads of books and filled the shopping baskets, and carried them to the back.

When I heard pounding on the back door I ran to unlock

it. Reed and Skylar stood in the rain. She grabbed me and held me in a hug. "Oh, Gram, are you okay? I can't lose you, too."

"Shush, shush. I'm fine." I patted her back. "It's the window that's broken."

"We need to get this window covered." Reed carried more books to the back and Skylar began filling baskets so quickly I barely had time to follow her lead.

Taking his phone out of his pocket, he said, "I'm calling Charlie. Then I'll get some sheeting from his warehouse."

The storm had torn branches from other trees, but it appeared mine was the only building damaged.

"Charlie's bringing a chain saw," Reed said when he'd ended the call. "He'll be here in a few minutes. Just stay away from the tree and the glass. We don't know if more of the branch will break off."

Obviously Reed knew what he was doing. I liked his take charge attitude. With the books safely off the shelves near the window and cleared from the table, I pulled the cart all the way to the back.

Skylar and I went upstairs. Satisfied that I'd saved as much merchandise in the front of the store as I could, there was nothing more for me to do that would help in the next phase of cleanup and repair. The storm was moving east and blowing itself out. My next big job would be filing an insurance claim. A name change on the insurance policy had been one of the papers Richard had prepared when I signed the deed for the building. Thank you.

I answered the phone when it rang and Richard's name appeared on the caller ID. "Hello, Richard."

"What's going on there? Nathan just called and said the Square suffered damage."

I told him what had happened, but that it was all being handled.

"I'm coming to the Square to help."

"No, no, Richard," I said as firmly as I could. "You stay in Green Bay. Like I said, Reed is here and as soon as the storm is over, Nolan and Charlie will cut the limb and clear it away. Reed's going to board up the window."

"Well, okay, but stay put. I don't think you have to go out and help."

I glanced at Skylar and rolled my eyes. "Like everyone else, I'll pitch in and help clear the mess off the Square, but don't worry, I won't try to install the glass."

Skylar grinned, knowing the other end of the conversation without having to hear it.

"I don't like this, Millie."

I scowled and shook my head. "Well, no one does. But I live here now, Richard. Where do you live?"

I punched the cancel button in frustration. "Oh, brother."

Skylar giggled.

"He's the nicest man," I said, "but I don't need him swooping in here like he's a super hero, you know, capable of singlehandedly installing the window."

Looking skeptical, she said, "If you say so."

Still wearing her sly smile, she went downstairs. A few minutes later I went to the window and saw her standing with Reed. She waved when she looked up and spotted me in the window. Not long after, the sounds of construction began.

A half hour later, I went downstairs to find a large sheet of wood covering the broken window. With only a drizzle left of the storm, I joined others on the Square, who were already gathering scattered branches and picking up clumps of flowers stripped from their beds. I added my loads of the debris to the growing piles on the walkway.

Elliot stopped by to reassure me that the town's trucks would clear the piles in the morning. We'd be back to business as usual.

In a strange twist the storm hadn't knocked out electrical service on the Square. Lucky us. I went upstairs to start water for tea. Skylar and Reed went off to get some dinner and as dusk turned to nightfall, I enjoyed the corner of my couch overlooking my new town.

I might have been tired physically, but my mind wouldn't quit. What was going through it wasn't pretty. I kept circling back to the idea that maybe the storm had been an omen—a bad omen. Maybe I should have taken more time before I bought the bookstore and moved to Wolf Creek. Nothing bad had happened before I purchased the shop.

I groaned inside over my ridiculous train of thought, nothing but silly superstition. In the end, I wrote off my dark train of thought to fatigue and to odd thought patterns that had formed when my grief over losing Mark had left me barely coping. Those days were behind me, though, and tomorrow the sun would shine and I'd still be the owner of BookMarks. I had a mess to clean up, but so what? I'd also have a sparkling new window. I grinned inside. Now that kind of thinking was more like the real me.

***

The following week the window was replaced and the cleanup crew dealt with the gooey mess of wet sawdust. The books in the window had been damaged, but a few of them would dry out and sell for next to nothing on the sale cart—it was almost like a badge of honor to put them out on the cart as evidence we'd survived. Sadly, I had to accept that the antique photo of Rosie couldn't be saved. I'd planned to give it to Sadie for the museum when I was done with the display, and fortunately, I knew there were modern reproductions of the original poster, so if I ever wanted one it would be easy to find.

Mess or no mess, I proudly displayed a notice that the book club meeting would be held the following week to organize and choose our first book. I was going to suggest *The Secret Life of Susan*, a recently published novel about family secrets and what happens when they come to light. Sounded intriguing to me, and it was up around six or seven on a couple of bestsellers lists. But if other ideas came forward, that would be okay.

My shop would be the meeting place, but I decided I wanted to stay in the background as much as possible and let the participants determine the agenda. In some book clubs the members took turns choosing books, but in others, librarians and bookstore owners made the selections.

I had only one nagging worry, and that was about not

having enough space, even if I had plenty of chairs. I'd had so many inquiries about the book club, I worried if everyone who had expressed interest actually showed up, I wouldn't be ready.

I'd come full circle when I remembered that Betsy and I never had enough chairs, and some of our attendees had to sit on our carpeted floor. That memory prompted me to give her a call.

Skipping the usual greetings, I started by teasing her. "Hey—you never called back after the school bus arrived."

She laughed. "I forgot. Must be getting old."

"Not you. I have news. I bought the bookstore. I'm calling it BookMarks."

"After Mark?"

"Yes." A wave of emotion surfaced, but I forced it aside. I didn't have time to be sidetracked. "But when we last talked you said you had some ideas about ways I can brand the store, make it mine, not just a slightly altered Pages and Toys."

Betsy laughed. "You're not wasting time. Typical of you, I'd say. But, this is your lucky day. I have an author friend, Alexa Winkler, who's planning a book tour this fall. She published her mystery series independently. She's trying to keep expenses down so she's scheduling stops in towns where she has a friend who can put her up for a night."

"Oh, sounds like fun. Maybe even unique for the Square. I haven't heard anyone mention an event featuring a visiting author. I want to clear it with the mayor first though, just in case there's another event scheduled I'm not aware of."

"Get back to me with some dates soon," Betsy said. "Maybe I'll arrange to come with her."

"Really? That would wonderful. It seems so long since we've really talked. We can share bookstore ideas." Betsy had lightened my mood.

***

A week or so later, Richard was in Wolf Creek on the night

of the first book club meeting. He asked me to have some dinner with him at Crossroads, and he didn't take my request for a rain check particularly well. Why would he think I could take time out for a leisurely dinner on an incredibly busy night? Richard had been my friend for years, but he could be so frustrating at times. I was too preoccupied to do anything about it just then.

Marianna quickly saw that I needed chairs, so she grabbed a couple of people coming in and took them to her shop. They came back with folding chairs from her classroom. Sarah took a seat back in the corner, next to an older man I didn't recognize.

It took about two hours for the group to figure out the who, what, when, and where for the group. Because of my limited space, both Marianna and Steph offered their places. Steph won over the group when she offered cookies and beverages, and she and I agreed to privately work out a fee for the service.

Six or seven titles were thrown into the mix of a possible first book. I recognized them as standard summer reads with predictable storylines. I knew it would be challenging to find a way to have an in-depth discussion about the story. For the most part, the discussion was a free for all, but when the man next to Sarah raised his hand like he was in a classroom, I nodded for him to begin.

"Most of you are too young to remember me, but I'm Trevor Sinclair, former editor of the *Wolf Creek Gazette*. May I suggest we read *The Darkness in the River*. It's about three children from Wolf Creek that found each other years after they had been separated. Many times their lives intersected, but I'm not going to spoil the story of *how* they discovered they had siblings and reunited."

Heads nodded at his suggestion.

"If that's the consensus," I said, "I'll order copies tomorrow. How many of you want one?"

Nearly every hand went up, but a few said they'd buy the e-book online.

"So, Trevor, would you like to lead the discussion next time?" I asked.

"Sure, I'll be happy to do that."

"Okay, then next time we'll meet at B and B, where Steph will have cookies," I said with a laugh. "I won't let a cookie-less night happen again." Just like I wouldn't go to a Square picnic without bringing a dish to pass. When in Rome and all that…

"So, thanks for coming. I didn't expect so much interest." I started passing a legal pad to collect names and contact information. "I'll start a list, so I can send emails or texts to everyone when the books arrive."

The group lingered in the shop for a few minutes, introducing themselves to each other and talking about favorite books. Sarah kept her distance until most of the group had left. Those sitting in Marianna's chairs were more than happy to carry them back to her shop.

"Quite a turn out tonight, Millie," Sarah said when the crowd began thinning. "I do have a favor to ask."

"Sure, if I can." What would the mayor of Wolf Creek and the Square want from me?

"I'm writing a history of Wolf Creek Square," Sarah said, "and including a section on each building. I know you're new to the area, but I'd like you to read what I've written about your building."

I rubbed my hands together. "Ooh, sounds good. I'm always interested in reading local history. In fact, Sadie was telling me about your project. She's in a hurry to get it published so it can be available for sale in the museum."

Sarah grinned. "She's a champion supporter. I still have sections that need to be included, but aren't yet even underway." Sarah opened her tote bag and pulled out a manila envelope. I noticed a slight hesitation when she gave it to me. That wasn't typical of the confident mayor.

"I'll let you know as soon as I'm done reading it," I said, "but right now I better move the group along and lock up. It's been a long day and it all starts again tomorrow."

Sarah took the hint and in her gentle, yet persuasive way, helped me steer everyone out the door. Then with a wave, she left herself.

I thought about calling Richard after I locked up. I quickly rejected that idea. I didn't feel like *defending* my plans for *my* bookstore.

I also decided against making that call because curiosity got the best of me. I wanted to read what Sarah had written about my building. I went upstairs and poured a glass of wine and sat on the couch ready for a good story. I wasn't disappointed.

FIRST THE PREACHER, THEN THE TEACHER

[*Historian's note:* The following poem was found in one of the old school textbooks in the museum. No other writings by the young man have been found.]

First the Preacher.
With Bible in hand,
He teaches us
Right from wrong.

Then the Teacher.
With books we learn
Numbers and cipher,
And maybe a song.

And together.
They make our town
Happy and strong.

By Luke Carpenter
Age 10

FIRST THE PREACHER

Brian Korth reined the horses to a stop as he entered the outskirts of Wolf Creek. He waited a minute and then snapped the reins. The mismatched team of horses lurched ahead to get the buckboard wagon moving. The load was heavy, mainly furniture, books, and household supplies. A small amount of food was packed under the seat. It was late, approaching darkness, and the road through town was nearly empty.

Brian was tired. It had been a long trip and he'd left later than planned. One more argument with his superior about him taking the boy had caused the delay. But now, his companion, the small orphan boy from the river bank area of Green Bay, leaned against him.

As the temperatures fell after sunset, Brian had wrapped his jacket around the thin body and snuggled him next to his side. Brian knew the boy would need clothes as the spring days warmed into summer. Perhaps the parishioners would help.

Brian drove the team down the street past the relay station, the general store and the Crawford Freight Line office. On the far west end of the town, beyond the last building, Brian stopped the horses in front of a white-washed, steepled building. Another smaller building, behind the church, was silhouetted in the light from the half-moon. He pulled the wagon to the front of the small building. Brian looked up to the dark sky and with a smile, he nodded. Yes, he'd arrived.

He stepped down from the wagon and while he lit the lantern hanging on the side of the wagon, two riders approached. "Hello, neighbor," he called out. He blew the match out before tossing it to the ground and then released the handle holding the glass chimney above the flame. Brian held the lantern high as the men approached.

"Your name, sir?" one of the two men asked as he dismounted.

"Brian Korth, the new preacher for Wolf

Creek."

"We were told you'd be coming next week." The man stepped forward and extended his hand. "Woodrow Day, mayor of Wolf Creek."

"Had a disagreement with my boss." Brian chuckled at his attempted joke. "Not that one, the earthly one."

With an easy smile and a friendly manner, the second man came down from his horse. "Sam Crawford. I run the relay station with my wife. We'll be glad to help you get settled."

"Just want to get a fire going. The boy's hungry and cold." He nodded toward the wooden seat of the wagon.

"Can offer you food and fire back at the station. Even a bed."

"This is our home now." Brian opened the door of the building behind the church. He held the lamp high. Cobwebs, an overturned chair and a broken bed told Brian it had been a long time since anyone had lived there. "Just needs a good cleaning."

"Let me get a fire going." Sam gathered a few pieces of wood from the small pile next to the hearth and took a handful of dried moss from the basket nearby. He struck a match and the flames crackled in the dry tinder, growing larger as the wood began to burn. "I'll get more from the pile outside."

Woodrow stepped to the open doorway. "I'll go fetch a pot of stew. I'm sure Annie has plenty."

"No, no. Please. Maybe another day. We'll heat some water and make jerky soup. I have bread in the wagon. But thank you for thinking of us."

The young boy had joined them by the fire. Brian stepped behind him and, in a gesture of love and protection, he put his hands on the small shoulders. "This is Luke Carpenter. We're partners no matter what anyone says." There was solid determination in his voice.

The boy reached toward the fire, rubbed his hands together, then leaned back against Brian.

"Well, we'll let you settle in for the night." Woodrow buttoned his coat. "I'm sure the ladies of the town will be here in the morning to help clean up this mess."

"Luke and I can manage."

"The ladies, and the town, have waited a long time for a preacher so I'll let you tell them they're not wanted."

Brian chuckled. "Point well taken."

Sam added two more logs to the fire. "See you Sunday, Parson."

Sam and Woodrow mounted their horses and left. Brian and Luke stood in the doorway looking toward the town. "This will be a good home for us." He ruffled the boy's hair. "Come, it's time for soup."

"The stew would have tasted mighty good."

***

For the next two years Pastor Brian tended his congregation, praying in the spring for fields to produce a bountiful harvest, for the people of Wolf Creek to be healthy, and for all of them to be thankful for their blessings.

The following spring, Woodrow Day stepped up to the pulpit after morning service and announced that he had donated land next to the church for a new, larger church to be built. "By the end of summer, we'll have hired a teacher for the children. This building will be the new school house."

The women clapped and the children groaned.

[Historian's note: The building on the west end of the Square, in the north corner, was built on the original location of the first church in Wolf Creek, later to become the school house. For many years the building was owned by Ralph and Doris Parker.]

***

Sometimes a good story needed to be savored and read slowly. Sarah's was that kind of story. Knowing my building stood on the same ground as the town's first church, then the school, I wanted to change the window displays to honor the heritage of education. It was September and after the excitement of the storm and Labor Day, "Back to School" was a terrific theme for the month.

Maybe with an Internet search I could find a book about the first recognized school teacher or established public school in the state. I made a note to remind myself in the morning. At the bottom of the note, I scribbled Betsy, Claire, bus tour, and bedroom. I had a lot of varied topics to keep me busy and I needed my rest. Then I thought of Richard.

I was still awake, tossing and turning past midnight. The more I tried to relax, the more ideas for the shop popped into my head. Finally, I gave in to sleeplessness and got up. I almost had to, really, because the notebook I usually kept by my bed was somewhere in the living room. Not wanting to disturb Skylar, I was extra quiet when I put water on for tea. Then it dawned on me that Skylar wasn't in my apartment, but was likely sleeping soundly next door in her own place. I let out an audible sigh.

After having Skylar close by for the last few weeks, the apartment felt oddly empty and lonely without her. Then I realized that, indeed, I *was* lonely. It wasn't simply a passing feeling.

The tea settled my middle-of-the-night musings, if that's what they were. Suddenly, I was too tired to name a cause for my restlessness, and went back to bed.

12

Over the next few days I felt Skylar's absence in the shop, especially her bright smile and the musical sound of her joyful laughter. As if filling a void, I played more up-beat sing-along music in the shop, and now and then a customer would hum the tune as well. Sometimes I'd join in.

While I had much to do to get ready for company, I was also conscious of the need to repair my relationship with Richard. We hadn't talked since the day of the storm. So I called to see if he was in Wolf Creek, and when he said he was, I asked him to come to my apartment for supper.

"You cooking, Millie?"

I laughed. "Take-out from Crossroads. Anything special you'd like?"

"Just your company."

I took his answer to mean whatever I ordered would be fine.

"How about if I save you a trip and pick up the food on my way over?" he asked.

"Sounds good. Let's make it 6:30."

"See you then."

In the shop that day, I tried to sort out what I wanted to say about where I was in my life and how he could fit in. Not that I'd put it quite that way. It wouldn't be an easy conversation, not given his take-control nature and his desire to have me as a friend. Or more.

Had I used the word *desire*? Was I referring to his desire, or mine?

Were my rapidly warming heart and body ahead of my mind?

No! I wanted Richard to be my friend and companion. Someone to share a dinner or a movie. Maybe a dance partner at festivals on the Square, or at one of the many weddings that seemed to happen so frequently in town.

Enough!

I snapped to an alert state of mind. Customers were standing around needing help while I'd been standing around like I didn't know one book from the next.

Between customers, I heard my phone beep. Megan called to say that she was bringing in a bride-to-be, along with her mother and her sister, who was going to be the maid of honor. They wanted to look at books, registries, and photo albums. They'd be stopping in around noon.

When I'd taken Megan's earlier hint to increase my selection of wedding-related books, I'd ordered an electronic photo album to go along with the traditional ones I carried. Technology was an area that could trip me up, and I didn't want to fall into any black holes and waste money.

When Megan and the wedding group arrived, the bride's sister was the first to comment on Megan's flowers on the counter.

"I contract with many of the shops to provide flowers and decorations throughout the year," Megan said with a note of pride in her voice.

I made a note and put it in my pocket. Flowers would soften the atmosphere in the shop, the same way the toys had. Maybe flowers or a green plant hanging in the window would enhance the appeal. I knew Megan would have some ideas.

As Megan directed the conversation with the women, I passed around a few of the books I carried on planning a wedding.

"I don't think we need any of them," the bride's mother said abruptly. "That's why we're hiring Megan. But, yes, a gift registry. We may need two considering the number of guests."

I assumed from the matter-of-fact tone of her remark that since she would be writing the checks to pay for the event, her decisions were final.

"This electronic photo album would be great for Dad's office. Don't you think, Mom?" The sister tried to smooth what seemed like tension in the air.

"I'd like one for Paul, too," the bride suggested. "His office is pretty bare right now."

"I don't know. They seem expensive." The mother turned away.

Megan caught my eye. "Paul is the groom. He works for the father-in-law-to-be."

I nodded as if I understood the broader picture. I didn't, but I bet Megan heard more about her clients' private lives than she cared to.

As they talked, Megan wrote reminders in her notebook. It looked clear to me she was avoiding further conversation with the mom.

"Thanks for your help." Megan held the door open for the group to file out. The bride and her sister waved good-bye, but Mom walked out without a word.

Megan tried, but couldn't look me in the eye. Just as well. We had connected with the chilly atmosphere in the bridal party, and if we'd caught each other's eye, we might have given each other a bad case of the giggles.

I watched Megan lead her group across the Square.

What a loss. The lady's beautiful daughter was getting married. It should have been a time of excitement and adventure for the family, especially with Megan handling the details.

The afternoon passed quickly. Visitors and shoppers familiar with the Square noticed the new signs and the brand new toy store next door. Many asked about Lily and I casually mentioned that her due date was approaching. That's as specific as I got.

Rather than writing a note to myself to contact Liz Pearson the next day, I took advantage of the time right after I locked the door that evening to call her. So many people had mentioned her graphic designs, and I'd seen evidence myself. Now that I owned BookMarks, I needed a new design for all my promotions, from bookmarks, gift certificates, and business cards to a fresh logo for the sales bags and my website and social media.

For the logo, I'd chosen a strap holding two books together like children carried in pioneer days. Liz, I'd been told, could do it all.

We started a brief conversation, during which she said she'd be happy to complete the design for every item. Only when I asked if she could manage various online accounts, like the mailing list and blogs and newsletters and posting notices on my website, did she stop saying yes. There was silence on the line.

"Liz, are you there?" I asked.

"Um, yes, but I've never managed those accounts for a client before."

"Oh, I see. I guess I assumed you did that on a monthly contract basis. From my point of view, I'd rather do business locally than go elsewhere."

"Thanks for the vote of confidence, Millie. Why don't I put together a proposal tonight and bring it by tomorrow." I enjoyed the note of excitement in her voice.

"I like your promptness."

"Um, Millie? Do you know if Skylar needs graphic work?"

I paused to think about that. "To tell you the truth, I'm not sure. She knows how to do a lot of the work herself, but she's awfully busy. I'd give her a call. She might be a little shy about asking. Or, she may want to work with someone she knows in Minnesota."

"She needs to come to morning coffee now and again," Liz said, "although it's true that Megan and a few of the others aren't always regulars, and Lily rarely had time to stop in. But as a shop owner now, joining us will help Skylar feel like she belongs to this community."

Hmm…I had a feeling Reed and Nolan, not to mention Rachel and Alan, had already accomplished that for Skylar. But I acknowledged Liz' words. "I agree, but I think she'd feel better about going if someone other than her grandmother suggested it. She might think she's too young to join us."

Liz chuckled. "I think I'll give Sarah that job."

My conversation with Liz lasted longer than I'd planned so I had only a few minutes to get ready for dinner with Richard.

When he knocked on the door, I was as ready as I was going to be. When it came to me, and the minor disarray of the shop and my apartment, I could only say it was what it was and would have to do.

Downstairs, I unlocked the door and held it wide open for him to enter. "Come in, come in." I noticed the coolness to the evening's air. An omen for my evening with Richard?

Ridiculous! And since when had I started to think omens had any credibility.

I wasn't afraid of him, but when I thought of the two of us upstairs alone, my mind shot out a question: Was I actually afraid of being alone with him?

"I brought a bottle of wine from Zoe's. She suggested a blush since I couldn't tell her what we'd be having for dinner."

"Blush will be good." My mind was locked onto my question.

I went up the stairs ahead of him and turned back to see his reaction to my living space. He'd been there before, but he'd been focused on a business meeting, not a social evening.

"This is…quaint. I hadn't noticed the last time."

I laughed at the old-fashioned word, but it aptly described my apartment. Doris' outdated, but comfortable furniture blended well with the modern amenities. I enjoyed my cozy space.

"There're the corkscrew and two glasses," I said, pointing to the counter. "I'll take care of the food." I put the hot dishes in the oven to stay warm and the cold containers in the refrigerator. We could eat whenever it suited us.

I walked to the front window, where Richard joined me with our glasses.

"This is different from my place in Minneapolis with its

trendy furniture, huh?" He'd visited several times over the years when he'd been in Minneapolis for a case.

"But this apartment fits you even better." Richard was good at reading people, what made them comfortable and what set their nerves on edge.

I turned and scanned the room, then stepped to the couch and ran my hand across the arm rest, enjoying the pleasant texture of the cotton fabric. "That's how I feel, too. As it turns out, I like it here a lot. Maybe I'll add a chair or two. Most of my furniture is too big for either up here or for downstairs."

"How did the book club meeting go?" He'd redirected our conversation, and from my point of view was breaking into the sensitive ground I wanted to discuss over dinner. I'd heard one of the Food Network chefs say "good food softens bad news." I wondered if it was going to work tonight.

"So many people showed up we had to go to Marianna's and borrow chairs from her classroom," I said, laughing.

Richard raised an eyebrow.

"Next month we're going to B and B. Steph's offered to provide beverages and cookies."

"Really? You had that many people?"

I smiled. "You should come next month. Trevor Sinclair, the former editor of the *Wolf Creek Gazette* is leading the discussion of the book he suggested, *The Darkness in the River*. It's a memoir about long-lost siblings finding each other." I imagined mentioning a prominent person in town would tickle his ego.

"I wonder if Gus Alexander knows him," he mused.

"Bring Gus along. I've ordered a few extra copies of the book, if you'd like to read it before you come."

Richard smirked. "So, you're inviting me? Even after I laughed at the idea the first time you mentioned it?"

I decided to ignore his sheepish remark. "It's open to everyone. Besides, I'm learning to read people very well, at least when they're looking for a book."

"I apologize for my attitude. The fact is, I don't know anything about running a bookstore."

"Thank you for your honesty."

"I'm finalizing the paperwork for your condo, by the way. Seems to be going easier than I expected." He'd turned the conversation again. "You and Bruce had most of the details about the unit outlined in the buy/sale papers on file with the co-op."

"As I remember, Bruce spent a long time on the paperwork before we signed the final contract."

"What about your furniture?"

"That's something I want to talk to you about, but right now I'm hungry. Let me get our supper on the table and we can continue this conversation." There was a lot more than furniture to talk about.

I had put out placemats and serving dishes earlier. The cartons in the refrigerator were filled to the top with salad greens, dressings, and relishes. Transferring the food to the serving dishes kept my hands busy.

Richard offered to handle the hot platters in the oven and the warmed bread. He seemed to need to do his part of the meal, maybe to show me he wasn't helpless. He lived by himself, so I imagined he'd figured out how to fix his meals when he didn't eat out. I handed him the pot holders and stood back.

With slow, precise movements he transferred the fish and vegetables from the oven to the plates I'd set out earlier.

I refilled our wine glasses and brought them to the table. Richard had pulled my chair out and was waiting for me to sit. He took his chair and laughed when our knees bumped.

"That wouldn't have happened with the table in the condo," I said.

"This was a wonderful idea, Millie. Seems every time we go to Crossroads we run into others from the Square so we never have dinner by ourselves."

"Does make it difficult to talk," I conceded, "but we always have fun." And I never wanted to discuss my personal business in a room full of people anyway.

"I don't want to share you with others all the time." There was a hint of poutiness in his voice.

Okay. Honesty time.

"Richard, I want to talk to you about our relationship. I

value our friendship, more than I can say. I have no plans for that to change."

He put his fork down. "Are you sure? Think of the good life we could have together."

"I bought this business with my eyes open. I know it's going to take a ton of work to make a go of it, not to mention getting used to the new town and my new place. I wouldn't have bought it if I hadn't wanted to focus all my time and energy on BookMarks." To bring home the point, I added, "That's how I'll make the shop into a great success—even more successful than the one in Minneapolis."

As much as I enjoyed his company, until he understood that he couldn't make demands on me or my time, that even our friendship would be strained, let alone changing the nature of it, I couldn't commit to more. Of course, he had his own life, too. As I spoke, I wondered if he perceived me as being focused mostly on my own life, just the way I saw him focused on his own needs.

Richard didn't comment so I had no way of knowing if he understood what I was saying. "I don't know what you're asking of me," he finally said.

Really? Hadn't I made myself clear?

"Okay," I said. "I need you to respect me and my ideas. I need you to respect my business and the time it takes. I can't drop things simply because you're in town."

"You are a beautiful woman, Millie." He reached across the table for my hand.

I left my hand on the table. If I pulled away too quickly, he might take the gesture as a sign of my pulling away from him completely, and I didn't want that, either. I found his response odd, to say the least.

Falling in love with Bruce had been easy. It had been love at first sight and transformed into a deep love that still lingered in my heart. Was that part of my resistance to Richard? Was I stuck in the past, living in yesterday? After Bruce died had I built a wall around myself that didn't allow new experiences in?

Like adventures with a new man?

He rubbed his thumb across the back of my hand—a

soft touch that spoke of more intimate feelings. With that, I pulled my hand back and put it in my lap. Apparently, I'd failed to explain what I wanted, *needed*, from him.

"This salmon sure is tasty," I remarked. "I wonder if Melanie will have it on the menu come winter?" I didn't know if she would or wouldn't, and didn't much care, but I had to fill the silence until I figured out another way to get through to him.

"Didn't know salmon was seasonal." He took a bite of the broiled fish.

"Seems to be served more in the summertime, but with the little cooking I do, I really don't know." I laughed to cover the false pretense of knowledge.

"Doesn't matter," he said. "Everything I've had at Crossroads is excellent."

"You eat there a lot?" I used my fork to emphasize my question.

He shrugged. "I'm not much of a cook. Can hardly make eggs without burning them." He laughed self-consciously. "Best if I let someone else do the cooking."

"Me, too," I said. "I was never much of a cook. And now after being in the shop all day, I'm sometimes too tired or I just don't feel like it. Skylar felt the same way. That's why we always had a supply of food from the deli at Farmer Foods ready in the fridge."

"Maybe I should get some ready-to-eat food and put it in the refrigerator in my apartment here."

"You mean it's empty?"

"Lily invites me for dinner when I'm in town."

"She has a child to take care of—and herself. Besides, from what I can see, Nathan doesn't treat her like cooking is part of her job as his wife. Lily even bragged about him being a pretty good cook." My words had grown in sharpness and volume. I raised my hands in surrender. "I'm sorry, Richard. It's not my place to comment."

Richard sighed. "It's true. Nathan and Lily invite me, but Nathan often gets the food ready in the house, especially now that Lily has to be off her feet." Another long sigh. "I admit I've got a lot to learn, Millie. It is thoughtless of me to somehow expect Lily to concern herself with me. I've made some horrible mistakes with my family, beginning years ago with my wife, Irene. Guess I haven't learned much through the years."

"At least you're being honest with me." I got up to remove the platters and dishes, and serve the chocolate mousse pie I'd ordered. I put the wedge in front of Richard and started the water for tea.

His first bite of pie brought a smile to his face. "Wonderful taste, every time."

Despite all my tough talk and the boundaries I had drawn around my life, his smile still had the power to send a rush of warmth through my body. But then, I began describing the way I saw my upcoming days with Betsy and Alexa coming. Richard seemed to tune out, as if he didn't care.

Ugh! No wonder I was ambivalent about him.

He left shortly after finishing dessert. I stepped back when he reached for me, apparently taking in nothing I'd said. When I relocked the door, it seemed like I was locking my heart. But it haunted me that I might have been setting up a false choice in my life.

13

The next few mornings I fielded numerous calls about the book signing I was planning for the visiting author, Alexa Winkler. When I'd mentioned it to Sarah, she'd been enthusiastic, as usual, and pointed out that the attendees in BookMarks would naturally spill over into the rest of the Square. The women at morning coffee had many questions of their own, which I answered as best I could. Not being familiar with the author's work, I used the blurb on the Internet to give me details to describe what her books were about. A white lie, I suppose, but not one I thought I needed to confess.

When I mentioned Betsy and the author would be staying overnight with me on Friday and Saturday night, the women said they'd talk to Steph and organize a Sunday morning brunch at B and B. That worked for me, since Sunday was the only day we opened at noon.

Megan groaned. "I won't be able to come to the bookstore for the signing. I'm all alone in the shop that day."

Fortunately, the other women said they'd manage to find coverage so they could attend. I was glad because we needed to swell the crowd to give the event an air of excitement.

Later that morning, I called Betsy to give her a heads up about the brunch, knowing it would need to be part of her scheduling. Betsy squealed in response, and asked if they needed any special kinds of clothes. If only she knew how casual the Square was, she would have laughed at herself, although Betsy seemed to have a genetic disposition for drama. She'd have hurried out to buy an unusual hat and white gloves if I'd told her we were doing a retro theme.

When Betsy and Alexa arrived in their separate cars on Friday afternoon the shop was filled with customers. Then one of my customers recognized Alexa, and a small buying frenzy began. What fun. I handed both women a bottle of water and offered Alexa a chair by the table she'd use the next day.

Dressed for a car ride in capris and a cotton shirt, she pushed her sunglasses to the top of her head, where they nestled into her curly dark brown hair. A gray streak didn't age her as much as give her the look of a sophisticated author. She began bantering with the shoppers like she did this sort of author-reader event every day.

Remembering the author visits in Minneapolis and the sales those days generated, I had ordered many more copies of her mystery series, especially the new one, than I expected to sell. I'd get Alexa to sign them before she left and keep the interest in her going after the weekend.

Later, the three of us shared dinner in my apartment. Betsy was her usual animated self, but Alexa was equally engaging and had already made a positive impression on me. I could see that book signings were a great marketing tool for her and admired her focus on expanding her success as an author. I was glad I had invited them to stay with me and we could stay up and talk as late as we pleased.

When Richard showed up at the shop on Saturday morning, he said, "I'm here to help out with the signing, Millie. Put me to work."

Although I groaned inside, he apparently believed he could be helpful. After the unsatisfactory conversation we'd had the other evening, I couldn't help but see him as an extra body taking up valuable space. Still, he offered, so I told him we could use his help as a greeter at the door when the event started.

Just before the signing was about to begin Betsy and Alexa came downstairs and Richard approached the two and introduced himself. "I'll be here all afternoon, so if you need anything, just ask and I'll take care of it. I'll also help replenish the stacks of books and make sure you have plenty of water."

He'd already put bottles of water on the table for Alexa and had one set aside for Betsy. I asked him to haul two full cartons of books from the back and arrange a dozen copies on the table. He then stowed the rest out of sight under the table, where the long cloth kept them out of sight. He'd appointed himself the author's assistant, which freed Betsy and me to chat with customers.

I knew the PR I'd done for the event had paid off when we started the signing with a line extending out into the Square. Richard began doing what he did best. He took charge and kept the line moving forward so each person had a moment to chat with Alexa. He had fairly good social patter himself, I noticed.

I'd feared Richard would expect me to pay attention to him, which I was far too busy to do. But he stayed in the background as he helped, forcing me to admit I might have misjudged him too quickly.

The first signing at BookMarks was a great success, in part because of Richard's help. He offered to take us all out for dinner at Crossroads, but Alexa and Betsy were both tired. They indicated they were ready to get comfortable upstairs and eat simple snacks. And wine, of course.

On Sunday morning, Richard and I unloaded a box of books into shopping bags and carried them to B and B. It was soon evident we didn't have enough for everyone who wanted to buy a copy. Many of the women owners and employees on the Square had joined us, and they'd brought their friends and relatives with them. Once again, it was another festive event. Skylar and Rachel sat together and it struck me how happy Skylar seemed. We didn't have a lot of time to chat, but it was such fun to be—each in our own way—part of our new community.

Seeing the crowd, Richard whispered, "You only have one box left."

He was right. I spoke, trying to be heard over the noise, but I'm sure not everyone heard me say, "We're getting low on books, but I'll have Alexa sign whatever is left and if that's not enough she can send me more."

A few who were paying attention groaned, but being shopkeepers they all knew that ordering for a first-time event was just a guess.

Alexa was flushing with excitement when we went back to the shop and she settled at the table to sign books for the afternoon crowd. Richard was a little clingy and I tried to keep my distance, but wasn't always successful.

Later, when Betsy touched my arm, I jumped. "Is something wrong?"

She shook her head. "No, not a thing. I wish I had a man waiting for me when I get home."

By closing time on Sunday, only three books were left. I told Alexa I would have more books delivered to her at my expense. She could sign them and send them back, and I was certain we'd sell more. She had a new release scheduled for next year, so before she left we made a plan to have her back. She was thrilled with the way the event had turned out. And so was I. Between the book club and Alexa's signing, I was putting my own stamp on the shop.

Alexa also mentioned going on a group book tour next summer with some other bestselling authors.

"Send me the tour organizer's contact info," I said, without a moment's hesitation. "This is exactly what I want to be part of."

As for Betsy, I suggested she come back in the fall, maybe bringing another author with her. But if not, I'd still welcome a visit.

"October is best—let's talk and arrange it." She laughed as she beeped the horn and drove down the alleyway. Alexa was right behind her, but headed south to Sheboygan to visit another friend who had arranged for a local signing at a book club gathering.

***

Monday morning coffee was abuzz with the bump in sales in all of the shops over the weekend. And the credit seemed to be given to me. Those accolades made me blush. But as I cleaned up the shop and restocked for the week, I thought a lot about Betsy's words, her wish to have someone waiting for her. The longing in her voice made me pause.

That afternoon, I checked my website and media sites and enjoyed the photos Liz had uploaded. Alexa looked every bit the author and I must say, Betsy and I looked pretty fine as well. Liz was already working to choose the best photos for a page I called "BookMarks Scrapbook" on my website.

For lunch, I ate leftover pizza and that night polished off the other salads and rolls. I was starting a new week fresh in every way. I wondered if Richard really understood why I needed privacy and quiet after the kind of whirlwind weekend I'd had. Maybe, maybe not. It was possible that he got his energy from people, rather than needing quiet time to refresh. I needed to feed my ability to be a creative and responsive shopkeeper by having periods of solitude.

Late Monday afternoon, after closing, I stepped next door to say hello to Skylar. I smiled when I saw a wooden Jack-in-the-Box in her front window. Only one man could have made that for her—Reed. From the minute they met I'd heard Skylar laugh when she was around him. Just maybe there was a future for them.

Okay, Grandma. Back off.

Hint taken.

She grinned when she let me inside and gave me a quick one-armed hug.

"My weekend was spectacular," I said with a laugh. "What about you? How was your weekend?"

"Thanks to you, it was terrific." She pointed to the door. "I loved the brunch. And some of the women standing in line to get their book signed came in here to look around. A couple of people commented about Doris and Lily, and they asked after them." Skylar absently picked up a dust cloth and ran it over a shelf, but she didn't stop talking. "The Square was busy, even without Alexa. I even asked Reed to unpack the latest shipment."

Now why would Reed understand Skylar and Richard not understand me?

Was it possible he did, but couldn't express it? Or, perhaps I didn't see it.

"Don't forget that Claire is flying in on Wednesday evening. Want to go to the airport with me?"

"Sure. Sounds like fun. I haven't seen my aunt in years." Skylar gave me a teasing sidelong glance. "I wonder what she'll be wearing."

I rolled my eyes. Claire was known for her flair of loose flowing clothes and wild combinations of color. Her style had been years in the making.

I was leaving to go back to my shop when Nathan and Toby entered The Toy Box, and the bell on her door made its happy tune.

"Well, hi you two," Skylar said. "Out for a stroll?"

"Mom sent us to get supper." Toby broke free from his dad's grip and went to take a closer look at what Skylar was dusting.

"Be careful," Nathan warned. "These aren't Mom's toys anymore."

"But Skylar said I could come visit and help her pick out the new ones."

Nathan raised his hands in surrender. "Sorry, Skylar. He's been asking to come for over a week."

"I'm glad to see you both," Skylar said, gesturing behind her. "You can look over my new inventory in the back, Toby."

The boy took off and within seconds, we heard Toby let out a whoop.

"Bet he found the new mechanical robot," Skylar said.

"How many batteries does it take?" Nathan asked.

I could see he'd fallen into one of the hazards of modern parenthood. I smiled, thinking about Mark and his fascination with battery operated toys. Toby would probably lose interest in these battery powered action figures soon, when he graduated to sophisticated planes and drones.

I asked about Lily.

"About the same," Nathan said. "She *hates* being bedridden, but she has to be patient for a little while longer."

"That must be so hard."

Nathan tilted his head back, gave it a little shake. “Tell me about it.”

Touching Nathan’s arm as I walked past, I left him and Skylar to explain to Toby that he could have only one toy.

I needed to focus on getting the apartment ready for Claire. My quaint, cozy apartment. And then Richard came to mind.

I thought about my good, steady life with Bruce. Steady being the operative word, with no extreme highs or lows, but always secure. An easy life. Until it became low, and then lower, when I lost Bruce first and then Mark.

Richard, on the other hand, had turned my world around with a phone call asking me to help his family. Already a friend, he’d been around, and then a little more, and then he made assumptions that made me uncomfortable. Still, he’d become a serious friend.

Serious friend?

Even I laughed at that phrasing.

14

Like I was running an inn, I got busy putting fresh sheets on the bed in the second bedroom to get ready for my next guest. I shoved aside more of my spillover clothing in the closet and emptied a couple of dresser drawers to make room for Claire's things, although how much could she have after organizing women's education projects in a small village in India? Of course, I didn't know how long Claire would be staying, but if past was prologue, I doubted she'd be around more than a couple of weeks.

After sharing the bathroom with Betsy and Alexa, I longed for at least another half bath. But it had been a long time since Claire and I had shared our childhood bedroom and bathroom. I hadn't even seen my sister for years, not since Bruce's funeral. She had been in a remote village in India when Mark and Carolyn were killed and was unable to come home.

Thinking about Claire brought back a flood of memories. Almost everyone who'd ever met Claire described her as a free spirit—and it was true. She was born with a spirit that couldn't be fenced in. She made friends by saying hello, and stayed connected to many for a lifetime.

When we were in school, Claire was a joiner, where I avoided the overload of belonging to every club and organization the school offered. She was flamboyant with her clothes and her laughter. In college, she'd finished a degree in international studies with a focus on human rights, and only days later, took off to take a series of jobs in poverty-stricken regions in the world.

We were a study in contrast, Claire and I. Conservative to a fault, I only updated my same tailored look, with its crisp shirts and wool blazers in the winter and linen jackets in the summer. Blessed with financial security, I could afford my hair touchups and manicures every five weeks.

Despite our differences, when she sent an email asking if she could stay with me, I immediately said yes, and began to look forward to seeing her. My condo, where I'd assumed I would still be when she was ready to return to the states, offered lots of room and two full baths. But in the apartment, space was more limited.

I couldn't deny wondering if Wolf Creek was ready for my sister. Likewise, after traveling the world, would Claire be ready for a small town and the tight-knit community of the Square? Not that it mattered much either way. I gave it about a week before she began talking about moving on, somewhere, anywhere, as long as it was different and new.

The next morning my time for speculation and worry over Claire and Wolf Creek ended abruptly when a text came in from Sarah to notify the shops that an unscheduled bus tour was on its way. Yikes.

As it happened, the bus had encountered a mechanical problem, but managed to make it into one of the parking lots near the Square. It would take several hours before the replacement bus would arrive, so that meant a long, leisurely visit to the Square for the tour group.

Lucky us. The visitors would have lots of time for browsing and buying.

I learned from some people in the group that the tour had been planned to make stops at historical monuments and a couple of regional museums. Most hadn't heard of Wolf Creek Square, but when I mentioned the town's museum, many said they'd head there next. Fortunately, this tour attracted history buffs and they were notoriously avid readers. Wisconsin and Great Lakes history and biographies were the big sellers that day.

One of the women especially interested in local history and lore noted a tag on the cover of a book that indicated a companion toy was available in the shop next door.

"Very clever of you," she remarked.

"My granddaughter just opened The Toy Box next door. The toys used to be part of this shop, but there wasn't space enough for both of us."

"Can I take this next door to see if she has the toy?"

"Just let me put a note inside. If you don't buy it, you can either bring it back or leave it with the owner. Her name is Skylar."

I hadn't considered that separating the toys from the books would create this type of challenge. Maybe I needed to have a few toys on my shelves or maybe photographs would do, as long as it was clear they were available right next door. Skylar and I needed to smooth out the details about the way we could make joint selling work.

A few minutes later, the customer came back with the toy and wanted to buy the book. "Thanks for trusting me. Not many shops would let merchandise leave without being sold." Handing cash over for the book, she said, "I've never met a young woman so knowledgeable about toys. I could have listened to her all day. I'll be sure to come back when I start buying for Christmas."

"Is there a reason, besides family, that you're so interested in toys?" I asked.

"I work in a small public library and we're expanding the children's department."

"Maybe Skylar would be willing to talk with the librarian, perhaps suggesting toys that correspond to books. Or, she could come up with ways to challenge young readers."

"Excuse me?" An older woman spoke as she approached me and the other customer. "Is that book in the window for sale?"

"Which one?" I asked. I wanted to sell every book in the shop, in the window, on the shelves, or on the tables. I didn't care where customers spotted the books as long as they were lured in.

"The one about the first school teacher."

"Were you a teacher?" I left that woman to reach into the window and hand the other woman the biography of Electa Quinney, the first recognized schoolteacher in Wisconsin.

The woman ran her hand across the cover and smiled. "I started teaching in a one-room school in a town up north on the Lake Superior shore. Not many one-room schools these days."

"No, there isn't. Could I get your name and number?" I asked. "The woman working in the museum is organizing a weekend of seminars and programs exploring regional history sometime next summer. I'm sure she would love to meet you and get your perspective. There's an oral history project sponsored by the foundation that's helping to upgrade the museum. I'm sure they'd love to hear more of your story."

"That could be fun." The lady printed in very precise lettering her name, address, and phone number on an index card I handed her.

I smiled. Yes, she'd been a teacher, probably a good one.

I turned around and saw Richard holding Alexa's book and talking to a customer about it. Selling right out of his hand, or so it seemed. I hadn't seen him come in, but above the noise I heard him say, "This author was here a couple of days ago for a book signing. Millie, the owner, is hoping to have other authors in for events." He went on to talk about the extensive selection of nonfiction and fiction books available.

Richard? Hand selling books?

I walked to his side on my way to the register. "When did you become an expert on books?"

He laughed. "Nowhere near an expert. I just happen to have a good friend who lives and breathes books."

In the background I heard, "I'd like to pay for a book. Can someone help me?" I touched Richard's arm. "Later."

The rest of the afternoon I was much too busy to talk with Richard. But then the buzz about the arrival of the replacement bus started and the shop emptied.

After closing, Skylar came into the shop and joined Richard and me in discussing the tour group and their choice of books.

"So, Gram, what do you think of my idea to generate joint sales?"

"What did you do?" Richard asked, interested.

"I put tags on the toys that had an image of a companion title in Gram's shop."

"And she did the same on the books." I put my arm around her shoulders and squeezed. "Clever lady, here."

Richard had reverted to lawyer mode. "It could get complicated keeping the sales separate for each shop."

He was right. Today worked out okay, but customers could get confused and not necessarily take the time to find out if the item was in stock. If we sold the items together, we'd have another bookkeeping step in the program. I was sure we'd figure something easier and safer. I didn't like stock leaving the shop that hadn't been purchased, no doubt Skylar felt the same way about her toys.

I cut our conversation short. I needed to keep moving. Claire's flight was due to land at 8:00, the last connecting flight of the day from Chicago. I'd Googled a map from Wolf Creek to the Green Bay airport for Skylar and me to use. Richard had offered to drive us there, but he was headed to Green Bay for the night and the next day, and we needed a car to get back to Wolf Creek. "You can follow me there if you like," he suggested.

I shook my head. "No, we'll be fine. But thank you for all your help at the signing, and then again today. You're a natural. Maybe *you* should have bought the shop."

Richard burst out in a hearty laugh. "Nathan keeps me busy enough." He gave Skylar a hug. "I'm counting on you to keep your Gram safe."

"That's a big job now, Richard. She's found her groove and her wings."

Richard bent forward and gave me a kiss on the cheek. Not a trace of shyness, even with Skylar watching.

"We'll see you when we get Claire settled," I said. "I'll call you and we can all go to dinner."

"I'll be waiting." He stepped out and I locked the door, batting the little bell to hear the jingle. What a great sales day it had been, and I was eager to see Claire.

Skylar and I allowed ourselves plenty of time to get to the airport, which involved navigating the roundabouts on

Highway 54, then merging onto Highway 172 going east into Green Bay. The roads were well marked and the airport was easy to find with all of the bright lights shining. The airport was smaller than the Minneapolis-St. Paul Airport, so we easily found Claire's arrival gate.

Claire burst through the automatic doors in an explosion of color. Her tie-dyed skirt and jacket were reminiscent of the 1960s, red colors bumped next to blue with spatters of green. Bright, in-your-face orange and turquoise sunbursts added to the rainbow spectrum.

Claire had always loved her curly, free-flowing hair, now salt and pepper, and she wore it well. Now and again, she tried to straighten it and calm the flurry of curls, but those attempts never lasted long. Sooner or later, she eventually gave in to its natural ways.

We waved and she found us in the crowd. "Millie! Skylar!"

People moved aside when the lady in the bright colors ran forward.

My joy at seeing my sister stopped me. She was simply an older version of the girl she'd been when we were kids in grade school. I ran forward and wrapped my arms around her and let the happy tears stream down. "Oh, Claire, how are you? Have you eaten? How much luggage do you have? Here, let me carry your bag."

"Millie. I'm here," Claire said with a laugh. "Slow down. I'm not leaving right away. We have so much to talk about, but first I need the bathroom."

"Me, too," I said.

Skylar laughed. "Me, three." She'd seen these reunions in the past and the insanity that occurred when Claire was involved.

"Oh, Sky, I was so sorry to hear about your mom and dad. I wish I'd been able to get back in time, but it wasn't that simple."

"I know," Skylar said. "Don't worry, I understand."

"Millie told me you're a toy expert now, not to mention a business maven." She wrapped Skylar in a huge head lock. "Now, find me a bathroom."

We took off and managed to get in the ladies room without waiting in a long line. Then we followed the arrows to the baggage claim. Claire's bags had bright red bows tied to the handles, so we found the three pieces easily. It was a squeeze to get the three of us and the bags into my car. Three women pushing and yanking the bags around in the trunk must have been a sight to see.

"I can call Richard," I offered. "He has a bigger car."

"What? And admit defeat?" Claire stood with her hands on her hips.

"Why don't I hold the smallest one in my lap and that will solve the problem," Skylar said, already pulling the smallest one out.

When Skylar had finished the maneuver, she and Claire did an enthusiastic high-five. "Smart lady," Claire said.

We made it home, but not without first stopping for ice cream cones. Claire hadn't eaten since Heathrow.

"You need a better meal than this. We've got your favorite food ready to stick in the oven, all done in twenty minutes or less."

"Pizza!" Claire bounced in her seat like a kid.

"Did you think I'd forget?" I asked.

"Not my kid sister."

When we pulled into the parking spot across the alleyway, I ran ahead to turn the oven on. Laughing over one thing or another, Claire and Skylar lugged the suitcases and the carryon bag upstairs and into the guest room. Claire had that effect on people—maybe because, although serious and committed to her projects of the moment, she was always up for some fun.

Claire poked around in each room while I opened a bottle of wine and filled our glasses.

"I love this place, Millie. But soon you have to tell me the long story of how you and Skylar ended up here." She lifted her glass to both Skylar and me. "Love you guys. I've missed you so much." She covered her mouth with her hand to stop the wave of emotion about to surface.

I had bought a large pizza, but I should have had two. We ate, we laughed, we listened to Claire's stories about her flight-from-hell out of India, with its four connections. When the pizza was gone I brought out cheese and crackers. Skylar filled our glasses and emptied the bottle.

When Skylar asked Claire about her long-term plans now that she was in the states and her time with the foundation had ended, I held my breath.

Claire threw back her head and laughed. "Since you asked, I'm counting on Millie to help me find my next adventure."

Then I froze.

October
15

When I turned the page, I was greeted with a field of pumpkins on the calendar photo. That triggered about a thousand thoughts. Had I been in Wolf Creek three months already? One-quarter of a year? When I'd agreed to six months as a favor, nothing more, I'd never imagined my life would change so rapidly. So far, not counting the broken window, the change had been good—really good.

As for Skylar, she'd found her footing faster than I had. From all accounts, it also looked like she'd found herself a circle of friends and a terrific man. Even with many days passing by in a blur, a tingling sensation still traveled through me whenever I thought about the moment I signed the ownership papers for an up and running bookstore in an historic building on Wolf Creek Square.

With Claire still adjusting from her rapid change in time zones, she opened her eyes and got going later in the day than I started mine. That meant my mornings were quiet, giving me time to reflect and plan, and get ready for my nonstop schedule. Claire and I overlapped at suppertime, which gave us an opportunity to reconnect.

"Millie, you never cease to amaze me," she said after dinner one evening as she washed and I dried the few dishes we used. "I went back overseas after Bruce's death, and then Mark died, but look what you and Skylar have done to create new lives. You two took a great leap forward, and far from home at that."

Her observation pleased me, mainly because it affirmed

my own feelings about the move. "Why, thank you. I'll tell you a small secret. Even with all of the day-to-day work and the expectations of being part of the Square, I love redoing the shop with my own ideas and style."

Claire squeezed the water from the sponge and put it back in its holder on the sink. "I'd love to do something like that." With no further explanation she turned away and went into her room.

The next morning, I poured a large cup of tea and went downstairs to begin another day. Claire's words gave me pause throughout the day, mainly because I had no idea what she meant. Approaching her mid-sixties now, I could imagine she wondered how long she could keep up her overseas work.

As festive and colorful as they were, the pumpkins on the calendar had reminded me that it was time to change the window displays. Again. I allowed myself a sigh. I had enjoyed the challenge three months ago, but now I had to find time to come up with new ideas on a regular basis. The look of the Square depended on all the shops having inviting windows. Now that the number of visitors expected for the fall and the holidays had increased, that also meant I'd have few lulls in the day to come up with something attractive and fresh.

By the time I completed a sizable sale to a family of four and listened to them assure me they'd be back soon, Claire was at the back of the shop browsing the small international travel section.

"Well, I'm surprised to see you up so early. Are you finally adjusting to being in the central time zone?" I asked.

She grinned. "I *need* to live on local time so I can help you down here."

I waved her off. "You don't need to do that. At least for now." But she hadn't given a hint for her future plans, nor did I know how I'd handle the masses of people I'd been told would be coming to the Square when the holiday shopping season began. "But on the other hand, you're welcome to be in the shop anytime you feel the need to interact with people again."

Claire smiled faintly and stared off into the distance. "I haven't done much talking these last months. The village we were based in was so remote that few people there spoke English, except for my fellow workers. One was from Spain and the other from France. They both spoke some English, though, but both left months before I did. Their contracts were up, and the organization was out of money."

That intrigued me. "Then how did you work with the teachers you were training?"

"A traveling religious leader stayed with us for a time. She spoke some English, and we used some interpreters that came through." Claire laughed. "Between that and hand gestures, we managed."

"I don't know how you managed," I said, shaking my head.

Claire rubbed her stomach. "See? You know I'm telling you I'm hungry." Then she moved her hand to her mouth. "You can tell I'm inviting you to sit down and eat. We did that sort of thing. But that's the part of English the kids picked up on very quickly." She turned away when the bell on the door jingled.

I looked at the door. "Don't go. When the customers leave, I want to hear more about your life over there." *And maybe you'd like to learn about these last few years of my life. Why is it neither of us kept in touch?*

"Good morning," I said to the two women, "and welcome to BookMarks. Is there something I can help you with?"

A woman pointed to herself and then to her companion. "We had dinner with Beverly and Virgie the other evening and they mentioned the book club you organized. Is it full or can we still join?" I detected a note of impatience when the woman waited for me to answer. She also looked past me into the space in the far corner that I'd crafted into a small reading area with one chair, a low table and a small lamp. All compliments of Doris' furniture. Thank you.

"We'll be meeting at Biscuits and Brew from now on," I said. "As it turned out, more people were interested than I can handle here."

"So there's room for us." She'd made her comment a statement.

"Any chair is free for the taking," I said with a laugh. "First come, first served as the saying goes, so come early."

One of the two ladies grabbed a business card, but I stopped them before they left. "I've ordered copies of the book, but you can get an ebook if you like." I pulled out my yellow pad and indicated they should add their names and email addresses to my growing book club and mailing list.

"We can't wait to come," the second woman said. "We tried to get Doris to have a reading club, but she wasn't interested."

The customers waved when they left, but stopped outside to look at the books in the window display. I'd taken one copy of *The Darkness in the River* and put it next to a sign that read: "*Book Club Selection for October.*" Maybe there would be even more interest as more people learned about the club.

With the two shoppers gone, Claire came to the register. "Would there be an extra copy for me?"

Really? "Sure, I can always order again. I'm placing book orders three times a week now and will probably need to stock more copies when holiday shopping is in full swing."

"That busy, huh?" She turned away clearly lost in thought.

I didn't see Claire the rest of the day, but when she came downstairs at closing time she looked rested and energized. "I'm hungry for a burger, big and juicy and messy with ketchup, mustard, pickles and anything else they can fit in the bun. And fries, lots of them."

I laughed. "I suppose it's hard to eat like that in a country where cows are sacred."

"You guessed it, Sis. But is there someplace off the Square we can go?"

Uh, oh. What was that all about? Maybe she didn't feel comfortable meeting the other shopkeepers and workers who often ate at Crossroads. "Skylar told me she and Reed went to an old bar called Creekside Pub and the hamburger was the best she'd ever eaten. Let me give her a call for directions."

"You close up and I'll go next door. I'll ask her if she can write the directions down," Claire said. She looked at me for a long moment.

She stepped out the door, but then stuck her head back in. "I know it's not my place to say this, but maybe you want to change clothes. I'd freeze to death in that outfit."

I looked down at the clothes I'd chosen to wear that morning. I'd seen the pieces in Styles' window as I went down the Square to B and B for morning coffee one day in August. After thinking about it, I'd stopped on the way home and bought the capri pants in a blue that matched the color of the decorative embroidery on the white tunic that had caught my eye. The look was more casual than my usual tailored fare, but I liked it. When I'd put it on that morning, I knew that with the summer heat gone, I'd probably not wear it again until next summer.

Claire was right. The late afternoon air was so cool I needed long pants and a sweater for the evening. I hurried to be ready by the time she returned.

***

Following Skylar's directions, I easily navigated the short trip to the outskirts of Wolf Creek. Creekside Pub itself looked like it would fall over in a strong wind, but if the number of cars in the parking lot was any indication of the quality of the food, we were about to sample some great fare. A poster just inside the door announced that the pub burger had been voted the "Best Local Burger" three years in a row by readers of the local paper.

We needed a moment for our eyes to adjust to the darkness inside. Claire stepped up to the bar and asked for a table, a pitcher of beer and two glasses.

"Help yourself to any open table, lady. I'll find you."

We found a table in a relatively quiet corner, and before we'd even settled in, the bartender, Bud, according to the name on his shirt, was at the table with cold frosted mugs. He gave us a one-page menu and a stack of napkins. This wasn't Crossroads. No linen tablecloths and multi-paged menu. I put both of our glasses on napkins to catch the melting frost before he poured the beer with just enough flourish to create an acceptable head of foam.

He looked at me first. "What'll you have?"

I waited for him to take a notepad and pencil to write our order.

He winked at Claire. "I'll remember."

Claire jumped right in and ordered a large burger smothered with the works and a giant order of fries.

I ordered a medium burger, and when he asked about fries, I shook my head. "I'll eat part of hers."

"Coming right up." He wiped his hands on the towel pinned to his apron—his clean apron, I noted—and went back to the bar. I heard him give the order to someone behind him, probably in the kitchen.

"A night on the town with my sister. What could be better than that?" She held her glass in a mock toast and I touched mine to hers. I'd never been much of a beer drinker and I couldn't remember the last time I'd enjoyed a frosty mug of brew. Months? No. More like years.

The old-fashioned jukebox started playing a tune that sounded vaguely familiar, but I couldn't have named the song or the artist. Claire was humming along, reminding me of Skylar, who had eclectic tastes and kept track of new artists bursting on the scene. Even with her coaching, though, I was at a loss to identify the singer most of the time.

"Remember this one, Millie?" Claire asked, bobbing her head back and forth to the beat. "Brings back lots of memories from the time I was in Mexico."

"That's too many years ago for me to remember one song."

"You're not that old. It's a Beatles' song, almost as old as we are."

Richard's favorite words were reassuring adages about aging not being important. He'd repeated that in one context or another when he'd called the other evening to let me know the documents for the sale of the condo in Minneapolis were ready to sign.

When our meals arrived, Bud pulled a bottle of ketchup from one apron pocket, mustard from a second and pickle relish from a side pocket. He did it with the kind of showmanship magicians were famous for, but since he'd carried everything we needed in one trip, Bud was walking efficiency. He put a small piece of paper under the ketchup. "Pay at the bar on your way out." He picked up the pitcher of beer and refilled our glasses, set the pitcher down and disappeared into the growing crowd.

Even with a table of six boisterous people nearby and the constant music from the jukebox, Claire and I enjoyed our dinner. With each bite, Claire let out an "oh," or "ah," or "mmm." I could see why. It was great food. I'd doubted the pub's reputation, but Skylar had been right.

Other than exclamations about the food, Claire hadn't talked much while we ate. But when she'd popped the last fry into her mouth, she leaned forward in her chair and rested her arms on the edge of the table. I knew she was about to begin the real reason for us having dinner together.

She took a deep breath and blurted, "It's time for me to come clean, Millie. The truth is, I'm nearly broke. I haven't had an apartment in the States for years and I've never made enough to have any real savings. Even worse, not-for-profits are just about as bad off. Very few have enough money in the coffers to pay people like me. More and more, they rely on volunteers."

Claire looked me in the eye as she talked, but glanced down when she paused to gather her thoughts. "I have only limited experience in retail, but I need a job." A few tears streaked down her cheeks, but her pride kept her from falling apart. "So, if you're willing to hire me for these next busy months, I'll work hard. I won't be a burden. I'll make you proud to be my sister. What do you say?"

I was blindsided, but not by the idea of her working in the shop. No, it astounded me that my usually strong, confident older sister had asked for my help. I couldn't remember the last time that had happened.

So, would I give her a try at BookMarks?

Well, why not? I needed the help during the holiday

shopping season anyway so having an in-house employee was the perfect solution.

Or was it? Claire's penchant for spur-of-the-moment decisions to run off to various parts of the world when disaster struck kept me from immediately saying yes.

"Okay," I started, tentatively, "my first impulse is to say yes, but there's more to it than that." Seeing Claire's frown, I quickly added, "Let's give it a month. You'll know by the end of October if you *like* working in the shop. Then we can talk about what comes next."

I grabbed the check before she had time to pick it up. I didn't want her spending what little money she had on our dinner. "Hey, the cost of the dinner is worth it to me," I said. "I got over my skeptical attitude toward this place. I like it a lot, and maybe next time I'll bring Richard." Richard probably spent way too much time in tonier places—as I had. Seeing his expression when I pulled into the parking lot would be worth the cost of the dinner. I also wagered that Bud was the kind of guy who'd remember his customers.

Claire quietly thanked me for dinner, but was quiet on the drive home. I used her silence to comment on how many houses and yards had fall and Halloween decorations. Pumpkins were abundant everywhere, just like in the calendar picture.

When we got to the top of the stairs at BookMarks, Claire gave me a tight hug, but she stayed silent. Somehow, I sensed she was hanging on by a thread. How stressful it must have been to come back to the United States knowing she had only a sister and grandniece to turn to for help until she got on her feet and figured out her next step.

Before she sent off to her room, I said, "Don't worry, Claire. You're safe here and you don't have to leave 'til you're ready."

I gave Claire time to settle in her room before calling Richard. I sat on the couch and looked at the trees decorated with small orange lights. When had that been done? Claire and I had been gone only a few hours and they hadn't been there last night.

Richard answered on the fourth ring. I was preparing a

voice-mail message when he answered, immediately asking after me—and Claire.

"Well, since you asked, she told me tonight that she's nearly broke and, of course, she has no home to go back to. She hasn't had an apartment in the States for years. So, she asked if she could work for me and earn some money."

"And?" he asked.

"I told her we would see how she liked retail selling for a month. After that, it's anybody's guess." I wanted to give her a chance. We both might be surprised. Me most of all.

"You are a smart businesswoman, honey."

Honey? We were in the endearment stage? Since when? Hadn't I told him we were friends, just friends?

Turning my thoughts back to Claire, it struck that for the first time, I'd seen Claire vulnerable, and at least for the moment, alone.

"Millie, are you there?" A note of concern edged Richard's words.

"I'm here. Sorry. Just got lost in my thoughts about Claire. I hope she enjoys working downstairs. I sure need the help."

"Time will tell. No use to worry. So, take good notes at the association meeting. I leave for Milwaukee in the morning."

"Travel safe, then. Good night."

I never asked Richard about his cases. That would always be a part of him he'd keep to himself. Bruce had been the same. The clients and the nature of the work was privileged and between him and his clients.

I sat on the couch a while longer thinking about the past and projecting myself into the future, especially the upcoming weeks. They would be my first holiday shopping season in a shop I proudly called mine.

16

Sleep came easily. But at some point in the night, I was jolted awake at the sound of a crash and Claire's voice saying, "Oh, dear."

I pushed the blanket aside and slid my feet into warm slippers. It wouldn't be long before I'd turn on the furnace to ward off the chill of autumn mornings. I opened my bedroom door and found Claire on her hands and knees picking up pieces of broken pottery.

"I'm sorry, Millie," she said, her voice plaintive. "I know it's your favorite teapot. I'll clean up this mess and replace it."

"Hush. No need for that—replacing it, I mean. But yes, we do need to get rid of the evidence."

Claire looked at me and we both burst out laughing.

"How many times did we 'get rid of the evidence' when we were kids?" I asked.

She pulled out a chair and sat down. "Oh, you don't know how good it feels to laugh. You can't know how scared I've been lately, knowing my project was coming to an end, and I'd be heading back empty-handed."

I waved her off. "You don't need to think about that anymore. You're young, you're smart, you like people, and Wolf Creek Square is all about people."

I sat in the chair across from her. "Having you in the shop with me changes things. It means that I'm freed up in a way. Sometimes being alone in the bookstore makes me feel like a *prisoner*."

Her eyes widened at my use of the term.

"The idea of owning the shop and moving to Wolf Creek happened so quickly I didn't think about being in the shop seven days a week. The hours get even longer during festivals and the holidays that roll around every month. Who was I to think I could do everything alone? I'm not young like Skylar who has energy to spare."

Claire eyed me skeptically. "You *are* superwoman, Millie. Always have been. I'm the one who ran away and chased a different life, one that was by design unstable and lacked settling down in one place."

This wasn't a conversation I cared to have in the middle of the night. Fortunately, Claire left the table and got out the handi-vac to clean up the last small shards of the broken pot. I was fully awake now and started a pot of coffee. I rarely drank the stuff, but sometimes I needed the extra caffeine. While every day brought something new for me to think about or deal with, I gave myself a free pass on those days when I didn't get my to-do list done. Lacking a full night's sleep, I figured tomorrow would be one of those days.

Claire had returned to the table before the brewing was done. I waited at the counter for the last spurt before pouring the rich, aromatic blend into two of my brightly-colored cups. I gave one to Claire and brought mine to the table with me.

"You didn't run away. You followed your dream and no one can fault you for that. Mom and Dad wanted grandchildren and they weren't shy about telling everyone their wish. I married Bruce and had Mark. We all were happy so none of us should have any regrets."

Her faint smile communicated satisfaction with my neat explanation of the past. "So, can I start working tomorrow?"

"Sure." I held up my hand to stop her next question. "Two things make BookMarks successful—having books on the shelves to sell and selling those books. It's that simple. But it isn't."

She grinned. "Zen."

"In a way, yes. The challenge is to get customers in the door to offer them the book they wanted or one they didn't know they wanted."

These weren't exactly Zen riddles, but still, Claire spoke in a sage tone when she added, "And it happens over and over and over."

"You make it sound like drudgery," I chided. "But it's the challenge that makes it interesting. Every customer is unique and so is each sale." I covered my mouth when a yawn tried to escape. "Today you can start by browsing the stock, so you're familiar with it, and you can greet the customers. You'll soon become comfortable in the shop, even if customers are packed shoulder to shoulder. This evening I'll show you the inventory system."

"If we're still awake."

I pointed to her. "Right you are. And tomorrow you can shelve the orders while you're browsing the stock." I stood up, noted the arriving dawn in the front window and groaned when my alarm beeped. "So much for getting any more sleep."

"We need a hearty breakfast to have the energy to work all day." Apparently, my plan had energized her. She opened the refrigerator door and surveyed the contents, while I headed to the shower.

***

All morning, I'd watched Claire timidly approach shoppers, but as she explained she was a new employee, leaving out the part about being my sister, her demeanor became more relaxed.

By the end of the busy day we were both running on adrenalin. Claire had done a great job. She seemed a little embarrassed when I told her so.

"Thank you, Sis. I don't want you to think you made a mistake having me here."

"I won't. Besides, you haven't exactly been hidden behind a computer for decades. You've been working with people all your life. And tomorrow you can go to Country Law and talk to Georgia about becoming an employee." I turned the lock on the door. "Whether it's a month or a year, you'll be paid like any other employee. And while you're there, you can ask Virgie to make a vest for you. If you're going to work here, customers need to know that."

"Georgia and Virgie." She said the names a couple of times to herself as if committing them to memory. Then she mentioned arranging to take a walk with Skylar before opening time. "Skylar said it's the only way she gets outside on these busy days. You want to join us?" Her sideways glance had the tease of a dare.

"Nope. I'll leave that to you." I enjoyed my easy, relaxed mornings too much to give them up.

Relaxed? Who was I kidding? I hadn't had time to relax since Richard had called in June. It would be a few years, if ever, before I could relax. Meanwhile, I intended to enjoy every day at whatever speed it arrived. I told Claire the inventory entries could wait. I was way too tired to concentrate.

"Thanks, boss," Claire said with a grin. "I don't know how I'd keep my eyes open tonight." Claire unlocked the door, saying, "I'll be right back. I'm going to see Skylar."

"Take my keys for now." I handed her the ring of keys.

She went out the door and I went up the stairs. I ate quickly and got ready for bed. I took my phone to bed with me and dialed Richard, only to get his voice mail. But I must have soon drifted off, because the sound of my phone startled me.

"Hi, Millie. Sorry to miss your call. I was out for dinner with a client and had my phone off."

"I dozed off right after I called," I said, struggling not to sound groggy. "Claire and I were up most of last night and the shop was busy today."

"So, how did she do?"

"Better than I expected, especially when the shop filled with people. She's not been in crowds much these last few years—even in India. She spent most of her time in remote small villages."

We talked about the big changes in her life and in mine, and I opened up about being nervous over the next few months. "From what I've heard, everyone is worn out and ready to collapse by Christmas. But I need to quit worrying about it, and stop whining. I might as well put on a happy face and enjoy myself."

"With Claire's help, you'll do fine," Richard said, with a laugh. "Maybe we can leave early one afternoon and get away for part of a day."

A good idea, but impossible, given all I had to do. "We'll have to see. I have almost no time to think."

"All the more reason to get away…and with someone who cares about you."

"It's true that I talk to you about things I'd never discuss with Claire or Skylar," I admitted.

"I've made myself clear, Millie. You're important to me," he said, his voice low, "but it's late now and you're tired. I can hear it in your voice. We can talk tomorrow."

"Tomorrow's the association meeting. Marianna and Liz asked me to join them for a late dessert after the meeting. Sounds like fun."

"Sweets for the sweet. Good night, honey." He'd said his parting words so easily.

I was learning that being around Richard was a series of highs and lows. Working for Nathan gave him a sense of belonging to Wolf Creek, but on the days he had extra time on his hands he wandered around like he was lost. That's what led him in the direction of BookMarks. And to me.

***

The next morning I took my large cup of tea to the front window upstairs. The trees in the courtyard had exploded with colors of yellow, rust, and bright red. The fir trees in their dark greens were a perfect backdrop for the splashes of color. I spotted Claire and Skylar doing a fast walk, pumping their arms to the rhythm created with their feet. Claire pointed to one of the scarecrows leaning against a bale of straw, and Skylar must have made an amusing comment because Claire burst out laughing.

A rush of memories deflated what had started out to be a pleasant morning. I might have known. The return of bittersweet, sharp images was as predictable as the trees shedding their leaves. Sometimes it seemed Bruce had lived for fall, usually spending two full weekends putting up the Halloween decorations around the house, inside and out. He wasn't shy about decorating the front door foyer with miniature bales of straw and pumpkins. When he'd finished he took me on a tour of the yard to see his new additions amongst the ones he used every year. For what would be his last fall, he arranged scarecrows like a choir, with pumpkins stacked like a snowman acting as the director. I meant to ask him where he got that idea, but it slipped my mind and I'd missed my chance. I'd never know if his choir was his own creation or if he'd picked it up in a magazine or party store. Wherever it had come from, it worked. I'd laughed at the sight, and he'd beamed.

From the time we were married, decorating for holidays was his arena, his baby. I didn't care about the holiday either way, but Bruce saw decorating as being part of the neighborhood.

I shook my head to distract myself from these tender memories of my old life. While I insisted I was moving forward, sometimes it seemed I'd only changed locations. The memories were always present. Now, Skylar had finally moved on. Lately, she hadn't asked my opinions about issues with her shop, which told me she had found a new circle of friends. She was doing fine. Better than fine when I saw her huge smile as she and Claire approached our corner, where they'd end their morning exercise.

The bell on the door jingled when Claire came inside, followed by the sound of her heavy steps running up the stairs.

"Morning, Millie. You should have come with us. Crispy air outside this morning."

"I'll leave that for you. Enjoy your breakfast," I said. "I'm going downstairs. Join me when you're ready."

"Yes, boss." She laughed and went into her room.

Claire's energy helped me get my focus back on the shop and I hurried down the stairs with a light step. Once in the shop, I startled when the phone rang even before I unlocked the door. Thinking it was Richard I answered in a husky, somewhat sexy and mysterious voice, "Good morning." His words of endearment had been with me all night, interrupted only by the morning's memories of Bruce. Clearly, I needed more time to allow my hesitant stance toward Richard to soften, but slowly, very slowly, Richard was becoming more than a casual friend.

"Millie? Sarah here. Just wanted Claire to know she's welcome to come to the meeting tonight. It would be a good chance for her to meet the other shopkeepers and employees on the Square."

As soon as she said her name, I laughed to myself. Sarah hadn't missed a beat, and if she'd noted my sultry actress voice, she didn't comment. Too busy to notice, most likely. My mind turned a corner and tried to catch up with what was on Sarah's mind.

"I'll let her know you called," I said. "I don't know what her plans are for tonight, but I'll be there."

"See you later, then. Bye."

Within in seconds of each other, Sarah hung up and Claire came to the register. I told her about Sarah's invitation.

"I'm going to pass. Maybe another time. Books are stacking up in the back room and I noticed on the flyer that bus tours are coming every weekend until the end of the year. Maybe we can sell more than your projections." She pointed to me. Claire was challenging us and making a game out of my sales projections. Maybe that *would be* a fun thing for us to do.

"Everything's taken care of with Georgia," Claire added, "and Virgie said she'd have my vest done within the week. They are busy with Halloween costumes now." She pulled a shiny key from her pocket.

So that was why she was busy right after the shop closed. Claire was showing me she was responsible and taking care of business, and actually doing what I'd told her to do.

Customers came in spurts, some browsing, others in need of a special gift or a book for themselves. We shared breaks for lunch. It had been an easy day, but a good one for Claire to gain confidence. I watched her step forward and help the customers find a book. Every now and then I heard her mention Skylar so she must have been connecting the books with the toys.

Since Claire wanted to process our latest delivery, we went over the inventory program so she could work on her own while I went to the association meeting.

"Text me if you have a question," I said on my way out the door.

"Got it." Claire finished slicing open the first of the seven boxes she'd signed for earlier that day.

I'd waited until the last minute to leave for the meeting, so I wasn't surprised to see that Skylar had already arrived. She waved to me to join her and Reed, but Sadie had gotten my attention first, so I told Skylar I'd catch up with her later. The soft chairs in the private dining room were almost too soft after a busy day. I forced myself to stay alert and tune into Sadie's description of the museum's newest display.

Sarah started the meeting with a tap on the microphone, and the room went quiet. "This month starts the holiday selling season and I want all of us to be ready for quite a ride. Never before has there been a bus tour every weekend this time of year."

My mind reeled with the idea of that many bus tours. In my years owning a store with Betsy, we'd never catered to that kind of shopping tours. Sarah pointed out that at times, more than one scheduled bus would overlap with another.

"That's terrific marketing, Sarah. Kuddos to you." Art Carlson started clapping after making his remark. We all joined him.

Sarah grinned, apparently surprised by the burst of gratitude. "It might seem like a bit too much for some, but we've worked for years to make the Square a popular shopping destination. So far, so good. Only time will tell if we need to be more careful with our scheduling in the future."

She took a sip of water, but quickly moved on to the Halloween plans for the kids. I made a note to get a supply of treats, and to put some Halloween picture books on the front display table.

"I'm going to be a Power Ranger." Rachel's son, who

was on his mom's lap clapped his hands.

"Go for it, Thomas." Clayton, who sat behind him, high-fived the little boy.

Somehow, the presence of a young child reminded the rest of us not to take ourselves so seriously. I kept that in mind when Sarah moved on to November and reiterated the policy to open an hour early and stay open an hour later for Black Friday and Small Business Saturday.

A mock groan rippled across the room.

"Enough of that," Sarah said with a laugh in her voice. "Happens every year. Then there's Christmas, but let's not get ahead of ourselves."

"Santa comes."

Once again, Thomas showed he was wide awake and paying attention, maybe even more closely than the rest of us.

"With packages for you," Sarah responded with a quick chuckle. "The rest of you keep in mind that weather could be an issue for any of our events."

I thought of the storm that had left me with a broken front window and how frequently Sarah had checked on me until the replacement work was done. She offered whatever help I needed. I was beginning to understand that in order to keep the Square running smoothly and looking good, Sarah stayed in constant touch with the shopkeepers. Although it could sometimes feel like interference, and I'd reacted that way, she was really motivated by her desire to make sure we all had what we needed to keep the Square in great shape.

"We have one more item tonight," Sarah said, "but I didn't put it on the agenda."

"Is it legal?" Elliot Reynolds quipped.

"Sort of. I'll let Jack explain."

Although Richard worked with Jack Pearson at Country Law, I'd not had any dealings with him other than to say hello. Jack wore a brown tweed sport coat over a plaid shirt. No tie, but he still had a professional look, albeit casual. And totally opposite of his wife in her brightly colored trendy clothes.

Jack stepped up to the microphone. "We all know Lily

is going to have the baby sometime this month, so to add a level of fun we are having four different pools for only owners and employees of the businesses on the Square."

"Is that really legal?" This time Elliot's tone was serious.

"It's legal because it's not open to the public and all of the money will go to Nathan and Lily for the baby. It is just like giving them a gift of money, but we get to have all the fun."

Jack held up four large white poster boards. "Each chance costs one dollar. The first board is for the baby being a boy or a girl. The second one is the date of birth. Next is the baby's weight and the last is for the length."

From the buzz, I could tell most everyone was on board with the plan and up for the fun of it. Lily was a colleague on the Square, current or not, and her family had deep roots in the community. The pools didn't particularly interest me, but I'd go along anyway. In the scheme of things what was four dollars?

The meeting ended and Jack and Sarah put the boards on the back tables, and announced that after that evening, they'd be moved to Square Spirits.

"I'll keep them in my back room so customers aren't involved," Zoe said.

I wondered if she was aware of the responsibility she'd taken on. I wouldn't have offered at all, being so new. But I had to ask myself if I'd have offered under any circumstance. It wasn't the kind of thing I was used to volunteering for. When Betsy and I had made contributions to our Minnesota community, it had usually been in the form of cash, or sometimes a gift certificate for a drawing.

The meeting over, I made my way to the dining room where Marianna and Liz were already waiting for me to join them. Sadie pulled out the last remaining chair of the four-top table, and Jessica pulled a chair over to the corner of the table and joined us.

And so the evening ended as it had begun, with talk about the holidays. After giving the waitress our order, Jessica told a story of a past holiday season when shipments from Europe arrived late because of major winter storms on the east coast. "Come May we ended up selling our entire winter collection for half-price."

We all laughed at Jessica's story, but although I tried to stay in the conversation, my heart wasn't in it. It was as if the flurry of events had caught up with me, mild anxiety about keeping up the pace over the next weeks, maybe a little skepticism lingering that Claire wouldn't rise to the occasion. I spoke to the others briefly about how different it was to own a business on the Square compared to being a shop in a small strip mall. "The holidays were always busy," I said, "but these bus tours are a whole new event for me."

"I'd had no experience with them either," Marianna said, "but when you see the bump in your sales figures, you'll begin to look forward to them like the rest of us do."

I had no doubt that was true, but I was worn out. I finished half my slice of apple pie, and when the waitress came around to refill our cups I stood and made up a story about Claire needing my help at home. That gave me an excuse to leave.

I enjoyed emerging from the busy restaurant into the quiet of the nearly empty Square, with the orange lights softening the darkness of the evening. As much as I wanted to make friends in the community, a part of me would probably always remain something of a loner. Or, perhaps I was simply tired after working so hard. The light in the window upstairs at BookMarks made me eager to see Claire's progress with the new deliveries so I hurried along.

I unlocked the door and yelled, "I'm home." After switching on the lights I noted the new titles lining the shelves filling in previously empty spaces. As I went into the back room, all the boxes were gone. Panic set in. How was it possible that Claire finished in one evening what I'd envisioned taking the rest of the week? I hurried up the stairs and found her asleep on the couch. A copy of *The Darkness in the River* lay open on her chest.

"Claire? Wake up, Claire." I squeezed her shoulder.

She opened her eyes and struggled to sit upright. "Home so soon?" She caught the book with both hands before it crashed to the floor.

"The meeting's over. Tomorrow's another big day. When

I left, the others were all still drinking coffee at Crossroads." I really wanted to ask her if someone helped her deal with all the new books.

"I didn't mean to fall asleep. I was waiting for you."

"It's okay. Tell me how it went with the books."

"The books are all checked in. I left a few on the cart. I didn't know which section to put them in. You can tell me in the morning and I'll finish up."

"You did all the boxes?" *Impossible.*

"It wasn't difficult once I got a system going. If you change a few steps in the process it will be easier." She frowned. "Oh, and you need more shelf space."

"I know. That's part of my do-over plan now that I own BookMarks."

"I can help with that if you'd like." She stretched her arms high over her head, but a large yawn escaped. "But maybe another day. I'm so bushed I'm nodding off again." She waved goodnight and padded off to her room.

Had Claire just handed me the long-term help I needed? I covered my own yawn as I readied for bed. I checked the clock and decided it was still early enough to call Richard. My heart raced a little faster. Why was that? It seemed so silly, yet I picked up my phone and hit his speed dial number.

17

The next day Claire suggested that one of the windows could feature some titles related to Columbus Day and U.S. history. "I saw quite a few relevant books when I was arranging the shelves." She'd set aside a couple books to support her idea.

"Sounds good. Why don't you take charge of the display?" That would be one item off my list. I realized windows were not my strong suit.

"Do you think I can do it?"

Would she actually doubt herself? "Of course you can do it. You've done all sorts of things in your life. So, go for it. If you need other supplies, we can order them or you can drive to Green Bay to pick out what you need."

"Really? You going to send me off in your car to a town I've never been to in my life?"

"Not really." I turned away so she couldn't see my smile.

Like me, Claire needed to venture out and find her way around the neighboring communities. Well, at least until she decided to leave town for another adventure. She was earning money now and had few expenses, so she might be able to save some money and be on her way.

Stop! I had no way to know if she had plans to leave, let alone a desire to. I actually knew very little about Claire, at least as the person she was now. It had been years since I'd seen her and we'd had little contact throughout our post-college years. I'd sent her birthday and Christmas cards if I had an address for her, but only received a post card now and then from her. I hadn't seen her in the five years since

Bruce's death, and even though she'd stayed with me at the house we'd talked very little. I'd kept the postcards, though, thinking they might be my only treasures from her. This could be a new beginning for us.

After sorting through the history titles, Claire and I decided to leave the books we chose on the cart and place it just inside the front door. Then we'd put a copy of the selected books in the window. Maybe this strategy would generate sales when people stopped to browse.

Claire rifled through the old box of decorations labeled "July" looking for items of a patriotic nature. "Everything in all the boxes looks old," she said, "but these July 4th type flags still work." She held up a couple of smaller ones that had probably been in the window a few times.

She arranged the flags around a few books featuring Columbus and other early explorers, including a few written for kids.

"It needs something more," she said. "Why don't I go to Rainbow Gardens to see if Megan has anything to fill it out? Is it okay if I spend some money?"

I shrugged. "Marianna calls that cross marketing and does it all the time. We can label anything from her store—Megan probably has some plant pots with an autumn theme." I explained Marianna's drawings and prizes as her way of building her newsletter list.

"Everyone wants to play a game and win," Claire said.

"Speaking of games of chance, the Square is having four private pools around the arrival of Nathan and Lily's baby. If you want to participate, the boards are over at Square Spirits." It occurred to me that Claire would find Zoe interesting. "You should go ahead and stop in. Introduce yourself to Zoe and look around. It's a fun shop."

"Seems like it," she said. "Skylar commented on it when we walked past yesterday morning. I'll go later this afternoon."

Even with the sun shining and warm temperatures, activity on the Square was slow. Claire and I took the time to go through the shelves and look through the newer titles. I still didn't know what kinds of topics would be big sellers.

Only time would help me learn more about the clientele for a shop like mine going into the holiday season.

"You can work on the Halloween windows soon," I said. I'd been collecting books with Halloween themes and stashing them under the counter. "Doris had a Halloween carton. It's in the back room. The other boxes have been pretty dull and way outdated, but maybe this one will be better."

Claire was about to go to the back when the bell jingled. We both looked up to see Richard walk in with Trevor Sinclair. A nice surprise. I introduced Claire to Trevor.

"Nice to meet you, Trevor. I was just reading the book club selection last night."

That pleased Trevor, and he and Claire began talking about the book, gradually moving toward the reading corner in the back of the shop. At one point, Claire ducked into the back room and came out with a folding chair. She offered him the reading chair and joined him.

"Slow day?" Richard asked with a note of interest.

"The quiet before the storm, at least according to what Sarah said at the meeting last night."

"I'd have liked to get back in time, but I couldn't move my evening meeting to the afternoon."

"I don't think you missed much," I said, smiling. "Except maybe Jack talking about the pools they formed for the baby."

Richard laughed. "That's all the chatter at Country Law this morning. Georgia and Virgie are going to Zoe's during lunch. I guess they want to buy more chances."

"You'd think this was the first baby ever born with all the attention it's getting."

My negative tone gave extra power to my sarcastic words.

Richard turned away. "It's a first for the Square."

Oops. I had to at least try to smooth things over. "And a new grandbaby for you. Are you getting excited?"

Glancing my way, he said, "Worried is a better word. I'm in Wolf Creek now until the baby is born and Lily is home. Toby will be staying with me so Nathan and Lily don't have to worry about him. We're making it seem like a big treat to be Grandpa's companion."

"And how is Lily's mom doing?" I asked. Richard wasn't the only extended family in town.

"Beverly," he said, as if reminding me. "She's offered to make meals for Toby and me, but she and Virgie are very busy now making Halloween vests, and they've been getting many orders for holiday gifts."

I don't think he understood all that went into the one-of-a-kind vests, which were more art than clothing. But I imagined he was happy to have another person to help look after Toby. I was the one who needed to get it through my head that this event wasn't only for the Connor family, but for the community on the Square. Many people had worried about the wellbeing of both Lily and Toby.

Wanting a quick change of subject, I reminded Richard of the book club meeting the following week.

"I haven't forgotten. My copy of the book is in my briefcase."

I was about to ask if he was enjoying the memoir, but the door opened and a group of six entered. The bell never stopped jingling until the last person shut the door.

"Dinner tonight?" he asked.

"Crossroads at 7:00. I'll meet you there."

He waved on his way out, and my focus switched to the six customers. The bell must have jingled, but I didn't hear it.

Trevor soon followed Richard out the door and Claire immediately began interacting with three women from the group of six. From her smile and hand motions, I was struck by the way a natural was revealing herself. Of course she liked people, but I hadn't fully appreciated the way they gravitated to her. When one of the women came to the register to complete her sale, she laughed as she pulled cash out of her wallet. "I came in because my friends wanted to stop. I didn't plan on buying anything, but look here, three books and a suggestion that I stop next door to get the companion toy for one of them."

I grinned, and exaggerating a note of pride, I said, "The Toy Box is my granddaughter's shop and we aim to please."

"That's for sure. I'll bring my daughter to the Square for a mom-daughter day. Every shop is different and unique. And lunch at Crossroads never disappoints."

I handed her the receipt and change for her money, and put her books in a bag, proud of the shopping bag imprinted with the logo Liz designed for me. She'd done an excellent job making my design match the sign on the outside of the shop. I made a note to connect with her so I could send out my first newsletter—time to start drumming up interest in my holiday specials.

Claire and I continued to help the customers all day, breaking only to refill our mugs with coffee for her and tea for me. We ate lunch a bite at a time on the run.

When she locked the door and switched off one bank of the overhead lights, she clapped her hands in front of her chest. "What a great day this has been, Millie."

"Fun, huh?"

"Now I understand Skylar's excitement. I told her I wanted to learn her inventory, too."

"Getting ready to jump ship?" I asked in obvious jest.

"No, *no*," she said, with no lack of emphasis. "I asked *you* for a job and I'm sticking to our agreement."

"Well, then, tomorrow I'll teach you how to work the register and you'll be more or less completely trained." I glanced at the clock above the door. "I better get moving. I'm meeting Richard for dinner in an hour."

Claire crossed her arms. "He really cares for you."

I was about to ask why she thought so, but she put out a hand to stop me. "It's written all over his face." She didn't wait for my response, but headed up the stairs.

Later, maybe because Claire had relieved some of my anxiety about the shop, I was able to relax with Richard. I'd never enjoyed myself with him more. Having Claire with me all day, I hadn't been rushed to help the next customer and the next and the one after that. Always thinking about getting the next sale. I told Richard about Claire being confident and quickly becoming familiar with the stock.

"And she's so patient when customers debate about buying one book or two, or maybe even more. She understands important decisions about spending money. Naturally, given her circumstances, she would have an affinity with people on a budget."

"I'm glad that's working out," he said. "I'm very happy myself. It will be fun having Toby around. And it's good he's in school, so I can work." He laughed. "I still need to stop at Zoe's tomorrow and sign up for those baby pools."

He'd offered an opening, and I decided to take it. "Speaking of the baby, let me apologize for my attitude and words the other day. I understand that everyone on the Square is important."

Richard was sitting next to me rather than across the table, and he didn't have to reach far to take my hand. His warmth reached all the way to his eyes. "You and I are both new to this community. We are still figuring out where we belong. We're forging into new territory."

"And it's all your fault," I said with a laugh. "If you hadn't called me for help…"

Richard laughed too, knowing how I'd finish the sentence. Then he signaled the waiter for the check and a few minutes later, we left Crossroads.

Since it was getting late, the peak of the crowd was long over and we were among the half dozen patrons left. We'd enjoyed a spicy stir fry, and with it being October, pumpkin chiffon pie had come with the meal.

We started a slow walk on the Square. "We've got two bus tours on Saturday," I said. "And depending on Claire's comfort level using the register, I'm going to Minneapolis on Monday morning. The co-op wants me to do a walk-through and sign the last papers. I'll stay with Betsy. You remember Betsy from the book signing?"

He nodded as he took my hand. "I do."

"I've also contacted the bank, so I'll empty the safety deposit boxes. The accounts have already been transferred here."

"So, you think Claire is ready to be in the shop alone?" His frown was skeptical.

I was surprised myself that I believed she was ready. "It'll be a test, but Skylar is next door if Claire gets into a jam. Monday and Tuesday are usually slower days on the Square, so I figure it's the best time to go."

Stopping in front of the shop, he said, "I wish I could go with you, but I promised Nathan I'd take care of Toby. I don't want to tell him I've changed my mind."

I wasn't prepared for Richard's offer to travel with me. Did I even want him to come? Not really. Once again, he was jumping in where I hadn't yet invited him. Besides, he wasn't part of my life in Minneapolis, and I wanted to spend time with Betsy and my friends. Having Richard there would change the atmosphere.

"I'll be fine," I said. "I have friends on both ends of the trip if something comes up and I need help." I squeezed his hand. "I want to go now before the weather gets bad. Besides, Ethel, the co-op manager, told me a couple is waiting to move into my place."

Richard grinned. "I know you can take care of yourself. But even so, you call me if you need help. Plenty of people on the Square will step in and help with Toby in an emergency."

As if it were routine, Richard held my face in his warm hands and lowered his head. His kiss spoke volumes of his feelings for me.

I backed away first and went up the steps to unlock the door. I thanked him and said goodnight.

He raised his hand in a quick wave. "I'd like to see you across the table every evening, Millie."

I had no response for that. What would I have said? I wasn't ready to see him or any man across the table every day. Not yet.

I returned his wave and went inside.

***

Friday was dead, but I called it the lull before the storm. Claire used the quiet hours to show me her streamlined inventory process, which involved a way to quickly scan the books a carton at a time and then separate the titles into stacks for easy shelving. Assembly-line fashion, almost like

Mr. Ford's invention itself. Easy and efficient.

When the tour buses arrived on Saturday, Claire and I could have used another person in the shop to help the customers. Fortunately, Virgie had delivered Claire's vest, the looser fit style that looked great on her. A couple of customers took the time to note the way it attached her to the shop.

Apparently, Sarah made a habit of checking in with shopkeepers on these especially high-traffic days, so I wasn't surprised to see her come in around noon. We had no time to chat, though. I could have kept the door open all day, given how many customers came in and out.

Claire worked like she had been in the book business a long time. I couldn't stop grinning. By the time we closed for the day, the shelves were in disarray, the sale cart was almost empty, and the toy samples weren't where they belonged. We'd done so well, we were left with a host of cleanup jobs demanding attention. It was a bookstore owners dream!

We both stared at the mess, and then Claire perched on the stool by the register. "I think we deserve a glass of wine tonight, and maybe have a pizza delivered. I'll buy, if management would give me a loan."

I laughed. "Great idea, and it's management's treat. Go ahead and make the call. I'm hungry and much too tired to straighten up this mess tonight. That's what early morning hours are for. We'll get a good system down to get the shop spruced up again."

After searching for the phone number for Wolf Creek Pizzeria, Claire ordered a large, thin-crust with the works. "It'll be here in thirty minutes. Can you stay awake that long?"

"I'll close out the register. Oh, that's something you need to learn tomorrow. It's easy enough and the accounting program is updated automatically. Remember, I'll be gone on Monday and Tuesday so you'll be in charge." Before she could refuse again, I walked up the stairs with the money bag under my arm.

She followed me up and while I counted the cash, the

checks, and the credit card receipts she poured the wine, brought the glasses to the table, and took a seat across from me. "How'd we do?"

"I'd have to check, but I think it's the best day of sales yet." I got up and opened the freezer door and brought out a notebook in a plastic bag. "Best safe in the world."

"Yeah, right. And everyone uses it. You need to get a permanent safe up here. And soon."

When the buzzer on the back door sounded, Claire grabbed cash from the stack on the table and ran downstairs. By the time she was back, I'd returned the money and book to the cold freezer.

"I'm so hungry and this smells wonderful. I'm drooling already." She put the box in the center of the table and opened the lid. The mixed aromas of tomato, cheese, and onions filled the room and made my mouth water. Neither of us sat down before we reached in for our first piece.

We didn't eat just one piece, either. By the time we sat back, more than half the pie was gone and our glasses were empty.

"What a fun day, Millie. I understand Skylar better now when she talks about finding a gold mine."

"She saw the potential faster than I did. She's claimed the lucky break and put her own stamp on it."

"Have you seen The Toy Box lately?" Claire asked.

I was embarrassed to admit it had been a couple of weeks. "I'm always tied up here during the hours she's open. And, I haven't wanted to intrude. But she seems happy here. Better than happy when I see the two of you speed walking around the Square in the morning."

"She has big plans to make The Toy Box so unique that people will drive to Wolf Creek just to buy toys and books."

"Really?" I sounded more surprised than it warranted. "I suppose I shouldn't be shocked that she'd have that kind of goal. After all, when I bought the bookstore, I told her I wanted to make BookMarks a top-level shop."

"I guess she's taken that as a goal for herself. I can't wait to see both of you make it happen."

Claire stood and transferred the rest of the pizza into a

container, then broke down the box and stuffed it deep into the wastebasket. She held the open bottle of wine toward me, but I'd had plenty and shook my head. After corking the bottle, she quickly washed up the scant dishes and the kitchen was clean again.

Coming over to my side of the table, she bent down to give me a hug. "Thank you, Millie." Her voice was soft, almost reverent. She left me sitting at the table and went to her room. I heard the door click shut and took that as a sign she wanted to be alone.

I needed some solitude as well. I moved to the couch and sat in peaceful silence until the Square and the room were completely dark.

18

Since Claire was such an excellent student, I had no second thoughts about leaving on Monday. I also texted Richard to let him know I was on my way and would let him know when I'd arrived at Betsy's.

Claire skipped the Monday walk with Skylar and fixed us a hearty breakfast. While I finished getting dressed, she carried my overnight bag and briefcase to my car.

After a quick goodbye hug, she said, "You be careful. I won't call or text unless absolutely necessary."

"You'll do fine. I'm not worried." I honked when I drove away, and returned Claire's wave when I saw her exaggerated wild arm wave in my rear view mirror.

As I drove along Highway 29 west toward the Minnesota-Wisconsin border I contemplated the possibility that this would be my last trip to the city I'd called home for many years. On the other hand, maybe I'd visit to see Betsy and a few friends, but with Wolf Creek Square becoming a four-season destination, I wouldn't have much time for travel. Especially when Claire left.

Since Claire had never stayed in one place for long, I needed to assume she'd leave again one day. It was a given. And that was fine, as long as I had some notice.

A few hours later, traffic increased when I crossed the Mississippi River, forcing me to put my meandering thoughts aside. I made a quick stop for an early lunch and to gas the car. I went straight to The Book Shelf and was greeted by Betsy's happy shrieks. The shop was a step back in time for me. She still had the vanilla infusion scent filling the room and books were stacked in every corner, just as it had been when I was a partner. Talk about a lack of space. I quickly realized I had nothing to complain about at BookMarks.

I'd scheduled an appointment at the condo for mid-afternoon so I stayed in the store with Betsy, chatting until she needed to tend to customers. Then it was time to go. Although I hadn't planned to stop at the cemetery on my way to the condo complex, the idea had passed through my mind. Hadn't I already said goodbye? Hadn't I shed enough tears? Truthfully, I'd tried to make peace with losing Bruce many times, but only recently had my heart begun to follow my head. Driving to the condo, I passed the first driveway entrance to the cemetery, but then I quickly changed lanes and turned in at the second gate.

I'd driven here day after day following Bruce's funeral so I knew the route by heart. I left the car in the same turnabout space I'd used many times before and walked to the headstone bearing his name. I stood in the warmth of the afternoon sun and mumbled a few words about my new home in Wisconsin. I touched the headstone and whispered my message. I was doing well and Claire and Skylar were with me and we were supporting each other. I told him about the challenge of BookMarks, and then I found I had nothing more to say. I'd said it all in the years past. I patted the cold granite. "Good-bye, Bruce. I loved you so."

I turned to leave with the realization flowing through my body that I'd put my love for him in the past. That's where it needed to be. My spirit was lighter as I walked to the car. Without regret for the past or fear for the future, I smiled when Richard's face flashed in my mind.

I checked my watch. It was time to put my home in the past, too. I texted Ethel and told her I'd be there in a few minutes. Driving to the condo, I told myself the trip was my way of really putting the past in the past. I had taken every possible step to make it so.

My meeting with Ethel was short and all business, involving a walk through the professionally cleaned empty rooms. I saw nothing that made it my house any longer. The furniture was scheduled to arrive in Wolf Creek before

Halloween, and Richard had taken care of the storage arrangements for me. When I signed the papers and gave Ethel a perfunctory hug, one more part of my old life was gone.

That evening, Betsy hosted a small gathering of friends at her place. "Nothing big. Snacks and wine." I would have preferred a quiet evening with my old friend, but true to her personality, she turned the occasion of my visit into a party.

It was disquieting that I found myself drifting out of the conversation and counting the hours before I'd be able to head back to Wolf Creek. Fortunately, the hours passed quickly, and I begged off visiting late into the night, using the excuse that I had a long drive back. I also used anxiety about leaving Claire alone in the shop as a reason I wasn't in a party mood. I wasn't all that anxious, but Betsy understood my inability to keep my mind on my old home when I was still adjusting to the new one.

After muffins and a few cups of my favorite tea early in the morning, I closed my bag and headed out in time to get to the bank when it opened. My business there took almost an hour, and then I re-traveled the same highway east toward home, all the while wishing I had a magic carpet to travel the distance faster.

I came in through the back door intending to help out in the afternoon. It was a good thing, too, because I walked into pandemonium. Customers stood shoulder-to-shoulder and lined up at the register. On a Tuesday?

I shouted to Claire that I'd be down in a minute and ran up the stairs, dropped the bag and the briefcase, and grabbed my vest.

Once downstairs, I fell in beside her.

"Whoa, glad to see you, Sis." She laughed as I grabbed a shopping bag and began loading it up with books from the last sale. "I'm just a little too busy at the moment to ask how your trip went." She punctuated the obvious with a burst of laughter.

"You're doing great," I said, touching her shoulder.

Over the next few minutes, I helped clear the line and went off to see if I could help customers browsing the shelves and the sale cart. The next few hours until closing passed in a blur.

Claire made a ceremony out of locking the door. "I was beginning to panic for a while there, but I didn't want you to think I wasn't capable of handling the shop." She went to the register and pulled out the cash, credit card slips, and checks, and ran totals on the register. "I hope everything matches."

When the register was closed out for the day, I put the bag under my arm and gave her a hug. "Thanks so much. I accomplished everything that needed to be done." And more. But I kept my visit to the cemetery to myself. It had been my private good-bye to Bruce and would stay that way.

"As promised, I'm going to call Richard and let him know I'm home. Then, dear sister, I want to hear about your two days as a retail queen."

I heard in my own voice that I was calm, settled, and no longer carried the past on my shoulders.

I went upstairs and made my call. In a few words, I gave the positive report of my trip.

Richard's response wasn't related to my safe return, though. "We're on baby watch. Lily's water broke last night. She and Nathan are at the hospital in Green Bay. I'm on pins and needles waiting to hear."

"Where's Toby?"

"He went from school to Sally's. They're painting faces on pumpkins this afternoon. I'm picking him up in a few minutes. So, I'll be the first to tell him he has a brother or sister, probably tonight."

The whole baby event had become tiresome for me before my trip to Minneapolis.

Now, though, having had a chance to think about the Square and put the people and activities in perspective, I reset my attitude. I realized why the women at morning coffee were cautious with their enthusiasm over Lily's baby when I was at the table. I'm sure they saw my lack of interest—I'd even changed the subject a couple of times. I'd only participated in the pool boards because I thought I had to as a member of the community.

I also thought about my seesaw claims of finding joy in being a shop owner, and then telling Claire selling was the same day after day. If I hadn't known better, I'd have thought I was second guessing my quick decision to buy the shop.

"Make sure you call when you hear you're a granddad of two. This will be a special day for you, too."

"I love you, Millie." His voice was soft, strong. There was a little hesitation when he spoke.

"Bye." I couldn't repeat his words to him. Maybe soon, but not when I'd just said good-bye to Bruce. And to the life I'd known for most of my life. Besides, I didn't yet trust that Richard understood—down deep—my drive to create my own success.

By the time I finished the call, Claire had set out cheese and crackers. She poured tea for me and wine for herself. We carried the tray to the couch and set it between us. The sun lit the shops on the other end of the Square casting long shadows into the courtyard from our buildings on the west end.

Looking content and comfortable in my home, Claire grabbed a pillow to make a table for herself on her legs.

My home. Not my residence, not my address or zip code, but my home. My sister was living with me and my granddaughter was next door. The extent of my family. And Richard was waiting for a new member for his.

A twinge of guilt shot through me. Once Skylar had made her move and began shaping her new life, my concern for her had lessened. Traveling solo, she was navigating her own ship. I hadn't seen or talked to her every day, nor had I stopped in to see what customers had raved about when they'd shopped there. But now I'd have more chances to visit because Claire could watch the shop.

Claire recited an account of her two days, almost hour by hour. She handily solved small problems, too. When two people wanted the same book, she noted the inventory systems reported two copies in the shop, which sent her on a hunt. She didn't have to look far, because the second copy was on the cart by the door. Just before I left she'd added a sign noting "New Arrivals," hoping to increase interest. So far it had, and books in that location had been selling well.

A few repeat customers asked about Lily and Doris. Thinking it best not to go into detail, Claire had given non-specific answers. "As if I had the latest news on either of them." She rolled her eyes and popped a cracker into her mouth.

"Richard told me Lily and Nathan are at the hospital now."

"Oh, how exciting." She clapped her hands. "A new baby was always a time of celebration in the villages—villages pretty much anywhere in the world I've been in." She had a faraway look in her eyes when she turned to the front window.

"Do you miss it? Being there with the people?"

"The people, yes. The poverty, no. And the realization that at least in some places the old conditions would come back was disheartening. But there was hope over the long term that life would be better because we were there."

"Are you ready to go back, or move on?" I hadn't planned to talk about her future so soon, but it was as good a time as any.

"Pushing me out the door?" She frowned, saying, "I promised you I'd work at least 'til the end of the month. You wanted me to try this out, see if I like it."

"I'm not pushing, Claire. Not at all. Take your time to decide what's right for you." I reached across the length of the couch to squeeze her hand. "Now, tell me about today."

"There I was, dusting shelves, when the door opened and this mass of humanity entered." She shook her head. "Unbelievable. They were laughing and talking and asking questions. Thank goodness, I had my vest on or I would have gotten lost in the crowd. I tried to multitask, but since I didn't want to make a mistake with the money we might have lost a sale or two."

She had said "we" so easily it surprised me. I waved her off, dismissing her concerns. "One customer at a time. That's Marianna Spencer's philosophy." Seeing Claire's quizzical expression, I refreshed her memory about the owner of Quilts Galore.

"The paperwork from yesterday is in a separate bag in the *safe*." She laughed when she swung her arm to indicated the freezer. "Does Richard know you keep it there?"

"Nooo. And don't you say a word."

We bantered back and forth until after dark. My second cup of herb tea had gone cold and I was too tired to make another. Fatigue accumulated over the two days washed over me. I braced my hands on my thighs and stood. "Bedtime for me."

Sometime after getting ready for bed, my phone rang.

"Her name is Emma Irene Connor," Richard said. "They named her after Nathan's mother."

I heard deep emotion in his words. He so rarely mentioned his late wife. "So, how are Emma and Lily doing?"

"Good. Both are good. Lily's tired, but they'll monitor her for an extra day."

"And Nathan?"

"For a guy who claimed he wanted to be a bachelor, he's changed his tune. He keeps saying, "I have a son *and* a daughter now."

Richard paused, probably in reflection, but I didn't interrupt. "I'm going to tag along to the hospital with Nathan and Toby tomorrow evening. Want to come along?"

That didn't feel right. I might send the wrong message, not just to Richard, but also to Nathan and Lily. "You need to be a family right now. I'll visit them when they get home."

"Maybe you're right." He paused. "But I bet others from the Square will be visiting her—them."

"But they've known Lily longer than I have."

Silence. Then he said, "Well, I understand. Another day will be good."

"Get some sleep, Richard. They will need your strength now more than before."

His next words came out rushed. "And to think I almost missed all of this because my drive to control everything in my life pushed my son and Toby away. Their move to Wolf Creek finally woke me up."

By reliving his past, sharing his mistakes and his change

in attitude, he was reminding me that he had been able to reunite his family. Maybe I needed to acknowledge my feelings toward him before he thought I didn't care about him or his family.

I said goodnight and promised to check in tomorrow.

He laughed. "I sure hope I can sleep like Toby. He's out cold and doesn't know he has a sister yet."

I had to laugh when I disconnected the call. Richard would have talked all night if I'd let him.

***

I told Claire about the new baby before she left for her walk with Skylar. She was as excited as if the baby was part of our family. "Oh, and would you tell Skylar her grandmother is coming for a visit this morning?"

"That's your business. I'll let you call her."

"Right." Claire wasn't my messenger any more than I was her caretaker.

After she left, it occurred to me that she wore the same outfit for her walk each day and had only what amounted to a couple of changes of clothing. I smacked the side of my head. She only had the clothes she brought with her, next to nothing, and no money for new ones until I paid her. She borrowed a sweater the other day and I still hadn't realized she had so little to wear.

My mood plummeted. I had no excuse for just noticing this problem. She'd admitted she was near penniless. She'd lived in a warm climate for years and hadn't once asked for a loan to buy warmer clothes. I did notice she was always busy when I suggested a trip to Farmer Foods for groceries. Like it or not, the next time I saw her I'd give her money, or, if she objected, I'd give her a loan, an advance on her salary.

I checked the calendar and noted the next evening's meeting of the book club at B and B. Since I hadn't been to morning coffee there for a week, I dressed quickly and went to join the other shopkeepers to catch up.

I opened the door and was greeted by Zoe's burst, "Millie! You won the weight pool. Free coffee for you today."

"Oh, well, I'll have tea, please," I said, painfully aware I'd shown almost no reaction.

Zoe grinned. "Hey, Steph, one tea please. For Millie."

"Coming right up." Steph, too, was excited and happy.

Zoe was still bubbly when she said, "Here's a list of the other winners. You're in good company."

Forcing a smile, I quickly scanned the list. Megan won the boy/girl pool by being the first to choose a girl. Rachel had guessed 7 lbs., 12 oz. Emma weighed in at 7 lbs, 13 oz. And Virgie had guessed Emma's length at 18 inches, spot on.

I looked at the men's table and was disappointed not to see Richard. He was probably on his way to school with Toby, or still asleep after the few, long days he had waited for the news that both Lily and the baby were safe.

Grinning, Steph handed me a large pink cup. I thanked her profusely, once again, trying to feign more interest in all this than was genuine. If there was a time to be an actor, this was it.

When I went to the table, I noticed every cup on the tables was pink. Emma's arrival was old news. Sadie slid into the open chair next to me, making it easier to join the group. Sarah nodded to me. "How did your trip go?"

As mayor, Sarah made a point of knowing the who, what, where, and when of the people in her community and on the Square. Of course, she knew I was gone. I found myself less irritated and more accepting that someone needed to be in charge to keep the Square thriving. And hers was a hands-on style.

I laughed. "Well, I sold my house, closed accounts at the bank, and turned in my library card. I guess Minneapolis can take me off the tax rolls."

Sarah quickly swallowed and covered her mouth, coughing twice.

Sadie chuckled. "I guess it was the amusing bit about the library card that caught her off-guard."

The conversation drifted into baby news and was in full swing when Nathan walked in. His eyes were tired and red, but his smile showed his happiness. He carried a pink gift bag with "It's a Girl" printed on the side. He passed a Hershey chocolate bar to each of us, thanking us for our interest and concern for Lily. I smiled when I saw the "she" part of the bar had been highlighted in pink.

"What? No cigar?" Elliot goaded.

"Smoking's illegal in Wisconsin in public establishments, my friend," Nathan countered. "Mother and daughter are doing fine." He gave a picture to Sarah and asked her to pass it around. Lily, Emma, and Nathan.

"And Toby?" Sarah asked.

Nathan smiled. "He wanted a brother, but said he'd share his toys."

Sarah's watch beeped and we gathered our mugs and napkins to put in the bins by the door.

Everyone from the Square gave Nathan a hug or handshake. Me, included.

Claire had already unlocked the door and had started an R&B CD, both upbeat and energizing—and loud. "I think it's going to rain today," she said over the music. "Those gray clouds are hanging really low."

I gave her the chocolate bar from Nathan. "A gift from Nathan and Lily. Their daughter's name is Emma Irene and the family is doing fine."

"Well, congratulations to them. Maybe I'll stop by Country Law later today and see Georgia. She must be happy about this." She turned away in thought, and also turned down the volume.

I stepped behind the counter, opened the register and pulled out some money. "I owe you an apology, Claire. You were forthright about your situation with money, but I knew you were safe with me and never gave it another thought. You need money for clothes and anything else you want to buy, so take this." I put the cash in her hand.

"I don't want to be a charity case." Her stubbornness was at the surface. "I was going to buy some clothes when I got paid."

"Your pride is showing, but I'm not worried about the money. You've already added a lot to the shop and besides, I feel better having my sister work for me than a stranger."

Moisture gathered in her eyes.

"Right now," I said, "I'm going next door to see another member of my family I've neglected."

"She's been busy, but she'll be happy to see you."

The drizzle began as I looked at the displays in Skylar's windows. I saw she'd cleverly eliminated the need to change one of the displays each month by making it permanent. She surrounded the wooden Jack-in-the-Box Reed had made with a variety of green plants. Nestled in the front corner of the window was an artistic Jack-O-Lantern. A sign noted the plants and pumpkin were from Rainbow Gardens. Toys, games and puzzles filled the other window. The drizzle had become a light rain so I stepped inside.

The train whistle and the click of the wheels on the track greeted me. Mirrors had been hung over the train so everyone could watch it go by. Skylar was unloading a box sitting on top of her counter. I waved and said, "When did you put the train up?"

We hugged each other warmly before I again asked about the train.

"Reed and Nolan have been tweaking it for a few days now. See the mirrors? They're a security system. Every time the train passes a switch, the cameras take a picture."

"You need security?" When had that happened?

"No, no," she laughed. "Nolan needs hidden security for a client and wanted to try it here first."

"Boy, that's a relief."

Then I noticed her shelves were arranged in pinwheel fashion. A Jack-in-the-Box had been painted on the floor as the center hub of the wheel. I thought it was unusual and took some getting used to, but I also recognized something modern and artistic in her design. "So, are you happy with this arrangement?"

"It was my idea. And having the low shelves makes the kids happy." She shrugged. "Happy kids, more sales."

The bell on the door jingled and a family in brightly colored raincoats and boots entered. I waved and left. I needn't have worried. My granddaughter was doing fine. I smiled to myself, thinking about the way she was returning the favor by making her own mark on Wolf Creek Square.

Back at BookMarks, Claire and I rearranged the books on the cart and debated titles for the next book order. The shop was essentially empty, so we sat in the back corner and ate the tuna sandwiches I made. The small lamp in the space added a circle of glowing light in the dark corner.

After lunch, we kept busy with cleaning up and placing online orders, but neither of us mentioned the fact that not one visitor or shopper came into BookMarks that day. A first!

The book club meeting was scheduled for 7:00, and at the end of the day I asked Claire to lock up while I hurried upstairs. I remembered I'd never confirmed with Steph for the treats for the evening. I dialed B and B, but when the call went to voice mail I left a quick message.

Within minutes, Steph called back. "My hands were full taking tonight's cookies out of the oven."

"That's a relief. I'll come a few minutes early."

Steph said an unceremonious "Later," and that ended the conversation. No doubt she was in a hurry to close up to get ready for the meeting. Steph was skilled at keeping things simple and efficient, but always managed to show some flair. I'd noticed she volunteered her help and her products for many activities and festivals on the Square. I remembered she'd made special cookies for the Fourth of July picnic.

I heated chicken soup I'd picked up from Farmer Foods, and Claire and I ate our easy supper in a hurry. Claire volunteered to clean up the kitchen, but was still ready to go before I was. Maybe that was because I changed my clothes twice before giving up on finding the exact right look. My conservative tailored style no longer seemed appropriate in this casual, and in some ways, artsy community. Then it dawned on me. My clothes represented my past and in my quest to move forward, I needed to change my style.

Claire was on the couch when I stepped out of my room. I wasted no time in announcing that we'd be going shopping at Styles tomorrow morning. "I hope I can convince Jessica or Mimi to open early for us."

"Road trip." Claire threw one of the pillows at me.

I caught the pillow and waved it at her. "Yeah, a road trip around the corner. Come on. Let's go meet Trevor."

We did a fast walk through the rain drops and found B and B already half full of book club readers. Without being prompted, Claire made the round of tables to introduce herself and ended up sitting next to Trevor.

Steph had set aside a table for the beverages, and small plates and napkins were ready for each table. Trays of cookies lined the counter and she asked some of the readers to pass them around. At 7:00, she took a seat at a nearby table to signal the kitchen was closed.

I sat next to Trevor, opposite Claire. I read from my note cards a short introduction of the book and let Trevor begin the discussion.

"This is the story of a Wolf Creek family," he said. "If Sadie did the genealogy I'm sure we'd find that I'm related to some branch of this family, but not these children."

A hush fell over the café.

"I think because these children were so close in age it's remarkable that they didn't note their similarities, even with favorite foods or interests. And they all lived here in town."

"I don't like the foods my sister eats," a woman at one of the tables remarked.

"But this goes beyond personal tastes," Trevor said. "All three of them worked in Farmer Foods at the same time. They had friends that overlapped."

"Weren't you surprised it was at a funeral that the two girls connected?" Virgie piped in.

Trevor considered his answer. "I suppose I wasn't surprised. Not really. Weddings and funerals tend to be times that people talk about their families. They might even reveal secrets, unwittingly or on purpose. In this case, both girls made passing remarks about being adopted."

"That just tells me to watch what I say the next time my family gets together," the woman at the table said.

The rest of us chuckled, probably wondering what secrets *her* family held.

"Weren't you surprised when Stephen and Margaret started dating?" Trevor was getting the readers involved with his questions.

He succeeded. The idea of siblings dating is like everyone's worst nightmare, and fortunately the two had not found each other interesting and had moved on to other classmates to ask to dances and such. The dominoes began falling at a funeral, and it was soon apparent that these children had been separated early in their lives and adopted to three different families, two of whom hadn't lived in Wolf Creek at the time. But somehow, they all ended up in town at some point.

Claire and I listened to the back and forth and the emotional response to the story. We didn't have to do a thing. Trevor took over the conversation and it only ended because we reached the end of the scheduled time. But that was okay. We left them wanting more.

We ended the evening with Beverly suggesting a short book about the first Thanksgiving. A consensus approved the choice as appropriate for November. The book chosen, Beverly volunteered to lead the discussion.

"Thank you all for coming. Let's thank Trevor for choosing the book and Steph for her hospitality." I waited for the clapping to end. "Let me know if you want me to order a copy of the November book for you. I'm happy to do that and appreciate your supporting BookMarks. If you haven't signed up for our mailing list or added your name to our book club list, please see Claire. She'll take care of it." I'd never felt more like the owner of the shop than I did at that moment. I even had an assistant.

A few of the women helped clear the tables while I settled the bill with Steph, telling her I expected to use her services often, because we'd be expanding the programs sponsored by BookMarks.

I caught Mini just as she was heading out the door, waving my arm to stop her. "I need a shopping spree," I said. "And so does my sister. Any chance we could come in early, before the Square is open for business."

"Shopping spree, huh? I like the sound of that word," she said, laughing. "How about nine o'clock tomorrow morning."

I touched Mimi's arm. "We'll be there. Count on it."

My next stop was Trevor. Claire was standing with him, and the two were chatting like old friends. I grinned and patted his shoulder. "Thanks for leading tonight. The book—and you—were extremely interesting."

Trevor walked along with Claire and me to BookMarks. I told Claire about our appointment with Mimi the next morning and left the two of them talking by the front door. The rain had stopped, leaving the orange lights on the trees reflecting in the puddles on the walkway. A lovely sight.

I thought about calling Richard, but decided against it. His hands were full over the last many days and he was probably sleeping. Besides, it had been a long day for me. But I decided never to complain about busy days in the shop. Having no customers at all had made this a *very* long day.

Weather certainly drove the sales up and down on the Square. Business was business no matter if it was in an open pedestrian Square or an indoor mall. Everyone had good days and bad days. Today had been one of the bad ones.

19

Claire was a chatterbox when she returned from her walk with Skylar the next morning. I had finished a call with Richard and was toasting an English muffin when she filled a cup with coffee and talked about getting ready to go to Styles. "You should really join Skylar and me for our walks. It's invigorating, and we have long talks about business and men."

"Business I can understand, but men?"

"Why not? We're women, and you can't blame us for having men on our minds."

Casting a pointed look her way, I said, "Speak for yourself."

"Don't deny it. Like Richard never crosses your mind. You talk to him almost every night." She put her hands on her hips. "The walls aren't that thick, dear sister. I try not to listen, but…"

I swallowed the last of my tea. "I don't want to discuss Richard with you, or anyone else." I did wonder, though, what Skylar contributed to the conversation. Was she as preoccupied with Reed as I was with Richard, always questioning my feelings and trying to figure out his place in my life? Or maybe for Skylar, it was a simple case of being young and falling in love.

"So quickly you deny what is so obvious." Waving, she headed off to her room. "I'll be ready at nine. Skylar told me she found some terrific clothes at Styles. Unique, but not real expensive, either."

Since I'd only shopped at the boutique once before, and

that had been in the spring, I didn't know what Mimi and Jessica would be showing for the fall. But later, when we walked inside, the store burst with color. I made quick introductions and pointed out that Mimi's family went way back in Wolf Creek history.

Mimi responded with an arched eyebrow. "You know my family's history?"

I laughed. "Well, that's according to Sadie. I'm not the historian of the town." Oops, I remembered Sarah's writings were still on my dresser for me to finish reading. They were sitting right on top of a stack of new mysteries I wanted to read—when I could stay awake.

The fall selections on the mannequins and racks were rich colors of brown, rust, marigold, and purple. I walked between the racks and found two casual, but professional pairs of slacks and matched them with easy-to-wear and loose-fit jackets, a style new to me and a contrast to the sharp angles and contoured fit of my usual fare. I also spotted a tunic-style blouse I wanted to try on. I'd come in with the idea that I wouldn't buy anymore tailored styles—unless I found an unusual piece.

I heard Claire tell Mimi she wanted to buy one of everything in the store. I put aside a lifelong struggle not to be envious that each item or outfit she tried on fit her perfectly. She had the tall, slender shape that favored ankle length skirts and boots, or long, colorful jackets of the same type Liz Pearson was known for. I watched her try on one outfit after another. Each created a combined mood of stylish and trendy. The rich colors and basic black and white were perfect for her colorful style.

More often than I cared to remember, my new clothes needed alterations. This time was no different. Mimi suggested I come back the next day when the seamstress would be in the shop and the slacks and the jacket sleeves could be shortened.

Claire paid for a couple of items from the money I'd given her as an advance on her salary, although I considered it a gift. As for the other items I insisted she buy, we agreed I'd pay for them and she'd pay me back directly from her paycheck. We still had to work out other details like the expense of room and board. I knew she'd never expect to live in my home without contributing, but I wanted to keep the money she put in to a minimum, at least to start.

We both enjoyed our new clothes over the next weeks, which became one long blur of activity that included the bus tours and early holiday shoppers. We fell into a system that developed as we went along. Each evening, Claire and I divided the work that needed to be done before the shop opened the next day. But overall, we were giddy with the excitement of one busy day following one another—we hardly had time to breathe. When I talked to Richard, he fell silent and listened to me laugh and giggle and reflect my joy.

One afternoon after locking the door, Claire asked if it would be okay if she came down in the morning to shelve the books.

That was fine with me, but why the change? "Sure. Don't you feel well? Are you working too hard?"

She turned away like she was hiding something from me. "I'm fine. More than fine. Trevor's taking me to Crossroads tonight."

"Trevor?"

She waved her hands in my face. "No, not like that. We're just friends enjoying each other's company."

I gave her a skeptical look. "And let's remember when I said that about Richard?"

"Well, that's not so anymore," she said with a laugh in her voice. "That horse left the barn a long time ago."

"Go on and get ready," I said, turning away, "and wear one of your new outfits."

"Yes, boss." Up the stairs she went.

I was in bed with one of my new novels before Claire returned from her evening out. Richard and I had just finished a conversation about the shop, and Lily and the new baby. He was keeping an eye on Toby, who was in the tub playing with a new submarine bath toy. I thought the boy was getting too old for toys in the tub, but it wasn't my place to give my opinion. Apparently, Toby didn't want to go home now that the baby was a girl and not a little brother. He'd rather stay with Granddad. Nathan and Lily, glad to have Toby safely cared for, agreed he could stay for two more days and then he was going home to get used to having a little sister. I suspected Richard would miss having Toby around the house.

"He's a handful, Millie, but we're having so much fun." There was life in his words.

I told Richard that maybe I could spend some time with him and Toby and get to know the little boy.

"I guess it's easier to get away now that Claire knows the ropes and is helping out."

"True. I won't be able to get away during these busy bus tour days, but I'm glad I realized early on that I couldn't manage the shop all alone. It's no wonder Doris became overwhelmed. When I got home from Minnesota, Claire was somehow managing a crowd of customers quite well." I laughed. "But she collapsed after we closed that night. And then she said she hadn't felt so good in a very long time. She's already connecting with repeat customers." I considered telling him about Trevor, but changed my mind. It wasn't any of my business in the first place.

"Has she talked about leaving yet?" Richard asked.

"No, but she promised she'd be here until the end of the month."

"That's not a long time for you to get help if she does head out of town again."

"I'll hire you," I quipped.

When he fell silent I laughed. It wasn't very often I caught top-tier-lawyer Richard Connor off guard. My sense of humor aside, I was beginning to doubt that Claire would be ready to move on in a matter of days. I suspected she'd stick around at least to the end of the holiday season. By that time, she'd have paid me back and probably accumulated a little money of her own.

***

Mother Nature played a trick on the children's Halloween

party on the Square. A slow soaking rain began mid-morning and continued all day. By late afternoon, the rain and wind stripped the trees of the remaining leaves and left behind puddles in the grass. Claire and I watched the rain stream down the windows of our mostly empty shop and amused ourselves eating the small candy bars I'd bought for the kids.

By dusk, the courtyard should have been filled with children dressed in their favorite costumes. From the description of last year's party at morning coffee the adults enjoyed the evening as much as the children. Now even the pumpkins scattered about the Square were drenched and the scarecrows looked bedraggled.

A few families ventured out under heavy raingear. When they stopped at BookMarks, we put double treats in their bags and the parents also got chocolate bars. If any of the miniature bars were left in the bowl, I'd put it on the counter for the shoppers.

If the trick was Friday night's children's party, then the treat was the Alexander open house held on Saturday after the shops closed. Matt and Nora, and Matt's granddad, Gus Alexander, had purchased the Sorenson home, a once decaying mansion not far from the Square. Gus had the eyesore renovated as part of his commitment to support historic Wolf Creek Square. The Matt and Gus Alexander Foundation had chosen the museum-on-the-Square as their first revitalization project.

Costumes were optional for the evening, and both Richard and I decided to exercise the option not to dress up. The younger adults showed much more enthusiasm for that part of the event. Richard decided to drive rather than chance us getting caught in the occasional showers still predicted for the evening.

We drove up to the imposing mansion-like home and parked in some designated spots on the opposite side of the street. If the mansion also had acres of land surrounding it, we might have quipped that it was like a gentleman's estate. It sat on the end of a regular street of sprawling older homes, and stood out as the largest among them.

The arched front door was outlined with pumpkin-shaped lights and black cats with glowing eyes were near the opening. Bunches of cornstalks stood like sentinels on both sides of the door. Orange lights marked the edges of the walkway punctuated with real pumpkins carved like Jack-O-Lanterns.

Nora stood in the doorway welcoming guests as they came in. "We're so glad you've come. Please help yourself to beverages on the side board, and you'll find various treats around the house." She pointed behind her. "If you're interested, we put out some games on the back porch. And don't forget to introduce yourself. Some of our friends from Green Bay have joined us tonight."

Nora turned to greet the next group of guests to arrive. I admired how she looked in her black taffeta dress, her skirt rustling as she moved. The tall peaked hat tipped to the side when she turned her head, but she grabbed for it before it slipped off. No one could miss her radiant smile.

Richard and I skirted the crowd to admire the decorations on the long table in the formal dining room. A cauldron kettle was bubbling, a vapor of blue mist rising like a geyser. Artificial lights arranged like the kettle's fire looked real.

We found Reed and Skylar bobbing for apples on the large screened-in back porch. Reed wore a Jack-in-the-Box costume, with the box formed by a cube of cardboard hanging from his shoulders. He wore a juggler's hat with a bell on the tip that jingled when he moved—even his shoes had bells attached.

When Skylar came up with an apple in her mouth, we all pointed and laughed. Her Raggedy Ann makeup ran together on her wet face and dripped from her chin, threatening to roll down the front of the traditional Raggedy Ann pinafore.

Richard handed Skylar a piece of toweling from a roll nearby. "Where did you find that costume?"

She grinned. "Online. Where else?"

"The youth of today." He shook his head. "Even Toby knows you can get just about everything with a simple click."

I waved goodbye to Skylar as Richard and I left the porch

and stopped for snacks in a small sitting room off the large living room. When we ran into Gus, Richard introduced me. I'd heard he was a spirited man, evident by an almost constant twinkle in his eye. At the moment, he was "holding court" in his big chair in a combination library-den. He wore a green cape and a funny-looking king's crown. "I'm the king of cards," he said.

When the bewitching hour of midnight arrived, we all gathered around the caldron in the dining room. Nora stood on a chair and pretended to stir the black kettle on the table. "Double, double, toil and trouble, fire burn and cauldron bubble."

She frowned, looking stumped. I concluded she'd forgotten the rest of the verse, so I called out, "Fillet of a fenny snake, in the caldron boil and bake."

Laughing, Nora reached out and touched my head with her wand.

She got off the chair and stood beside Gus as Matt spoke briefly about the renovation, but spent most of the time talking about the foundation and the museum.

After saying good-night to our hosts, Richard and I were about to leave when we met Trevor and Claire at the door. Since Claire hadn't mentioned going to the open house, I figured they decided to come at the last minute.

Acting on impulse, and maybe because I'd had a tad too much of Nora's witch's brew, I invited Richard and Trevor to join Claire and me for a nightcap. We'd had such fun, it seemed a shame to cut the evening short. I had only tea, coffee, or wine, but I didn't see how that mattered. It was so pleasant just to think about the four of us being together.

Back in my apartment, we sat around the table all drinking tea. I don't know what prompted it, but Claire and I began telling stories about ourselves as two kids always arguing over space in our shared closet or over whose turn it was to do the dinner dishes. We must have driven our parents nearly mad, but somehow it all seemed funny after so many decades.

Trevor told tales about getting in trouble for reporting the truth about a prominent Wolf Creek citizen not so artfully skirting the law in his business. "The guy thought for sure he'd get away with it, too, but what good is investigative reporting if we don't follow the information wherever it leads."

It was hard to argue with that.

Richard was the quietest among us, sharing very little, probably because Toby had worn him out. Time passed quickly and it took Richard to break up our gathering by noting that Claire and I would be opening the shop in a matter of a few hours.

At the door, Richard asked Claire about her plans now that the month had ended. He kept his voice casual, as if he had only passing interest. I was annoyed with him for delving into that, but I was more curious what she would say.

"Me? Leave? I want to stay here forever."

Well, why not?

November 20

When I turned the page on the calendar, the picture showed American Indians greeting the Pilgrims. In the background, the moored *Mayflower* was shining in the setting sun. Two words instantly came to mind: thankful and grateful. And not just for the month. I was thankful to be healthy and the owner of a business I found fulfilling. My gratitude list would cover many pages. Claire and Skylar would be at the top of the list, and Richard would be next.

Yes, Richard.

After Trevor and Richard left my apartment on Halloween night, I went to bed, but couldn't fall asleep. My mixed up thoughts were all about Richard. It was so easy to picture the two of us together as a couple and think years into the future.. But when I added marriage into the mix, the picture became kind of fuzzy. I wasn't ready for that discussion yet. I could still enjoy his company, couldn't I? Well, why not?

Richard had come on too strong, and too soon, with his declarations of his feelings for me. He'd said he loved me.

The more I settled into my new life and put the past behind me, the more my feelings for Richard grew. Surprise, surprise.

To mark November, Claire left the flag from her Columbus Day window display and replaced some of the history books with military themes for Veteran's Day. We didn't have too many titles from current wars, but she settled for what we had in stock and advised me to fill in the gaps. At one point I heard her mumble, "Terrible times, those wars." No doubt she'd been in some of the major conflict zones, and for all I knew, she'd witnessed fighting in the remote places she'd been. When Claire put the books from the October display on the sale table, I was sorry to see that even with fewer daylight hours some of the book covers and jackets had faded.

"We need to show abundance, Millie." With her hands on her hips she stared into the other window. "We could fill this other window with some kind of harvest theme. We could have one of those…what is it? A kind of horn-like thing?"

"A cornucopia."

"Yes! And fill it with books spilling out." She illustrated a flowing line with her hands. "Fiction and non-fiction for adults and children covering the whole area. Maybe we… oh, I don't know." She let her arms slap to her sides.

"I think it's a great idea. Why don't you run to Rainbow Gardens and see if they have any for sale. We can order a large one with Express delivery if they don't." I handed her some money from the till.

"Back in a minute." The bell jingled her departure.

While she was gone I called Richard—feeling like a school girl. Something had changed since my trip to Minneapolis. No, not something. *Me*. I had changed. I wanted to hear Richard's voice, to hear him laugh. Now I welcomed his hand touching mine. I'd no longer pull away from his affectionate gestures. I wanted to brighten his day. Most of all, I wanted him to know I cared about him. Maybe I had been working hard to resist him, using his annoying ways to deny my feelings for him had gone beyond simple friendship.

Claire returned with empty hands, but immediately searched the Internet with sites Nora had suggested. "I thanked her for including me in her party. She is such a giving person. Not my experience with the super wealthy."

"When did you work with wealthy people?" I thought Claire worked with the impoverished.

"They'd come to our work sites for a photo shoot. Most never touched the people or went into their homes. Well, they weren't all like that." She waved away her own words.

"Some of the donors rolled up their sleeves and helped. In some of the villages the people would gather around the visitors and let them hold their babies."

"I'm glad Nora and Matt are part of the Square," I said. "And Gus, of course, although I don't really know him."

"Gus and Trevor have done some interviews with people in the community as a way of creating an oral history of Wolf Creek. Trevor said they have to work quickly to get this done before they're all gone." Claire laughed. "He calls Gus spooky smart."

"I'd say that's quite a compliment."

That was the last chance to chat that day. After closing, Claire stayed downstairs to order the wicker cornucopia. She was upstairs before I had our tomato soup and grilled cheese sandwiches ready. "We're running low on food. Here's a list I started. Add anything you'd like."

"I got paid today, so I'll get the groceries after Skylar and I finish our walk tomorrow."

Richard called later and I accepted his invitation. I was happy to be heading to Nathan and Lily's for a late—adults only—dinner. "Can you believe we're three generations, Millie? Not like some of the Wolf Creek families that go back more generations than fingers on one hand."

"We Fergusons are three generations, too. We just happen to be missing the one in the middle."

"I never thought of family as being particularly important," Richard blurted. "I only wanted money and what I thought it'd bring me. That's why I became a lawyer."

"Every generation, every person, has regrets about past choices," I said with a sigh. "That's why the present and the future are so important to all of us. Especially you and me."

"What are you saying, Millie?"

"I can't put it into words yet. But soon. I've been doing a lot of thinking."

"I love talking with you. You make me see things differently."

We ended our conversation, leaving me thinking about the link between the generations, and the history of so many Wolf Creek families. That reminded me of Sarah's pages.

No doubt she would be stopping in soon for them and I hadn't read the second section yet. I settled into bed after locating the envelope and began reading.

THEN THE TEACHER

On a beautiful September afternoon the stagecoach from Green Bay arrived on time in Wolf Creek. As soon as it came to a stop, Florence Busher stepped down. Her clothes were coated with a layer of dust, and her tired body ached from the constant jarring from the rutted road.

She made no effort to hide the excitement behind her smile.

Florence, who, for better or for worse, was known to her family and friends as a free spirit, had traveled all the way from Indiana by herself. And against her family's wishes. Her mother had shuddered and cried when she left. "No proper young lady travels alone, Flory." That hadn't stopped the newly graduated teacher.

A neatly dressed man approached Florence. "Excuse me, miss. Would you be...?"

"Florence Busher. Yes, I am." She put her hand in his.

"Um. Welcome to Wolf Creek. I'm Pastor Korth." He was surprised at her boldness.

"Oh, Pastor. I'm so excited to be here." She removed her hand from his.

Brian smiled. "I'm sure the children feel the same way."

Florence laughed.

Brian noticed her voice was happy, like water in a creek bubbling over smooth stones. Her eyes were as blue as the autumn sky, her golden hair like the standing wheat fields.

"Your luggage?" he asked, recovering well from being dazzled and tongue-tied.

"I'll be staying at the hotel until I can find a more permanent place. I have a trunk filled with books that can be delivered directly to the school house."

"I'll have someone take care of that. Perhaps you'd like to freshen up before dinner. The mayor, Woodrow Day, and his wife are expecting us at seven."

Florence looked across the street, and then to her left.

"Is there something you need, Miss Busher?"

"Call me Flory, please. I'm looking for the school house."

Brian stepped to the edge of the boarded walk. He pointed toward the setting sun. "It's down there. The building with the steeple. We haven't built the steeple on the new church yet."

"I see." In the glare, Flory didn't see what he was pointing to, but she needed to wash up and change out of her traveling clothes. "The hotel?"

"Oh, yes. This way." Brian picked up her traveling bag and extended his arm for the short walk down the street.

They went inside and Brian stood back and waited for Miss Busher—Flory—to register. "I'll be by around at six-thirty. It's a short walk to the mayor's house."

"Thank you, Pastor Korth."

"If it's Flory for you, it's Brian for me."

"Brian."

That casual meeting started a long friendship that had many of the townspeople smiling.

With faith on one side and education on the other, Luke, the little boy from Green Bay, thrived in the community. No one would have believed that when Brian found him on the river bank, the small boy didn't even know his name. At the time, Brian figured that his Father in heaven had been a carpenter, and since Brian liked the Gospel of Luke, he put the two together for the young boy and called him Luke Carpenter.

"Why didn't you use your name?" Flory asked one day.

"He's not mine. He's a child of God."

Brian didn't preach fire and brimstone, and Flory didn't teach with a ruler and harsh words. Under their tutelage, the town and the children thrived.

Year after year, deeper feelings grew between Brian and Flory. When they announced their engagement and upcoming wedding, the townspeople gave the church a new coat of paint.

For three days under crystal blue skies and the brilliant colors of autumn, the town of Wolf Creek celebrated Brian and Flory's wedding. Luke stood between them at the altar.

Brian and Flory added three children to their family, but unfortunately two of their children only lived a few years. Then, Brian and Flory left Wolf Creek when he was assigned to a larger parish in western Wisconsin. Luke moved along with them and their other surviving child, a daughter. It's known that Luke enlisted into the military, but no records exist in Wolf Creek with information about their daughter.

[Historians note: Many of the events included in this story have been taken from Florence Busher's journals. They are located in the museum at Wolf Creek Square.]

***

My days with Claire became richer and more exciting, at

least in part because we agreed not to tip-toe around our personal lives. She knew the way my feelings for Richard were growing, along with wanting to have him around more. No longer could I claim Richard as a casual friend. I laughed when our relationship began to become a noteworthy topic-of-the-day at morning coffee.

As we chatted at breakfast one morning I suggested she join me—us—at morning coffee.

"I'm an employee, not a shopkeeper."

"Well, that doesn't matter. Georgia goes, and she doesn't own the law firm. Others work in the shops—Nora and Nora's sister, JoAnne. Have you met her yet?"

"I think I waved to her as we passed Square Spirits a while back."

"You're a fixture here now, Claire. Plan on coming with me tomorrow."

Since it was my turn to clean up the kitchen, I took my plate and cup to the sink. Claire stayed at the table twirling her mug.

Uh, oh. Claire had been quiet and distant the last couple of days. The dishes could wait. I pulled out a chair and sat across from her. "Tell me, what's on your mind?"

She grabbed my hand and squeezed it. "Okay, I'll say it right out."

I swallowed hard.

"I don't want to leave Wolf Creek. I want to stay and work for you. I love the customers—well, most of them—and being around all the books I want to read. We both know you can't run the shop alone."

Interesting development. "Well, I told Richard the other day that I think you need to stay here and put down some roots."

Claire's features relaxed in relief. "Whew—I'm glad that's out of the way. But I don't have enough money to move into my own place yet. As soon as I can, I will."

That puzzled me. "Why would you do that? You're welcome to live here—and it's much cheaper than finding your own place. And you're contributing some to expenses."

She waved that off. "I want to pay my own way, Sis."

"Okay, that's reasonable. Let's figure out which of our expenses you want to pay and we'll come up with a monthly amount. I want you to save some for yourself—you still need clothes and maybe you'll want to buy a car."

Claire stared off into the middle of the room. "When I mentioned staying to Skylar, she said she wants our family to be together."

I nodded, knowing where that came from. "She said something like that to me when she first came to visit and then stayed on to help me. It's not surprising, really. Losing her mom and dad made me even more important to her. And now she has you, too. She never got to know her great-aunt very well, and now she has that chance."

"And there's Reed. Seems she'd be lost without him."

I agreed and went back to the dishes. I was sure Claire and I would talk more about the arrangements now that I knew she wanted to stay. Lucky me.

As the days passed, we saw an increase of shoppers, and after a few mornings at B and B Claire noted the importance of each shop to the whole Square. "The shops all complement each other," she said. "No wonder Megan had the unique idea of featuring the whole Square in the Weddings at Wolf Creek business."

"That's why we carry wedding planning books, registries, and photo albums. I wouldn't have any need or interest in carrying anything but a couple of wedding planning titles were it not for the wedding business."

"Maybe I could help her—you know, part-time in the evening."

Before I had a chance to respond, Claire turned to help a pair of women coming into the shop.

I stayed at the register through lunch and Claire took over until closing. Shoppers and browsers had formed a steady stream throughout the day. I went upstairs early when the afternoon lull arrived and left Claire to close the shop. I suggested she come to the business association meeting with me.

She begged off, mostly because she had a headache. Forgetting to eat had that effect on her. Richard was out-of-town on a case, so I called Sadie to see if she wanted to join me for coffee after the meeting.

"You bet," Sadie said in her usual upbeat, cheerful way, "and a piece of pumpkin pie sounds mighty good."

"Then we can hope the meeting will be short," I teased.

"I'm sure it will mostly be the usual reminders for the days after Thanksgiving."

Sure enough, Sadie was right. Sarah's agenda noted a bus tour the Saturday before the holiday, Black Friday and Small Business Saturday.

"In years past, we've had more activity on Saturday than Friday," Sarah said. "That's because we don't try to compete with the big box stores that stay open twenty-four hours starting on Thanksgiving. Our shops will open at 9:00 both days and close at 7:00. On Sunday, it's back to normal hours—noon to six." She paused. "Any questions?" She paused again. "I've said enough for tonight. Go enjoy yourselves."

By the time I joined her, Sadie had already captured a table. I'd been sidetracked by Georgia Reynolds, who'd stopped me to extend an invitation for Thanksgiving dinner at the new house she and Elliot built. Sarah soon joined us, and we chatted like we'd been friends for years. Sadie and I had established a friendship early in my arrival to the Square, and when it came to Sarah, I appreciated her more as I came to understand her responsibility to the town. Given enough time, I figured we'd become friends.

"Georgia invited Claire and me for Thanksgiving," I said. "Can you tell me a little about her open house policy?"

When Sadie touched my arm, the colors of her bracelets danced in the spotlight for the table. "It's a food free-for-all. Georgia cooks a traditional American Thanksgiving dinner. She must cook for days with all the food that's served. And we all bring something to share."

"Last year Zoe brought wine," Sarah said. "She'll probably do that again this year. I bring a pasta salad that's my secret recipe. What'd you bring, Sadie?"

"Gosh, I don't remember, but I'll think of something."

"If you have a family favorite, by all means bring it,"

Sarah said. "Always fun to have a new dish to taste."

I smiled to myself. Sarah was always the diplomat to make people feel welcome. "You know, Claire was so impressed with your "Welcome to Wolf Creek" brochure. When she and Skylar stopped at B and B for to-go coffees the other morning, Steph told her you were writing a book on the history of the Square's buildings. She talked about it all day between customers. I didn't tell her I'd read the part about my building."

"I'm not ready to go public yet," Sarah said, showing a hitch in her confidence. "I'll stop over soon and get the pages from you—make notes on them if you'd like."

Sadie picked up the decanter and topped off our cups. "I told Sarah I want the book done by next summer so we can sell it in the museum."

"I'll be sure to stock copies in BookMarks to help promote it."

"Oops, look at the time," Sadie said, catching a glance at her watch. "I have an early meeting with Gus and Matt tomorrow. Matt's always early so we get started and then brief Gus when he arrives."

"Your work must be very satisfying." I didn't like bringing the conversation to an end. I'd have preferred to linger and get to know these two women better.

With a smile, Sadie nodded, and then gulped the coffee she had poured. "I'll pay for mine on the way out," she said, getting to her feet. "Don't rush on my account."

I was glad when Sarah poured herself another cup of decaf, because I wanted to keep talking.

"I see Skylar's shop is making a splash." Sarah made her point with a statement, not a question, but I could tell she wanted me to comment.

"I see it getting busier every day," I said. "I'm so proud of her. She's had a few rough years, but when Lily needed to change her life because of the baby, Skylar zeroed in on the potential almost immediately and *went* for it." I chuckled. "Have you seen her shop lately? She has the train overhead and the Jack-in-the-box on the floor?"

"Of course, I've seen it," Sarah said, a laugh in her voice.

"I manage to stop at each shop at least once a week just to say hello and see what's new."

"I might have known," I said. Yes, the mayor knew her town.

"We've filled all but one of the vacant storefronts in the last few years, and that's what's brought so many changes to the Square."

"All good, or has there been a downside?"

"Well, mostly good, because we attract so many more shoppers, including the tour buses. By themselves, they make up a good portion of our visitor sector. You know how crazy the Square becomes when they arrive. And now everyone is involved with Weddings at Wolf Creek, which means we market to a younger demographic." She grinned. "I sure get energized when I talk about the Square."

"So I've noticed," I teased. "So what isn't so positive about the changes?"

"We haven't kept up in some ways. The number of rooms at the Inn is limited. I'm sure we're losing business when people can't make a weekend get-away to our Square. I get emailed complaints all the time about parking, especially when the tour buses are here taking up multiple spaces."

Knowing all this could affect me directly, I asked, "Any solutions on the horizon?"

She started to say something, but stopped and clamped her mouth. I guessed that she was going somewhere with her train of thought, but maybe she wasn't at liberty to share still private information.

Making it easy for her, I checked the time on the clock on the wall behind her. "I'd better go. I tend to get carried away and forget the time, but I've enjoyed talking with you. I'm sure we'll have more chances to catch up." I reached into my purse and took out cash to pay my bill. Sarah did the same.

We walked to the front of the dining room and waited to pay. Sarah absently rubbed the counter at the register. "Sure wish Melanie would let us run accounts like Steph does, but she said she's too busy to take on one more job."

I shrugged. "I can understand that. It's an excellent

restaurant. No wonder so many of us come for dinner often." I was stating the obvious.

When we left, Sarah went off to the left and I turned toward the far end of the Square. As I got closer to BookMarks, I saw Claire at the window. She was on the phone. She waved back when I waved. In minutes, I was upstairs ready for the day to end.

"Richard and Skylar called, both with the same news," Claire said when I joined her at the window. "It seems Richard and Lily are bringing Toby and Emma to the Square tomorrow. According to Richard, it's a chance to show off the baby, and Lily has promised Toby a new toy for being helpful at home, so that means a trip to The Toy Box. Skylar is beyond words, she's so eager to show Lily what she has done in the shop."

"I guess Richard is pretty proud of that girl."

"Lily or Emma?"

I laughed. "Both I guess, but I suppose Emma has all of his attention right now."

"I doubt that." She raised one eyebrow in a knowing look.

"No need to tease. I'm not denying it anymore. Richard is important to me. I never saw myself with another man after Bruce died, so it took me a while to adjust to the idea."

"Well, that would have been your loss. Anyway, I'm happy for you. Now, off to bed. You need your beauty rest for tomorrow."

"Oh, really?"

"You have to mind me. I'm the older sister."

I gave her a hug and, like she said, off to bed I went. It would be another busy day tomorrow.

21

My day began with a warm, sunny morning. As I dressed in one of my new comfortable outfits from Styles, my thoughts were focused on seeing Richard later.

Following the routine that had evolved, Claire opened the shop by unlocking the door and turning on the lights, while I opened the register for the day. But that morning, I found the money drawer full from the day before, which didn't match our routine.

Oh, my. "Claire? Was there a problem yesterday closing out the register?"

Her face drained of color. She grabbed the counter to steady herself. "I *couldn't* have forgotten. But the evidence doesn't lie. I'm *so* sorry, Millie."

What a puzzle. "Was there a problem you wanted me to know about before you removed the money and the checks?" We kept the credit card receipts handy, next to the checks.

"I don't think so. You went up early. I said I'd lock up."

Mentally I could see she was going through her steps from the night before.

"Door, lights…" She stopped. "Trevor called…"

"And?"

"I walked upstairs still on the phone with him."

"And never went back down?" I tried not to be sharp.

"I ate a sandwich, watched a movie, Richard called, and then Skylar called. And you came home." She leaned on the counter. "I'm so sorry, Millie. I know that's being irresponsible." She went into the back room and began processing the new deliveries.

I didn't know how to handle the situation. If Claire had been an employee and not my sister I would have said a few words about responsibility.

But this was Claire. My sister. No doubt this incident brought up the day from our childhood when Claire was sent to the store to buy some food for the family and lost the money. In our family at the time, this was no small event. Money was tight. An understatement. Every penny was accounted for. Even worse, our parents had branded Claire as irresponsible, as if one mistake defined her. This lapse, this mistake, brought that all back. Even for me.

Claire went about the business of the day straightening the shop, adding new books to the cart by the front door and keeping her distance from me.

At least until Richard arrived with his granddaughter.

"So, Millie, I'd like to introduce you to Emma Irene Connor." He put the carrier on the counter, and I peeked at a tiny bundle in a pink hat, wrapped in a pink and white blanket sleeping inside. The sides of the carrier surrounding her looked huge.

"Gorgeous," I said, grinning. I called out to Claire, who was dusting books at the far end of the shelves. "Richard's here with Emma."

"Be right there." Her voice was neutral, no sign of emotion one way or another.

"Where are Lily and Toby?" I asked.

"Next door. We stopped there first, but it's going to take Toby some time to decide on his new toy. I couldn't wait for you to see her."

Claire came along aside me and peered into the carrier. "Oh, isn't she just precious." Claire ran a fingertip across her tiny hand. At that moment, the baby opened her eyes. "She's beautiful, absolutely beautiful. Look at those eyes, Millie."

"Georgia says that dark blue makes them Owen eyes," Richard said. "Passed from one generation to the next. Lily's grandmother—she was an Owen—to Beverly to Lily. Toby has them and now so does Emma."

When the bell jingled, we looked up to see Lily and Toby

coming inside.

Lily approached, holding out her hand. "Well, well, you must be Claire. Welcome to Wolf Creek."

"Thank you." Claire shook Lily's hand and then bent down to offer her hand to Toby. "I've heard a lot of nice things about this young man. And what did you find next door?"

"It's a schooner," the boy said, patting the side of the bag he carried with a large box inside. "They were ships that sailed the high seas way back when there were pirates."

Claire squeezed the young boy's shoulder and led him away.

"I think he's tired of all the talk about the baby," Lily whispered, "and sometimes I miss his cues."

Claire wasn't aware of it, and I didn't know the whole story, but Lily had never taken care of a baby before. Through a series of family dramas, Lily had left Toby with her grandmother to raise him, and he'd soon ended up in the Connor family, adopted by Nathan's late brother and sister-in-law. It was quite a story.

"New parenting is a challenge no matter how many children there are," I said, stating a fact of life. I grinned at the baby, who was squirming a little and looking around with her big blue Owen eyes.

"Okay, Granddad. Best be going to the next shop," Lily said. "With Emma awake now, I'll need to feed her soon."

Toby came back in time to hear the conversation, and added his two cents. "Then Mom tells me to play quietly and she goes into the bedroom." He spoke with authority.

Lily ruffled the boy's hair. "That's the routine. Say good-bye now."

Toby waved companionably. "Bye, Millie. Bye, Claire."

"You come back for a visit soon," Claire said, "so we can talk about pirates again."

He winked at Claire and followed Lily out the door.

Richard bent down and kissed my cheek. "Surrounded by my favorite women. I'll call tonight." Carrier in hand, he followed Lily out the door, but stepped aside to hold the door open for the first customers of the day.

Claire went back to shelving books and we interacted little over the next hours. After a day of steady traffic, she went upstairs late in the afternoon and left me to close the shop. She was standing by the front window after I finished climbing the stairs.

I went to stand next to her. "Claire, it's not the end of the world."

She shrugged. "Maybe not. But you remember what happened when we were kids and I lost the grocery money. I once made a mistake that could have cost some people their lives if it hadn't been caught. I left a shipment of vaccines out overnight, rather than putting them in our cooler. They were ruined in the heat and we barely had enough. I never got over it." She stared at the floor. "More to the point, I never stopped doubting myself."

I realized how little she said about her decades overseas and how rarely I'd asked her about her experiences. We'd been so out of touch for so long. "Well, fortunately, we're dealing with books here, Claire, not people's lives. I'm not denying I was surprised when I opened the drawer, but it's not the first time it's happened."

She turned to me with a quizzical look.

"Before the baby came, Lily was sick a lot, and Skylar was still in Minnesota. I tried to do everything myself. As you know, this isn't a one-person shop and will never be again. The Square has gotten too busy. So I made mistakes, including forgetting the money in the register. That's when I began putting it in the freezer."

"Thanks, Millie. I really didn't want my sister to fire me."

"And have to train a new person?" I asked, teasing her.

She gave me a pointed look. "I can always count on you."

"Want pizza? I'm tired of deli salads, and there's nothing like hot pizza with all that spice and melted cheese."

She took a coupon out of her pocket. "I picked up coupons from the rack in B and B. I'll call."

"By the way, what were you talking to Trevor about?" I asked.

She held up her finger to respond to the person taking the order.

When she was done, I said, "I'm taking back my question. You have a personal life and it's not my place to ask about your phone calls."

"No mind." She smiled and shrugged. "But let me ask you something. I read Sarah's 'Welcome to Wolf Creek' brochure and then I said something about it to Steph. She said Sarah is writing a history about the town and the buildings on the Square."

"I've heard the same thing," I said. "I'm looking forward to stocking copies when it's done and published."

"Sarah's book-in-progress made me think of Trevor's work, so I suggested he put some of his editorials together and publish a book."

That sounded like a great idea. "And what did he say?"

"He asked me to help him."

"Hey, my sister, an editor-in-the-making."

She held up her hand, palm out. "Not so fast. I haven't given him my answer yet."

"As I like to say, well, why not?"

She planted a hand on her hip. "Because I was talking to him about it when I forgot to clear the money from the register."

The buzzer on the back door rang, and she picked up her wallet as she hurried down to get our delivered supper. I didn't bring up the issue again until we were done eating.

"I have an idea," I said, as we settled at the table with mugs of hot herbal tea, "and it's not just because you forgot. Some days we're going to be too tired to think about anything but locking the door and going to bed. So earlier, during a lull, I jotted a checklist for us." I reached into the pocket of my vest hanging on the back of the chair next to me and pulled out a folded piece of paper. "Here, have a look. See what you think."

She took the paper and read the numbers and the tasks that went with them. "Well, I see taking care of the register is first on the list…and after that, locking up and turning out the lights and storing the CD, then we're supposed to smile." Once more, a pointed look.

"Well, what do you think?" I asked.

"This is good, but one and two should be reversed. Lock the door and then empty the register."

"Right. Flip one and two, and I'll make a copy on the computer and print it out. Then we can laminate it and put it by the stairs." I grinned.

"Consider it done."

***

The next day all my talk about being busy and too tired to take a deep breath summoned the masses. Of people, that is. Even without a tour bus, Saturday on the Square was crowded. Once again, I took a risk and doubled my book orders and the print run on BookMarks shopping bags. I checked in with Liz about updates on Facebook featuring some key new releases we'd just put out. By the time we closed, Claire and I laughed all the way to the bank—the freezer.

Some of that money was already earmarked for expenses. I was investing heavily in inventory, and had Claire's fulltime salary to cover, along with utilities and incidentals. To say nothing about my new clothes from Styles and our frequent takeout dinners.

A few days later, I told Richard about my good fortune over the last weeks. He suggested he review my income/output spreadsheets.

"I'd like to see those books before the end of the year. Maybe you need to make some adjustments, like increasing your salary, or adding more to your retirement fund."

"We're so busy I don't feel right leaving Claire alone during shop hours."

"Well then, come to my place next Saturday after closing. I'll get dinner for us from Crossroads. Bring your laptop, so we can have a look."

"Okay, I'm game."

"Call me when you leave and I'll meet you at the front door."

We chatted a few minutes more before disconnecting, with his last words being "I love you, Millie."

He hung up before I had a chance to reply. I wasn't exactly sure what I would have said.

***

My schedule kept getting busier. Ironically, the bookstore owner barely had time to read. First, I had the book club meeting a few days before my working dinner with Richard. A combination of business and pleasure. Not a date, but not a non-date either. Hearing me playing semantic games, Claire just laughed.

As had happened the previous month, November's book club night again turned out to be rainy and cold. I was surprised by the dozen or so women and a few men who came anyway.

Beverly had suggested the book, *Simply Thanks,* which was a basic book about the lore surrounding the first harvest feast that Americans came to call Thanksgiving. In a way, though, the discussion evolved to the dual ideas of simplicity, an almost foreign concept in modern life, and gratitude.

As an extra feature, Beverly placed five kernels of corn on each plate Steph had set out on the tables. "If you were a Pilgrim and had landed at Plymouth Rock after an arduous voyage from Europe," she said, "this is the amount of food left for each person to eat. We've glamorized this historical event over the years, and because of the commercialization surrounding Christmas, Thanksgiving is almost a forgotten holiday."

Beverly's words launched a serious discussion of the number of Pilgrims that died from pneumonia the first year and how the Indians shared their seeds and planting skills. Had the Indians been hostile, probably no Pilgrims would have survived. Relating the concept of simplicity to the stark reality the early settlers faced produced an interesting back and forth, and did what book club discussions are supposed to do—raise questions and stimulate ideas.

Meanwhile, Steph's hot mulled cider and pumpkin mini-muffins were a perfect symbol of the abundance most of us enjoyed. As in October, that night our time at B and B ran out before the discussion ended. When I suggested skipping December, a resounding "Nooo" rippled through the room.

I laughed. "Okay, message received. How about if we read the book *Christmas Trees to Chicago*? It's about the legendary Christmas ship that disappeared on the way to delivering trees. It's part of the Great Lakes folklore. No trace of the ship was ever found. I tried to get the author out here for a book signing, but his weekends were full. I'll call him about coming for the book club meeting. I'll send out an email to everyone as soon as I know."

A show of hands indicated that everyone was fine with the book choice, and after that, we all helped Steph straighten the tables and chairs for morning.

As we stood by the door, Steph said, "Imagine five kernels of corn. I throw so much food away because of health regulations. Good food people could use." Steph shook her head at the waste.

The group gathered to file out into the stormy night. "I know," one woman said, "we take so much for granted and don't pause often enough to appreciate what we have." The words simplicity and gratitude came to my mind again.

Trevor and Claire had gone on ahead leaving Richard and me to travel at our own pace under his umbrella. Richard had come in after Beverly started the discussion and took the closest seat to the door.

"I'm looking forward to Saturday," I said. "Claire and I need to find some space apart from each other. We live and work together like a husband and wife."

He laughed. "If I was your husband I wouldn't be underfoot all the time."

Ignoring his remark, I said, "Don't get me wrong. I love having my sister in the shop, even though we hit a bad spot the other day."

"What about?" He immediately became serious.

We'd come close enough to the shop that we could hear Claire's animated voice and see her arms in motion.

"Saturday." I hoped he got my message.

"I can't wait to be alone with you, Millie. Just to sit

across the table and talk freely without having to worry about who's sitting nearby at the next table."

"'Til then, Richard. Good night."

"Not before this." He wrapped me in his arms and didn't care that Trevor and Claire were close.

With my head pressed against his chest, I needed to back away for air.

22

Since Georgia had invited Claire to bring a guest to Thanksgiving dinner, she'd quickly decided to ask Trevor to go with her. The day was fast approaching. As we made our respective coffee and tea one morning, we exchanged notes about what we were bringing. Claire had decided to make her sweet-sour meatballs, and Richard offered to bring homemade chocolate cornucopias filled with whipped sweet cream. One of his clients was building her cottage industry making specialized candy. So, we were all set.

"Trevor's going to drive," Claire said. "Want to join us?"

"We'll pass this time." I wanted some time alone with Richard, especially on the holiday.

That day, if Claire and I hadn't worn our vests at the shop we would have been lost in the crowd. Between the bus tour and early holiday shoppers, I smiled through every minute of that wonderful day. At one point, Sarah waved from outside, but apparently, seeing how busy we were, she decided not to come in.

At closing, Claire held up five fingers for our five steps to close the shop. "You go up and get ready. This is a special night for you."

I gave her a hug. "Love you, Claire."

At the appointed time, Richard met me at the door, fidgety and tugging on the lapels of his sport coat. Once inside his apartment above Country Law, he took off his jacket and visibly relaxed. I had the feeling he didn't have many adults up in his place. Toby was likely his main visitor.

He grinned when I saw the fireplace and lamented that I didn't have one. "You're welcome to come anytime. I'll share mine with you." I soon learned that Nathan had the apartment first, then Eli Reynolds, and now him. He loved it.

When he showed me the bedroom with the built-in race car bed, I laughed. "Yours?"

He relaxed a little more. "Funny, lady. Wine?"

"Sure." I saw the linen tablecloth and candles, crystal stemware and silver-rimmed dinner plates. "Quite the setting." I pointed to the table.

"Compliments of Melanie from Crossroads. I told her I wanted a little elegance and she went a little overboard, but we'll enjoy her efforts."

He was still talking a little too fast, a sign of self-consciousness, but I assured him the elegance would help make it special. "It's like dressing up now and then. We don't go to the trouble every day, but it's nice sometimes."

Suddenly, he blurted, "You know how I feel about you, Millie. I'd marry you tomorrow if you said yes."

"Not tonight," I said with a laugh. My face warmed as I thought about the idea of marriage. "On the other hand, Richard, my feelings run deeper as the days pass."

Thankfully, the path of our conversation was interrupted by the buzzer on the oven.

"Melanie called this meal an Evening for Two. Two small steaks, two lobster tails, two salads and hand-twisted baked bread. Of course there's dessert, but it's a surprise."

Since the food was ready, we sat down to eat right away. The meal was delicious, from the touch of Cajun on the steak, to the DmZ cabernet. We talked about Zoe's family winery and her brother being a wine master teaching Eli Reynolds. Eli was growing grapes at the family farm and wanted to make wine for his own label.

"Quite the enterprising community, this little Square," I said.

"Now for the treat of the evening." He cleared away the dishes and brought a small crystal plate from the refrigerator. Miniature chocolate cornucopias filled the center, with whipped cream overflowing and covering the surface. "I thought we should taste them before we bring them for Thanksgiving."

He sat down and popped a whole treat into his mouth. His expression said it all.

I tried to be polite and take a small bite, but the fragile shell broke into little pieces. So, with no finesse, I shoved all the pieces into my mouth. A small bit of cream hung on the corner of my mouth. Richard's finger wiped it away before I could capture it with my tongue.

"I'd kiss it off, but you're too far away."

"Another time." I put enthusiasm into nodding my head. "These chocolates are perfect to bring."

I stood up and began to help clear the table.

"No, no. I'll do that," he said. "Get your computer out. You need to show me those books of yours."

I went to get my laptop off the counter where I'd left it while he cleared space on the table. "You know, it's not important now, but Claire made a mistake the other day and forgot to empty the register one night. She was very upset with herself, and I was upset with her, at least at first."

He looked at me expectantly, as if waiting for me to finish the story. He had no way to know that was the story. It sounded so trivial in the retelling. He didn't know how one incident in childhood had affected her—and not in a good way.

"I got over it, though. I told her everyone makes mistakes and we needed to let it go. Obviously, we don't want to make the same mistakes again."

"That's the story of my life," Richard said sadly. "I've made my share of mistakes more than once. But in recent years, anyway, I've tried not to keep repeating them."

"True, but some lessons are harder to learn than others."

Maybe I'd hit too close to home, because he didn't respond. I opened the accounting files and turned the screen so he could have a look. Richard made notes and periodically shook his head. I forced myself not to ask why—yet. He asked a few questions as he scrolled through the pages.

I sat back and surreptitiously studied Richard's profile.

He'd kept himself fit through the years and even though his temples had grayed, his face carried few wrinkles. Those around his eyes added character. His fingers were long and thin, giving him attractive hands.

Finally, he laughed out loud. "I should have bought this bookstore, Millie. You have a gold mine here. Little loss or spoilage of your product, and despite the changes in publishing, print books haven't gone out of style. There are always new releases to encourage repeat sales."

"Skylar said almost those same words when she bought Lily's inventory."

"When Lily wants to get back to work again, she should be a business consultant. She sees potential and pitfalls. I saw that a few years back."

"Maybe I should have her review my business." I was kidding, but Richard took my words to heart.

"Maybe so. After all, I'm your attorney, not your accountant. Things are looking good. I suppose I'd wait to raise your salary until the first of the year when you have the first six months of sales to judge and evaluate."

"I'm hoping to beat all my daily sales before the end of the year. Claire thinks we need to have an ongoing contest with each other. She'd win, of course. People love to talk to her, so they end up buying something before they leave."

Richard clicked out of the accounting program. He held out his hand. "Dance with me."

Soft music had played through dinner, but Richard changed the CD to slow dancing music from the 70s. An instrumental version of "You Are So Beautiful to Me" played. I recognized it as a song full of romance, and judging from the way he hummed along, so did Richard.

"I haven't danced in years," Richard said, "so watch your toes."

"No weddings, no parties in all that time?"

"Not so many. I've kept to myself a lot."

I took his outstretched hand and let him pull me into his arms. I believed I belonged there. With my whole heart.

We danced through a few more songs before I decided it was time to leave. We, well, I, still needed to take this relationship slow, unlike the way I'd jumped into BookMarks.

***

On Sunday afternoon, Claire was beside herself when large, fluffy snowflakes hung in the air over the Square. And why not? She hadn't been back to the states for a long time, and when she had, she'd been close to one of the charities headquarters in Florida. No wonder winter's first dusting became a reason to celebrate. And for us, that meant pizza and wine.

Claire called Skylar to join us, which gave us all a chance to talk about the three men in our lives. Although, Claire insisted Trevor wasn't really in her life in a romantic sense. He was too old for her, she claimed. Besides, they were just friends.

Right, sure, okay. That's what I'd said about Richard. Only Skylar was a bit more circumspect about Reed, brushing us off if we asked too many questions. I didn't blame her. What young woman welcomes questions about her romances from her grandma and a great-aunt?

When we'd had our fill of pizza, I pulled out the box of chocolate cornucopias Richard had sent home with me. Skylar's eyes opened wide at the sight of the chocolate, and Claire rubbed her stomach like a kid after the first bite.

"Oh, Millie. These are sooo good. And I'm so full." Claire raised her arms in the air.

After Skylar had eaten every morsel of a couple of pieces of the rich chocolate and cream, she stood to leave. "If I don't go home now I'll be too stuffed to move!"

I cleared away our mess and Claire followed Skylar downstairs. As I went off to get ready for bed, I smiled to myself. Another wonderful day on the Square.

Monday and Tuesday passed quickly with steady traffic on the Square and in the shop. I'd been led to believe that Wednesday would bring browsers getting ready for Black Friday, but at BookMarks we had buyers, too.

At coffee that morning, I overheard Claire ask Megan

about the wedding business. Marianna had drawn my attention away from their conversation so I waited until we were back in the shop and had a break before I asked her about what I'd overheard.

"I told Megan that BookMarks was my first priority, of course, but most of my evenings were free, so I could help her if she needed it."

"What about Trevor's book?" I asked.

"He's proceeding really slow, gathering his old writings and deciding which he'll use. Megan doesn't expect me to be available every evening. Besides, I'm doing my share of the work to keep us in clean clothes and food. I want to keep making some money so I'm never so broke again." She grinned. "It's about time I learned that lesson. I'll leave the overseas work to younger people now and put down some roots."

That ended the conversation, because three generations of women came in, laughing and chatting. The younger women reminded me of Skylar. I imagined they were probably home from college and shopping with their moms and grandmas.

"Gram, you have to read this book," one of the young women said. "It's exceptional—I've read all the novels by this author—she's all the rage in Denmark." She handed her white-haired grandmother one of the grisly European mysteries from the "New Arrivals" cart. The whole lot of those newish mysteries from Europe were more popular than I'd realized until I started featuring them.

"I'll take your word for it," the older woman said. "Put it in the basket. I want to find a few more before we leave." Side by side, the two moved deeper into the store.

A man and boy entered, a father and son I surmised. "Can I help you?" I asked.

"Maybe," he said. "A year ago my family stopped here on a rainy afternoon and the kids found toys and games. I don't see them here." He twisted around to look down the aisle where the toys had been.

I smiled at the boy. "Well, good news. The toys are next door now. We ran out of room for both shops being in the same building. My granddaughter runs The Toy Box." I handed the dad one of Skylar's business cards. "She'll be happy to help you."

The man glanced out the window. "My wife and daughter are at Styles. They will be coming soon."

"Go on. I'll tell them you're next door."

Unfortunately, I never had the opportunity to single out his wife and daughter from the groups that entered. But near closing, the whole family returned and left with two shopping bags filled to the top with books. A great final sale for the day.

Claire locked the door when the family left. "Millie, I don't know how it happened, but everything I had ready to go for Black Friday now needs updating. I even sold books that I was going to pull for the sale table."

"And your complaint would be?"

"None. Absolutely none," Claire said, her face opening up in a big smile. "Luckily, you ordered plenty of books to fill those empty spaces. Shall we do the stocking tonight?"

"Sure. Tomorrow is Thanksgiving and we aren't working down here at all. I need a whole day off, and so do you."

Claire made her version of a Cobb salad using whatever odds and ends she could find in the refrigerator. "This food isn't going to be wasted during my watch," she said with a solemn nod. "Beverly sure made a point with me by putting those corn kernels on our plates at book club." She cleared her throat. "Not that I needed any reminder of scarcity."

While I was on the couch talking to Richard, she used every morsel of fresh vegetables we had. She shredded and chopped and sliced, and we ended up with a full meal.

I said goodbye to Richard when she called out, "Done. Dinner's ready."

As we ate, we chatted about handling what we hoped would be Friday and Saturday crowds.

"I'm not going to worry about it, though," I said. "Let's focus on having a fun time tomorrow at our first Wolf Creek Thanksgiving. I have so much abundance in my life. So much to be thankful for." I'd managed to hang on to my sense of gratitude even after Bruce died way too young. At least, I'd thought, I'd had a chance to have a great love. But after Mark died, I had no such comfort. It had taken me a long time to feel deep gratitude again. Now that I was whole again, I reveled in being thankful for my life.

"I can relate to a full life," Claire said, taking our empty plates to the sink and rinsing them off. "The maid can finish them up when she comes in."

"Would her name be Millie?" I joked.

Before we ran out of steam, we headed downstairs to put things right for Friday and came back upstairs late in the evening, more than ready for our day off.

23

Thanksgiving morning started with low-hanging gray clouds and fog. Every time I glanced out the window my mind wanted to be negative about the weather. I could have rattled on about this or that not being the way I wanted it. Laughing at myself, I made a decision to be bright and cheerful, even if the weather wasn't.

"No big breakfast for us today," I said, refilling Claire's coffee mug. "I'll make us some toast to tide us over."

"Aw…and here I was hoping we'd have pancakes and omelets."

"And be too full to eat at Georgia's?" I asked in mock scolding.

She laughed.

We spent our morning sitting on the couch and reminiscing about our childhood, our long-gone parents, and talking about our new life in Wolf Creek. Claire drank coffee and made a huge number of meatballs for the pot luck. While she worked, I watched the clouds break apart and on a westerly wind, move out of the area. The gloom was soon replaced with bright sunshine.

I noticed she took extra care preparing for the afternoon, choosing clothes she'd bought at Styles on her own. A long, gray tweed skirt hung gracefully to her ankles and she'd accented the rust-colored sweater with a multi-colored, flowing scarf. I hadn't seen her earrings before, but I assumed they'd come from India. They had dramatically large beads that hung in the circle of the gold loop.

She looked terrific and I told her so.

I waited awhile to dress. Richard was coming around 1:30. The short drive to the Reynolds' farm would only take a few minutes.

Trying not to compare my pretty, but not particularly dramatic blue silk pantsuit to Claire's look, I put it on without looking in the mirror. But when Richard held my coat for me, he let out one of his low whistles, the kind Nathan specialized in when he felt like teasing Lily.

On the drive, our conversation became stilted with talk about the pleasantly changing weather. Richard seemed especially anxious to get there. "What's the hurry?" I finally asked. "We aren't running late, are we?"

"Game started at noon."

I groaned inside. I'd never given any thought to the Thanksgiving football mania.

We might not have been running late, but many people had arrived ahead of us. I was surprised by the number of vehicles parked around the new house.

Inside the open concept space, nearly every person I saw was in some way connected to the Square and I was now part of that special group. The large dining room table was an hors d'oeuvre wonderland. Claire had arrived first and her dish of meat balls already sat on a warmer plate.

When Georgia stepped out of the kitchen to great us, Richard handed her the large flat box. "Dessert."

We found ourselves absorbed into the group as a stream of people entered the house. Richard grabbed a plate and filled it with a variety of hot and cold snacks for us to share. Eli and Zoe walked around with a tray of wine-filled glasses. I chose a white and Richard took a red.

From a distant corner, I heard Elliot call out to ask if we wanted to be part of the football pool. I shook my head, but Richard called back, "Who gets the money?"

"Historical society. Matt's in charge."

"I'll take two squares on the grid," Richard responded, his voice raised to be heard in the loud buzz of conversation. "Doesn't matter what the numbers are. I'll pay Matt when I see him."

The football business out of the way, we moved around the

room, greeting those we knew and introducing ourselves to people who turned out to be Elliot and Georgia's neighbors. I spotted Skylar standing with Reed, but it would have meant going through a maze of people and tables and chairs to reach her, so we settled for a quick wave across the room.

All of a sudden a loud metal clanging sound came from the kitchen area. I saw the metal lid from a kettle high in the air. Someone—I couldn't see who—was hitting it with a metal spoon. Talk about getting everyone's attention.

Then I heard Georgia's voice, although I couldn't see her. "Quiet everyone. Elliot?"

"Coming, Peaches." The husky voice came from a corner where the television was mounted on the wall.

"Mute the sound, Eli," Elliot said.

The crowd quieted and the television went silent.

With his height, I could see Elliot put his arm around Georgia's shoulders. I'd seen him do that at the association meetings and at B and B in the morning. Charming.

"Grab a glass, folks. Georgia and I want to thank you all for sharing our new home with us on this special holiday of thankfulness. We are all blessed with family and friends that make our lives richer. Salute to Thanksgiving."

I raised my glass high. Elliot had echoed my feelings about the day.

"Salute" rippled around the room.

Richard put his arm around my shoulders, akin to Elliot. "I'm grateful you're with me, Millie." He bent close to my ear, "And more."

Georgia started the feast. "Okay, everyone. Let's eat, drink and be merry. Buffet line starts here."

"Let's hold back and allow a few others to go first." Richard waved to the people close to us to go ahead to the buffet in the kitchen. The counters were covered with dishes and trays overflowing with food.

But as it turned out when those nearby moved into line, we fell in behind them. Soon Richard and I were loading our plates with turkey, ham, dressing, and all manner of vegetables. I'd seen many of the salads at Farmer Foods.

Sadie grabbed my arm when I looked for a place to sit

and enjoy the meal. "I told Clayton to save seats for us in the sunroom. Those younger people can stand while they eat."

Clayton gave his seat to his mother and those he'd saved for Richard and me were about to be taken when Clayton pointed for me to sit. The other chair was taken by an elderly man. Richard found an empty seat nearby.

There I sat, glass in one hand and plate in the other. So I followed Sadie's lead and set my glass on the floor beside me. I laughed inside when as soon as the chair next to me was vacated, Richard scurried over.

"Isn't this something, Millie? Imagine knowing all these people and welcoming them into your home," Richard said, his voice filled with awe. "What a rich life Georgia and Elliot have—and such deep roots in Wolf Creek."

I looked up when Toby came running—well not quite running, what with the crowd—toward us. "Grandpa, is it dessert time yet? We're late because of you-know-who." Toby did a big eye roll.

"Let's get you some turkey and mashed potatoes first." Richard was about to hand his plate to me when Nathan joined us. "Keep your chair, Dad. Toby and I will get a plate and head for the football game. We have a wager going."

"Green Bay's going to win." Toby left as fast as he'd appeared, skirting between the people standing nearby. Nathan was quick to follow.

"Did I tell you his grandparents from Ohio are coming right after Christmas?" Richard asked me.

"Oh, boy. Does Toby know that?"

"Oh, boy, is right. Nathan and Lily want to wait a week or more before telling him so they don't have to answer questions every day about how long it will be before they come."

The crowd shifted again and soon new people were standing in front of us, more longtime friends and neighbors of the Reynolds. I couldn't even hope to remember the names of all the new people I'd met.

When the buzz in the room turned to desserts, I told Sadie she had to try one of the chocolate cornucopias. Sadie handed me her glass. “Save my seat, I’ll be right back.”

She returned with a dinner plate filled with an assortment of desserts, miniature cheesecakes, chocolate-dipped pretzels, sugared grapes, the cornucopia, and many more. A dessert lover’s banquet. “I shouldn’t have eaten so much healthy food,” she quipped.

Richard decided to join the football group to check on his pool numbers and pay Matt if he spotted him.

I also think he wanted to spend time with Toby, who was hanging out with the men. That boy filled his granddad’s heart with joy. Given Skylar’s effect on me from the day she was born, I sure understood.

I left Sadie to finish her desserts and made my way into the kitchen. Certainly I could help rinse and load the dishwasher for the first load, but I could never repay their generosity in kind. Megan was washing some delicate crystal bowls as fast as she was talking, and Claire was next to her with a towel in hand. I heard talk about “weddings and free evenings,” so I assumed Claire was angling to pick up extra money by helping with the Square’s wedding business. With the kitchen work covered, I decided it was best to get out of the way.

The crowd shifted and Georgia, once again the gracious hostess, was thanking those who were getting ready to leave. She turned to me when she closed the door and offered me a cup of tea.

“That would be great,” I said, “but I’d like to help clean up if there’s something I can do for you.”

“My job is done,” Georgia said with a laugh. “Megan and Clayton, along with Eli and Zoe are the clean-up crew. I imagine Clayton and Eli will get there eventually, but their big game is tied in the fourth quarter, so it might be a while.”

“Living in Minnesota most of my life, the only thing I know about football is that the Vikings and the Packers have a decades-long rivalry.”

“Today the Packers are playing the Detroit Lions. It’s somewhat of a Thanksgiving tradition to watch the game and eat turkey.”

That explained why Richard had been eager to head off.

"So, let's sit at the table and watch the others do their magic." Georgia gestured for me to follow her.

As if anticipating our purpose for settling at the table, Claire brought Georgia and me hot cups of tea.

"Isn't it great having a sister close by?" Georgia said. "Beverly and I were apart for many years, but I don't know what I'd do now if we had to separate again."

"That's also true for Claire and me," I said. "Our paths diverged and we rarely saw each other for many years." I'd heard bits and pieces of Georgia and Beverly's lives, mostly in connection to Lily's situation. It all came down to being sisters, like Claire and me, and finding their way back to each other. I looked over to Claire and saw that Skylar had joined her and Megan, with Zoe delivering more glasses to be rinsed. My family.

Georgia left the table when more people gathered their coats and the dishes they'd brought and prepared to leave. Elliot appeared from the football marathon and stood next to his wife to send their guests on their way.

Georgia did a quick, little shiver when she joined me and a few others who were normally at the table at B and B. It was strange to see Steph sitting rather than behind the counter. "Brrr...the weather's changing. Frost on the pumpkins tonight," Georgia said.

Lily had joined us saying they could stay as long as Emma was sleeping.

"Pumpkins froze the other night," Megan said. "Whatever the weather, the rush is on for Christmas. I need to find something special for Clayton this year."

"Maybe saying yes to a wedding?" Marianna nudged Sarah.

Megan stopped and her eyes got very large. "You think that would be a good gift?"

No one at the table believed she didn't know Clayton was getting tired of their long engagement.

"Well, if you don't marry him soon, I'll push you out of line and take your place," Mimi teased.

The women hooted, probably because Mimi was usually very careful with her words. She'd even surprised me.

"Who's standing in line for what?" Clayton had ventured into the kitchen and the conversation.

"Um, nothing, honey." Megan covered her mouth before she said more.

"Who won?"

I smiled at the way Sarah ably redirected the conversation to the football game.

"Detroit. Last minute field goal. We should have won."

With the game over, Eli came in and he and Clayton began putting the dining room and kitchen back in order, with the help of a steady stream of men gathering around to lend a hand before heading home. Jessica and Mimi also said their goodbyes, wishing everyone a good Black Friday and Small Business Saturday. I suppose they knew better than I that we'd have little time for small talk over the next couple of days.

Their leaving brought the day to an end for the rest of us. Richard gathered our coats. We exchanged hugs and thanked Elliot and Georgia, and headed back to Wolf Creek Square. It had been a wonderful day.

The drive was short, but the ice pellets and sleet collecting on the windshield meant Richard used both hands to grip the steering wheel.

To avoid distracting him, I didn't talk at all. I thought of Claire and Trevor and Reed and Skylar coming on the same roads only a few minutes behind us. I wouldn't fully exhale until I knew for sure they were home safe.

Richard dropped me off at the back door. "I wanted us to have a walk around the Square, but it's treacherous underfoot. We don't want to fall on this ice."

"You call when you get home," I said.

Before I got out, he reached across the seat and brought my hand to his lips. "My queen."

His words stayed with me as I went up the stairs. Minutes later, Richard called. He was safe in his warm apartment. We ended the call when Claire came in.

Skylar was laughing when she called to let me know she was home. She and Reed had been sliding on the ice on the walkway of the Square, and Reed wiped out. She was still laughing about it.

I said good-night to Claire and went off to get ready for bed. My family was safe.

24

Black Friday began with the color gray. Thick, dark clouds hung low over the Square. After a night of drizzle, sleet, and freezing rain, the trees and walkway were bending with the weight of a thick layer of ice.

My mood dropped just as low. Not the launch I'd planned for the holiday season. I had wanted to break all of my sales projections, even challenging Claire to sell every book in the shop.

Within minutes, Claire came to my side at the front window. She handed me my favorite mug filled to the top with my favorite breakfast tea blend. Bad times required major comforts. She had coffee in her mug and touched mine in a toast. "Maybe it'll melt early."

With hope, we watched the local weather report, which gave us no cause for happy talk. The dark clouds didn't lift. Nor did the sun shine.

We opened an hour early, following the holiday schedule mandate. Then we waited.

A few hardy shoppers stopped in. For the most part, they were people who lived within walking distance of the shops. Even so, they apparently wanted to get out of the house because they weren't in a buying mood, mostly looking for super-bargains or browsing.

I could have handled the day myself. Claire could have handled it without me. At one point, she went next door to check on Skylar. She returned with the grim news that Skylar was putting a jigsaw puzzle together to pass the time. Richard called twice. He was watching football highlights of the games as a time passer as he went over some paperwork for clients who couldn't make the drive to the office.

Claire fixed us a sandwich for lunch, but after eating quickly, I couldn't sit around any longer. I went off to visit the other shops and see what my friends were up to. "I'm going to the quilt shop and then to Styles."

"You be careful on the ice."

"I'm not going far, and I'm sure you will be the first to know if I meet the pavement." I made a funny motion with my arms like I was falling.

She pointed a finger at me. "That's not funny."

The sound of the bell at my leaving gave me a boost of energy. Little did Claire know that I was shopping for her.

I went to Quilts Galore first. Last week Marianna had described a quilt she was making for a client, which gave me the idea to give Claire and Skylar quilts for Christmas. It was too late to ask Marianna to make them, but she had quilts hanging on the walls that might be for sale.

When I went inside the quilt shop, I was greeted with "Jingle Bells" playing on the CD. Marianna, Liz, and Rachel were singing along. They missed some high notes, but they didn't seem to care. Liz and Rachel were arranging bolts of Christmas fabric by the front door. Marianna was bent over her sewing machine, the motor whizzing at a high speed.

"Hi, Millie. Busy in your shop?" Liz laughed at her own absurd question.

"Same as here, so I've come to buy. I'm looking for quilts for Claire and Skylar."

"We're jammed with special orders, but…" Liz looked around the shop. "We've already sold a few of the finished ones." She pointed to the two bare spots on the wall.

Marianna soon joined us.

"Millie's looking for quilts," Rachel said.

I laughed. "I'm starting my Christmas shopping. Hoping the spirits will notice and change the weather."

"Please don't ask for snow yet. Come on, let me show you what's left." Marianna touched my arm so I'd follow her while Liz and Rachel went back to their singing and displays.

I found a quilt made in my favorite colors of mint green and peach, in a pattern Marianna called a Double Irish Chain. I could see it brightening my bedroom. "I guess that'll be a gift to myself. Can I pick it up later—after Christmas?"

"Sure. Better for me to have it hang here than have another empty space."

I didn't see any other pieces that intrigued me, but when I left the shop Liz and Rachel were busy changing the displays in the front windows. Out with autumn and its rich colors of yellow and rust and in with Christmas with bright red and green and gold and silver.

Now why hadn't Claire and I thought of changing the windows? Because we'd planned to be too busy.

I decided to skip Styles, mostly because I saw Jessica and Mimi redoing their window. I hurried back to BookMarks to deal with our window displays, but as I rushed up our steps I almost ran into Trevor coming out. "So sorry. My mind was on using our free time to change our windows."

"Easy, Millie. The steps are a little slippery yet."

"I'm being careful. Is there something you need?" Like Claire? I smiled to myself.

"Just talked with Claire. I've given her the first part of the book."

"Wow. You're not wasting any time." And he looked very pleased with himself.

Trevor grinned. "I'm having fun again and I have Claire to thank for that."

"Well, good luck." Luck with what? Why had I said that?

Trevor held the door for me. The little bell jingled and reminded me of Christmas and my mission.

"Claire?" Where had she gone?

"Right here." She came out of the backroom with a full mug of coffee. The aroma filled the shop.

"Put your cup down," I said, feigning a stern tone. "We've got work to do. Marianna and Jessica and Mimi are changing their windows for Christmas."

She frowned. "I thought you scheduled that for next week."

"Change of plans. Why waste this dead day?"

She gave me a mock salute. "Need orders, Captain."

"Go to Rainbow Gardens and get evergreen boughs and lots of ribbon. If they have artificial snow, we need some of that, too. And a tree. Not too small."

Claire grabbed a notepad and began to list the items.

"I wanted to use my tree ornaments, but with everything from the condo in storage, I wouldn't know where to begin looking."

"We can make our own ornaments," Claire said, her face brightening. "We can cut up book flyers and some sample bookmarks and hang them on the tree with yarn."

I clapped my hands. "Go, go. Time's a wasting."

Claire ran upstairs to get her coat as I got money out of the drawer so she could pay in cash.

"Buy a variety," I said as she headed out the front door. "Let's make our windows shine."

While she was gone, I dismantled the cornucopia and put all the books on the sale table. I left the other window intact because we were still celebrating Thanksgiving for the weekend.

About half an hour later, Claire returned with her arms full. She dropped the bags on the floor. "Have to make a second trip."

When she came back, she was carrying the tree over her shoulder and a bag of decorations. "Don't ever send me on a buying trip again. Rainbow Gardens is stuffed with decorations we could use, down here or upstairs. And for every occasion."

"Whatever we don't use in the windows or around the shop, we'll use upstairs."

I left Claire to figure out the display by herself, and by the time she was done, a few boughs and one spool of ribbon were all that remained of the supplies.

"Not much left, Millie. The window needed all of it. You know, Christmas gifts and more gifts. That's why I used all the space for the books under the tree."

"You sound like a kid," I said, wanting to keep her good humored.

"I feel like one," she said, waving her arms in the air.

"After all, I haven't had Christmas with my sister for years."

"Remember when mom used to wrap each piece of a gift, or she disguised the item, like putting a paperback book into a box big enough for a pair of boots? She always managed to lead us astray."

"Yeah, and we'd have one special book or toy, or later, those record albums that are now collectors' items, and all the rest clothes." She seemed far away, as if searching for a memory.

I stepped outside to look at Claire's handiwork—and I was pleasantly surprised. She'd featured the book *Christmas Trees to Chicago* next to the tree in the center of the window. She'd put a placard next to the book giving the time and place of the book club meeting. To add a touch of magic, she'd strung a set of white tea lights through the boughs and ribbon to give the window a festive look.

I went back inside. "You did a terrific job, and so fast. You're a natural."

"If I over-think something it becomes too much with too many points of interest."

I nodded. "I noticed Jessica and Mimi keep their windows uncluttered."

"They plan it so we see the clothing, but aren't distracted by the surrounding stuff."

We stayed busy with shop maintenance jobs the rest of the afternoon and that was the point. It wasn't long before dusk approached and we had some accomplishments to count for the day.

We each had a prepackaged meal from Farmer Foods for dinner. Marianna had warned me about being too tired to eat after the busy day.

Right.

Our leisurely dinner gave Claire a chance to tell me about Trevor's book. She could hardly wait to begin reading the pages he'd brought.

Later, after listening to another uncertain weather report, I called Richard and we talked about the way the Connor family was going to celebrate Christmas.

But now, with my feelings for Richard growing stronger every day, he didn't say anything about including me.

25

Mother Nature changed her ways on Saturday and so did the shoppers. As if celebrating their release from an ice-covered day, they arrived on the Square early and with their lists. Claire and I were ready for what seemed like very eager buyers. We wore our vests proudly and we weren't shy about promoting the first holiday season of the *new* bookstore on the Square. I filed away a note to myself to thank Marianna for showing me the fabric, and Virgie and Beverly for making these connections to my book business.

Shoppers came all day, mostly in family and friend groups, but occasionally a solo shopper would come in and wander. Claire's people skills were evident in the way she enjoyed them, and they returned the attitude. At the end of the day Claire was still ready to help more customers. I had to lock the door on her and shut off the lights. She finished our numbered list and smiled all the way up the stairs.

She looked crestfallen when she added up sales though, having assumed it would be much more. I laughed loud and long when I handed her the second bag I'd held back. "Fooled you, didn't I?"

"Gave me a heart attack." She put her hand over her heart and groaned. "Okay, go away and let me count."

I fixed Farmer Foods' homemade potato soup and cheese and crackers for our dinner. It was hot and satisfying to eat while we chatted.

"Wow, Millie. Look at these totals. Let's make a chart for each day. Like kids do."

"Hey. That sounds like fun. Not that I want to flaunt our

success, but no one will see it but us."

"If every day is this good maybe you'll need a partner instead of an employee."

Partner? I wanted to ask her a million questions, but I held back. My knee-jerk reaction would have been, *well, why not?* But, as much as I wanted Claire to stay in Wolf Creek and work in BookMarks, I wasn't necessarily ready to have my sister be my business partner. "Well, your conservative sister isn't ready to expand into partnership yet."

"Sorry, Millie," Claire said softly, "I shouldn't have blurted out that idea. But I can't deny it. I see potential here for me to do better all around, including financially, and I can also make a contribution to the business."

I took a bite of a cracker. "Well, for right now, maybe management could give you a raise."

"Ah, now that would be much appreciated."

By the time Richard called, it seemed so much later into the evening. Closing an hour later made a big difference. When I mentioned my offer to give Claire a raise, he immediately agreed.

"I'll take care of it on Monday. I don't think we'll be as busy as today."

But when Monday rolled around, I saw immediately my prediction had been wrong. Every time the register made an audible ring, Claire's smiled widened. By the end of the day she was tired, but joked, "I smiled so much today my face hurts."

"Need a doctor?"

"Only to tell him to go away." She laughed at her attempted humor. "I'm calling Trevor to tell him I need a good meal, my treat. Want to call Richard and join us?"

"You're going to buy for all of us?" My sister—penniless and homeless no more.

"I'm flush tonight."

"Okay with me." I called Richard and he was agreeable to a spur-of-the-moment dinner.

So the four of us, with Trevor driving, headed to the Creekside Pub, and sure enough, the bartender, Bud, remembered Claire and me.

"Beer?" Bud asked.

"A pitcher and four glasses." Trevor remarked that he'd been to the pub often during his newspaper days, and never had a bad meal there.

On the other hand, Richard kept his opinion to himself. I hadn't said anything, but his hesitation once we stepped inside wasn't lost on me. It might have been years since he'd been in an old-fashioned pub like Creekside, even though all the TV screens showed one of the ESPN stations and I'd learned he was quite a sports fan.

Trevor and Richard were soon into a conversation about who'd end up at the Super Bowl. Claire added a few comments, but I stayed quiet. My knowledge of football extended to the names of books I'd included in my small sports section of the shop. Maybe I needed to expand my selection.

To keep it simple, we all chose the burger platter. Richard relaxed and dug into the bowl of peanuts Bud had brought with the beer.

Bud filled our glasses and with a nod, asked if we wanted the pitcher refilled. "Who gets the bill tonight?"

Claire raised her hand. "Yes to another pitcher, and this is my treat tonight."

Bud nodded and moved away, blending into the crowd.

Claire reached across the table to touch Trevor's arm. "Tell Millie and Richard your news."

"Well, because of Claire's enthusiasm and willingness to help, I'm going to publish some of my old columns about the town and the Square. A little trip down nostalgia lane—the town went through some hard times before the Square came roaring back."

"Then tell it all," I prodded.

"Maybe," Trevor said. "I mentioned the project to Gus at lunch the other day and he said the Matt and Gus Foundation would underwrite production costs. They're doing the same for Sarah's book. They want these books available for sale in the museum as soon as possible."

"Terrific." Richard was excited, more than I expected him to be. "Fits in with the historical interviews Gus is doing.

That'll be another attraction for the museum."

"Any book signings planned?" I asked.

Trevor laughed. "We need a book first."

"We've been brainstorming how to put it together and what to include," Claire added, her enthusiasm evident on her face and in her voice.

Our platters arrived, the fries still snapping from the hot oil. Then Bud handed Claire the bill. "Pay at the bar before leaving." He winked at her.

Laughing, she winked back. "Will do."

We finished our meal and headed back to the Square. While Claire rode in the front with Trevor, Richard held my hand as we sat close together in the backseat. His fingers danced a rhythm on my palm. I couldn't place the song or recognize a pattern in the rhythm, but maybe it was only in his mind. Still, familiar or not, I echoed his finger movements with mine. We played the game all the way home.

Trevor parked behind BookMarks, and after saying our good nights to them, Richard and I walked around the building to the courtyard in the Square.

He pointed to the bench opposite the shop. "This has been an interesting evening, wouldn't you say?"

"Lots to look forward to in the months to come." We settled on the bench.

"You mean Trevor's book?" he asked.

"That, but also Sarah's book. And now Claire wanting to stay and be a partner. Funny, Claire and I were both such bookworms as girls. Now, after decades apart, here we are selling books together. We also get to watch Skylar develop her shop. Such fun days." I sighed with contentment. "Just think, we have front row seats to all the action as it unfolds."

Richard squeezed my hand. "What about you, Millie?"

"Well, now that I'm here with no plans to leave, I'd say there's a future for us."

"You really mean that?" He turned sideways and brought his hands up to cradle my face. "When did you realize that could happen?"

"On the drive back from Minneapolis. Once I'd said good-bye to my old life and home, I had a sense of freedom and wanting to enjoy life again. And maybe not be alone any longer."

He punctuated my words with a soft kiss.

"You've been open about your feelings for me, Richard, but I wasn't ready to hear them. A part of me was still living in the past. Even a little afraid of the future."

"You don't have to be afraid, Millie." He chuckled. "Let me rephrase that and say it this way. At long last, I'm learning to at least try to stand back and let people live their own lives without my running commentary. But, I admit that sometimes I jump in before they can decide what's right for them."

I smiled. "I think that's called learning patience."

"I wouldn't say I've become a patient man, but you've given me a reason to wait and now, look at the gift you've given me." He wrapped me in his arms and kissed me like we would never see tomorrow.

When I finally broke away, I stood. "As they say, I hate to run, but tomorrow is closing in. It's been a great evening, though. I'll tell Claire thanks for dinner from both of us." I patted his arm. "I could tell being able to pay for a dinner meant a lot to her."

Richard sat a minute longer before rising. "What do we do next, Millie? About us?"

"Let's not rush. We can take our time to get to know each other better. We can dance by the fireplace, or share a bowl of popcorn and watch a movie. Or, let's just enjoy whatever happens to come our way, like tonight with Trevor and Claire."

"I want to do all those things and more. Much more. And I want to do them all with you." He put my hands in his and their warmth traveled to my heart.

"Time for me to go." I stepped across the walkway to the front door of BookMarks. Richard was by my side and holding my hand. "You know, each time I see you my heart loves you a little more."

"Let me know when your heart is full." He sealed his words with a kiss. "I'll call tomorrow night. We can talk if you can stay awake."

"That's a chance you'll have to take." I unlocked the door and stepped inside. When I turned to relock the door Richard was on the top step. I opened the door.

"Oops, I almost forgot," he said. "The tree lighting on the Square is tomorrow night. It's a special event. Will you go with me?"

"Sure, I'd love to." I bent forward and gave him a kiss. "'Night."

He waved when he stepped down and started on his way home.

I didn't need lights to walk to the back of the shop to the stairs. My feet knew the way. On the way up, I considered what I'd said. True, my heart was filling with love for him. But marriage? He'd mentioned it, so I knew it was on his mind. I had no answer to that dilemma yet. Maybe I found my "new beginning" a little too new to know where it would go.

***

Since Sarah had publicized the tree lighting event, many shoppers remained on the Square for the official kickoff of the Christmas season.

From her place standing at the window Claire said, "Wouldn't it be just perfect if snow started to fall when the tree was lit?"

I grinned. Claire had been waiting for days to see more snow. The first dusting had only whetted her appetite. "It could happen, I suppose."

"Are you ready to go, Millie?"

It had been my turn to finish the dishes. Earlier, Claire had joked that "Millie the maid" had taken a few days off, so I was hurrying to catch up with the clutter we'd created during the last couple of busy days. "Two minutes. I'll be ready in two minutes."

"Here come Richard and Trevor. I'll go down to meet them." She grabbed her new winter coat and long, fringed neck scarf purchased on the Square from Styles and Square Spirits.

I took a minute to put my coat on and made sure my gloves were in the pockets. While not icy cold, the temperature had fallen during the day reminding me that my hands would need to be covered to stay warm. I laughed to myself. Maybe I could play the ingénue and ask Richard to hold my hands.

Now, where did that foolish thought come from? I knew perfectly well Richard would take my hand without needing to be asked.

I joined the three of them at the front door and we made our way the short distance down the walkway to the flag pole area where the tree was located.

Within minutes we were surrounded by fellow residents of the Square and a large crowd of people we didn't know. Some faces were familiar, though, likely because they'd been in the shop that day. I absorbed the energy of the festive mood and joined the spontaneous singing of Christmas songs.

Richard put his arm around my shoulders and drew me next to him. I leaned in and snuggled closer to his body. When he looked down at me and smiled, my heart filled with joy.

Sarah tapped the portable microphone to quiet the crowd. "Welcome, everyone. This year Wolf Creek Square is bringing back the tradition of an official tree lighting. It's been absent too long."

There was a round of applause and a few whistles pierced the air.

"I've asked Jamison Brunette, the oldest resident of Wolf Creek, and Emma Connor, the newest resident, to light the tree."

Another round of clapping sounded. Jamison proudly rolled his wheelchair next to Sarah and raised his arms in victory.

Lily placed what looked like a bundle of blankets in Jamison's arms. Only Emma's tiny arm and mitten were visible, but that was enough for a hush to fall over the crowd. I was touched as well, as the meeting of the old and the new marked the return of a tradition.

Sarah stood beside them. "Okay Jamison, whenever

you're ready to light the tree."

We all held our breaths.

Within seconds, every light on the tree became a star of brightness, and on the top, the biggest star glowed brilliantly.

The crowd began its steady murmurs of approval. Someone began to clap. I saw flashes from cameras and people holding their cell phones up to capture the moment.

Richard bent down and whispered in my ear, "Just think, Millie, this will be our first Christmas together."

I squeezed his hand. My gloves were still in my pockets. I should have left them at home. I wasn't cold at all.

Claire's wish was granted when small snowflakes began falling as the four of us walked back to BookMarks. She kept turning back to look at the tree with a wide smile lighting up her face. I wondered what she was thinking when she looked at me, but I didn't ask.

***

As a veteran bookstore owner, I knew that bookstores usually made a huge percentage of their annual profits in just six weeks of the year. Books were good gift items, as a planned choice or something grabbed off the shelf as a last minute impulse buy. Knowing the next weeks were critical, I'd ordered more copies of each title, and using suggestions from Claire, I'd expanded the variety. She thought we needed more how-to and craft books, which were really safe gifts, along with international travel guides and narratives and volumes of photographic history. We both saw a need for more books about Wisconsin lore, including legends about haunted ships and lighthouses, and even some about old hotels and inns. Since Zoe carried few books focused on local phenomena, we were easily able not to infringe on her New Age titles.

In short order, Claire had become an inventory specialist, probably because processing the deliveries and shelving the books gave her an edge. When we were super busy and I struggled to locate a title for a customer, I found myself asking her. Sure enough, nearly every time, there it was, on a particular shelf, or in the window, or on the "New Arrival" cart, just as she'd said.

Beginning on the Sunday after Thanksgiving, the crowds arrived with the sole intent to buy. The bargain hunters from Thanksgiving had become Santa's elves.

Although I'd always offered complimentary gift wrapping, it seemed impractical for the space we had on our counter. Plus, we didn't have the personnel. I couldn't spare Claire to wrap gifts when the store was crowded. Instead, we decided to use our shopping bags, and add extra sheets of tissue paper customers could later unfold and embellish from there. The embossed envelopes I'd ordered for the gift certificates looked good enough as a wrap.

We also took time to remind every customer to sign up for the newsletter, because we planned to offer coupons good for the entire coming year. Thanks to Marianna's idea, we also created a gift basket for a drawing. Claire had picked out eight books and arranged them in a woven basket. It was small enough to sit on our counter with a bowl to gather the business cards or slips of paper we provided for customers who wanted a chance to win it.

We found our days beginning slowly, but gaining speed in the afternoon. Some days we had customers in the shop beyond closing time. But did we ever ask them to leave? Not a chance.

Claire had begun saying "Gold Mine" at the end of the day when she locked the door.

"Stop saying that," I said, showing genuine disapproval of that kind of brash remark. "Someday, you're going to make a mistake and mention our good fortune in the wrong crowd."

"Everyone on the Square is saying the same thing," she replied. "Haven't you been listening?"

In truth, she was listening more than I was. She and Skylar had begun stopping at B and B during their morning walk so they could visit with the other women. I walked over for morning coffee less often. I still didn't find it all that enjoyable, but mostly I liked starting my day more slowly, and alone.

Claire was my stand-in, and passed on all of the day's gossip or the little buzz that became gossip during the busy days. She'd tuned into the Square's pulse quicker than I had, easily using the unique people skills she'd developed from so many years of traveling the world, not to mention being based for long periods of time in small villages with their own ways to spread the news.

Richard and I talked on the phone every evening of that busy week. I couldn't see him in the evening and still have the energy and focus I needed to make the most of whatever the next day had in store. I concluded he finally understood me and accepted that BookMarks was my first priority. More than my living, it had become my passion.

One morning, just before the end of the month, Richard stopped in as soon as I'd unlocked the door. Glad to see him, I asked what brought him by so early.

"I'm heading to Green Bay for a few days. End of year evaluations at the firm, although it is only November." He laughed. "Business stuff. That sort of thing. But sometimes you'll see the lights on at Country Law. Charlie Crawford and his crew will be doing some work both upstairs and in the offices."

Our conversation was cut short when a family of three arrived, and then a pair of women came into the shop behind them.

I squeezed his hand. "We'll talk more tonight. Travel safe."

He bent forward as if to kiss me, but then reconsidered. Instead, he grabbed my hand and squeezed it like I had his.

I would have preferred the kiss.

December
26

When I turned the calendar page to December, I was greeted by a photo of a winter wonderland that matched the scene outside the front window. During the night, a layer of snow had fallen and covered the foliage and walkways on the Square. Claire laughed at the sight of it. After Thanksgiving weekend the Wolf Creek maintenance crew had replaced the scarecrows, pumpkins, and bales of straw with full-size cutouts of Santa and his elves. Huge bouquets of artificial poinsettias marked the entrances of the walkways. Giant stars hung from the bare branches of the trees.

As the days blended one into the next, Claire and I became all-around efficiency experts, working all day and eating hot and cold deli dishes from Farmer Foods at night. At B and B one morning, Claire mentioned the wonderful meat loaf we'd brought home the night before, which brought murmurs of agreement from everyone assembled. The conversation soon became a rundown of what specials Farmer Foods ran each day of the week. It was funny, but useful over the next few weeks.

Claire laughed at Jessica, who'd quipped, "Eli and Elliot and their crew support us, so we support them."

True enough. Nearly everything Claire and I needed was at our fingertips, either on the Square or on the streets just behind it. Ordering items online filled in the rest of what we used day-to-day. I hadn't had my car on the road since my trip to Minneapolis.

I enjoyed my solitude on the many evenings Claire left to work with Trevor on his book, or when they went out for coffee with some of the others who were cooped up all day in their shops. Meanwhile, I looked forward to my chance to lose myself in a book and share a nightly conversation with Richard. He was surprised we had so much to talk about, and he listened to my funny stories from the day in the shop. Hmm…so unlike the way he'd been months ago when he brushed off my day—and my plans for the shop—as if not particularly important.

"I can't wait to get back to Wolf Creek and see you," he said. "The work here is going slower than planned, so I have to stay a few days longer."

I laughed. "I won't be sitting around twiddling my thumbs waiting for you. That's for sure. By the way, the book club meets next week, so maybe you can get back for that."

"I'm halfway through the book. As interesting as the story is, I don't think the author did it justice. Any job on a boat is dangerous and not something to be glamorized."

"Save your comments for the meeting, honey." I got up from the table to stretch my legs and wandered over to the front window. "Oh, Richard, there are carolers on the Square."

"I remember Sarah mentioning they'd be around all month," he said, "but I don't remember if she mentioned exactly when. It's time for me to go to bed. I have an early morning meeting tomorrow and I want to be sharp."

Even over the phone I could hear the sound of a stifled yawn, but he continued, "You know I love it when you call me 'honey'. I can tell you mean it and aren't just repeating my words."

"I do mean it. Good night, *honey*." I chuckled as I ended the call.

Claire came in a while later. She was humming Christmas carols and didn't realize I was sitting on the couch in the dark.

"Hi, I'm still up."

"Millie! You scared the bejeebies out of me."

"Sorry. I was talking to Richard and the carolers were

singing, so I stayed put after we ended the call. It's so peaceful here."

"Yes, I heard them singing when I came home." She moved closer and stood by the window. "When will Richard be back?"

I shrugged. "Couple more days, I guess. The case is going slower than he'd like. He is taking it all in stride, though."

Claire stretched her arms over her head. "I'm bushed. Trevor works all day writing introductions to each editorial he's putting in his book, then he's eager for me to read them right away."

"Is it any good?" I asked.

She bobbed her head back and forth as if unsure how to answer. "Some of his columns are better than others, but I think we can smooth out his selections. He wrote so many during his time at the paper. I'm thinking we can press the delete button on a few."

"Ouch. Such a harsh critic you are." I chuckled. "You sound like Richard. He said the book club author could have told his story better."

"That was my reaction to the book, too, but I won't say any more tonight. Too tired."

"Remember, there's a bus tour on Saturday."

"Right. And then it will be Christmas." She waved her arms over her head. It was a gesture I'd come to recognize as her way of celebrating.

"Do you think we need a tree up here besides the one downstairs?" I asked, hoping she'd say no.

"Nah. I'll carry the one from downstairs up here for Christmas Eve. Then we can take our time dismantling it afterwards." She headed to her room. "Marianna said something the other day about the way she and Rachel raided their store decorations for their apartment the first year they were on the Square. It's not like we'll be doing a lot of entertaining, other than having Richard and Trevor around—and Skylar."

"You're right," I said. "We don't need a tree to make Christmas special for you and me."

Claire waved, and then I heard the door to her room click

shut.

Even though fatigue was working through my body, I stayed on the couch a while longer, mostly marveling at the rate of the passage of time. Six months ago I'd agreed to help Richard's family, and if that had been the extent of it, I'd soon be packing my bags and heading back to Minneapolis. Someone else would have bought the bookstore or it would be closing. Instead, I was the one who was succeeding with my own shop and was the proud owner of the building on the corner of the Square.

Equally rewarding, Skylar was well and happy in her own independent venture. No matter what happened in the future, my granddaughter's strength and joy for life would be a solid foundation. To add to the positive developments, Claire was happy in Wolf Creek and had no intention of leaving. She'd been all over the world, but found the little community on the Square so much to her liking she wanted to put her wandering days behind her.

Did my future look as bright as theirs?

Richard's face popped into my mind. I smiled. Well, why not?

27

When he knew he was coming back to town, Richard asked me to have dinner at his place, rather than Crossroads. "I have things to tell you and show you, and I don't want other people to hear me."

Hints of news and excitement heightened my curiosity. "As long as you don't go to any trouble," I said. "I'll bring dessert. What time?"

"We can plan that later after I get back."

When Claire came in, I mentioned the dinner.

"Well, I guess absence makes the heart grow fonder." She laughed and gave me a hug. "Bring home the leftover dessert."

I laughed, knowing she was referring to the chocolate cornucopias, but I dismissed that idea with a hand wave when she padded off to bed.

The next morning, more books arrived. Even as Christmas neared, we still needed many deliveries to fill the rapidly emptying spaces on the shelves. That night, I went upstairs after closing. Claire said she was going keep working to get the books entered into the inventory for the next day. It was ten o'clock before she came up.

"Why so late tonight?" I asked.

"Trevor. We're working tomorrow night."

The next evening after Claire went out I had time to wrap a few gifts. I hadn't outgrown the desire to make each gift unique, so I got down on my hands and knees and pulled out the Christmas trappings from under my bed where I'd stored them. I bought the cheerful paper and colorful bows from a holiday shelf at Farmer Foods and hid them from Claire. I'd put my gift purchases under the bed, too. Claire would never have reason to look under there. Would she?

It had been years since Claire and I exchanged gifts, and that had been through the mail. I didn't want her to think she needed to spend a lot of money on gifts for me, especially because she was finally getting back to having a regular job and income. We both had a lot of years to make up. After Bruce died, I hadn't wanted to celebrate the holiday at all.

I struggled to free two packages that ended up wedged against the wall. Nothing to do but stretch out flat on the floor to grab them. I laughed at myself at how ridiculous I probably looked.

Continuing—or really, restarting—our mother's tradition, I bought Claire mittens, T-shirts, and a sweater. I began wrapping, but then stopped to turn on the CD player. Claire had been playing "Songs of the Season" by various artists and I soon found myself singing along.

Like our mother used to do, I wrapped the gifts in such a way they wouldn't be recognized. The mittens could make a small and compact package, but I put them a good-size box so she'd never guess. I rolled one of the T-shirts so it would fit in a cylindrical mailer. No chance she'd guess what that gift was either. The other shirt went into a padded envelope that I wrapped in paper printed with colorful wreaths.

I made an elaborate package of her sweater with metallic gold paper and a white lace bow I'd ordered on line. The bow had crystals on the loops that reflected the light, making it shine like a star. When I was finished, I stepped back to look at the gift I'd created. It was even prettier than I'd thought it would be.

I had one more gift for Claire, but I needed to talk to Richard about it first.

Skylar's gifts had been a little more challenging. One day, I stopped at Styles and Mimi mentioned that Skylar had been looking at a particular dressy sweater. I bought it right then. It would be perfect for the holidays either in the shop or for a dinner out, and I'd learned my granddaughter kept a full social calendar. Like young people everywhere, she could put in very long workdays and still have leftover energy to go out with Reed and their friends most nights. As I folded the long sleeves of the hand-knit wool piece I knew how much she loved that bright shade of green. The knitter had attached dark green gemstones in the shape of an evergreen tree, and by chance, I'd found matching emerald earrings at Art&Son. Perfect gifts for a granddaughter whose tastes I'd come to know well.

I was finishing with Skylar's packages when Claire came in. She didn't hesitate to begin looking at the name tags. "Woo hoo. I have more packages than Skylar." She broke into a mock dance.

"How do you know that's all I have for her?" I grinned. "Besides, how old are you? Five?"

She spun around, her features feigning defeat. "Oh, darn. You're right. Maybe Santa will bring her more on Christmas Eve." She pulled a chair out from the table and began to re-spool the ribbons I'd used. "So what are you getting Richard?"

"Want to see? It came a couple of days ago."

"You bet."

I opened the shipping carton and removed the gift box. Claire stretched her neck to look inside when I took the cover off the box.

"Oh, Millie, it's beautiful." She rubbed her hands over the tooled soft leather briefcase.

I flipped the case over to show her the monogrammed initials done in gold.

"He's going to love it, Sis."

"He can't keep using that worn out one he carries around. It's so far gone it doesn't look professional, and I checked with Lily so we wouldn't get him the same gift."

I recapped the box and started to unroll red paper with dancing reindeer printed on it.

"No, no," Claire said. "That paper is for children." Sifting through the pile, she pulled out deep blue paper flocked with snowflakes.

I snickered. "I might have known. You're obsessed with snow."

"Now that I've seen the lovely white blankets covering everything, I can't get enough of it." She held the box as I unrolled the paper.

"What are you getting Trevor?"

Still holding the box, she plopped down in the chair. "Don't have a clue. The man has everything."

I put out my hand for the box. "You'll think of something." I finished with Richard's gift and carried it to the front window, nestling it on the floor next to the others. "There. At least it's a start."

Once again, I had a sense of satisfaction about my day.

28

Another book club night, another stormy day. For the third month in a row, we were greeted with rain. This month a drizzly mist became freezing rain by mid-morning. By early afternoon the Square was empty, and we'd heard from many of the readers who'd called to say they wouldn't be attending but hoped we'd pick a snow date. As long as the speaker hadn't cancelled, I was still inclined to hold the meeting.

By mid-afternoon, I checked with him. We decided it made no sense for him to come twenty-five miles on icy roads when many of the readers had already called to say they wouldn't be coming.

Not to be defeated, I called Steph and told her I'd show up and have some kind of discussion with whoever arrived. Then I told Claire we might have a lively back and forth if she and Richard spoke up. I hadn't heard from Richard, but he'd promised to be back for the meeting. The bad weather might have interfered with his trip home, though.

"Has Richard called?" I asked Claire.

"Haven't heard from him. Is he driving in this mess?"

I grabbed my phone and hit his speed dial number. There was no response, not even his voice mail activated. For the first time that day, I was uneasy. "Oh, Richard, where are you?" I whispered.

As my mind traveled to the worst possible scenarios, my heart cried out *I love you.*

Claire was on her phone at the same time. "See you soon, Trevor." She came alongside me. "I told him to stay home and be safe."

By the time Claire and I put on our boots and left for B and B, I still hadn't heard from Richard. I carried my phone in my hand so I could quickly pick up a call. Claire held my other hand, so if one of us went down, we'd take the other along for the crash to the ice.

"The beauty of the snow aside," Claire said, "I haven't tried to get around in this kind of weather for a long time."

We walked—sort of—in silence. Mostly, we shuffled and slid. Finally, Claire squeezed my gloved hand. "He's okay, Millie. I'm sure he would've called if he could."

When we arrived at B and B three women and one man were already there. They'd all come together in one car, driven by the man. His wife had insisted a little ice shouldn't keep them away.

"I told Frank my friends and I weren't going to miss tonight and he said I wasn't going without him. I'm really grateful he offered to drive. It's nasty out there." She grabbed his hand.

Steph stepped forward with a tray of frosted cookies shaped like Christmas trees, complete with green sprinkles over the white frosting and one red-hot candy pressed into the frosting at the peak of the tree. She offered everyone a dish of vanilla ice cream to go with the cookies, and pots of hot tea and coffee were ready.

We put a couple of tables together so we were one group, no matter how small.

"Well, thanks for coming tonight," I started. Steph was behind the counter pouring our beverages, but she nodded when I paused to wait for her. "Seems like Mother Nature isn't supporting our group getting together. First the rain and now this ice." I shivered to make my point.

Steph joined us, filling the last empty chair and put her book, *Christmas Trees to Chicago*, on the table. "Let's go around the table and give our overall impressions of the book," she said.

"It was awful." The woman, Maxine, sat between me and her driver-husband. She shook her head. "He made the whole story read like a children's fairy tale. I wanted to come tonight and let the other readers know that working on a ship in wintertime is dangerous. I lost my dad in a maritime accident. It was similar to the *Edmund Fitzgerald* disaster, and we all remember that."

"I agree," Claire said. "The author made it sound like only his family gave gifts to the poor of the city. And a tree isn't the same as getting food."

The door of B and B opened and Richard came in. I rushed from my chair. "Are you all right? I tried calling, but there was no answer." I kept patting his face, not believing he wasn't hurt.

"I'm sorry you were worried. I turned my phone off so I wouldn't be distracted driving," he explained, wrapping his arms around me. "I put it in my briefcase in the back seat. I didn't want to stop and get it out when I spun around on the ice and slid off the road. I just wanted to get back on the road and get home. To you."

"You slid off the road? Where? When?"

"No harm, Millie. Just onto the shoulder."

I linked my arm in his and led him to the table. I wanted to hear more about his trip to Wolf Creek, but I'd wait until we were alone. "Come join the discussion. So far, no one's been generous about the book or the author."

Claire added a chair and moved over one seat so Richard could sit next to me. Steph brought him ice cream and coffee, and slid the tray of cookies toward him. He nodded his appreciation.

Each reader added comments about their disappointment in the book. I generally agreed, but since I'd chosen the book before reading it I had to admit it was my mistake. It was a fairly famous book, so I didn't think we could go wrong. I'd read my next recommendation first.

We ended the evening early when freezing rain peppered the front window of the coffee shop. Nor did we choose a book for January.

One woman at the table suggested we read something lighter, a novel, maybe one on the funny side. "January is such a dark, dreary month we need something brighter. Something to make us laugh," she said.

I volunteered to send the members an email with three choices to vote on. We thanked Steph and helped her put the tables and chairs back in place for morning. The husband hurried his group out the door.

I settled the bill with Steph. As we strode out, Richard offered Claire and me an arm and we slid across the layer of ice toward home. When we reached BookMarks, Claire immediately said goodnight and went inside and on upstairs.

Richard and I followed her into the shop. As I thought back on the evening, I don't know if he made the first move or if I did but without prelude or pretense, we were in each other's arms. The kiss became two, then three. Finally we separated.

"Claire was right," I said. "She said absence makes the heart grow fonder."

"Fonder?" He laughed.

I looked him in the eye. "I love you, Richard. It's just taken me awhile to realize I want to be with you."

"Oh, Millie. It seems I've waited so long for you to say that." He circled my face with his hands and leaned in for another kiss. "We need to celebrate. Come to my place Saturday. I have so much to tell you."

I laughed. He was like a kid at Christmas. "Go home. Call me when you get there or flash the lights."

He wouldn't leave without another kiss.

My heart jingled with the bell when I shut the door.

***

By opening time the next day, the Square was back in full holiday shopping mode. The maintenance crew had spread a layer of ice-melt and between that and the bright sunshine the walkways were nearly clear.

Every time Claire looked at me she smiled. "You have a glow about you, Millie. You look happy."

I stretched my arms up into the air, like she often did. "I am, and it feels good."

That was the last we chatted until the end of the day when I mentioned going to Richard's for dinner on Saturday.

"You are a lucky lady, Sis." She went upstairs to assemble our evening meal from our stash of containers.

Even though our days were busy, my mind kept rushing ahead to Saturday. I enjoyed my evening calls with Richard as much as I enjoyed being on Wolf Creek Square and owning BookMarks. Being with him, having him nearby, was what I wanted now. I was sure of it.

On Saturday after closing, I took extra care and time with my clothes and makeup as I got ready for dinner. A couple of days earlier, I'd seen a soft wool pantsuit in royal blue in Styles' window, and decided I had to have it. I left Claire to open the shop alone because I wanted to try it on and have the pants and sleeves measured for alternations. I was eager to wear it to Richard's.

Claire was still cleaning up the shop when I came downstairs all dressed up and ready to go. "Wow, Millie. The new outfit is beautiful. It makes your eyes look even bluer and brings out the color in your face." She held my coat for me and wished me a wonderful evening.

Richard met me at Country Law's front door. I smelled raw wood and fresh paint when I stepped inside.

"Let me show you what Charlie did." He took my coat and put it on the front desk and locked the door. He led the way down the hallway and opened a door on the right. The nameplate on the desk read "Richard Connor."

"An office? You have your own office now?"

His smile was my answer. "We took part of the storage room and moved the outdated boxes to the basement." His arm swept the interior of his new space. His diplomas had been hung on the wall to make it official. "When Nathan and Jack left my firm in Green Bay and moved to Wolf Creek, they joined Miles Owens' practice. Miles was Georgia and Beverly's uncle. Then, just days after the new firm was formed, Miles suffered a stroke and soon died."

I frowned, trying to make sense of all the connections—there were so many complex family situations on the Square. "Sometimes it's hard for me to keep all these family relationships connected to the right people."

Richard covered my hands. "No matter now. I've sold

my share in the Green Bay firm and am now part of this office. We're Connor, Pearson and Connor. I'm the second Connor." He laughed. "Isn't that terrific? That I can work for Nathan and with Jack again?"

"But what about your home in Green Bay?" He was getting ahead of me with his news.

"Well, Millie, I decided I want to live in Wolf Creek now. I have my house in Green Bay for sale. I'm here for good. I'm with my family, but, most importantly, I'm here with you."

"Wow, that's huge, Richard."

"It's meant to be a big change. It's letting go of the past and changing my life." He sighed. "I think I'm finally ready to put my mistakes behind me, and enjoy my family—big or small, they're all the family I have."

"Like Skylar and Claire and me," I said, nodding.

Richard led the way upstairs to his apartment, and I immediately noted his changes. A love seat replaced the two chairs in front of the fireplace, its soft glow adding warmth to the room. On the wall by a reading chair were new pictures; one of Nathan, Lily and Emma and one of Richard with Toby. A small Christmas tree stood by the front window.

"Come look over here." Richard stood by the door of what had been Toby's room when Nathan lived above his office. "I had Charlie take out Toby's race car bed and redo the room."

I peeked in and found a bedroom with a single bed. The faint smell of fresh paint lingered in the room.

"Eventually, you can add a bed for Emma, too," I said.

He grinned. "That's the plan. By the way, Toby's grandparents are coming for a visit after New Year's. The Inn is full that week so I've invited them to stay here. They can have the big room and I'll stay in this one."

"You sound excited."

"I am. It'll be the first time Toby's whole family will be together, but I'm a little nervous, too."

"You'll do fine. From what you said, his other grandparents are great people to be around."

"I'm hoping you'll be able to get away and join us for a couple of lunches and dinners while they're here."

"Sure. I can juggle some hours with Claire. We'll be slower anyway. I think we can work it out." I glanced around again. "I can't believe you made such a big decision. Sure didn't take you long."

"No, and that's because of you. Wolf Creek feels like my real home."

We'd moved back into the open kitchen where Richard poured us each a glass of wine. He held out a chair for me to sit. I couldn't miss the yeasty smell of Crossroads twisted bread, and Richard grabbed a bowl of salad greens from the refrigerator to go with the crusted pork chops and roasted vegetables. "And dessert for later."

Richard told me every detail of his week in Green Bay and the funny stories that came about with the evaluations at the firm, his last official duty in Green Bay. He'd used the extra days to meet with a realtor and to pack his personal belongings at the house.

After we cleaned up the kitchen, we settled on the loveseat before the fire. We could see the Christmas tree across the Square and, to make the scene complete, snow flurries filled the air.

"What are your plans for Christmas, Millie?"

I shrugged one shoulder. "I don't have any yet. I'm sure over the couple of days Claire will spend some time with Trevor. I think Skylar and Reed will be together part of the day."

"I'll be at Nathan's on Christmas Eve. I'm sure you'd be welcome to join us."

"Maybe next year. I do want to get to know them better, but Claire and Skylar and I haven't been together for years, nor have we talked specifics yet. We're all so busy in the shops right now."

"I know you are, but I just want to be with you all the time. Let's plan on being together Christmas Day evening. Here at my house." He hesitated. "My home."

"I'd like that. Together with you." I held his hand.

It was almost midnight when Richard walked me home.

"Welcome to Wolf Creek Square, honey."

"Back at you." He laughed. "Toby says that all the time. Good night to you, honey."

I went upstairs and remembered we never had dessert.

29

The week before Christmas neither Claire nor I could have said what day of the week it was. We were that busy. My midday trip to the bank behind the Square became part of the routine, because we didn't want such large amounts of cash and checks in the freezer anymore and we didn't want to go to the bank in the dark at the end of the day, either. Not a bad problem to have. I declared BookMarks a success after five and a half months. That meant I needed to talk about future finances with my accountant and Richard. I trusted their judgment.

On Christmas Eve, the shop became crowded like a bus tour day. Last minute gift buyers grabbed books off the shelves. It seemed some shoppers were so desperate, they cared little about the subject or the title. I saw Claire reach into the window for books with a holiday theme and then, inside a BookMarks bag, the books went out the door.

We locked our door long after closing time when the last customer left with a shopping bag filled to the top. Claire turned to me and quietly said, "Gold mine."

She was so right.

I was the first up the stairs and handed Claire a glass of wine when she joined me with the receipts and money that we collected after my afternoon trip to the bank. Claire had never forgotten the cash drawer again after her first mistake. We thought every day deserved a celebration and I had changed from drinking tea to having wine most days after we locked our door. Was that part of becoming a member of the community? Maybe so, because everyone talked about the wine Zoe carried in her shop.

Claire changed her clothes and was ready to meet Trevor when the back door buzzer rang. "I'll be home late, so don't wait up for me."

"Tell Trevor I said Merry Christmas."

"Will do." She gave me a hug as she passed by.

I walked to the window and saw the dark windows of Richard's place above Country Law. I was relieved to have the evening to myself and not need to rush to the Connor house. I could only imagine Toby running around excited with all the packages under the tree. I was tired from my long day. I sat on the couch to finish my wine and reminisce about Mark when he was Toby's age. So many years ago. A different lifetime. Losing him was an ache that would never go away completely.

The packages looked forlorn without a tree over them so I went downstairs, and with a little maneuvering, got the tree out of the front window and upstairs. Claire had volunteered to carry it up, but I was the younger sister and if she could do it, then surely so could I.

As I arranged the packages, I noticed Claire had added a few of her own. I shook one with my name on it to see if it rattled. It didn't. Darn. I needed to wait until morning to find out what was inside.

I went to my room and brought out two large Christmas stockings, one for Claire and one for Skylar. I figured my sister and granddaughter would be very surprised with the gifts.

Richard didn't call. He'd hinted that he might overnight at Nathan's if the time got late. If he came home, he'd go back early in the morning as planned.

I toasted my new town and finished the last of the wine in my glass. I turned on the light over the stove for Claire.

I went to bed and said goodnight to my family. And to Richard, my new love.

***

Christmas Day started with Claire in the kitchen brewing

coffee and steeping a pot of tea for me. "Morning, Sis. Isn't it a beautiful day?"

She wore a bright red sweater embroidered with snowflakes and a long chain necklace of gold discs and beads. Her earrings matched the necklace, except that the beads were smaller.

I wrapped my hands around the mug Claire put in front of me. "I haven't seen that sweater and jewelry before."

A soft blush instantly appeared on her neck. "Gifts from Trevor." She busied herself gathering ingredients from the fridge for breakfast.

"No need to be shy about it. I know you and he are close. What did you get him?" I spoke as I walked to the front window, not ignoring her, but the bright sunlight was too inviting.

"I gave him an anthology of British poets and a sweater. It's Scottish wool with leather on the elbows. I told him that if he was going to be a writer then he needed to look like one."

I nodded in approval. "Nice."

"I wanted to get him a writing pen set, but didn't think of it soon enough. After I saw Richard's initials on his briefcase, I wanted the pens monogrammed for Trevor."

"There'll be another time." I was distracted by the lack of sound and activity on the Square. For weeks, Christmas songs had played throughout the day and filled the courtyard with holiday spirit. On that morning, every shop on the Square was closed. No early morning gathering at B and B, no last minute reservations at Crossroads, no jingling of the bells on the shops' doors.

I thought it felt lonely, but the longer I stood there the more I realized it wasn't lonely. It was peaceful. It was as if the Square itself could rest for a day after a stretch of hyperactivity.

"Millie? You okay?" Claire had stepped next to me.

"Oh, sure." I turned to give her a smile. "Just thinking about last Christmas when Skylar and I were alone. It wasn't a good day for either of us, and we were glad when it was over."

"Well, Skylar will be here in an hour if you'd like to get dressed. Or not. Maybe you want to spend all day in your jammies."

"Haven't done that…ever." I playfully slapped her shoulder and went to get ready for a beautiful day.

Skylar showed up right on time and helped Claire fix us a breakfast fit for Paul Bunyan. Since our kitchen area was too small for three people to move about, I sat at our table to stay out of the way as they created the rhythm of their own dance.

Skylar wanted pancakes—a tradition we'd started years back when she was little and her parents and Bruce were still alive. Claire thought veggie and cheese omelets were needed. "Protein to balance the carbs," she said. "And thick slices of bacon just for fun."

"It's a holiday. I don't care about balanced nutrition today," Skylar teased back. "But we need fruit." She opened the refrigerator door. "Gram always has strawberries." She wasn't disappointed.

I could only laugh at the two of them and revel in the joy of having them with me. Not only today, but every day.

My mind jumped to Richard when my phone rang and I saw his name on the screen. "Merry Christmas, honey."

"Hey, the same to you. What's happening at your house?"

"Breakfast is in the making, thanks to Skylar and Claire. And you?"

Richard groaned. "Toby's been up since five and the house is in shambles. But who cares? Right? We're with family."

Claire's loud voice drew my attention. "Breakfast is ready."

"Gotta go. Food's on the table, and I'm starved. Call me when you get home."

We said quick goodbyes and I headed to the kitchen. We lingered over our food, coffee and tea, but eventually I shooed Claire and Skylar out of the kitchen so I could clean it up. It was only fair, since they'd done all the cooking.

Behaving like excited kids, they said I was taking too

long. They each grabbed a towel and dried as fast as I could wash.

So there we were, three adult women acting as if we were children on Christmas morning. Skylar had separated the gifts into three piles and sat cross-legged on the floor. Claire and I had taken our favorite places on the couch.

I pointed to the two stockings. "Those are to be opened last."

"Well then, let's get started." Claire clapped her hands. "These look so interesting. She picked up the large box. "What could this be?"

"You'll never guess, so you better go ahead and open it," I said with laughter in my voice. I knew that mittens would never make her list of guesses.

Claire tore through the wrapping, lifted the lid and then pulled out handfuls of tissue until she finally found the red mittens. She held them up. "Wonderful! These are perfect. " She gave me a pointed look. "I see your old habit of gift wrapping subterfuge hasn't gone away."

"Not on your life. You might as well stop guessing."

Skylar chose to open the large box from Claire. Inside was a cardigan sweater with an intricate design knit with natural yarn. She held the sweater against her cheek. "Oh, my. Thank you so much."

"Tracie, from The Fiber Barn, knit it so if you don't like the wooden buttons she'll change them."

"I think they're perfect." She stood up and put it on. It fit so perfectly, she left it on and sat back down. "Your turn, Gram."

I, too, opened a box from Claire to find a brightly colored teapot. "You didn't have to…"

"I know, I know," she interrupted. "It was done by a local potter. I heard shoppers talking about him Labor Day weekend. He was one of the vendors so I hurried to buy one."

"I don't remember you leaving the shop."

She just smiled. "I didn't. I called Virgie to get it for me."

I ran my hand over the smooth red glaze. So unusual.

"It was worth the effort. I love it." I nodded to the pile of presents. "Now, your turn."

Claire ripped off the paper on the cylinder package, surprised to see a purple Tee she could wear with all kinds of jackets. "Clever packaging," she said. When she opened her gift from Skylar—a sweater in soft gray wool—she let out a hoot. "I don't think any of us are going to get cold this winter. And the purple top is perfect with it." She nodded to me. "You're next, Millie."

I opened my package from Skylar to find a hand-knit shawl in natural colors.

"It's for when you're resting in the evenings this winter." Skylar looked at Claire. "Seems The Fiber Barn was our go-to shopping store this year. Katie was just finishing this when I stopped in." She gestured to my shawl.

"It's beautiful." I wrapped it around my shoulders and snuggled into its warmth.

Skylar turned to the packages from me.

"Open the large box first," I said, "and then the little one."

She was careful undoing the ribbon and paper on the oversized box, keeping the suspense high.

Claire bounced on the couch in anticipation. "Hurry up, girl."

Skylar laughed, but kept going at her own slow pace. And then she peeked under the lid. "Oh, Gram. For weeks I've wanted to buy this, but it is so not practical."

I chuckled. "Christmas doesn't have to practical—except for mittens and T-shirts."

Claire moved to the edge of the cushion eager to see inside Skylar's box.

Skylar pulled out the green sweater with the crystals and held it across her chest. "Thank you, Gram."

"Now, the little package before you put the sweater away."

It didn't take her long to unwrap the blue Art&Son box. I wish I had a picture of her face when she opened the lid and saw the emerald earrings.

"Ohhhh. Really?" Her eyes glistened when she looked at me.

Claire sat back in her corner of the couch. "Lucky lady, I'd say." She reached across to give my hand a squeeze. "Merry Christmas, Sis."

"I never thought I'd enjoy this holiday again, but having both of you with me has made all the difference." The feeling of warmth in my heart was overwhelming.

Skylar made Claire and me stand up for a family hug. "Merry Christmas to us."

All that remained were the stockings when we sat down.

"This one is for you, Skylar." I handed her the stocking with her name embroidered on the cuff.

She carefully undid the ribbon and reached inside. She looked at the papers. All she said was, "Oh, Gram." Tears balanced in her eyes, again, ready to spill down her cheeks. "How did you know?"

"Well, tell me what it is." Claire stretched over to see.

"An all-expense paid trip to the Toy Expo for me and a friend."

"Oh, what fun." Claire was back in her festive mood.

"Gram, I never mentioned I wanted to go. But I did. I do. So, how did you know?"

"You and Lily talked about it and she told me. She said she always wanted to go, but now with Emma…" I didn't need to finish. We all knew her time for professional trips had passed, at least for now.

"Maybe Reed would go with me." Skylar held the papers to her chest. "I'll ask him this afternoon." She got up and gave me a hug. "Thank you, Gram. You're the best," she whispered.

Then it was Claire's turn. I handed her the same kind of stocking that had her name on the front. I noticed her hand shook a little when she opened it and brought out the papers inside.

She began to read, "Certificate of Ownership." She stopped and looked at me.

"Keep reading," I said. "You can skip all the legalese on the first page. The important part is on page two."

She turned the page and began to read aloud the paragraph I'd highlighted. "The receiver—Claire Powers—is given

10% ownership of the business known as BookMarks located on Wolf Creek Square in the town of Wolf Creek, Wisconsin."

Her voice had become a whisper. She brought her hand to her mouth.

"When you decided to stay, I thought as long as we were partners up here, we might as well be partners downstairs." I wanted to keep the mood light. "Anyway, good help is hard to find."

Claire reached across the length of the couch and squeezed my hand. "This is the best Christmas I've ever had."

I smiled. "Welcome home, Claire."

Skylar began the American tradition of gathering the discarded wrapping paper and returning her gifts to their boxes. The silence echoed in the room.

"Hey, you guys. What's wrong?" I asked.

"You blew us away, Gram. You surprised both of us."

"Shocked is a better word." Claire had gotten her voice back. "I can't wait to tell Trevor."

Claire stepped over to turn on the CD of instrumental Christmas music I'd planned to play while we exchanged gifts, but had forgotten all about it.

Did it matter? No. Seems we'd made our own music.

Later, we all had calls to handle on our respective phones—Claire returned Trevor's call, Skylar called Reed, and I left a message for Richard. After another group hug, it wasn't long before Skylar and Claire left for the rest of the day.

I waited impatiently for Richard to come home.

When my phone rang I answered immediately.

"I'm home. I'll be waiting at the front door," he said.

"I'm on my way." I hurried to put on my coat and grabbed the shopping bag with his gifts. I almost forgot to lock the door when I left. *Almost.* Fortunately, I remembered before I started down the street.

I was less than half way across the courtyard to Country Law when Richard stepped outside. He wasn't wearing a coat so I knew he hadn't planned on coming to join me. As soon as we met, he kissed me and took the bag. He wasn't hesitant to look inside.

"For me?"

I suddenly could picture him as a little boy asking the same question. "Who else?"

The temperature had fallen throughout the day and with the gray sky, we both bet we'd have snow that night. Once inside, a small light at the end of the shadowed hallway provided enough light for us to make it up the stairs. We hadn't made the first step before he pulled me into a long, heartfelt kiss. "Only two days without seeing you and it feels like a lifetime."

"I've missed you, too, Richard." I stared into his eyes. "You look tired."

"It's the kids." He laughed. "Toby went to sleep late and woke up early. Emma must have sensed the excitement, because she fussed most of the night. I think they'll all nap this afternoon."

"Hmm…then maybe I'd better go and let you rest."

"You're joking, right?" Even in the dim light, his eyes twinkled. We kept going up the stairs and into his apartment, where he put my bag of gifts under his tree next to the other gifts already there. We sat on the loveseat in front of the fire and held hands.

"So tell me what you got from Toby."

"He drew two pictures for me." He got up and brought back a double picture frame, hinged like a book. Inside were the pictures. "This is the dog Toby wants. He asks for one every day. And this is his family." He pointed to the second picture. Toby had made five stick figures, three large and two small, and all five were holding hands.

"Can't Toby count?"

"I thought the same thing, but Toby told me this one was me." There was a catch in his voice when he pointed to the stick figure man on the end.

I squeezed his hand. "Made you feel good, huh?"

"More than I can say." He rubbed his fingers over the figures behind the glass. He cleared his throat with a small cough. "I've got old-fashioned chicken soup from Farmer

Foods for us. Are you hungry, or should we open our gifts first?"

Richard was a top-tier lawyer, but inside there was still a small boy that not many people got to see.

"We can open the gifts first and eat later." I couldn't keep a chuckle from escaping.

"Tell me what you got from Claire and Skylar." Richard went to the tree.

"Claire gave me a teapot to replace the one she broke and Skylar gave me a hand-knit shawl."

Richard nodded. "That's great."

He seemed a little distracted, and probably hadn't paid much attention to what I'd said.

As if unable to contain himself, he reached under the tree. "Here's one from me."

I unwrapped the thin box and took out a framed picture of Richard and me that Marianna had taken at Rachel's birthday party. Sitting close together, we both were smiling for the camera. No doubt about it, we looked like a couple. "This is really nice."

I held it up in front of me. "I'll hang it in my room next to my mirror. I think this is the *only* picture of the two of us together. We'll have to rectify that." Laughing, I pointed to the smaller of the two boxes I'd brought. "Open that one."

He quickly removed the wrapping paper and hooted when he removed the picture inside. It was the same photo of the two of us that he'd given me. "Too funny," he said, "Marianna obviously gave each of us a copy." His face showed that he wasn't disappointed.

"Now you can open the big package."

He tore into the wrapping with the same enthusiasm I'd imagined Toby had used for his packages. When he lifted the cover off the box his eyes grew large. "Oh, Millie, it's beautiful. *Handsome*." He lifted the briefcase from the box and looked at it from every angle.

"I thought you'd like a new case to go with your new office."

"And for my new life on Wolf Creek Square." Putting the briefcase next to him, he stood up and turned on the CD player. "Dance with me, Millie."

I laughed. The song was "Silent Night." It didn't matter. Our dancing was more swaying to the music than moving of our feet, but when the song ended we were standing in front of the window. The lights on the trees in the courtyard created a winter scene worthy of a painting, especially when the snow began to fall.

Richard bent down and reached under the tree. He picked up a blue box with Art&Son embossed on the top. Then he opened the cover and held it out for me to see. "Art has created a new collection of brooches he's named 'Crowns.' I told him I wanted the first one for you—for my queen."

He lifted the arch of jewels from the box. Emeralds alternated with garnets along the curve with a diamond positioned at the peak in the middle.

"Oh, Richard," I said with a sigh. "This is beautiful."

He pinned it to my jacket. Then gave me a kiss, strong and long.

I pulled away first and touched his face. "Remember when you called in June and said that coming to Wolf Creek Square would be a new beginning for me?"

"I do." His soft kiss touched my lips.

I gave him a kiss in return. "Well, that was partially true. As it turned out, it was a new beginning—for us."

He put his arms around me and rested my head against his chest. I sighed with happiness and contentment. I was exactly where I belonged.

If you enjoyed *BookMarks* by Gini Athey, you may enjoy these books from other Wisconsin writers...

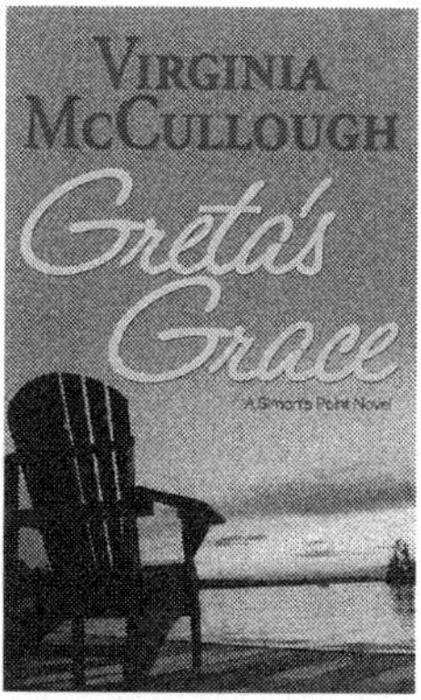

Greta's Grace

Virginia McCullough

Everyone deserves a second chance!

Professional speaker Lindsey Foster is looking for a second chance to repair an emotionally distant relationship with her daughter, Greta McKenzie-Iverson, who herself is hoping endure her cancer treatment and then grab her second chance at life itself. Greta's dad, Brian McKenzie, works to heal the past and win a second chance to find happiness with Lindsey.

But Sam Iverson, Greta's father-in-law, also has hopes of finding love again. In the small town of Simon's Point, on the shore of Lake Michigan, two families search for hope, healing, and their second chances.

Noble Assassin

Reluctant Heroes Book 4

Lily Silver

Reluctant Heroes:
Bold Men, Independent Women,
Finding True Love was Never in Their Plans!

Former assassin Ambrose Duchamp believes he is unworthy of love. He lives a quiet, secluded life in the Caribbean and keeps his heart locked in a steel box. When his friend warns him Aphrodite will find him no matter where he hides, Ambrose scoffs at the idea. After a frightened governess asks him to protect her, Ambrose faces a new challenge: keeping cupid's arrow from piercing his heart.

Juliet is a woman alone in a brutal world. As a fugitive, she takes a position as a governess on a tropical island far from England's shores. As her enemy hunts for her in the Caribbean, Juliet has one hope of surviving his wicked plan of revenge—by securing the protective services of an imposing Frenchman. But when Mr. Duchamp suggests a feigned courtship to protect Juliet's reputation as he shadows her, Juliet secretly wishes it isn't a ruse. How can this dark and deadly man be charming and yet so vexing?

The Countess of Denwick

Nancy Sweetland

On board the *Falcon* in the West Indies seas, Anne Landry is furious when she learns her father has agreed with the Duke of Denwick that she will marry the Duke's son, Earl Reginald Rumford. The Earl is a pompous, self-centered sot; she has no intention of ever marrying him. But just before her father is swept overboard in a wild storm that sinks the ship, he makes her promise to honor his agreement with the Duke.

Survival on a tropical island, rescue by pirates, lecherous sailors, two murders, a guilty midwife, a handsome seaman and a spunky heroine with a mind of her own... Will speaking with the Duke himself get her out of this unacceptable marriage? Or will he hold her to her father's agreement? And how can she stop dreaming about seaman Anthony Clearhaven, who is everything she's always dreamed of in a man? Will she become the Countess of Denwick against her will? Or will she follow her heart?

Acknowledgements

It is never easy to decide who to include in this section of the book because as the story develops more and more people become involved.

As always, I would like to thank my husband, Gary, who stands by my side with encouragement to follow my dreams. Not a reader himself, he knows writing makes me happy and he supports my efforts. I love you.

I'd also like to thank Peggy O., former bookstore owner, for explaining that the mundane daily grind becomes the challenge of being a bookstore owner. But she never forgot the joy books brought to her customers.

Having friends as critique partners strengthens the camaraderie and trust. I will be forever in debt to Kate Bowman, Shirley Cayer, Virginia McCullough, and Barbara Raffin. You're the best.

To members of the Romance Writers of America, my friends in the Greater Green Bay Area of the Wisconsin chapter and all the individuals associated with these organizations, thank you.

To Brittiany Koren and the Written Dreams team, once again your attention to detail has produced an outstanding product. My readers thank you, as do I.

Gini Athey
2016

About the Author

Gini Athey grew up in a house of readers, so much so it wasn't unusual for members of her family to sit around the table and read while they were eating. But early on, she showed limited interest in the pastime. In fact, on one trip to the library to pick out a book for a book report, she recalls telling the librarian, "I want books with thick pages and big print."

Eventually that all changed. Today Gini usually reads three or four books at the same time, and her to-be-read pile towers next to her favorite chair. She reads widely in many genres, but her favorite books focus on families, with all their various challenges and rewards.

For many years, Gini has been a member of the Wisconsin chapter (WisRWA) of the Romance Writers of America and has served in a variety of administrative positions.

Avid travelers, Gini and her husband live in a rural area west of Green Bay, Wisconsin.

BookMarks is the fifth book in her Wolf Creek Square series: *Quilts Galore*, Book 1; *Country Law*, Book 2; *Rainbow Gardens*, Book 3; and *Square Spirits*, Book 4.

Made in the USA
Middletown, DE
05 July 2022

68513187R00177